Shipley's Secrets

JEN SIMMONS

Shipley's Secrets

Published by Jen Simmons

ISBN: 978-0-578-60832-7

Published: Jen Simmons 2019
jensimmonsauthor@gmail.com

Cover Design: Ari @ CoverIt! Designs, coveritdesigns.net

Editing by Duane Lindsay @ Books and the Bear
www.booksandthebear.com

Interior Design and formatting by Stacey @ Champagne Book Design
champagnebookdesign.com

For Jason

Your love and loyalty are why this book has made it to this stage.
Thank you for loving me enough to help me make this happen.

Shipley's Secrets

To Aurilla

Prologue

Malcolm

1993

At a quarter past 2 am, my life changed. At a quarter past 2 am, I became a father.

I'm now the father of my best friend and brother's newborn daughter. Both her parents died before she ever met them.

Now, I will stand in that pivotal role and pray I don't fuck her up. God knows she's entering a world that is damaged and broken, her birthright a hard-handed fate. While rewarding, saving the world is never an easy task, even if you were born to achieve the impossible.

As I pace back and forth, my brown Cole Haan's steadily thud on the wood floor. With my eyes dancing from the floor to the clock, my head pounds with the need for another cigarette and a stiff scotch.

Stopping at the small table next to my favorite reclining chair, I pick up the pack of cigarettes I left there earlier. I pull one out and lift it to my lips. All the while once again glancing up at the clock on the wall.

3:15 am. She should be here by now.

The protocol was to have the child here no later than 0315 hundred hours. 1 hour. Delivery was planned for 1 hour after birth. The only way to ensure the safety of my brother's offspring is to complete this mission and deliver the child in the span of 1 hour.

Pulling another drag off my cigarette, I remove the fedora felt hat I always wear and wipe the sweat accumulating on my brow.

Knowing I am not ready for this, I stub out the remainder of the cigarette in my hand just as I hear a knock on the front door.

"Finally."

With measured determined strides, I march toward the front door.

The thudding from my shoes is louder now that my stride has purpose. One hand moves the red curtain on the small window aside, allowing me to peer out the window to ensure this is the delivery I have been waiting on. The other is around my back, gently resting on the Glock hidden in my waistband.

In the light from the street lamp, I can just make out the outline of a person. Not wanting to draw attention by turning on the porch light, I gently tap three times on the window. Then I wait for the required taps to be returned, letting me know an agent is on the other side of the door.

Tap. Tap.

Letting the curtain fall back into place, I quickly turn the deadbolts one by one until all three are unlocked and the door opens.

Ushering in my guests, I shut the door quickly behind them and turn the deadbolts to lock in record time. Turning, I follow them down the hallway to the living area, where I was just pacing back and forth a few short seconds ago. I feel a sense of urgency to meet this tiny human that has newly infiltrated my life.

Stopping at the entrance of the living area but still standing in the hallway, I lean up against the wall and survey the scene unfolding in front of me.

Rebecca is holding the baby in one arm and unloading a black tote bag from her shoulder. She lays it to rest on my recliner, then turns to face me. Now that her arms are free from holding the bag, I get my first glance of the child.

Only an hour old and she already has me wrapped around her finger. I haven't even held her yet, but somehow, I feel great admiration for her. All because she is the daughter of my best friend, my brother and the one I will never get to see again.

Rebecca looks at me with a small smile on her face.

"Malcolm, meet London." She circles the infants face with her first finger, moving the blanket wrapped tight around her tiny body away from her face so I can get a good look.

Not able to refrain any longer, I reach out and take the bundle of blankets from Rebecca's arms. I cradle the child close to my chest and stare down into her small face.

"Mission completed without incident. We were able to get an agent who is an MD to the hospital to deliver the child and attempt resuscitation on Clara completely anonymously. Your directive to put Clara on the abandoned VIP floor and surround the hospital with agents assisted in this mission succeeding." Rebecca walks back to my recliner, moves the bag to the floor and sits down.

"Were you successful in transporting Clara's body as directed? Was the hospital record cleared to ensure no one will ever know Clara was in the emergency department?"

Rebecca nods her answer. She then watches me as I walk into the room and take a seat on the bench I left abandoned in front of the piano. I pushed off the piano keys when the call came in that Clara was in the ER. I had been playing a haunted Mozart melody, when the phone began to ring. Intuition told me a promise I had made many years ago was about to be called in.

Looking up at Rebecca I ask sternly, "And you were able to leave the hospital without being seen? Can you guarantee me that no one saw you leaving with the child?"

"Tate led us out through the service entrance in the basement. We exited into the dark alley just off the basement's main door, where another agent was waiting in an unmarked town car to transport us here. I had him drop me a block west of here, and I walked the rest of the way. No one saw a thing, Malcolm."

Looking back down at London, I can see the resemblance gifted to her from her parents. Moving the blanket off her head, I push the hat that was placed on her tiny head back a bit. Just as I thought, she has what looks like fussy dark hair, slightly curling at the end. I use my first finger to trace around her closed eyes and tiny little peach nose. My skin color is darker against the milky white of the infant's skin.

Her tiny lips pucker up and an adorable wrinkle forms on her forehead between her eyes. She doesn't wake up, just keeps puckering her lips, her fist coming up to rest on her tiny chest.

"Did you bring the appropriate paperwork with you?"

Rebecca reaches down and opens the black tote bag. Putting her hand in, she pulls out a manila envelope.

Handing it over to me, I slide the important documents under my thigh on the bench.

"The assigned MS4 Soldiers will be here in 30 minutes, with all the supplies you need. One soldier will stay with you around the clock to help out with the baby." As she looks down at her watch, realizing the time, she rises from the recliner to leave.

"I have to go; Tate is waiting for me. Brian has the flu and is being a pain in the ass; something for you to look forward to." She smirks as she walks down the hallway towards the door.

Rebecca moves the red curtain as I had earlier when she arrived, making sure the street is clear before unlocking the deadbolts and heading out onto the porch. Pulling the hood of her coat over her head, she turns and gives me a smile and a wave, as I shut the door and lock it behind her. I don't peek out the window again to make sure she is safe. Rebecca is one of the finest trained agents in my organization. Quickest draw and shot with a 9 mm I've ever seen.

Not to mention she's married to Tate; that Scottish bastard is the toughest of us all.

Just as Rebecca had said, thirty minutes later, MS4 Soldiers arrived with a crib, baby supplies, and formula. My soldiers know better than to be late; tardiness isn't something that is tolerated in MS4 Nexus. Once the task at hand is completed, the soldiers are dismissed, except for one.

Still holding a now awake London in my arms, the tension in my neck becomes almost too much to bear. Gently laying London down in the crib, I reach above my head and stretch to release the tension in my sore muscles. Grabbing the top of my hat, I remove the soft fabric of my fedora and run my hand across my face and up over my head. My thin buzzed hair is slightly wet with sweat.

Laying the hat on the small changing table attached to London's crib, I lean over and rest my elbows on the white wood rails. Reaching down, I run my finger down her nose and apply slight pressure to the pacifier lodged in her mouth. As London looks up at me, all I can think about is the promise I made to her father all those years ago. The promise I made to him and the promise he is cashing in on right now.

Even in death, my brother changes my life in the biggest of possible ways, just like he always did.

Standing over the crib, I look up and see the manila envelope sitting on the bench where I left it. Picking up the envelope, I separate the seal that keeps the documents safe and pull out the top page. With a big seal from the Department of Human Services stamped onto the paper, I peruse the document closely, ensuring no errors were made.

With sweaty palms, I replace the birth certificate back into the envelope.

Walking to the bedroom, my footfalls fast but quiet, I open the safe hidden behind a painting that's hanging on the wall.

Placing the documents inside on top of another 9 mm and a stack of one hundred-dollar bills, I close the safe and secure the lock, keeping my most important documents secure.

Taking a deep breath, I go back to the little girl that is likely to be the death of me.

At a quarter past 2 am, my life has changed.

At a quarter past 2 am, I've become a father.

PART I

1980

Chapter 1

Malcolm

"Dude, watch out!"

I duck to the left as a shoe comes flying from the hand of the fourth foster father I've had this month.

This place is even worse than the last. I never thought that would be possible. It's all because of Jeff Turner.

Jeff. "The man of the house".

No, "The scum of the house".

I've been here all of three days and already have a black eye.

My black eye the result of pulling, "THE Scum of the house", off a 6-year-old girl who was placed here by social services just yesterday. While I don't enjoy a beating, I did welcome it; because it keeps him away from her.

My twelve years may not be many but it's enough to know that jackass should not be anywhere near her bed, especially after dark.

I may not have been around long, but I do know that even in 1968 when I was born, this treatment would never have been ok.

ANYWHERE.

ANYTIME.

Jeff yells, spewing Milwaukee's Best from his mouth, the liquid foaming up in the corners as he screams at me to leave the room. My only prayer is that the alcohol has poisoned him enough that he'll fall over and drown in his own puke.

God, hear me, please.

Once again ducking, I dodge the second shoe, and manage to roll out into the hallway. The shoe barely misses the back of my thigh as I lunge forward into a roll.

With my back now against the wall, deep breaths soothe my soreness but do nothing to calm my nerves.

This place gives me a feeling, but not a good one.

Then I hear a thud. It's the sound of Jeff as he hits the floor and passes out. Half of his body is in the room and half of it out as he snores loudly.

Across the hallway, nestled into a corner is a boy about my age.

His hair is dark, and dirty. He has glasses perched on his nose, surprisingly not broken yet. His skin is shiny with sweat. The summer heat almost too much. With no running water and no A/C to cool us off the heat is unbearable.

He stares at me, like he's scared I'm gonna attack him. Places like these cause us to be scared all the time.

"Hey." I give him a small wave, hoping to break the tension; making his back straighten at my voice.

Ready for battle. Always ready to fight. Always ready to take cover.

"H-I-I-I." It's slow and broken but he manages the friendly words, even tilts the side of his mouth.

Maybe a smile? No. Probably not. Kids like us don't smile. Not that often at least.

The iron rod in his spine loosens as he slouches slightly. Telling me it's ok to continue.

"How long you been here?" My voice is strong, betraying the dread I feel just knowing he's been here for a while.

"Umm, I dunno know. A week… Maybe." Looking to the other side of the hallway as he speaks, he pushes his glasses up his nose once again. There's a slight red tint on his face. He lifts his left leg, bending it at the knee and wrapping his arms around it.

"You, youuu just got here right?"

The question catches me by surprise. I thought for sure he would cower into himself.

They always do when I first try to talk to them.

"Yeah, three days ago. I'm Malcolm. Who are you?"

"Adler." He doesn't make eye contact when he says his name, only continues to look down the hallway.

His eyes focus on the shadows from where Jeff still lies partially in the room. I nod, even knowing he doesn't see me because his head is constantly searching.

Trying to ease Adler's tension, I say, "You know, that guy's dick is smaller than a tootsie roll. He couldn't find it if he tried." I look down one side of the hallway and then back toward where the boy sits across from me, a small smile cracking my lips.

Adler looks back at me, all the fear leaving his body, but only for a second. He smiles, the action bringing a shine into his eyes I'm sure doesn't come around too much.

It's at that moment, I know this kid will be the first friend I make in this God forsaken situation I now call home.

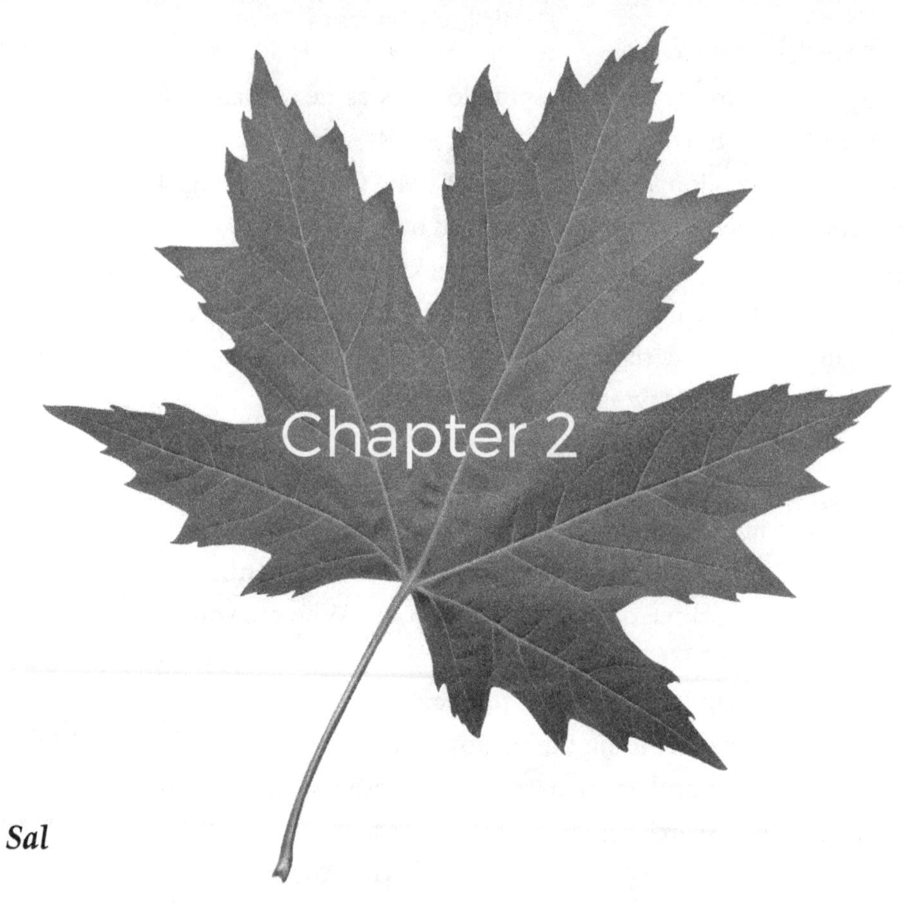

Sal

Walking through the living room, I hear Mrs. Johnson's whisper coming from the kitchen. It's low; so low I think I mishear her.

"Carl, he skipped school again. We can't keep letting this kid influence the others."

Mr. and Mrs. Johnson are nice people. They've just been a little unhappy with my lack of interest in school. In a five-day week, I actually show up to school only three of those days.

Tops.

I hate this school. It's boring and slow. No matter what kind of sleep I get, I still can't stay awake in class. Plopping down on the couch, I sit on the side closest to the kitchen.

My leather jacket bunches behind me, so I sit up with my elbows resting on my knees.

"I know honey, that's why I called social services this morning about getting him placed in another home."

Mr. Johnson shuffles his feet; I can hear his shoes squeak slightly on the linoleum.

He's always shuffling his feet; like he's nervous or something.

"Good, I worry about the other children. They're such good kids and I would hate for Sal to be the reason they're removed from us."

Wow. What a bitch.

I don't want to be here anyway.

Pulling the back of my jacket down under me, I sit back on the couch and continue to listen.

The phone starts ringing and I hear Mr. Johnson answer on the second ring.

"Hello? Yes, this is Carl Johnson." He pauses before continuing, "Yes, we did call, thank you for getting back to us so soon."

I lean forward again, peeking into the kitchen and seeing Mrs. Johnson making motions with her hands. She's trying to guide the conversation her husband is having on the phone.

"Well, it's not just him skipping school that's the problem, you see. The other children are influenced so easily; we fear this behavior is going to rub off on them. We want to avoid that, if possible. We explained to you when we started out as foster parents, we want children we can raise and possibly adopt. Salvatore is just not working out to be who we want in our family."

Carl covers the receiver with his hand while listening to Mrs. Johnson whisper in his ear.

"Tell them he stole from us. That should help convince them to re-home him."

God, these people are assholes. They want to re-home me. I'm not a dog. Or a thief.

"We had twenty-five dollars go missing yesterday. Sal came home acting as if maybe he had been doing some drugs. That is our true fear. The boy has a problem."

Now I'm a drug addict too.

I curl my lip in disgust, the anger rising in my body so fast I can feel my face heating.

"Ok, that sounds great. Thank you for calling back so quickly. We will have him get his things together now."

I try to keep calm, knowing they are coming around the corner any minute now.

Mrs. Johnson whispers one last time, "Now just be nice Carl. Let's get him ready and get him out of the house without any fuss."

They enter the living room, Mrs. Johnson first with Mr. Johnson trailing behind her.

She stops abruptly causing Mr. Johnson to run into her from behind.

If I weren't so pissed that would actually be funny.

"Oh. Hello Salvatore. I didn't realize you were in here." She smooths out her dress as she avoids eye contact with me.

Laughing, I say, "Yeah, I noticed."

"Well, Social Services called and they have a new placement for you, dear. Go on now. Pack your things. A car will be here soon to get you." She smiles as she rushes me off the couch. Getting up slowly, I don't return her smile. It doesn't take long for me to gather my stuff; I keep it all in my black duffle bag anyway. Slinging the bag over my shoulder, I go back into the living room.

Mr. and Mrs. Johnson stand there, talking. An awkward silence settles in the room. They whisper, and then look over at me, acting as if I can't tell they hate me. Plopping down on the couch again, I double-check my bag. Everything I own is right here in this bag or on my back.

Twenty tense and awkward minutes later, the doorbell rings.

Mrs. Johnson straightens out her dress again, nodding to Mr. Johnson to open the front door. A police officer waits at the door for me.

"Oh dear, a police officer, honey? Did they tell you a police officer was picking him up? What will the neighbors think? Thank goodness the children aren't home from school yet."

"It's routine, Miss. When an accusation of theft is made on a foster kid, it's standard procedure to pick them up in a police cruiser." I look out at the officer, happy when I see it's Hank.

I grab my bag, and head toward the door. Mrs. Johnson places a hand on my shoulder, smiles at me with straight white teeth. "Good luck to you sweetie, none of this is your fault, it just isn't going to work out. Okay."

My lip sneers as so many things I want to say run through my head.

I turn to leave but can't help myself and say, "I suppose not, cause having a money stealing, drug addict, stray dog isn't good for the other children. Don't worry about me, I'll be just fine on my own."

I walk out the front door and take two steps down to where Hank stands.

"Hey man, how are ya?" My hand goes up to meet his in a high five.

"Salvatore De Luca. So, you're at it again huh?" He has his hands on his hips, and a huge smile on his face.

"Let's go kiddo, you have new fosters to get home to." Great, they already have a place for me.

Just great. I can only imagine what the next place will be like.

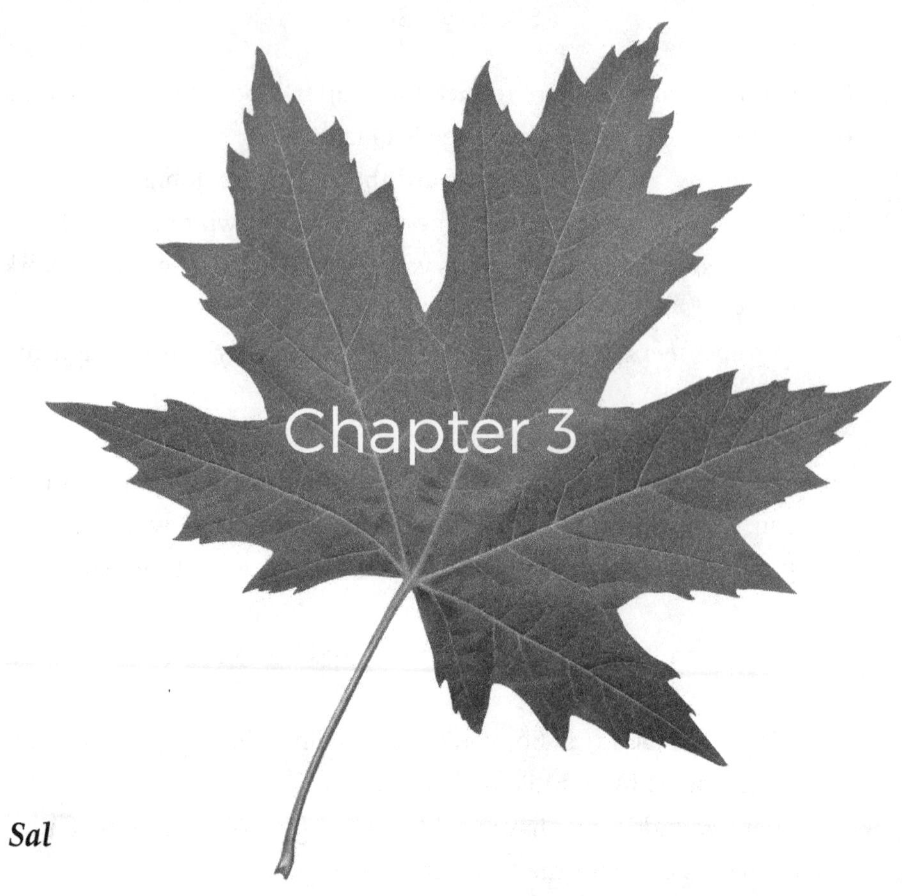

Sal

Hank takes me to the station, my usual hotel for the night when changing foster homes. I sink down into the hard-plastic chair outside the Social Services office. *Jefferson County, Colorado Police Department* in bold letters on the sign above my head. It feels like I was just here. I guess I was.

Two months ago. Man, times flies when you're stealing money and doin' drugs. I laugh to myself. Mr. and Mrs. Johnson were a joke. They want children they can adopt. My ass.

They want children they can manipulate and make into dolls that behave and wear perfect clothes.

If only they knew why I hated that school so much.

That my mind works faster and smarter than any of those lessons the teachers thought they were teaching me. It's so boring because I could teach those lessons with my eyes closed. I've always been smart.

The kind of smart where numbers and letters just fall into place and I know exactly what I'm supposed to do with them, long before anyone even shows me.

But I keep those things to myself. Hoping no one will try and take advantage of me for my skill with numbers.

Coming over to sit next to me, Hank hands me a can of soda. It's cold and smooth as I guzzle it down. I didn't realize how thirsty I was. I can tell out of the corner of my eye that Hank is staring at me.

"What? Do I have something on my face?"

Wiping my face with my hands, I don't feel anything wet.

"No; son. I was just trying to decide how to tell you about the next place your going."

"That bad huh?" Now I'm curious.

"It's not that bad, just not ideal."

"What part of foster care is ideal, Hank?"

Nodding he pats my shoulder and turns to walk back to his office, "You're a smart kid Sal. Too smart for your own good sometimes. As usual, the bunk in the locker-room is set up and ready when you are."

Knowing I can't change what happens tomorrow and where I go, I head into the locker-room to toss and turn all night just waiting for what hell comes next.

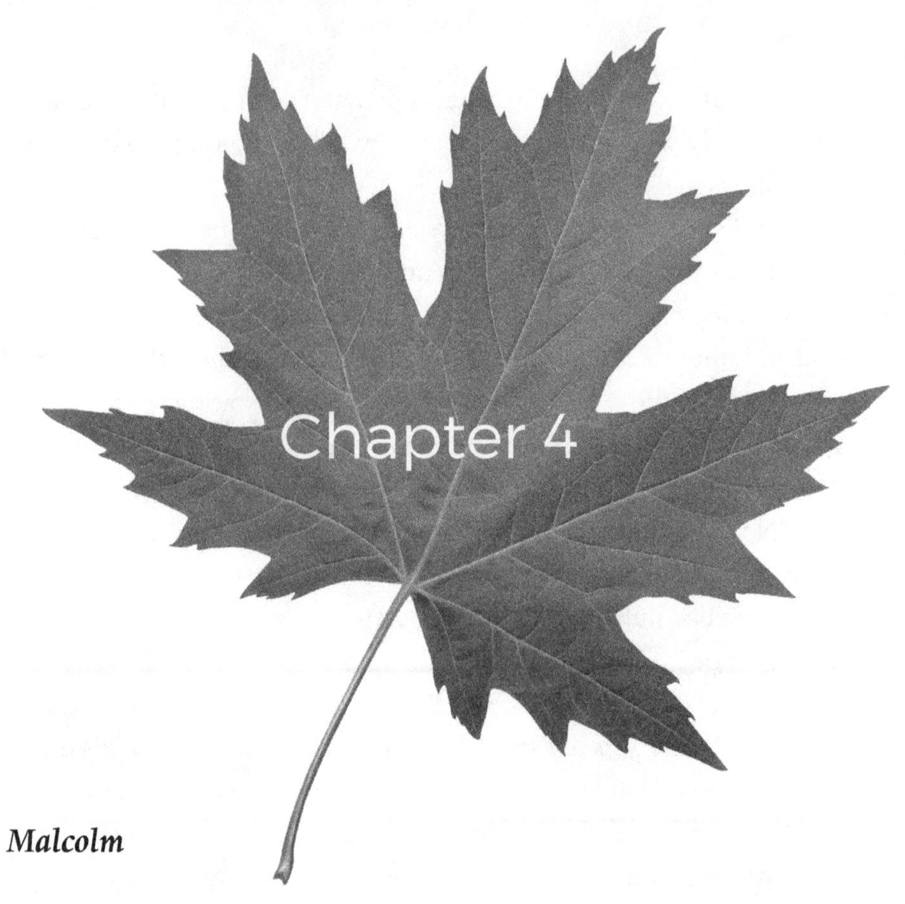

Malcolm

The days seem longer here than they did at the last place. I hate it here. The only thing making it bearable is Adler. He's not real bright but seems to be able to keep a settled calm around anyone in the room.

Except for Jeff, that is. That guy has two speeds, jackass or passed the fuck out. I prefer passed out. Seems to be happening more often these days. The foster mom here, her name is Jenny. She's nice enough, when she doesn't have a needle in her arm. When she's not speeding, we get food and sometimes water. But both are rare around here.

Today, social services are coming, to "inspect". That's what they call it, but really, it's just a visit to make sure we're all alive. All three of us kids sit at the old kitchen table; wood chips and splinters stabbing our skin. We're wearing the only "nice" clothing we have. Not sure who would agree anything here is nice.

Before the visit, Jeff scolds us on what to say and how to act.

"You little bastards better behave; we need this goddamn check." In true Jeff form, spit sprays from between his decayed teeth. The smell of his breath is like rotten milk. Fostering keeps the money coming in for all the drugs and alcohol they use.

Glaring, I stare right at him with all the hate and anger I feel. Heat rises from my chest, creeping up my neck and begins to redden my face. My anger is palpable, but he doesn't seem to notice.

Looking over at Adler, I can see the panic on his face. He slightly shakes his head, the motion telling me to cool it and not start any trouble. With my nose flaring, deep breaths steady my anger.

I really hate that guy.

Just as I settle myself enough not to look so pissed, there's a knock on the door.

Instead of coming inside to "inspect" as they usually do, the social worker asks for Jenny and Jeff to step outside. The three of us scramble from the table, tripping over each other, frantic to hear if this is the visit that takes us out of here for good.

No such luck. The door starts to open, us kids hurrying back to our seat at the table.

"Well kids, it's your lucky day!" Jeff walks back inside, his arms wide like he has a secret to share.

We all turn, curious despite the disappointment that social services once again didn't pull thru and take us out of here. Just inside the door, stands another boy. He looks about the same age as me and maybe Adler too.

He has a black duffle bag slung over his right shoulder, wearing a black leather jacket that's seen better days.

He's taller than me, with wide shoulders. His hair is jet black and his eyes are dark. The only thing not dark is his skin. The parts that are pale, a sharp contrast to his dark features. My favorite part about this whole thing, what stands out to me, is the kiss my ass smile, he has written on his face! His message is clear.

You can all kiss my ass and go to hell.

Chapter 5

Malcolm

The next few days go by surprisingly uneventful. Jeff and Jenny continue their downward spiral. The additional body gives them an extra paycheck. That means extra dope and more Milwaukee's Best for Jeff. We haven't eaten anything but stale cereal in days, not minding so much though, since the fosters are minding to their own.

The new guy, Sal, or whatever his name is, keeps to himself and doesn't say much. But no one really tries talking to him either. I noticed that in the last few days, he hasn't taken off that jacket and he doesn't let his bag out of his sight either. I don't judge. I have nothing to be protective over, except myself. Adler has started talking a bit more, to me at least. The kid's growing on me, every day.

Last night, we heard that school was starting. Another new school. Another way to be treated like shit, just not by the adults. I've gotta make it six more years. Seems like a lifetime but if I can get through the next six years, I can sign up to join the Marine's. I came across a few men talking to some kids at my last school about the Marine Corps.

They said when you turn eighteen you can join. Becoming a Marine could change your life forever. At least that's what the guy in the uniform said. Only six more years and I'll turn eighteen, and then I'll be out of this shit hole they call foster care. Shaking my head at the thought, I move from lying on my back into a sitting position. We all sit, hanging out in what is considered "our room", a room we share.

All of us. That includes the girl.

We all have a nice comfy spot on the floor. My bed, if you can call it that, is an old sheet with holes in the fabric and stains haphazardly placed. No telling what those are from. I try not to think about it. At least I have a small pillow. Something I can lay my head on. Not that it's soft, but it's not the floor.

Outside I can hear muffled voices with a car idling in the background. Then, the sound of the front door makes us jump. Sal, sitting with his back against the wall, hanging out on his comfy sheet, doesn't move. He just looks up at me then back down at the book in his hand. When he pulled that out, we all looked at him like he had two heads. Where the hell he got that book from, I don't know

A few minutes later, Jenny stumbles into the room, a little shaky. Her last hit wearing off.

No words come from her. She just throws a grocery bag, full of something lumpy, to the floor in the middle of the room. Then she walks out like she didn't even see us. None of us move.

We look around at each other, each wondering who will be brave enough to look in the bag. Adler sits cross-legged next to me, his back also against the wall. My position on my sheet, now matching his and Sal's. He looks at me, pushes his glasses up his nose and motions with his head at the bag. I shrug.

Looking back at the bag, I see Sal rise from his spot on the floor and walk toward the bag. He's the only one willing to make the first move. He grabs the bag with confidence and looks up at me just before he opens it to look inside. A small glint of sweat on his brow. Maybe he thinks it's a dead person chopped into pieces. Maybe its bats. Ok, not bats. But something to kill us, eat us or torture us.

Licking his top lip, Sal opens the bag with both hands. Pulling at the top of the bag where someone has tied a knot to keep it closed, he pulls the ends apart and the knot gives.

He peers into the bag and immediately drops it to the ground.

Not impressed, he walks back to his spot on the floor, sitting back down with a huff. Resuming the reading he was doing before. Always the tough guy.

"It's just clothes and stuff." His attitude trying to mask his true feelings. Lucy, the little girl, looks at Sal, a small smile on her face.

Shyly she crawls on her hands and knees to the bag. Pulling out clothes that are obviously not new, but clean. "Wow, look." She says as she holds up a t-shirt with a unicorn on the front. Looks to be just her size. Her smile widens as she continues to pull girls clothes out of the bag. Then her smile fades as she sits back on her ankles studying the clothes spread out in front of her.

"The rest are boy's clothes." Her voice is soft and hesitant, like she's scared talking to us will end with her being hit or worse. She grabs the girl's items and slides back on the dirty carpet to her mat on the opposite side of the floor.

Adler and I look up at each other but neither of us move; until I nod my head in the direction of the bag. Adler nods along with me and together we move to the bag of clothes. We look through them to see if any of it will fit either of us.

After pulling out a pair of jeans my size, a small hole and grass stains on the knee, I pull out two plain blue t-shirts and two plain black t-shirts.

It's been a long time since I had something new. Or at least new to me.

Adler has gone back to his wall and is folding his new-found prizes, stuffing them under the sheet he was just sitting on. Obviously hiding them, to keep them safe.

I return to my spot and look over at Sal. He tries to look like he's not curious, but I can see him looking up from his book every few seconds.

"I think the rest of those are for you." Looking over at him, I lay my clothes over my lap and see Sal put his book down next to his black duffle bag.

Glancing at the black grocery bag from his spot on the floor, Sal sits at war with himself.

Thinking better of it, he picks up his book and continues to read. Or pretends to read. I look over again. My clothes now folded and under my sheet like Adler's.

"They won't fit anyone else. You might as well take them. Could be the last clean clothes you get for a while." Sal looks up at me as I lay back down on my sheet, just as I was before. Now staring up at the ceiling.

The rest of the clothes go untouched on the floor.

Chapter 6

Clara

My whole life I've lived in North Carolina. I don't understand why Daddy is making us move. I don't want to move. I have a life in North Carolina. I have friends in North Carolina.

Standing in front of my full-length mirror, I stomp my feet and hope that Mama and Daddy can hear my feet hitting the floor. Hoping they will understand just how mad I am about this whole movin' business, I stomp my feet as hard as my legs will let me. Daddy says this job will give us financial freedom. Why do I care about financial freedom? I'm a twelve-year-old girl. Oh, wait. Young woman, as Mama always says.

And, I have a life. Argh.

"IT ISN'T FAIR!" I scream for good measure, trying to add icing onto the cake. I know throwing this tantrum won't change anything, but I don't care.

Throwing clothes from my closet into the big box Mama brought up this morning, my tantrum continues. After fifteen minutes, no one comes to comfort me like usual so I decide to take my tantrum downstairs.

Opening my door with force, and standing at the top of the stairs, I ball my fists ready to fight as I take each step down. However, my tantrum fades once my feet hit the hard wood floor at the bottom of the stairs. Mama and Daddy are in the kitchen, Daddy holding Mama as she cries into his chest.

I don't say a word; just stand there in the middle of the hallway staring at them. My daddy is comforting her, Mama's face buried in his white newly pressed button up shirt. Her fists wrapped around the material at his waist.

I can't see her tears or his, but I can hear them.

"It's going to be all right Gayle, I know it. That's why we're going to Denver. They have the best facilities and treatment centers. I'll take care of it all. I promise."

"What about Clara, Stan? She doesn't know any of this. We have to tell her. We have to tell her soon." My mama's tears grow larger and come faster now. The worry as clear as a summer Carolina sky on her face.

What's going on? I don't understand why they're so upset. What does Daddy have to take care of? Treatment Centers? What treatment center and why does Mama need treatment?

My mind wanders as I slide into the laundry room just off the stairs before the kitchen.

Hiding, I concentrate on their voices. Hoping to hear more before they realize I'm here listening.

Drying her eyes, Mama stands straight and begins working to fix my Daddy's wrinkled shirt. Taking deep breaths and releasing them slowly, she says "Ok. It's all going to be ok. Yes, you're right Stan. I just have to be strong. For us all."

"We'll be strong together; you just get better. I'll take care of you and Clara; I promise."

He kisses her gently, her smile small. The relief my daddy's strength brings her is visible in how she shakes off the emotion and goes back to packing the kitchen.

It's now that I realize my life is changing in a whole different way than I thought. I may not have the details, but I have a feeling; the details will bring us all to our knees. Stanley and Gayle Abernathy have always been the perfect image of strength and power. Seeing them broken and crying today is scary.

Heading back to my room, Daddy sees me leaving the laundry room. "Hey honey, what are you doing in the laundry room? Do you need any help before I go to the office?"

You'd never know by looking at him that there was any worry or concern at all.

His smile is big and real. But now I can see the fear behind the smile and his blue eyes.

"No Daddy. I'm ok. I'm just heading back upstairs to finish packing."

"Ok, listen for your mother to call in case she needs help in the kitchen. I'll see you tonight." Kissing my forehead, he grabs his briefcase, and walks back towards Mama.

He smiles and winks at her, his hand sliding across her hip as he walks by.

"I love you."

"I love you; see you tonight darling." Mama continues pulling dishes out of the cabinets and wraps them in plastic wrap. She's singing along quietly to the country music playing on the FM radio on the windowsill.

As I head back upstairs, my steps just as heavy as before but this time for a very different reason.

The tantrum I was having earlier, the one my parents never noticed. Is now forgotten. So, I go back to pulling clothes down from the hangers, folding and stacking them into the boxes.

As tears swell in my eyes, I resolve myself to accept that we are moving to Denver.

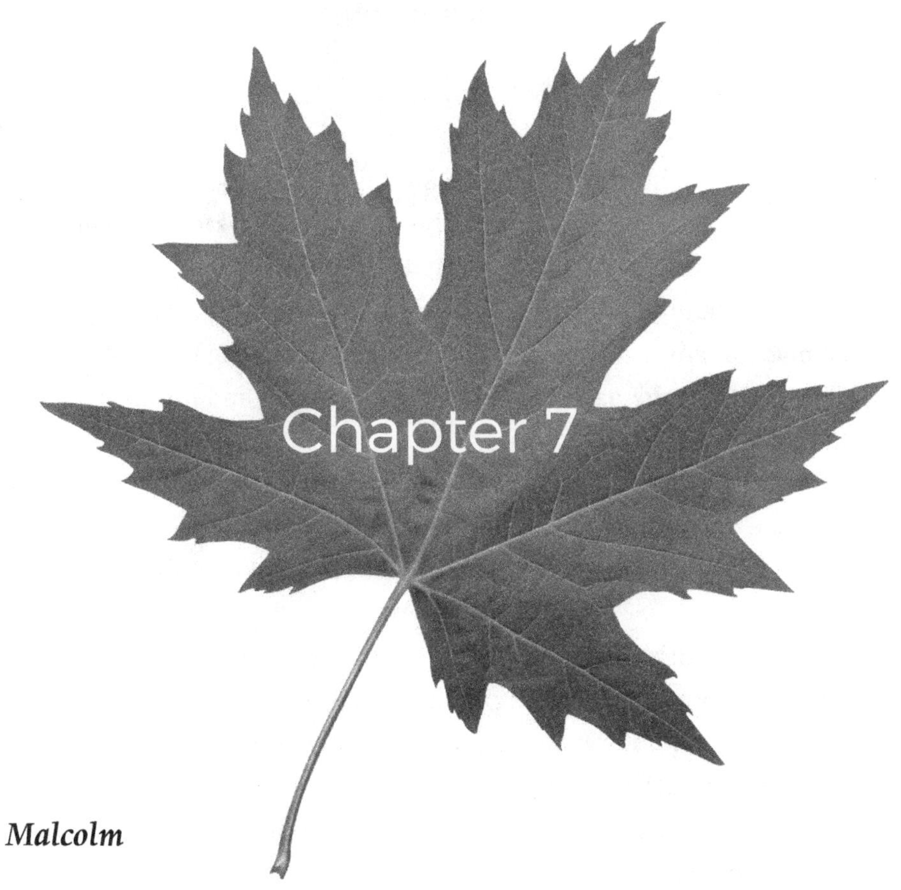

Chapter 7

Malcolm

The only thing I look forward to about going to school is being out of that house.

Just being away from the fosters for a few hours each day will be the highlight of every day. Adler and I walk slowly down the hall. Sal walks behind us, his leather jacket in place, black duffle bag hanging from his right hand. Classrooms are on each side, with kids spilling out into the hallway. It's loud. So loud I can't hear myself think. Being around all these people makes me uncomfortable.

As we walk down the crowded hallway, it feels like thousands of eyes are staring us down. The weight of it making heat rise from my chest up my neck to redden my face.

We don't have backpacks like everyone else here or any supplies to speak of. Adler walks beside me, his arms at his sides. My stride is wide, my hands hiding in my pockets, as I walk toward the sign hanging from the ceiling that says "OFFICE".

Sal, still behind us, looks around as Adler opens the door and together, we enter the room.

There's a short line of students waiting to talk with the lady standing at the counter. She just looks bored as the first kid complains that he doesn't like the schedule provided to him.

"You can talk to your counselor if you want, but no changes will be made to any schedules until next week." Chewing gum like her life depends on it, she hands the kid a piece of paper and motions for him to sit and wait.

The next few are quicker and get what they need without any annoyance from the lady.

We come up to the counter, and its then I notice, this lady isn't a lady at all.

She's clearly a student; working in here must be punishment for her. Detention or something. Not looking up at us, she smacks her gum louder. She's drawing hearts and flowers on some paper lying in front of her on the counter.

"Hi; we're supposed to ask for Mr. Keating." She looks up then, meeting my eyes briefly.

"Have a seat, I'll tell him you're asking for him. What's your name?" Somehow, she manages to continue chewing while she talks. If she had to walk too, I bet she'd fall flat on her face.

"Malcolm Shipley. This is Adler Beckett, and behind us, that's Sal De Luca. We're new here."

Looking unimpressed, she nods and turns to walk around a few desks that have been placed poorly in the room. There are a couple of offices behind the desks. One has PRINCIPAL written on the door, the other VICE PRINCIPAL, and the third door says COUNSELOR.

She walks to the third door, and knocks.

"Aye?"

"Mr. Keating, there's three boys out here saying they were told to ask for you. Don't remember their names." She shrugs her shoulders as she looks in at the counselor.

"Aye, have the lads come in." His accent is strong and hard to understand. She waves at us to come in.

One at a time, we enter the small room. A huge desk takes up the middle of the room; books are stacked up to the ceiling in shelves on the back wall. The desk is covered with papers and a huge TV that's perched on the corner, pointing diagonally so that the man behind it can see it at any angle. Why he has a TV in his office, I don't know. He is rapidly typing on what appears to be a typewriter but looks different from any I've ever seen. As he types, he looks up and down from the TV on the desk. Weird guy. He looks annoyed and frankly, pissed.

He stabs the keys muttering under his breath as he does. "Bugger. Hate this thing. Waste of money if ye ask me." He pushes the huge typewriter looking contraption over and turns toward us.

"Hello lads, welcome to Jefferson Middle School. Sit." He motions to the chairs in front of his desk. The three of us sit as we've been told, but don't say a word.

"The county is supplying you with pens, paper and such." He rummages behind his desk, picking up three backpacks, hefting them up onto the desk. Papers under them crinkle from the weight.

"Here's your schedule. Malcolm, Adler, Sal." Each of our names slurred out in his heavy Scottish accent as he hands us the piece of paper with our classes outlined. He has fire red, curly hair, green eyes and pale white skin. He's a large guy, tall and broad. He wears jeans and a button up blue shirt, a red tie hanging from his neck. The strangest thing, his belt is thick brown leather, held on by the biggest belt buckle I have ever seen. The words "JeffCo County Stock Show Champion" are written out on the gold medal.

He comes around the desk, sitting on the corner across from us. One boot covered foot is touching the ground, the other is up on the desk, knee bent with his leg dangling to the ground.

"I know yer stories, no shame or blame; we don't get to choose our lives or our families. Keep in mind, I don't want any trouble here, Aye? Keep to yourselves and ignore the wee scunner's, Aye? Let me know how I can help. Get on to class you wee laddies." Grabbing our backpacks, doing as we're told, we head back into the main office. The girl is sitting on a stool at the counter, her back to us now that we're behind her. She twirls a strand of hair around her finger, barely looking up as we walk by. Her doodles are more important than us walking past.

Just outside the door, Sal turns to the right and begins walking down the hall toward his first class. Adler and I stand watching his back as he leaves us in the hallway. All the other students are already in their required classes. I didn't even hear a bell ring.

"Bye man, see you later." Holding my bag on my shoulder, I wave at Sal as he continues to walk, not that he could see my wave, but I do the motion anyway. Then to my surprise, he lifts his left hand in the air, a quick wave in return. "Later."

Looking at Adler, I smile and shrug. Turning, we head down the hall in the opposite direction of Sal. We go to our classes, dread in my stomach knowing that at the end of the day, we'll return to the fosters, and the hellhole we now call home.

Chapter 8

Malcolm

The next few weeks pass so fast and surprisingly without any major problems or unexpected punishments from the fosters. They seem to enjoy our absence during the day as much as we do. I've begun to like Jefferson Middle School. It's nice to have the option to eat breakfast and lunch every day.

Sal's even opened up a little more. He's really taken to Lucy. Gives her a piggyback ride home every day after school. He's been calling her Lulu. She seems to like it, if the huge smile on her face is telling the truth.

Her laughter is infectious. We all laugh as she tells us the stories her teacher told during group reading. Every day, the three of us meet in the corridor by the main office and head to the lunchroom together. Naturally, we get some looks. Sal is the most put together, his leather jacket hiding the tear in his shirt at his right shoulder.

I get the most looks; my hair has grown out. People stare at me like they think I might break out and start singing *I Want you Back by Jackson 5;* all while dancing around like a lunatic.

That has to be the worst song in history.

Grabbing our trays of food, we walk to the back of the cafeteria to sit at the same table we've been sitting at for breakfast and lunch since the first day.

"I'm starving. Cereal at breakfast just isn't enough," Adler says while shoveling French fries in his mouth.

"Dude, slow down; you'll choke," says Sal as he reaches over the table to pull Adler's plate from under his face. I look on, watching Sal; his dark brown eyebrows coming together at the middle of his forehead. He looks away quickly, trying to act like he doesn't care.

Sal's friendship with Lucy has made him open up to us more. He tries to act like he doesn't care but we catch him looking at us from under the long hair covering his eyes.

He reminds me of a parent, always watching. Or at least I think that's what a real parent does. Dickhead Jeff has even stayed out of our room at night. I suspect it's because Jeff knows Sal will protect Lucy and keep her away from him.

"You guys wanna hit up Rocky Mountain Soda on the way home?" I pull out the five-dollar bill I found in the bathroom this morning, holding it up for them to see.

"We'll get Lucy first, that should be enough for four milkshakes," mentions Sal.

"Yeah, let's go," Adler says, talking again with his mouth full.

"Dude, that's gross. Don't talk with your mouth full." Mumbling out the words, Sal gets onto Adler. Just like I said; always the parent. He then looks at me, nodding his head in response to my question about the milkshakes.

"Yeah, sounds good." After the final bell rings, I meet Sal and Adler out on the steps of the school at our usual meeting spot.

We walk toward the elementary school to get Lucy, all excited about getting that shake.

As we walk, the three of us side by side covering the width of the street, we hear laughing and the sound of tires squeaking on asphalt.

A group of boys ride up behind us, speeding up as they get closer, their laughter increasing. Sal turns to look behind him, keeping his pace steady and unfazed by the change in mood around us.

We all turn and look. There's two of them, one on a green bike, the other orange with blue lightning bolts on the side of the metal. Both bikes have pegs on the back wheels, probably for their friends to ride on.

The boy on the orange and blue bike yells out, "Hey Wasteland, where'd you get the jacket, out of a dumpster?" He's laughing with his friend as they ride up to us. What an asshole.

The boy spitting out hate is short and skinny, with blond hair. His eyes are huge on his little head, I laugh under my breath. He makes fun of Sal's jacket all while he looks like he swallowed a fly.

As they ride past in a hurry, the one on the orange and blue bike reaches out and hits Sal on the back of the head. "Watch it Wasteland, you'll get your ass kicked if you're not careful."

"Come on Baker, let's get out of here!" The kid on the green bike yells at his friend.

"Don't worry, we won't waste our time here, with these cheesedicks". As they ride off, I look at Sal. As usual he's calm and seems unaffected by what Baker was saying to us.

"That guys an asshole. You should've said something, Sal." I don't try to hide the anger in my voice.

"Nah, he's lame. He'll one day get what's comin' to him." He keeps his head down, hands in his pockets as he continues to walk down the street towards Lucy's school.

As we get closer, I can see Lucy standing on the curb. Her school funded backpack that matches ours weighing down her tiny body. She bounces where she stands, excitement on her tiny face.

"Hey Lulu! How was your day?" Sal leans down in front of her, grabs her bag from her shoulders and hands it over to me. Smiling down at her, I shoulder her bag on my right arm and mine on my left.

"Hey Lucy. I found five dollars today. You wanna milkshake?"

"Can I get chocolate?" Her blue eyes are wide with excitement, waiting for my answer.

"Of course, you can. You can have any kind you want," Sal answers, as he lifts Lucy up onto his back.

"Hey, it's Malcolm's money, Sal," Adler finally chimes in. He's been quiet since the bike boys came hounding us earlier. Always avoiding conflict and argument, Adler never speaks up unless it's something one of us has done.

"Can I get chocolate, Malcolm? Please?" Lucy looks over, hope making her eyes shine the bluest I've ever seen.

"You bet Lulu, anything for you." Sal looks at me out of the corner of his eye, slight smile on his face. This is the first time I've used his nickname for her. Her smile gets wider and she bounces more on Sal's back in excitement.

"Ok, Lulu. Tell us what story Mrs. Jones told today." And so, Lucy begins to tell the story she heard today about a small dog that doesn't have a home, and the awesome people who bring him into their family, leaving us all hoping for the same thing one day.

Chapter 9

Clara

They still haven't told me anything. They act as if nothing is wrong and nothing has happened. Because I guess, nothing *has* happened and there is nothing for them to tell me.

Just knowing that something is going on, has me on alert and focusing on everything around me.

Every time Mama coughs, sneezes or falls asleep on this long drive, I worry. All I know is that she needs some kind of treatment. And, that treatment has to be in Denver.

Packing up our house and driving away was so hard. I sat turned around in the seat as we drove away. My childhood and my dreams were both left there in the house I grew up in. I can't shake the feeling that life is about to get much harder. Mama and Daddy try to be excited and happy about this move, trying repeatedly to get me excited too. They're constantly talking about how beautiful the mountains are and what we will do there. Like fishing in the rivers and going hiking.

I just want to say, "Really Daddy, fishing? When have I ever wanted to go fishing?"

I know he loves it; I will miss our days out on the pier. Daddy fishing; me sun bathing on a towel just below him on the beach. As the baby oil increases the tan on my legs and the blonde in my hair. I will miss the sun and the beach; the sound of the waves crashing to the shore hard and heavy.

This drive is long. Even stopping every eight hours to get a hotel room to sleep, I'm exhausted from sitting in one place for too long. It takes us twenty-five total hours of driving. That's three and half days, three nights, three hotels, and a total of twenty-five hours in the car.

I was actually excited to see the mountains to the west. They're huge. Never would I have ever thought they would be that big. For as long as I can see, there are mountains.

It really is beautiful.

The first stop is at the storage place, where we leave the moving truck to unload our stuff into the storage. Our new house won't be ready for at least two weeks. Daddy's company has a house somewhere in Denver that we're staying in. He says it'll only be temporary; I sure hope so.

When we pull into the driveway, the house is spread out in front of me. It has huge windows in the front, a big porch that covers the entire front of the house. It's two story, tan and white siding with a red front door. I thought only houses in North Carolina had front porches.

Surprise covers my face with pure excitement because the porch faces the west with a field across the street that lends us a perfect view of the Rockies. It's a little tough to breath here but Mama says that's just the elevation and I'll get used to it. I'm more worried she won't get used to it. Her breaths are coming faster than usual, like it's harder to catch her breath.

Since leaving North Carolina and being with them every waking hour, I've noticed that Mama is definitely sick. I don't know from what, but seeing what I have has me worried even more. She sleeps more than I thought and her skin is a paler white than I've ever noticed. She tries to hide it with makeup, but I can tell. I tried asking her about it a few times somewhere between here and North Carolina.

She would just say it was nothing, and for me not to worry.

A few days later, I awake to my mother's hand rubbing small circles on my back.

Rolling over in bed, I rub my eyes and look at her. She is sitting on the edge, her left arm resting on the bed to prop herself up. She looks tired. Very tired.

The house is furnished and clean so I know that's not what has her looking so worn.

"Daddy is taking me to an appointment. Will you be ok here by yourself?"

"Sure, I'll be fine. But I'd like to go." I move quickly to get up and get dressed but she stops me, a hand on my leg that's still covered with the yellow comforter on my bed.

"I really want to go Mama. Please?"

"Sweetie, it's better if you stay. We won't be gone long, ok. Just a few hours. That'll give you some time to shower and get ready. When we get back, we'll go site seeing and explore Denver." She smiles wide, trying to calm me. I know she's scared that I'll have another tantrum.

Tantrum's used to occur often, when I didn't get my way. Now that just seems stupid, with everything that's going on. God; I really was a brat.

I lay back into the pillows and smile at her. "Ok Mama, I'll stay here."

Her surprise at my reaction makes me feel even guiltier for the way I have been acting. Something tells me I should do exactly what she says and be ready for whatever news they bring home today.

I have a feeling this may be the day I find out what has Mama so weary. Today could be the day I find out just exactly how our lives are changing.

Chapter 10

Malcolm

Our routine continued to be the same each day. Get up, shower, and go to school.

Showering always depends on whose turn it is for that day. The fosters only let us shower on opposite days of each other. We've developed a system. It works most days.

Having three boys in the same room, the smell gets really bad. We try to alternate and give each other two days in the shower, determined by the stench in the room. Some days, our ripeness determines the system. At times, Adler, Sal or I will give up our day to shower so Lucy can have an extra day.

Not that it matters that much since our clothes rarely get washed. Sometimes, we take them into the shower; use the soap to wash our bodies and our clothes. Then on the days when it's not too cold, they dry on the walk to school.

Then the routine continues. Breakfast at our table in the cafeteria, classes, then lunch at the same table as breakfast. After lunch it's back to class and then at the end of the day we all walk together to get Lucy from school.

The four of us have gotten much closer. Jeff the scum mostly leaves Lucy alone and we never let her out of our sight. One of us is with her all the time. The best part of our daily routine is the time away from Jeff and Jenny's. Today's routine has been the same as always. But something feels off. There's a cloud over us. I can't seem to shake this feeling.

Adler and Sal don't seem to notice. But I think Lucy feels it too. She's quiet on the way to school today. She holds onto my hand while we walk, deciding to pass on the usual piggyback ride from Sal.

"You ok, Lulu?" I ask.

"Yeah, my tummy hurts a little, that's all." Her face a little pale, she smiles slightly up at me.

"I can carry you if you want?" Not knowing what to do, Sal offers the only thing he can.

"That's ok, Sal." She looks down at her feet, shrugging her backpack up her shoulders a little higher.

The walk to school is boring as usual. The only difference today is, we're all worried about little Lucy. Once we get to the front door of the elementary school, Lucy lets go of my hand and starts up the path. Sal runs after her.

"Hey Lulu, if you want, we can skip school. Maybe go hang out at Rocky Mountain Soda Shop? Maybe Bill will let me do some dishes so I can buy you your favorite milkshake. I bet that will help you feel better." His concern is clear on his face.

Bill, the owner, has let Sal and I work jobs around the shop. He slips us money in a thankful handshake. It helps keep us out of the fosters house for a little longer.

Using her tiny hand, Lucy touches Sal on the cheek, trying to ease his worry about her; she gives him a small smile. Her crystal blue eyes glossy with an emotion I don't understand but seem to feel just like she does.

"I'm ok, Sal. Really. See you after school." She turns, going up the walk. As she mixes in with the other students, we're unable to see her curly blond hair and small frame anymore.

Even with our worry about Lucy, we make it to school on time.

Walking into the main doors of the middle school, the feeling to turn and run back to Lucy's school grabs me by the shoulder.

Down the hallway towards our lockers, Adler, Sal and I walk side by side when that kid Baker comes up behind us. He's up to no good, as usual.

Baker's a bully. He spends most of his days in the Principal's office, which usually results in detention. Even though he's at least a head shorter than Sal and not near as big, Baker comes right up behind Sal, pushing him into the locker.

Sal loses his balance, the push catching him by surprise. As he falls to the floor on his hands and knees, laughter breaks out.

"I already told you once Wasteland, you're gonna get your ass kicked one day." Baker stands over Sal, the look in his eye angry.

Damn, what the hell did Sal do to him? That kid is such an asshole.

Sal moves from his position on all fours, to sitting with knees bent in front of him, his kiss my ass smile showing on his face as he looks up at Baker.

I know this kid is getting to Sal. How could he not be?

"Landry the Lame, you *twally-washer*. Bugger off. Leave the lad alone, or I'll show you a real wasteland while I kick your arse all the way there." We all turn to look at the kid standing across the hallway. He leans against the lockers, with one knee bent. He is tall and broad, has bushy red hair and pale white skin covered in freckles. His clothes look new, not a wrinkle on 'em. Clearly, he's not from around here. He sounds just like Mr. Keating.

He leans back into the lockers, pushing off to walk over to Sal. He reaches down offering Sal his hand.

Surprising both Adler and me, Sal takes his offering and the bushy red headed kid helps our friend to his feet. By now, Baker and his friends have taken off down the hallway.

"What does *twally-washer* mean?" Sal asks the redhead with the funny accent, a smile on his face.

Chuckling, the redhead answers, his accent stronger with the laugh behind it.

"Means cocksucker. At least that's what my *Seanair* says." His smile is wide, and he laughs at the expression on Sal's face. A big laugh, the kind that shakes his body.

That makes Sal smile the biggest smile I've seen on him. Adler and I laugh too, causing the new kid to turn to us.

"I guess ye two are gonna ask what a *Seanair* is, Aye?"

Looking at Adler then back at him, I nod and look at Sal. His attention is on this funny weird kid standing in front of us.

"*Seaniar* is Gaelic for what ye American's call grandpa." At the look on our faces, he continues before we can ask; "Oh bloody hell, ye've never heard of Gaelic? I bet ye gonna ask what that is too," Laughing again, he reaches out his right hand for me to shake.

"Tate Keating at ye service." My hand meets his, griping tightly as we shake.

"Malcolm Shipley, this here is Sal De Luca and Adler Beckett."

The two shake hands with Tate as well before he says, "Well, on to class wee laddies."

I chuckle again, this guy's accent keeping a smile on all our faces. Tate walks with us down the hallway, stopping at each door to wave at the students as we walk by. Adler's class is first then Sal's. Tate continues to walk with me, until we reach room 124, Mrs. Barker's seventh grade class.

"Nice to meet ye, Malcolm, see ya!" Turning to continue down the hallway, he stops.

"Oh, and Gaelic is Scottish. I'm from Scotland. And as ye can tell I can't stand that arsehole Baker Landry." Tate then disappears into the next classroom.

Even with the distraction of Baker and our introduction to Tate, I still can't shake the feeling I have today.

Chapter 11

Malcolm

I look up at the clock. Only an hour left. I'm so ready to get Lucy and head to the soda shop. I'm hoping seeing Lucy feeling better will get rid of my bad feeling. I jump up as soon as the bell chimes, signaling the end of the day. I head out to meet Adler and Sal on the steps as usual. I find them right where I always do, only this time, Tate's there waiting too.

"Hey guys, you ready to get Lulu?" I squint as I look out across the parking lot toward Lucy's school. Not sure what I think I'm gonna see. Nothing looks different. It just feels different.

"Yep, let's go." Sal heads down the steps first; Adler and I follow behind him.

"You comin?" I ask Tate as he stands, his bike propped up against his leg as he leans on the stair railing.

"Aye. Where ye goin?"

"Pick up our foster sister then head to Rocky Mountain Soda shop. You been there?" Tate walks up next to me, pushing his bike along as I pick up my walking speed, trying to catch up with the guys. "Canna say I have."

As we get to the steps of Jefferson Elementary, the feeling I've had all day, grows bigger, a pit of fear and worry deep in my belly. My heart kicks up speed as we wait for Lulu to come out of the school. Sal keeps looking back at me, then back at the main door.

After waiting longer than usual, Sal looks back at me again. Worry, just as clear on his face as it is on mine. With that look, we both know she's not coming out.

Sal takes off, a slow jog to the main door. Just as he reaches for the handle, Mrs. Jones rushes the last few students out the door.

"Hey Salvatore, how are you sweetheart?" Sal is tall enough that she doesn't have to look down at him. He stands eye level with her 5'6" height. Standing far away enough to barely hear them is Adler, Tate and I.

"Mrs. Jones, where's Lucy? Is she still in your classroom? Is she waiting in there for us to come get her?"

"Oh Salvatore, I sent a message over to the office at your school and I thought for sure social services would have been by there already." Her worry is now written in fear on her pretty face.

Swallowing she replies, "Salvatore, Lucy went home early today. She wasn't feeling well; the nurse called your foster parents to pick her up. When Jeff arrived, he was in no condition to be driving. We called social services but he insisted that Jenny was able to drive. Lucy left with them a few hours ago."

The blood in Sal's face drains and his breathing comes faster as his panic rises. Although I can't hear much, I can see from the look on Sal's face, something is wrong.

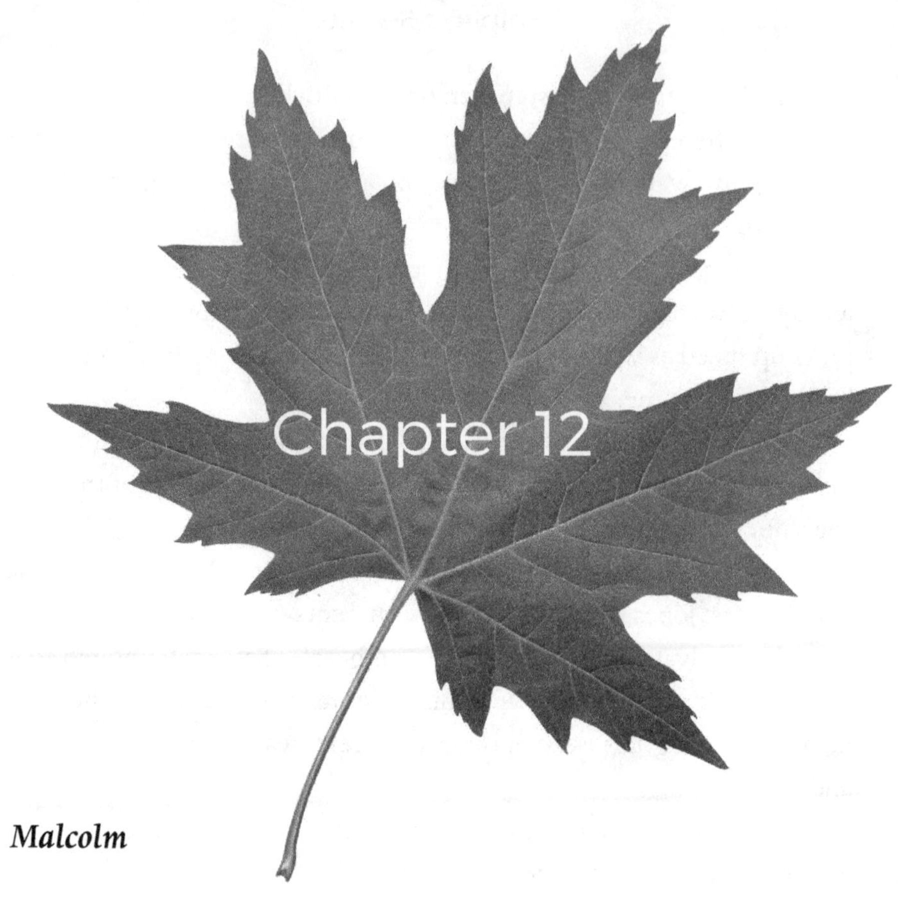

Chapter 12

Malcolm

My heart beats fast, heat and fear climbing up my body, threatening to burn me alive. My panic is real.

As that fear causes me to react, I start running, full speed towards the fosters as fast as my twelve-year-old legs will take me. Sal runs up behind me.

His speed incredibly faster, his legs take him towards what I know and feel will be a horrible discovery.

Lucy's alone with Jeff.

I can hear Tate behind us. Delayed in his shock to our reaction at the school, he trails behind us. Having a bike gives him the advantage to catch Sal and I quickly. Adler is somewhere behind us.

I know, because I can hear him crying. He feels the fear and worry now too.

Lucy's alone with Jeff. Worry and fear are a dark lake above, threatening to drown us in its deep water. Turning the corner and coming up the hill, we all stop at the top and look down at the fosters house. I see the old run-down Wagoneer Jeff drives parked out front.

He missed part of the asphalt, the front end of the jeep up on one curb, the other in the grass. There's no movement outside and no noise in the street. It's weird, and it's quiet. That is until Sal, who now continues to run toward the house, is screaming all the way. Going full speed toward the house, Tate and I following close behind.

Sal is screaming out Lucy's name, calling to her over and over as he runs down the hill and up the steps onto the front porch. Adler, stopping on top of the hill, he hasn't moved an inch. I can feel tears threatening to fall as I follow up the steps after Sal.

The door crashes open, wood splintering in the doorway from the force. Sal's true strength is showing as he punishes the door on his fight to get inside. We enter, Sal, me and then Tate.

I look back out the window and see Adler has made it down the hill and stands in the yard, tears constantly falling down his face.

Just inside the door, Jenny lies on the floor. No movement and no signs of life.

The rug under her, soiled with urine and what looks like throw up. White foam covers her mouth, coming across her cheek and down her neck.

Her eyes are open, and she looks like she's dead. Her eyes are wide, unblinking.

My heart pounds as Sal jumps over her, rushing towards the hallway and into what's supposed to be our bedroom.

I follow him, Tate stops on the doorstep, his red hair shining brightly in the sun coming in from the doorway. Sal enters the room first, his head and eyes looking frantically around for our Lulu. His eyes stop on movement coming from the corner of the room. In the corner where Sal's sheets and bags lie in. His normal space to sleep in this hellhole. I look to where Sal's eyes are, and I see him.

Jeff.

And I see Lucy.

It feels like hours, but I know its only seconds.

Sal breathes deep, a growl coming up his throat as he rushes toward Jeff, his body on top of Lucy. She doesn't move, his hands around her tiny throat.

"NNNOOOOOO!" He rushes toward them, jumping on Jeff's large back. Sal tightens his grip, one arm wrapped securely around Jeff's neck, the other being used as leverage to squeeze tighter.

Jeff looks up, the pressure on his own neck making him loosen up on Lucy's. With Sal on his back, Jeff rears up, sitting on his knees, still on top of Lucy. Her tiny legs are sticking out from under him, her lifeless arms splayed out to the sides. Sal screams as he continues to choke Jeff. "You son of a bitch," Sal screams.

Jeff stands, his naked back blanketed by the twelve-year-old body of the bravest kid I know. I run toward Lucy, sliding to stop at her feet. On my knees beside her, my hand slides under her head, protecting her from any further hurt. I cover her small body with one of the sheets that used to be a bed. Jeff stumbles back, hitting the opposite wall frantically trying to get air. He's naked except his dirty boxer shorts that are pulled down slightly.

Sal continues to apply pressure around Jeff's neck while Jeff is slamming Sal against the wall over and over again trying to stop him from chocking him. His face is red, eyes blood shot, fear showing in his brown eyes.

Jeff slams just hard enough and Sal's breath leaves him in a whoosh of air. His arms loosen enough for Jeff to pull Sal free from his neck. Jeff shoves at Sal's arms, spinning around to face his attacker. The look on his face is murderous and angry. He quickly kicks, landing it in Sal's right rib cage. Sal cries out in pain as Jeff grabs him by the shirt and lifts him in the air, his left fist connecting with Sal's face.

Blood splatters from Sal's nose as Jeff lands another punch, this time to Sal's right eye.

Sal's head hits the wall each time Jeff hits him, causing Sal to cry out louder in pain.

"How do you like that, you little pussy? You can dish it but you can't take it? Be a fucking man, you piece of shit!" Jeff continues his beating, hitting Sal twice more before letting his limp body hit the floor. Jeff then kicks him once more before turning around toward me and Lucy's lifeless body.

"What the fuck do you think you're doing with my girl?"

Jeff spits the words, looking at me with so much hate, eyes wild, evil, and sick. His baldhead shines with sweat in the light coming from the window.

I slide my arms under Lucy's armpits, scooting as far back against the wall as I can while protecting her head. I lay her head down on Sal's pillow in the corner then stand.

Scared and drowning in my own tears, I stand up tall and look Jeff in the eye. Trying to fake courage I don't feel.

"Leave us alone, Jeff." My voice betrays my fear, coming out strong and clipped.

Sal continues to lie motionless on the floor behind Jeff.

"You little fuckers ruined EVERYTHING!" Jeff roars, his face red, words spitting from his lips in anger. I hear sirens in the distance; I just hope they can get here before he kills us all. He stands in front of me, his stance defensive.

"Now's your chance, Jeff. The cops are on their way, you better hurry or you'll get caught." I try to convince him to flee, knowing that if he does, I could help Sal.

"I DON'T CARE, CAN'T YOU SEE THAT!" Jeff's eyes are wild and unfocused. He charges now, his back bent to gain some force. As he lunges hard towards me, I duck down at the last second towards Lucy, covering her body with my own. As he plows his body straight through the glass window above my head, the glass shatters.

I cover my head with my arms, the glass pieces cutting and stabbing me as they fall to the floor.

The sirens outside get closer and I see the flashing red and blue lights just as darkness is coming through the house, the sun descending to its final resting place for the night.

The room grows quiet. I don't move or say a word. Fear still clutches at me, leaving my tears dry on my face, the cuts on my arms stinging from the glass shards.

I hear shouts and see shadows from the flashlights down the hallway. I can see Sal still on the floor, not moving. I still don't move, protecting Lulu for as long as I can.

Voices break through my thoughts. The flashlights are in the room now. Someone leans over Sal. My first thought is protecting them both, so I scream out.

"Don't touch him!"

"It's ok, kiddo; I'm an officer with the Denver Police Department. I'm not here to hurt you, I promise." The officer touches his fingers to Sal's neck, and then shifts his entire focus on me and Lucy.

"I need you to move toward me, kiddo. Just slide this way on the floor. Slowly."

"I can't. No; I can't."

The officer moves closer, holding his hand out to me. His face is showing kindness and sympathy.

"You have to, son. There's a large piece of glass, dangerously close to falling on you from the broken window above your head. I need you to slowly move this way, or you could get seriously injured when that glass falls."

"But what about Lucy?" I can feel the tears coming back, threatening to fall again.

The officer looks confused, like he doesn't understand why I am so upset.

"Who is Lucy, son? I didn't see anyone else in the room." The officer looks back toward the doorway, another officer just reaching the room, gun drawn.

"Casey, stay there. Don't come closer, any movement could make the glass from the broken window fall on the kid." The first officer moves closer to me, confusion still on his face.

"Ok son; who's Lucy?"

Slightly I move my body up and away from Lucy under me. The cop shakes his head for me to not move until he realizes that I have a small child under me.

"Oh God. Casey! Never mind, get your ass in here and help me move the glass. There's a little girl in here." Panic settles in to the officer as he moves quickly now.

The two officers work to free the glass from under Jeff's dead body, ensuring safety for Lucy and me to leave this room. Paramedics have already taken Sal out of the room on a stretcher.

As I lift up, revealing a sleeping Lucy under me, the officer grabs my arm and pulls me to my feet. As he drags me away, I plead to stay with her, but he continues to pull me away.

"No, I have to stay; I can't leave her alone with him. Please!"

"It's ok son; he's dead." Even though I already know that, it's hard not to fight the officer so I can stay here with Lucy. She needs my protection. She will always need my protection.

Chapter 13

Clara

I was right. Yesterday our lives changed forever.

Mama and Daddy pulled in the drive, exactly two hours after they left for Mama's appointment. The second I saw Mama's splotchy tear streaked face; I knew the news was bad. She had the visor down, working as fast as her fingers could to hide the redness and swelling of her eyes, her Merle Norman compact getting good use. The powder was just barely coloring the white of her cheeks and covering the redness around her eyes.

She pushed the loose blond hair back into the clip holding her hair in a chignon.

She looked at me when she lifted the visor, a small smile on her red lips, like she hadn't just been crying the whole drive home.

Daddy walked to her side of the car and opened the door for her to climb out. But unlike all the other times he's opened the door for her, this time he reached down, helping her climb out. I stood staring at them. Just waiting for them to climb the porch stairs and finally tell me what was going on.

Mama sat in the wooden porch swing, patting the seat next to her for me to sit. Daddy stood next to her, his hand lightly holding onto her right shoulder. Hearing Mama's fate from her mouth left me feeling as if there's a dark cloud around this house and our family.

Breast cancer.

Stage 4.

Spread to other places in her body.

Prognosis is terminal. I now know what that means.

Six months to two years to live.

The rest was just a blur of appointments, surgeries, chemotherapy treatments, and all the things the doctors wanted to do that wouldn't save her life.

Now, lying here in bed, a bed that's not mine, I'm angry.

I'm angry this is what we've got to live with, looking up at the ceiling wanting to be anywhere but here at this moment.

I know going back to North Carolina won't change anything, but my mind keeps trying to tell me that if we'd just go home, Mama would get better. Being in her house, in her own bed, with us around her. She'd get better. She'd be healed. She'd live.

My heart fights to tell me the truth, pushing me to grow up a little faster. I know now, I need to focus on helping Mama get better. This is what is most important. The best quality of life we can give her. For the life she has left.

I head down the stairs to begin my duty as the daughter of a terminally ill breast cancer patient. I pray I can keep this family together for as long as her body allows.

I pray I can keep my anger in while I watch my mother slip away.

Chapter 14

Malcolm

Standing outside the house, a paramedic is putting some kind of goop on my cuts and then wrapping my arms in gauze. Taping the white fluffy cotton with tape.

They still haven't brought Lucy, Jeff or Jenny out. I keep asking where Lucy is and why she's still in there, but no one has an answer.

Nobody will tell me if Sal is ok either. The cops just tell me social services will be here soon.

Cops go in and out of the door. Yellow tape hangs from the Waggoner around the mailbox and is tied to the front door of the house. The lights shine and flash. Red and blue, red and blue. Just as the medic finishes with my arms, I see the officer who brought me out heading my way.

"Why haven't you brought Lucy out? If she wakes up and we're not there, she'll be scared." I look frantically around him, hoping to get a glimpse of my friend and sister.

He stops in front of me, kneels down on his right knee. The look on his face making my heart beat faster again with fear.

"They'll bring her out in a minute. Malcolm. There's something you need to know, son."

"What is your name?" My fear has me asking questions I really don't care the answer too, trying to delay the news I'm scared I'm about to hear.

"John." He smiles a little at me, waiting to see if I will keep on with the small talk.

Instead I pull the band-aid off quick.

"John, is Lucy still asleep? Why is she still in there? Where is Salvatore?" I feel the tears gathering in my eyes as I plead with John for answers.

He grabs my shoulders, "Malcolm, Lucy wasn't sleeping in there. At least not when we got here. I'm sorry to tell you this, but Malcolm; Lucy is dead."

Lowering my head, I close my eyes and let the tears fall. I cover my face with my hands and lean into John.

"It's ok, kiddo; you're safe and so is Salvatore. He's at the hospital with your other foster brother Adler. I'll take you there." He stands to his full height but never releases his grip on my shoulder.

It feels good to have someone comforting me, to finally have someone who isn't looking at me like I'm a freak.

John leads me to his police car.

Denver Metro Police is written on the side of the car. The lights continue to flash even after we get into the seats.

I look down at my arms, covered in the white dressings. How am I gonna tell Sal? I turn my head to look out the window just as John climbs into the seat next to me. That's when I see her. Lucy. Her body is covered with a white sheet, but I know it's her.

As John pulls off down the road, I can't think of anything but Lucy and her pretty blue eyes and long blonde curls. At least that is how I will remember her, forever.

"Malcolm, this is Janine Campbell, from social services. She will get you something to eat, then take you to see Sal, ok?" The doctor in the emergency room smiles before leaving the room.

He says I'm lucky, that the cuts on my arms will heal fine as long as I keep them clean.

Yeah, right. Keep them clean; that's easier said than done. Now that my fear has gone, I feel nothing but anger.

Anger at this system. Anger at this whole thing. Especially knowing that I'll be placed in another new foster home. Another hellhole I will call home. The only thing giving me relief is that the next one can't be as bad as Jeff and Jenny's.

Can it?

Once in the cafeteria, Janine gets a cup of coffee then hands me a chocolate milk from the sliding cooler.

"Do you like turkey and cheddar?" Her look is hopeful. Like she thinks I'd actually say no.

I nod as she hands me the sandwich, pays the cashier and we walk towards the exit.

"Would you like to sit in here, or just go on upstairs to see Sal?"

"I wanna see Sal, I can eat and walk at the same time."

She smiles and guides me to the elevator. She gives me a quick update on Sal, stating he has some bruises on his face, a broken nose and a head concussion. The doctors say he'll be just fine though.

We exit the elevator and I can hear muted arguing in the hallway.

My mind must be playing tricks on me, because I think I see Mr. Keating in a heated talk with our normal social services worker. Then I notice Tate sitting on the plastic chair across the hall. His red hair is glowing in the hallway lights. When he turns that's when I see bruises covering his right eye and cheek.

"How can ye people place kids with twats like that? What the hell is wrong with this system? Ye never thought of pulling 'em out of there before someone gets murdered? I can't believe this." Mr. Keating is pacing the floor back and forth in front of the social worker and Tate, his Scottish accent stronger than ever.

"Mr. Keating, we had no idea how severe the abuse to the children was. I assure you, the State of Colorado would never leave children in conditions as bad as this. I know you're upset, but I need you to calm down, for the sake of your son and these boys."

Our footfalls are just loud enough for the social worker, Mr. Keating and Tate to hear. They turn to look down the hallway, all turning at the same time. Once they realize it's me, Mr. Keating starts toward me quickly.

"Thank God Malcolm, we've been worried sick. Sal's been asking for ye. Go on in. Adler is with him now." I can hear him resume his angry talk as I go inside.

Shutting the door behind me, I see Adler sitting at Sal's bedside. His head is back, lips parted, sleeping soundly.

I move in further and get my first look at Sal.

His head is wrapped in the same white cotton my arms are, his right eye is swollen shut and badly bruised. White tape stretches across his nose. His head is turned slightly to the left, his good eye closed in sleep.

As I pull up the plastic chair from the corner to the side of the bed, Sal wakes and turns to look at me.

"Hey. You're ok?" Sal's words are slurred and hard to understand, his face turning in pain as he shifts in the bed.

"Yeah, I'm all right, I guess." I look down, not able to look him in the eye.

Knowing he will be pissed when he finds out I didn't save Lucy. Knowing that I lost my friend and sister tonight and will likely lose my best friend and brother too.

I play with the bandages on my arm and try to keep from meeting his gaze. Sal reaches down with his left hand, resting it on top of mine.

"It's ok, Malcolm. You couldn't save her."

My head shoots up, meeting his gaze without hesitation.

"I tried Sal. I tried to protect her. I covered her until someone could help us, I thought I had saved her." The tears are again falling, sadness so strong my body shakes from it.

"Malcolm, she was already dead when we got there. There was nothing you could've done."

"How do you know Sal? How do you know she was dead? She looked like she was sleeping!"

I'm begging Sal to change what's just happened, but he just blinks slowly. Pain and sadness are covering his battered face.

"Because they all look the same Malcolm, I happen to know that. One day I'll tell you how, but for now, I'm so tired." His breathing has become faster. A single tear escapes as he shuts his good eye and slips off into sleep.

The light shines through the window waking me from a deep, dreamless sleep.

I sit up, my body fights with me to lean back over. Somehow, I managed to fall asleep right next to Sal, my head laying comfortably on the soft hospital mattress. The door to the room opens, creaking slightly on its hinges.

I know I'm safe but the noise, not loud enough to wake Sal or Adler, causes me to flinch a little. Man, I'm jumpy.

Mr. Keating and Tate enter with a different social worker than before. I think it's the same lady who got me the food earlier. Jane or something?

Tate comes over to sit next to me, sitting on the edge of Sal's bed, one leg touching the ground, the other up on the bed, knee bent. His usual smile is gone, there is nothing to be happy about here.

"What happened to your face?" I ask. Tate looks at me, his eye the same color as his hair.

"Ah, Baker. The twat, tried to push me around when I was trying to get here. I left him redder in the face then he left me." He doesn't smile or make jabs about his win over Baker. Just slightly shifts on the bed, and looks at Mr. Keating then at Sal.

Mr. Keating shifts at the foot of bed; "Yeah, and now we gotta keep his Lawyer Pappy off our tails. He'll have ye put in juvie for ruffling his boy's feathers."

Sal comes to at the movement of the mattress. Adler begins to stir in the chair across from us, rubbing his eyes under his glasses.

Mr. Keating grabs the last chair by the window and slides it over to sit next to Adler, at the foot of Sal's bed.

"This here is Janine Campbell; Malcolm ye met her earlier. She's here to give us an update." Mr. Keating looks at me then Sal.

"I'm sure you know that Jeffery Turner was found deceased after the altercation you had with him yesterday afternoon. Jennifer Turner was also found dead in the home." The clipboard she holds is pressed tightly against her chest. The more she talks, the tighter she holds it.

I can't help but feel like she's telling us some secret. Something that could get us in trouble later. She looks at each of us as she continues on.

"The condition of your foster home was worse than your regular case manager was aware of. She didn't realize the abuse you were subjected to by the Turners was that severe. The State is fully prepared to place the three of you in a better, shall I say, more appropriate guardianship upon discharge from the hospital." She finally drops one arm, grabbing on to the foot of the bed.

The anger Mr. Keating had on his face before in the hallway, is no longer there.

Now he stares at me, then Sal. It's like he's waiting for one of us to make a run for it.

"An investigation into the Department of Children's Services has been started in the hopes of preventing this sort of thing from happening again." She shifts her weight from her left foot to her right.

Sal is the first to speak. He licks his lips and moves slightly higher in the bed before saying the words we are all afraid to hear.

"Are they putting us in another home? Can we go together? We want to stay together this time." I look over at Adler. His head is moving up and down so fast; his glasses slide completely off his nose, landing in his lap. He quickly places them back on his face then returns his attention back to Sal.

"Yeah, we want to stay together. We're brothers, Ms. Campbell. Please let us go together to a new place." Adler's tears look huge under the lenses of his glasses.

"Well, that's what Mr. Keating and Tate wanted to discuss with you." She looks over at Tate's father, nods at him, telling him to explain.

"Ye wee lads have been through a lot in your short twelve years. I never thought I'd come to America and ever be in a situation like this, but here I am. And I can help ye three out. Tate and I been talking. We'd ask ye to come live with us, on our ranch." Tate's eyes show hope and he smiles for the first time since entering in the room.

"But how? How can we do that? We're fosters, Mr. Keating. We've no family, no parents. We've gotta go where Ms. Campbell tells us." My voice cracks as I look over at Ms. Campbell, my hope climbing as I look up at her.

She answers me without pausing.

"Malcolm; that was what Mr. Keating was working on when you and I came up here last night. He was applying with the State of Colorado to become your new foster parent."

Sal looks at her, his bruised face hopeful for the first time since I met him.

"That's impossible, it takes months and sometimes years to become a foster parent in Colorado." We all look at him, wondering how he even knows that.

"When my mom died, we had a neighbor she trusted. She tried to get approved to be a foster parent but they said she couldn't. She had a record or something. It took months to find out I wasn't gonna move in with her."

That's the most Sal has ever spoken at one time. The shock must be written on our faces, because Sal looks away. Trying to hide now, after he let us know a bit more about him.

"That is true, Salvatore, but Mr. Keating requested this as an emergent injunction and was appointed guardianship just before we came here. If you guys want to, you can go with Mr. Keating and Tate. The judge did an immediate placement that says the three of you can't be taken out of his custody without a court order and a judge's signature. The only thing stopping this right now is you three. You say the word if you want to be placed elsewhere and you'll be put back into the system, but you won't be together."

I feel like this is a dream or some kind of a joke. Mr. Keating to foster us? Three kids from nowhere and from nobody who cares. At least not until now.

Sal, Adler and I look at each other. Shock and surprise are keeping us from saying anything else.

"Come on, Ye wankers. It'll be fun! There's lots of room for all ye!" Tate slaps at the mattress in excitement at the idea of this crazy dream. The bruise on his eye is as shiny as his red hair.

Mr. Keating smiles, and encourages us to say yes. Excitement about where they live and all the land they have is clouding the room. He tells us about the horses, goats, and chickens they have on the farm. And about how the corn grows oh so high toward the end of summer.

"Come on, it'll be work and hard at times, but we want ye to join us. Live with us. We'll expose ye to some culture and Scottish tradition. Do ye some good."

I look over at Sal then at Adler. No words are needed as our smiles answer for us.

"Ok. Mr. Keating. I think you just gained three new sons. I'll go finish the court documents and get you a copy in a few days.

The doctor says Sal is free to go. You can take the boys home." Ms. Campbell's smile is big, true, and real.

We sit, waiting for the nurse to come in and help Sal get dressed. Excited about the new future ahead of us, we didn't have until about five minutes ago.

The idea of moving in with Mr. Keating and Tate is scary. The unknown we have lived with thick in the air. "We'll go pull around in the truck. See ye out front." Mr. Keating and Tate leave us there alone in the room, staring at each other, not believing what just happened.

"I can't believe it. We're really moving to Mr. Keating's? Together?" Sal's expression is hard to read. The bruises blue and purple, keep him hidden behind them.

In the past, trust has been a hard thing for us, but believing in the thought that this Scottish stranger, and his funny son might actually be trustworthy, is exactly what happens.

And our lives change forever.

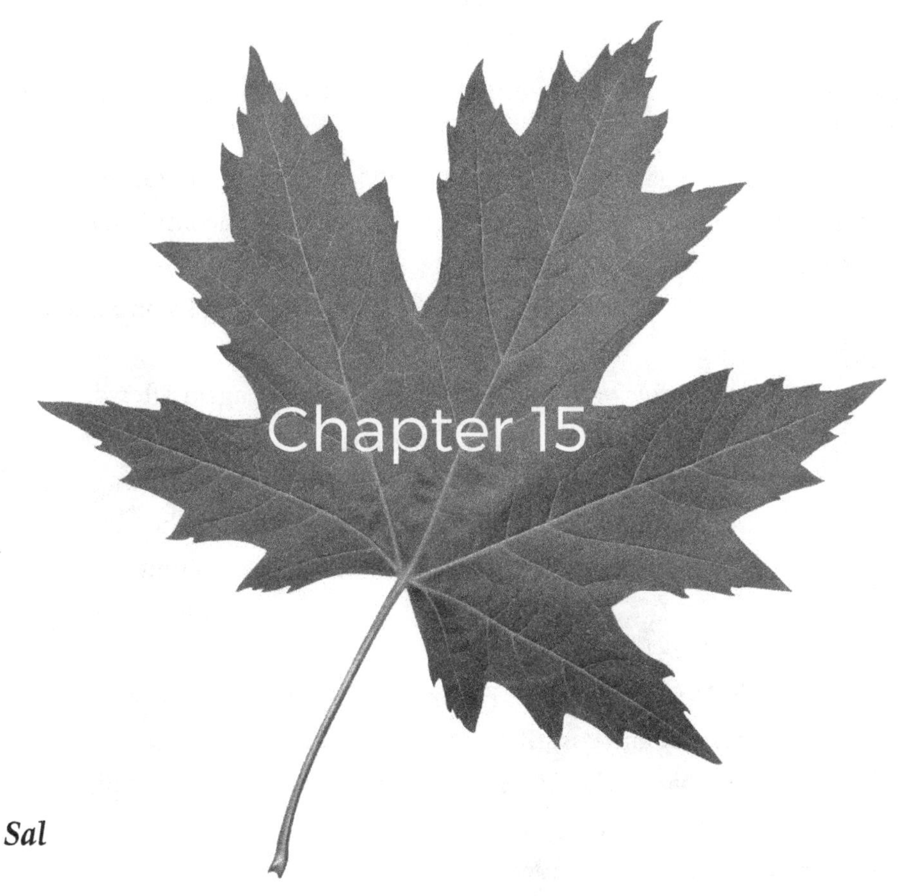

Chapter 15

Sal

I thought the hardest day of my life was when my mother died. I was wrong. So wrong to think life couldn't get worse. And then I saw Lulu lying there under Jeff. I've never been that angry. Never wanted to hurt someone as bad as I wanted to hurt him.

The thing is, I've always been the one to get hurt, not the one to cause it.

When my mother died, I felt anger, I felt sadness. I felt betrayed and abandoned. But I was only six at the time. I didn't understand why I felt those things; I only knew I felt them. But standing on that sidewalk, talking to Mrs. Jones, I felt something I've never felt before.

Terror.

I knew what we'd find when we got to the fosters. I knew Jeff would be drunk and that Lulu would be his target. I didn't even notice Malcolm running behind me. But he was there. He was just as scared as I was. He seemed to know the whole day that something was off.

Malcolm has something not many people do. He senses things. Things I would never sense in a million years. Malcolm knew something was off that day.

Me? All I knew was that Lulu didn't feel well and I wanted to help her.

I never would've thought I'd never see Lulu again after dropping her on the sidewalk at school that day. Now, we stand here. Her brothers. Dressed in all black, standing over the tiny box Mr. Keating paid to have her buried in. I still haven't figured out what he wants with us. Three boys from broken abusive homes with no family; except for each other.

At least we have that.

Now that Lulu is gone, I've made a promise to myself to protect my brothers, at any cost. If this is how I take the first steps to protect them, then living with Mr. Keating and Tate is what we will do. My only fear is being separated from the only two living souls who know exactly how I feel right now.

Looking over at Adler, my eyes catch the tear ready to fall from his eye.

All I know is, they need me, and I need them. I never thought I'd need anyone again. We stand side by side watching as the groundskeeper lowers the box into the ground.

Lulu, like us, didn't have any family. There's no one else here but us, Mr. Keating and Tate. Oh, and the priest who keeps tossing finger full amounts of dirt into the hole.

He's speaking the words *"Ashes to Ashes, Dust to Dust. From dirt we come, and to dirt we shall return. Go be with God, child"*, his fingers are wrapped around a cross that hangs from his wrist.

He makes some motion in front of his chest then closes his bible, kisses the cross in his hand and then turns to walk away from the gravesite.

We continue standing there, staring down at the ground. Looking over at Malcolm, I can tell he has as much on his mind as I do. Mr. Keating lays a hand on my shoulder, squeezing lightly. "Tate and I, will meet ye all in the truck. Take ye time boys."

The three of us are now alone at the gravesite. There's a slight breeze coming off the canopy covering the burial site. I think it's my job to mention that we need a plan. A strong plan that will guarantee that if this living arrangement doesn't work, that we do whatever we can to stay together.

No matter the cost.

Just as I'm about to turn toward them, Malcolm beats me to it. "I think it's time we make each other some promises; what about you?" His hands are in the pockets of his black slacks. His white shirt is bright against his dark skin.

Mr. Keating helped Malcolm cut his hair this morning. Dude looks different with a buzz cut. He looks sharp and older in his suit and tie. We all look older now; our clothes aren't torn and faded. Glancing down at my shoes, I wait for Malcolm to continue. Adler says nothing, just pushes his glasses up his nose for the twentieth time today. The cuffs on his jacket that cover half his palms, are too big for his small frame.

"I'm leaving in six years, no matter what happens. But I want you both to know, you're my family now. I will work my ass off the rest of my life to protect you and whatever family you create."

"Agreed. I promise the same. No matter where I am, no matter where you two are, I vow to protect you and your family too." I turn toward Malcolm and make another promise.

"I'm coming with you, brother. To the Marines. I promise to find a way for us to protect our families together. Adler, what do you say?"

Adler steps up, standing between us. He has to look up at us, his body a few inches shorter than ours. "I'm coming with y'all. I'm with you, I promise. We're family."

I reach my hand out to Malcolm, knowing that the only way to seal this is with a handshake.

He reaches out and clasps his hand in mine, squeezing tightly. Our arms move with the power of our shake. Adler looks up at us, and nods. A small smile on his face, he pushes up his glasses once again.

"If you shake my hand, you might break it. So, let's not shake, but I promise too ok guys?" Malcolm and I laugh at the expression on his face.

"Sounds good, Adler; sounds good." I smile for the first time today, knowing that our promises to each other will mold the rest of our lives.

Malcolm reaches up, places his hand on Adler's shoulder. He gives a reassuring squeeze as he laughs and turns to walk toward the truck.

I take a deep breath, and let it out slowly, no longer feeling the weight of the world on my shoulders alone. Now I'm sharing that weight with the only other two people in this world that understand what that really feels like.

For the first time in a long time, I look forward to going home.

PART II

1985

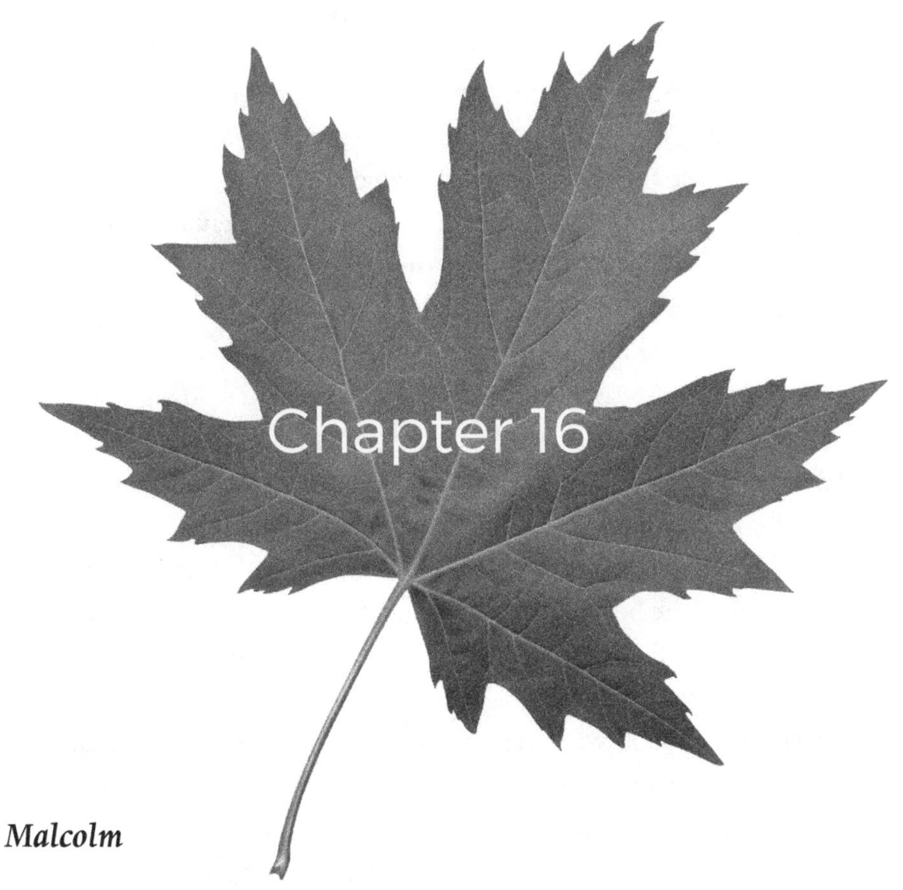

Chapter 16

Malcolm

Today's the anniversary of Lucy's death. The anniversary of us having a real home for the first time in our lives. It's been five years. Hard to believe, but true. Five years that have flown by in a haze of hard work and growing up. Mr. Keating keeps us busy when we're not at school. He says being idle makes you lazy. Being lazy makes you a bugger. Whatever that means.

Being here's been better than I could've imagined. The farmhouse is so big, we actually get to have our own room. I've never had my own room, let alone my own bed. Sal chose to live out in the barn. There's a small tack house in the back, under the loft. It only has one room and a one bathroom but it's just big enough for him.

Adler sleeps in the room right next to mine. We share the bathroom down the hall with Tate whose room is at the far end. Adler seems to be having more trouble settling in than Sal and I. In the last couple of years, some nights I would hear him screaming and crying in his sleep. There were other times I would awaken to find Adler sleeping on the floor at the foot of my bed.

I tried once to ask him about it, just before we went down for breakfast. He was rubbing his eyes, still tired from lack of sleep and a nightmare hangover. Just as he was putting his glasses on, I opened my mouth to ask if he wanted to talk about his dream. He just put up his hand and said, "No, I don't want to talk about it, Malcolm. It's no big deal."

He then took off down the stairs, his footfalls loud and heavy from his work boots. So, for now I just don't mention it. But I'm watching out for him, and if he needs me, I'll be here.

I love the work we do out here. It's hard work and I'm exhausted every night. The best part, it's making my two years before I can enlist go by so much faster now. Really, it's a year and half to be exact.

We also get paid for the work we do. Old Man Keating says he won't have anyone work on his farm and not get compensated. Not even his family. I don't mind, I like having my own money. At first, all three of us refused, saying room and board was enough pay.

That didn't go over so well. Old Man Keating just cussed a few words in Gaelic, ending that fight before it even got started. We've never discussed it since. He even gives us raises each year we get older. Says we can do more as we grow.

With us out of school for summer break, our work hours have increased. Mr. Keating says to get ready; this summer is shaping up to be the busiest season this farm has ever seen. He says having so many hands to work has increased Old Man Keating's productivity and increased his revenue from corn and other produce.

The land has to be prepared for the corn that they plant at the beginning of summer. That's how Old Man Keating, Tate's Grandfather, makes his money. He owns this farm and lets us all live and work here. In addition to the crops he produces, he preps the land at the end of every harvest for a corn maze and fall festival. The last few years, that day has been the only day we don't work. I guess technically, we still work. If guided tours through the maze and hay rides count as work. It doesn't for us. We love this part of living here. The pay is just a bonus.

The week the farm is open to the public, Old Man Keating holds a barn dance.

We spend two weeks prepping the barn, clearing out the hay bales, sweeping the floors and assembling a stage for the live band. Adler has even discovered he has a talent for electronics. He has the task of connecting all the wires and equipment that provides the music and entertainment for the dance.

Adler still has nightmares from time to time. He doesn't wake up screaming and crying anymore though; now he wakes up angry. I still haven't told anyone about his nightmares or the fact that I still find him at the foot of my bed after five years.

When this happens, he's even more pissed. Pissed at himself, pissed at me, who knows but I'll keep his secret as long as he needs me to.

Sal spends most of his time in the barn and in the fields. He's either reading, writing in his journal or working somewhere on the farm. That guy has so much energy. He works constantly. If he's not at school working to keep his grades up, then he's working here. He gets up to man his chores at least two hours before anyone else.

We tease him about it, but really, we're all jealous he's able to keep going like that.

Today, we've been tasked to stop by the Tractor Supply to pick up some feed Old Man Keating ordered last week. Tate is off with Mr. Keating at a Farmer's Expo, trying to keep up with updated ways to run this farm and generate more income.

Adler hops up into the back seat of Old Man Keating's black Ford pickup. Sal drives us into town, me sitting at shotgun. With the windows down, the humid mountain air fills the truck.

Even in the summer months the mountains have a layer of snow covering the tips, making for great scenery. This time of year, we depend on the water running off the mountains to fill the reservoirs and aid in irrigating the crops.

Pulling into the parking lot, Sal motions with his left hand out the window, triggering us to look in the direction he's pointing. Baker stands next to the sliding doors, two of his buddies standing with him. They're laughing and pointing at something we're unable to see. I don't really care what though. He hasn't bothered us in the last few years. Tate got into it with him the day Lucy died. Tate beat him up pretty good and left him bloody and bruised with the threat of more if he didn't leave us all be. He has so far. We try to avoid him, but sometimes that's harder said than done. Today could be one of those times.

Sal pulls into a space, jumping out of the truck. Adler and I follow. Sal has increased in size in the last few years. Towering over us all at six foot three inches. Because of the work we do on the farm, he's stacked with muscle. My six-foot frame is smaller than Sal's but I'm packed with muscle from my work on the farm as well.

Adler hasn't changed much though. His height has increased so he stands as tall as me, but where the work on the farm boosted strength and muscle for Sal and me, Adler is still stick thin. Strong as hell, but super thin and lanky.

Sal walks up toward the store entrance, his red bandana hanging loosely from the back pocket of his Wranglers. His black cowboy hat is the same dark color of his t-shirt.

My steps are even and steady behind Sal, my boots falling heavy on the concrete. Adler is slower out of the truck so he's trailing behind. Coming up to the door, Baker looks over at us. On his face is a sarcastic smile.

"Well, well. Look who we have here. Where's Tate? Aren't y'all scared to come out without him?" Baker and his friends laugh, walking off toward the side of the store.

We ignore him, finding it's the best way to keep him from getting himself hurt or one of us in a lot of trouble.

Grabbing the pre-ordered feed, each of us with a bag over our shoulder, the lady checking us out stops Sal just before he goes out the door.

"Mr. Keating ordered twenty-five of those, son. Can you pull around to the back so we can load the rest up."

"Sure. We're in a black Ford truck." Sal says.

"K, back up to the dock. I'll let receiving know. They'll help you load."

Nodding, we head back out to the truck and hop in. Baker and his friends are nowhere to be found. Thank god. Knowing we only have a couple years left of putting up with that asshole is the only thing keeping me from tearing him apart.

Sal starts the truck, maneuvering the massive brick of steal through the parking lot.

Just as he's about to turn the corner toward the back of the store, a flash of yellow, blue and white in front of the grill of the truck causes Sal to slam on the brakes.

There's a girl standing in front of us, her hands flat on the hood, eyes blue and wide with fear, her long curly blond hair blowing slightly in the breeze.

She waves at us mouthing an "I'm so sorry." Tears are sliding down her face as she continues her sprint across the parking lot.

"Damn, what the hell was that?" Sal looks around, trying to find the girl he almost ran over. I look to my right, see the yellow of her hair and the blue of her dress barely visible as she slides into a white Dodge.

Sal accelerates, turning the corner now that the girl has crossed the parking lot.

"She came out of nowhere. Damn, I almost hit her," Sal exclaims.

"Good thing is you didn't," I say.

We all get out of the truck and start loading up the feed bags. I can't get my mind off the girl. Man, she had the bluest eyes I've ever seen. I don't know why she was crying, but I know I felt her pain deep in my chest. Crazy, I've never had a feeling like that before.

Shaking it off, I continue loading the bags of feed, wishing somehow, I could've gotten her name. I'm not sure why, but I have a feeling I will see that girl again soon.

Chapter 17

Clara

I didn't think today could get any worse. Boy, was I wrong. Leaving home and coming to work this morning had been hard enough. I was so surprised by the call from Daddy, because Mama seemed so good today. She seemed in good spirits, with a small light in her eyes. We haven't seen that in months. But now Daddy's called to say the worst is happening.

Five years ago, they gave her a prognosis of terminal; they said she had six months to two years to live. Here we are five years later. The first three were manageable, but the last two? Treatment stopped working; radiation has now been deemed as Palliative in nature. Hospice care has been set up. She fought for five hard years, against the odds.

Mama hasn't been able to recognize me lately. Her mind is full of sickness and fear. I just hope she can hold on until I get there. Please hold on Mama; I'm on my way. It's a seventeen-minute drive from the

Tractor Supply to the house. I have seventeen minutes to prepare myself for the hardest thing I'll ever do.

Say goodbye to my mother.

Mama took her last breath only seven minutes after I got home. A mumbled "I love you, Clara" leaving her lips as she closed her eyes and slipped away. My tears stained the white gown covering her body.

Even with her face so pale, with dark circles under her eyes, she passed in peace, her smooth head covered in the scarf I got her for Christmas last year. Daddy was holding her hand while the chaplain was saying a prayer.

The funeral services were beautiful. Friends and family came from North Carolina to say goodbye. Now as Daddy and I clean up the kitchen, exhaustion takes over him. Resting his palms on the edge of the sink, he lowers his head down in sorrow. It's now that I see the neglect this has had on him. He's lost weight, his back sags with sharper edges around his bone structure.

Running my hand up his back, across his shoulder blade, I can feel just how much weight he's lost recently. I rest my hand on his shoulder, hoping the tiny bit of strength I have left will transfer from me to him. I can't lose two parents.

"Daddy, let's get this finished and get you to bed. You're so tired." Lifting his head, he wipes a single tear from his cheek and looks at me.

"Sweetie, we have to figure out what we're doing next. The house has to be cleared out in fifteen days. My company was kind enough to allow us to stay in this house while your mother was sick, but now…"

"I know and we'll get a plan, but for now, you need sleep. Let's go. I'll finish this up, and you go on to bed."

"All right, all right; I'll go." Kissing me on the forehead, my father moves toward the staircase, reluctantly climbing the stairs rubbing his neck as he goes.

I'm holding on by a thread, my emotions trying to take me under, making me wish I could go up to my room and sleep for the next four years. I've been good at bottling my feelings, being the strong one of the family for the last five years. But I can feel my walls beginning to come down as the day continues.

I walk around the kitchen, living and dining area, picking up half full coffee cups, plates still covered in food, just waiting to be eaten, but instead wasted as I toss them into the trash bin.

I stop as I pass the bookshelf that surrounds the television. Looking at our family pictures on the shelves, I suddenly feel suffocated and unable to breathe. Overwhelming sadness, heartache and pain stab like a knife into my stomach causing me to fall to my knees.

Dry heaves rack my body, shaking me violently. My empty stomach isn't able to produce anything since I haven't eaten all day. Tears burn the back of my throat with the little bile my stomach has protesting against me. Taking deep breaths is hard, but manageable and slowly the heaves stop. My now weak and tired body falls to the floor, tears coming so fast and hard my whole-body shudders. The trash bin I had in my hand, now fallen over, is spilling its contents next to me.

I try giving myself a pep talk, hoping I can convince myself to keep going.

"Come on, get yourself up off the floor, Clara." After a few more deep breaths, I rise up, grab the trash bin and continue my chores.

One breakdown is all I get.

Heading back into the kitchen, I pull out a pen and paper from the drawer we use for random junk. I list out our next steps.

To do list:

1. *Find an apartment*
2. *Get Daddy back to work*
3. *Move*
4. *Back to school*
5. *Begin to live life*

Number four and five make me the most nervous. When Mama got sick and we moved here, it was better that I did home schooling, I was needed at home to help with Mama's care.

Now the idea of going back to school is scary. Maybe a little exciting but still scary. It's not like I haven't had any social exposure since we moved here. I've had a couple of jobs at various places to help supplement our family income but it's been three years since I've gone to an actual school.

Working is different; working makes me feel more like an adult. I'm not sure I know how to be seventeen. Living would mean I could be a teenager again. I could just be seventeen.

Well maybe, after I get Daddy settled, and he has worked through some of his grief. There. Having a list helps. At least I have some goals set now.

I decide after making the list and finishing up cleaning, to head down to the corner store.

A newspaper and an apartment guide will help check the first thing off my list.

I grab the last two days of papers, the apartment guide and turn to walk back to my car. Flipping through the pages, I see that apartments are very expensive. Since Daddy hasn't worked in the last two years, the money coming in is limited, and only from his retirement fund.

While the house we live in now is a corporate home and paid for by my fathers' company, we have outstayed that free arrangement. Daddy can go back to work though, so at least we'll have that income again.

With the little I make at the Tractor supply, we should be able to get a good place. With my head down looking at the pictures on the brochure, I don't see the uneven surface of the sidewalk. My toe catches the edge of the concrete and I start to fall forward.

I feel the humid mountain air fast on my face as I stumble toward the ground. Luckily, strong hands grab a hold of my shoulders, catching me in time to right myself after tripping.

"Oh, careful there, this concrete is in need of some serious work," a deep voice says. My eyes latch onto the hand still holding me up by my left shoulder. They follow up his arm, taking note of his dark skin, muscled forearm and bicep. My eyes meet his; blue to light clear green, his eyes shadowed slightly behind a black cowboy hat.

He's tall, dark and very handsome. Towering over me, he looks down at my shocked face, his hand still resting on my shoulder.

To my surprise, I feel his touch all the way to my toes. What is wrong with me?

"Wow; that could've been bad. Thank you for catching me," I say. He steps back, his hand falling away from me. I miss the warmth as soon as it's gone. Shaking my head, I straighten out my dress and stand tall. Even at my full height of five-foot seven, I have to look up to meet his gaze.

"You ok? Did you hurt yourself?" His voice is deep and smooth and I get the same feeling I felt when he touched my shoulder.

"No, I'm fine. Just wasn't paying attention that's all."

"All right." Tipping his hat, he smiles and moves to walk past me. For reason's I can't understand, I don't want him to leave. I want to keep talking to him. I can't place it, but it seems like I know him from somewhere. He's familiar somehow.

"Hey, wait!" I turn back toward where he is walking away from me. "You seem familiar to me, have we met before?"

Recognition comes to his face; he smiles showing me slightly crooked white teeth.

"Yeah; we've met. Now I remember. Well, not really met but my brother did almost run you over in our truck a few days ago." His smile is bigger now.

"That was you?! Yeah, you weren't wearing a cowboy hat that day, were you?"

"No, but you were crying. How could you even see me?"

"It was a really long, hard day." Looking around I try to act casual so he doesn't ask questions as to why I was upset that day. Like he really needs me crying hysterically in the middle of the parking lot.

Then I go with the obvious distraction; "I'm Clara. What's your name?" Lifting my hand, I reach out to shake his. Our palms meet, his large to my small. My fingers tingle at the touch.

"Malcolm Shipley."

"Well, it's nice to meet you, Malcolm Shipley. Thanks again for earlier." Walking away, I hear what sounds like a growl coming from him and I turn.

"I…I." He looks nervous now. He's even cuter when he's nervous.

"Yes, Malcolm?" I smile while I watch him squirm. I'm feeling better in this moment here with him then I've felt in months.

"I just… I was wondering if I could give you a ride home?" Sliding both hands into the back pockets of his jeans, he stands legs wide apart. His boots are covered in dirt and mud like he's been out working all day in a field.

"Well, my car is parked right over there." I point toward my white Dodge. "But maybe I'll see you at the Tractor Supply. You look like someone who shops there often. Again, thanks for saving me, Malcolm." Smiling, I slowly begin to walk away toward my car, looking over my shoulder the whole time.

He just nods, walking backwards in the other direction, our eyes locked on each other.

Feeling a bit proud of myself that I started working on my checklist, I get into the car and mark a circle around number five. Maybe living life at seventeen will be easier and better than I originally thought.

Chapter 18

Malcolm

Damn, I'm so glad Tate forgot to fill up with gas before coming back to the farm this afternoon. I've never been as happy to come back into town as I am right now. Usually I'd be pissed, this putting me late for the hay delivery again. Mr. Keating will just have to understand; some things are more important.

Clara's way more important than any hay delivery. The second I saw her walking, her head in that magazine, I knew she was the girl Sal almost hit with the truck. I played it off; at least I think I did. Man, Clara makes me nervous. That girl is dangerous.

I can feel it in my gut.

She'll be the cause of heartache and happiness all at the same time. My brothers always say I have a sixth sense. A way of knowing things before they happen.

Just like that day after school. When we found Lucy with Jeff.

I felt off and uncomfortable the whole day. Then the unthinkable happened.

The feeling I get from Clara is different. Maybe my senses are off somehow. When I grabbed her to keep her from falling, I felt something through my entire body. A power. A force. I've never felt anything like that in my entire life. My heart is pounding, the temperature around my neck rising from the look in her eye.

My fight or flight response triggering but not because of fear. Because of something else I can't explain. Something else I definitely want to experience again. I guess I'll just have to see her again to figure out what it is about this girl that has me so unwound.

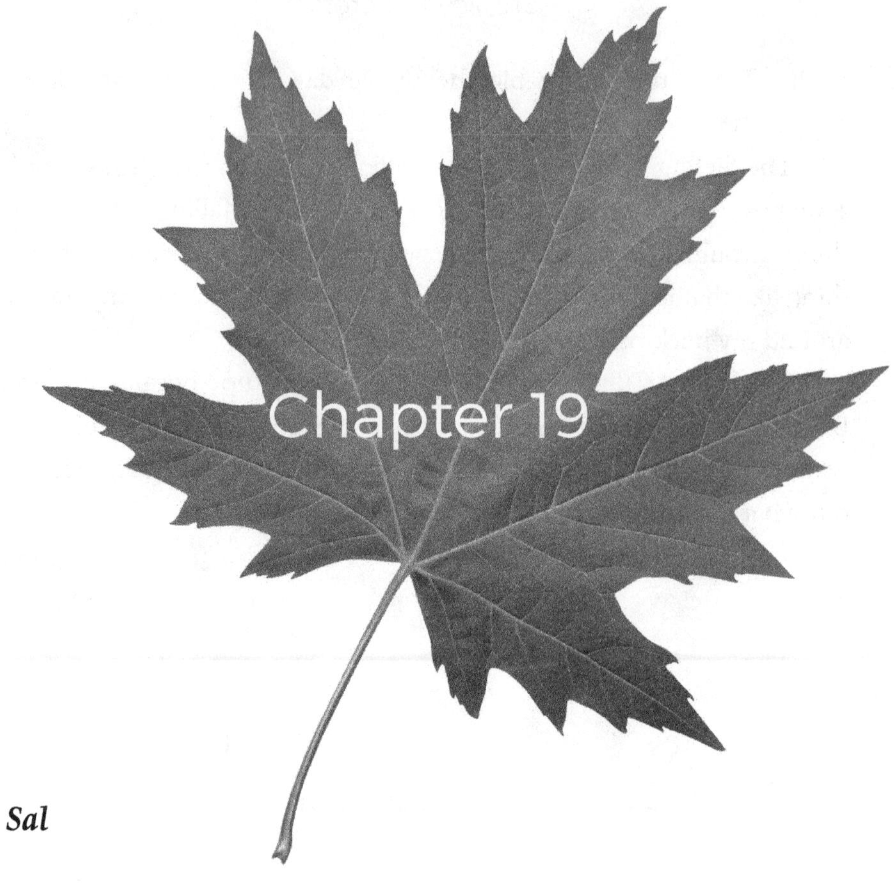

Chapter 19

Sal

I couldn't sleep last night. My thoughts kept coming back to that parking lot and the blonde I almost ran over last week. I can't figure out why I feel like I know her, but I do. I can barely remember her, it all happened so fast. The truck slamming to a stop, her hands flat on the hood with tears in her eyes. Her big blue eyes.

Why did it make me feel like I'd been gutted? Like my heart was breaking into a million pieces. Just like I did on that day five years ago.

My thoughts turn to Lucy. Turning again in the bed, I try to think of something else. Something other than this mystery girl. Finishing up high school, enlisting with the Marine Corps, the work still needed to be done on the farm. Nothing is working.

Tossing and turning is only pissing me off.

Getting up, I grab the jeans off the old wingback chair next to my bed, slip them up my legs, and then push my feet into my boots.

Grabbing my leather jacket, I slip it on over the black t-shirt I've chosen to wear today. Sliding open the door to my bedroom, I see the barn full of fall festival decorations, all still in boxes waiting to be put up. They're stacked in a corner behind the tractor, ready to be opened, sorted and hung, but still too far from the festival to make an appearance.

The main barn door sits halfway open, the light from the house porch shining through to light up the pathway the door uncovers. I can hear the rooster so I know it's early morning. Just before the sun will appear in the east and heat everything up.

I stand in my jeans, boots, and jacket as I look out at the work still to be done in the barn.

I go over to the utility cabinets set along the wall. At the opposite side of the barn is where Adler has been working tirelessly on building a stage for the festival this year. Grabbing three large buckets off the counter I fill two of them with horse feed and one with chicken seeds. I grab the two for the horses and head outside toward the horse pens.

After the horses are fed and I've filled their trough with fresh water, I go back to the barn to get the last bucket.

The sun has now come up to peak just above the horizon in the east. The heat of it, warm and inviting on my face and arms, my jacket now perched on the fence post by the horse pin.

Sweat covers my arms even though a light mist covers the ground at my boots.

As I turn to enter the barn, I see Mr. Keating turning a table over to pull the legs out so it will stand on its own.

"Morning lad, ye up awfully early eh?"

"Couldn't sleep, thought I'd get a head start on chores." I brush my dark hair back out of my eyes as I walk past him to return the two used buckets.

Grabbing the chicken seeds, I hold up the bucket to show him my intent.

"Mind if I walk with ye?" He stops what he's doing with the table, one leg up in the air, the others still lying flat in place.

"Yeah, sure."

We walk silently toward the enclosure the chickens and roosters live in. Opening the latch that holds the door tight to the chicken coop, I pull, so it releases, allowing me to go in the enclosure. The chickens peck at my feet, eating up the seeds I throw down quickly. They act like they haven't eaten in days even though I did this same thing last night.

Mr. Keating stands outside, leaning his left shoulder against the chicken coop, his red hair bright and shiny in the morning sun. A hint of gray hair speckled behind his ears.

"What's on ye mind, lad? Ye've been quiet since you came back last night."

"Ahh, nothing." I don't meet his eyes as I lie to him. I just keep throwing out seeds to the chickens.

"Something's going on in that head of ye's. Ye've just given those chickens twice the morning rations." I look up at him and see his red bushy eyebrows raised in question.

Mr. Keating has aged quickly over the last five years. Taking care of four teenage boys is taking its toll on him. He looks more and more like Old Man Keating every day.

"It's nothing really, just had something happen that got me thinking of Lucy. It's fine really. Don't worry about me."

"Oh, but I do lad. I worry about all of ye. Ye boys have lived here five years now, and I sure hope ye know ye can talk to me, about anything. When ye're ready, all ye have to do is tell me, ye hear." He looks slightly down at me, his height a few inches taller than mine.

"Yeah; I know," I say as Mr. Keating heads back to the barn.

He tells each of us this every day, it's become routine. Making sure we always know he wants to be our sounding board, even though we have each other and don't need one.

I have a sudden need to thank him, for taking us in. For being our guardian the last five years and for being the father that none of us knew we needed.

"Mr. Keating, Thank you. Thanks for ah, ah… For everything." Kicking the dirt with my foot, suddenly shy to relay my thanks to him.

He stops and turns back to me, "Hey lad; no thanks needed. But I'd be happy if ye and yer brothers would address me as Pop like Tate does. No more Mr. Keating, eh? Let's leave that for the Old Man," he says, walking away and leaving me stunned.

All I can do is stand there, not knowing what this feeling is I have. A smile spreads across my face and I all I can say is, "Ok, Pop."

He's mentioned this before when we're all together but I've never taken him seriously. Not until now. This is different. It's just the two of us. For the first time, I feel accepted by him and accepted by this place.

Even after five years, I've never been able to shake the feeling that I've been a guest here somehow. But today changes that feeling.

When this day started out sleepless with only the thoughts of a beautiful blonde hair, blue-eyed ghost, there was no way to salvage the mood my mind was putting me in.

But now, after the validation I just got, I know I'm part of this family, and this could turn into one of the best days of my life.

Chapter 20

Clara

It's been a few weeks since the day I saw Malcolm in the parking lot. I really hoped he'd show up here at Tractor Supply to see me. If he did and I were brave enough, I might get the urge to ask him out. Maybe check another item off my list. I keep adding to it, the idea of new and bold things making my seemingly boring life more interesting.

Daddy and I moved into an apartment just off the interstate a few days ago.

He finally went back to work today. Solemn and sad but he went all the same. I'm worried about him, but I'm keeping faith he'll bounce back into normal life just as I'm trying to do.

I have an appointment at Jefferson High School to see if I can get in for next year.

School is out for the summer now, so I'm hoping to get a head start and do an early enrollment.

I'm sure Jefferson County School District will need all my records in order to attend this fall. I should be a senior but with the last two years of home school, I likely didn't earn enough credits which could result in them holding me back a year. I was upset by that thought at first, but now I think maybe it's for the best. It should give me some time to settle back into life. Settle back into finding me again. Before I have to be an adult for real.

The store's busy today, helping the time fly by. No matter how busy though, I find myself looking over at the front entrance every few minutes.

Hoping to see light green eyes, beautiful smooth dark skin, and crooked white teeth staring back at me. Disappointment drowns me, every time the door opens and closes.

Get a grip Clara. He probably doesn't even remember me after the day in the parking lot. I bet he didn't even think twice about me after that day. Boys my age are assholes. Out for only one thing and one thing only. Telling myself this doesn't stop my head from turning towards the door every time it opens. The double doors open once again, this time revealing Baker and his friends.

Once again, not Malcolm. My disappointment even greater now, that I see Baker coming in. Baker's that douche bag, the one I saw outside the store a few weeks ago with his three friends. Oh, the day I almost got ran over. Baker and his friends were pushing around an elderly man, homeless I think by what he was wearing.

The homeless man appeared to be a Veteran. His hat displayed the logo for the United States Army. *Vietnam* printed in proud bold letters under the seal of the National Emblem.

His age unknown, but the years of mental torment and heartache written on his face seem to make him appear older. While he was large and strong enough to defend himself from assholes like those guys, he just took their torment. Too tired to care and just drunk enough not to put up a fight even when they start to tear him down.

It's been twelve years since the war ended, but there are still people out there who treat Vets that served as if they were filth instead of heroes. I don't remember the war much as I was just seven years old, but what I've read in my home classes make me appreciate what those soldiers did all those years ago. What they did to lose a horrible war. Thousands of Americans died.

I've found a deep interest in the military and how the government works.

The complexity of it confuses me, but unable to stop myself from studying it never the less. The ins and outs of war and the structure of the military are two topics that pique my curiosity when I study. Seeing as how my father has worked in political analysis for years, my love for government isn't surprising in the least.

Thinking back to that day when Baker and his friends were harassing the Vet, I can't believe I didn't do anything to stop them. But after receiving the call about my mother's impending death, all my thoughts became distracted and focused on her. Now my guilt hangs heavy on me that I didn't try to stop them, somehow. When I think of what happened, I vow to do something next time. What? I don't know, but something.

Baker and his friends laugh and push each other through the doors and down aisle number 1, their voices loud and unwelcome in the store. Shoppers look over at them in disappointment, wishing they could have back their quiet afternoon.

My line fills up, bringing me a rush of new customers coming through. Somehow, I even manage to forget to check the door for Malcolm every few minutes.

Just as the last customer leaves my line, I hear a crash on aisle 2. Startled, I look back in the direction of the commotion trying to place the noise that now has my pulse racing, sweat clinging to my brow. The sound resonating through the front of the store, sounding like a tornado just went through the aisles, breaking everything in its path.

I hear men shouting, but can't make out the words. Then I hear the sound of the door at the back-dock slamming shut. And just as quickly as the tornado entered, the store goes quiet.

Customers stand around looking at each other, waiting for more of the chaos of the last few minutes. When all seems quiet again, my line begins filling up with customers eager to get home. Fifteen minutes later, all hell breaks loose outside. The chaos from earlier starts up again as a commotion starts just outside the front entrance.

Checkers from each line run up to the double doors, trying to get a look at what's going on. My mind says to stay put at my register. I'm safer in here, and out of the way. But my body is having a different opinion and guides me forward with the other employees trying to steal a look outside. The pressure of so many people leaning on the inside of the door, pushes the doors wide open with a gush of air. People spill out onto the sidewalk and the very pavement where I was almost run over.

Looking around, the crowd is thick, everyone trying to get a glimpse of what's going on. Adrenaline rages through my veins, pushing me to get closer. Something tells me I need to see what's happening in that crowd of people. I push up through where two men have created a small opening. As I reach the center of the crowd, my boss Louie stops me short.

"Hey little lady, you don't want to see this." Trying to pull me away from the crowd, I say, "But what's happening? I need to see!"

"This won't last much longer; the police are on the way," he says.

He releases me and walks away, saying, "Damn kids these days."

I make my way between the two men standing at the entrance of the circle that's been created. Shock and disbelief register as I stare out at Malcolm fighting with fists flying. Punches landing fast and hard at the body lying limp under his jean clad legs and cowboy boots.

His hat is mangled and tossed aside, forgotten in his surge of violence. The other boy still fighting under him but losing power and strength with every punch Malcolm lands to his face and torso.

I look over across the circle, surprised to see the Veteran I was just thinking about sitting a few feet away, wiping his nose with a cloth. The whiskey bottle he always has with him shattered at his feet. What has Malcolm done? Why is he so angry? What did the Veteran and this boy under him do to deserve this?

Then out of nowhere, two other boys and a redheaded older man with an Irish accent, come barreling through the swarm of people. One of the boys, standing at least six-foot-tall and wearing wranglers, brown cowboy boots and a tan suede cowboy hat tackles Malcolm.

Grabbing him by the waist as the other boy and older man watch from above. The tall guy pulls Malcolm away, his body fighting to get back at the boy bloody on the pavement. I watch and don't hide my disappointment in what I just witnessed as Malcolm looks over at me standing in the crowd.

Chapter 21

Clara

As the people standing around clears, the police urge people back into the store or to their vehicles. I stand and watch as Malcolm pushes the big guy off of him and jumps into the black Ford truck I remember all too well.

The redheaded older guy hits Malcolm on the head and points at him, words coming out of his mouth so fast I can't understand them due to his heavy accent. He stands outside the passenger front window, clearly scolding Malcolm for his actions.

Malcolm argues something I can't hear, his bottom lip now swelling from the few hits the other guy landed. He wipes his lip and says something that looks like "Sorry P" or something like that. His lips are hard to read with all the swelling and the blood.

The older man's demeanor suddenly changes. He pats the side of Malcolm's head a bit, clearly in affection but with disappointment still on his face. He then climbs into the back seat of the black Ford truck. Standing on the sidewalk closest to the front door and near where the fight occurred, I stare at the truck as it drives off.

I stand with my hands on my hips, my work apron open but still hanging from my neck. Just hoping Malcolm will turn his eyes this way. Wanting to connect with him even though, I'm worried and afraid of the violence I just witnessed from him. As the black Ford truck turns out of the parking lot and onto the busy street, Malcolm looks out his window.

He sees me standing there, and watches me until the truck is completely out of sight.

All the days I would stand in this very place and wait for Malcolm to come into the store, I never thought I'd see him like I did yesterday. My mind hasn't been able to leave that circle and everything that happened. I dreamed last night of American flags, fighting cowboys and clear light green eyes. In my dream, I couldn't see Malcolm's face, just his back as he was beating the boy below him on the ground. His muscles bulging and contracting with the force of each punch.

I also pictured the Veteran on the ground next to the shattered whiskey bottle, acting like nothing really happened. The Vet is laughing the whole time; not caring about the beating Malcolm is giving some innocent kid. The whole crowd just laughs, not a single person trying to stop what's happening.

Shaking my head to try and clear the thoughts, I straighten my apron, running my hands over the knees of my jeans. I feel nervous and off balance today.

I took a page out of the Tractor Supply catalog and wore blue jeans and boots to work today. Not cowboy boots; combat, but whatever. Boots are boots, right? My hair is braided, the ponytail draped over my shoulder. Sometimes this is the only way to keep my wild blonde curls under control. I'd cut it short if I didn't think I'd look like a toad. I've never really been confident in myself and sometimes I wonder if that's why I was such a fucking brat before moving here. I look back at the last five years and regret so many things.

Today has been so hard. I miss Mama. I miss her smell, her laugh and the way she hugged me. Everything worrisome and bad in the world went away when she held me. Not that I had much to worry about back then. Before she got sick, or before I knew she was sick, my life revolved around getting my way. Making everyone else miserable while I threw tantrums.

Man, I was a fucking brat. At least I can admit that and say I regret my behavior. Now, I just want to live life and not feel lost or sad that she's gone. Move on. Now I just have to work on Daddy. He's not doing so well. This week, he's come home from work early three straight days. I'm really worried. It's only been a few weeks and his grief is so strong still, he's drowning in the ocean it's created around him. I'll find a way to help him, somehow.

Standing at my register, I look at the customers shopping in the store today. Just like every day, so many people come in and out gathering supplies for so many different reasons. Cattle supplies, horse supplies, gardening and animal feed. Every time someone comes in for feed, it's for a different animal. I've never been on a farm before so I have no idea how many different farm animals there are.

Looking at my watch, I realize it's time for my lunch break. My stomach growls at the idea of food, and I realize I'm starving. Daddy slept through dinner again so all I had was cheese and few crackers. Walking into the break room, I over hear a couple of guys talking about the fight yesterday. They work on the lot pushing buggies and carts back inside for new customers.

"Dude, it was crazy! That black dude had Baker crying and shitting in his pants. It was awesome." Laughing, he pushes his friends' shoulder playfully. Showing his enthusiasm for the topic they're discussing.

His friend laughs along, "I know! That guy deserves everything he got handed to him. He's such a dick. It's about time someone caught Baker and his posse messing with that homeless guy."

Hearing this stops me in my tracks. My heart sinks. My lunch is now forgotten. Did he say the homeless guy? I walk over, my urgency obvious in the small break room.

"What homeless guy? What are you talking about? The fight from yesterday? The black guy you mentioned, the one fighting, he was wearing a cowboy hat, right?" Both guys look down at me, surly thinking I'm crazy for interrupting their conversation.

"Yeah, he was wearing a cowboy hat. He beat the crap out of Baker; it was great!"

"What did you mean when you said that Baker kid was messing with a homeless guy?" My voice increases with every word. They can hear me fine, but my need for the information is making my voice rise with each syllable.

"Those assholes were messing with the Veteran again. Baker and his buddies always mess with the homeless guy that hangs out here. You know, the guy with the Vietnam hat?"

I feel the blood drain from my face.

The realization Malcolm was defending someone and isn't actually violent and aggressive washes over me in relief. And anger. Anger for the Veteran. So, it was Baker that I saw outside in the parking lot that day. He was pushing the Veteran around then.

It all makes sense now.

How could I have been so stupid? Now I feel incredibly guilty for assuming Malcolm is a violent and angry person. Now that I know Malcolm was just defending the Veteran, it shows his heart is big enough to defend someone who clearly can't defend themself. He protects those who need protecting. I find myself wanting to know everything about him.

And I will.

Chapter 22

Malcolm

My head is pounding this morning, the few hits Baker got in taking its toll. I'm dreading getting out of this bed, my body and head needing just a little more recovery. No matter what I feel this morning though, that guy got what he deserved. He was lucky that Sal pulled me off of him. If he hadn't, I wouldn't have been able to stop. The realization scares me less than it should. I've never been a violent person. After what happened with Lucy, I've always been the levelheaded one. But seeing Baker and his buddies push around that homeless vet, set me off.

All I could see was red. The blood was rushing hard and fast through my veins. My anger grew heavy as I watched them, making me see nothing but red. I couldn't control it anymore. I've never felt that before. Then to make things worse, Clara was there. She saw everything; disappointment and confusion written plainly on her beautiful face. All I could do was stare at her blue eyes that were staring back at me. I'm hoping I haven't missed my chance with Clara. Now, I'll have to explain myself. She'll want to know everything. I've never been good at sharing pieces of myself with anyone.

I went to the Tractor Supply yesterday hoping to see Clara. I was thrilled when Pop asked the three of us to ride along. He needed more posts for the cattle corrals we're building behind the barn. Pop knew he would need help loading them into the truck.

Adler had stayed behind, not wanting to leave while he was working on the flooring of the new stage. I'm relieved he wasn't there. It's bad enough Tate and Sal had to witness my anger.

And Pop, God; he was pissed. I thought he was going to kill me as I walked back to the truck. My head already hurt but Pop scolding me was way more painful than my pounding head. There's nothing worse than Clara seeing Baker and I fight. Except for Pop's disappointment in me. But even with his disappointment, I would do it again. I would beat Baker over and over with no regret.

That's what I told Pop at the truck and he was still furious with me. Yelling at me in Gaelic. His words fast and loud, the smack he delivered telling me how stupid it was to be fighting outside a public place. Repeating himself in English, his concerns about my behavior not quite what I thought he was going to say.

"Stupid, stupid, lad. Ye trying to get yourself banned from the Marine Corp?"

"No, Pop. I know it was stupid, but Baker was being an asshole to Vinnie, that Vietnam Vet that lives behind the store. I couldn't let him keep treating him like that. Baker and his buddies are always pushing him around." I could feel the blood dripping down my chin as I tried to explain myself.

"Ye have a good soul son. But ye gotta watch yer'self." He patted the side of my head lightly this time, with love and understanding behind the gesture. Pop's anger fizzled out as he hopped into the back seat with Tate.

"Yer future is more important than anything else. Be smarter Malcolm on ye efforts to help. Ye can help those who need ye in more productive ways, not with ye fists. Remember that."

That's when I saw Clara. Standing there, her hands on her hips staring back at me with so much confusion.

"Ok, Pop. I gotcha," I say.

Tate and Sal both were equally happy about my outburst at Baker. They didn't express that around Pop but they sure did once we got back home. Tate had the first chance and gave it to Baker really good the day Lucy died. That one act, on the worst day any of us had ever had, kept Baker away from us for five years. Now I worry I've opened a floodgate, one that has been shut and locked for so long until yesterday.

The consequences of us opening the gate aren't known yet. Pop reiterates Baker Landry's father will be looking for any reason to bring trouble to us, especially after Tate's fight with him years ago. Not to mention my fight with Baker yesterday.

Baker's father is a judge in Jefferson County, with hopes of becoming a Congressman soon and he'll likely use any and all power he has to ruin our family.

Today I've got to go find Clara, see if I can explain exactly what happened. Hopefully she doesn't think I'm too violent and unpredictable to spend her time with. If I can just convince her I'm not the violent man she saw yesterday, I know I can show her who I really am.

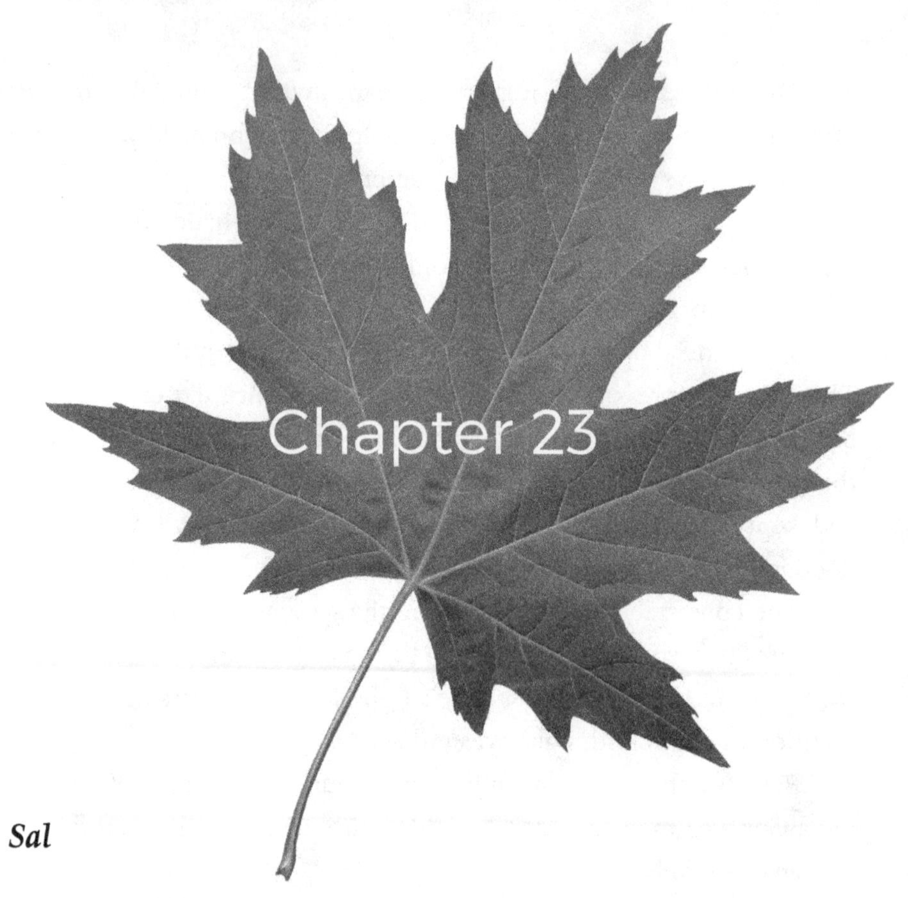

Chapter 23

Sal

While I'm both shocked and surprised that Malcolm was fighting with Baker in a store parking lot, I've never been prouder of my brother than I am right now.

God knows we came from rough beginnings. But since moving to the ranch with Pop and Tate, life has been easier. Allowing us to grow into men and to help us discover what paths our lives will likely take after high school.

Hell, if anyone had asked me five years ago, I would've said I'd be in jail or dead by now. But that hasn't happened, and I'm not dead yet. Like Pop said, we've got to keep straight and narrow. The military has strict and specific guidelines to be eligible to enlist. There won't be another draft; at least not anytime soon. So, staying on the right path is our only way to fulfill the dreams we've had since leaving the fosters.

Even Tate has decided to join the military. Pop and Old Man Keating are excited at the idea of having a Keating fighting for the country they have grown to love so much. My only concern is Adler. He wants to join with us but my fear being that he's just not military material. It's the same fear we all share.

The guy is smart. Adler can do things with electronics I don't think have ever been done before. That kid could probably one day cure cancer, he's that smart.

But the Marines?

Could he even survive basic training with all the pressure and force of the work? I don't think so. So, now we've gotta find a way to convince him that staying here and going to college is what's best for him. How do we do that without him hating us for it? Malcolm walks into my room and I'm glad for the distraction.

"Hey," he says. Dazed from yesterday's events.

"Morning. How's your head?" Standing in the open bathroom doorway, pulling my boots on, Malcolm moves to sit in the wingback chair in the corner, next to the bed.

"Hurts like hell," he exhales, leaning back on the chair and shutting his eyes.

I laugh. "Yeah but I bet you wouldn't hesitate getting that headache all over again just to have another chance to beat the hell out of Baker."

Keeping his head back he says, "God, he's such an asshole. I couldn't control it, Sal. My anger. My hate. That guy just finally set me off."

Slowly I move toward Malcolm, taking a seat on my bed.

"Dude, you can control your anger. Baker just happens to bring out the not so happy part of you." Resting my elbows on my knees and my head in my hands. I push my long dark hair away from my eyes and look up at Malcolm. Damn, I need a haircut.

"Yeah, he sure does; he brings out the worst in me," Malcolm says as he sits up. "Hey; I'm headed into town. Got a couple errands to run. What's your plan for today?" Looking up I reply, "Actually, if you don't mind, I'll tag along?"

Malcolm hesitates, his eyes narrowing, "Yeah, ok. But I don't know how long I'll be gone." Standing up, he walks toward the door.

"Well, I've got nothing else to do. I just want to get a haircut."

"All right, I'll meet you in the truck," Malcolm says, pulling the door open as he leaves.

I grab my leather jacket, putting my arms through. I love the smell of the leather just as much as I did the first day I got this jacket. The smell is more subtle, but still strong enough to help me remember. To always remember.

I jump up into the truck and roll down the window to rest my arm on the windowsill.

My curiosity at why he doesn't seem to want my company today is getting the better of me. I look over at him, hoping he'll spill it. He doesn't.

Malcolm has always been more secretive and private than the rest of us, but this is different. It's got me wondering what he's hiding.

We ride with only the soft sound of the music coming out of the speakers.

It's on a jazz station. The smooth sounds of a saxophone, electric guitar and piano fills my ears. It's Malcolm's favorite. Always has been, since we moved to the farm, anyway. He may dress, work and look like a cowboy, but he's a crooner in reality. Old Man Keating introduced us to music not long after we moved to the farm. All kinds of music. Country, Rock, R&B, Classic Jazz and of course, Scottish Folk Music. He even has bagpipes. I laugh at the thought.

That gets Malcolm's attention. He looks over at me, annoyance on his face.

"What's so funny?" he asks.

"This music. It makes me think about the Old Man and his bagpipes." I laugh again. This time meaning for him to hear me and hope it lightens his mood.

He smiles. "He looks ridiculous in that kilt too." Our joint laughter fills the truck.

"Nah man, he looks sexy to the lassies," I say in my best Scottish accent.

"Ha, and we wonder why he's not married." Malcolm's mood is better now that we're talking about Pop.

"If you'll just drop me off at Sonny's, I'll wait for you to come back to pick me up." I say.

Sonny's is a local barbershop. It's the only one left in this area, the rest bought out by chain companies and franchising ideas. All crooks, if you ask me. Pop says its modern-day assholes changing up investments and making them no longer trustworthy.

He pulls up to the curb, and puts the truck into park, "I won't be too long; give me thirty minutes or so, k?"

Nodding, I jump out of the truck and head in. This haircut is way overdue.

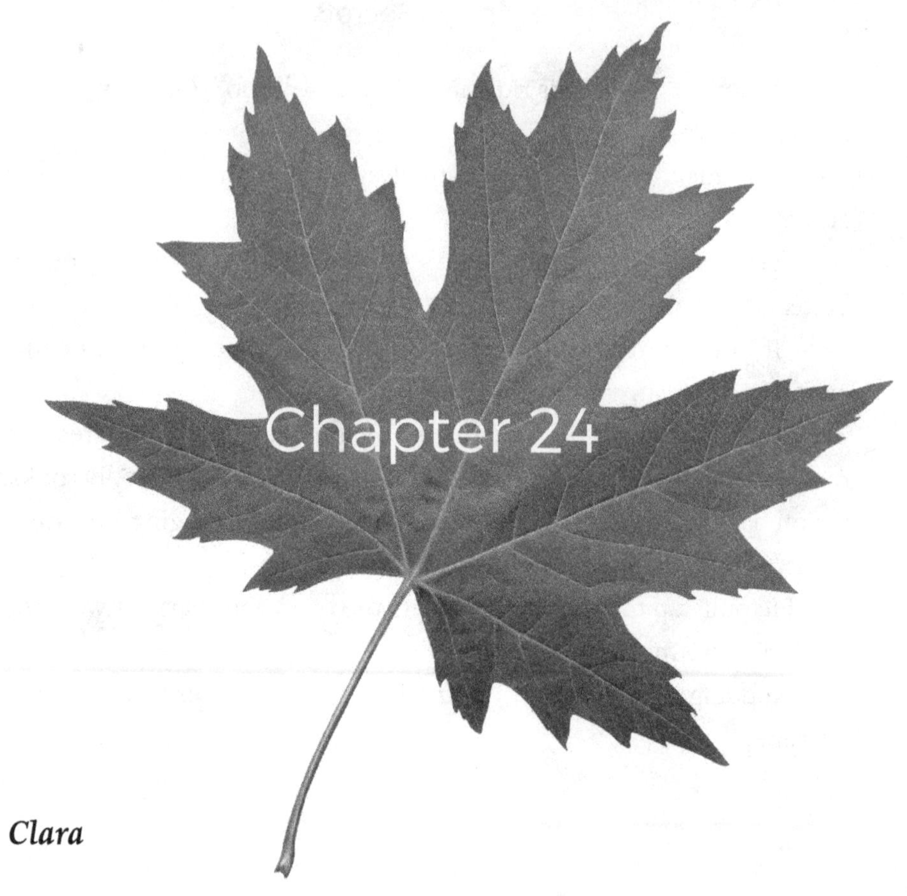

Chapter 24

Clara

Louie comes through the break room doors as I'm turning to leave.

He stops just inside, the door slightly open and says, "Clara; there you are. There's someone asking for you. I'm not sure you should go anywhere with him though. I could stay with you if you want." Worry flashes on his face.

Trying to look around him and out the crack in the door I say, "Why? Who is it?"

All I can see is a shadow of someone standing outside the door. My braid is falling down my back from the strain of my body trying to see around Louie.

"It's that boy from yesterday, the one that was fighting in the parking lot."

Now my heart races for a totally different reason than before. Not out of fear or apprehension that Malcolm is here, but out of excitement. Pure excitement that he's here to see me.

"Oh, Louie; thanks for the offer, but I'll be just fine." He winces as I move past him.

Grabbing my arm, he says "Clara, be careful. That boy is nothing but trouble."

I give his arm a pat, "I could argue with you on that, Louie. Be careful who you judge when you don't know the whole story."

Really Clara? That's exactly the same thing I've been telling myself for the last few minutes. Taking a step forward, I push the door open and walk out. Malcolm stands just outside the door, his hands in his pockets. He's wearing jeans and boots, his cowboy hat nowhere to be found. "No hat today, cowboy?" I ask.

Shrugging he says, "Nah. I really only wear one when I'm working. Can we talk? Are you on break?"

"Yeah, let's go outside. I still have thirty minutes. Want to get something to eat next door at the café?"

"Sure." He says.

Wiping my hands on my jeans to clear the sweat, I walk ahead. A few seconds later Malcolm walks up next to me. Our strides are equal in pace and speed. Leaving the store and heading toward the café, Malcolm doesn't wait to explain what happened yesterday.

While looking right at me, his light green eyes are full of apology. "I'm sorry you had to see that yesterday. I'm not even sure what happened really, it all happened so fast. I just knew I had to do something when I saw Baker and his buddies pushing around Vinnie."

The fact that he knows his name makes me like him even more. Malcolm continues to explain, but I've already heard enough. "I just couldn't let it go on anymore. My anger got the best of me and I reacted. I'm so sorry you saw that."

I ask, "Who were those two boys who pulled you off of Baker? That older man? Were they friends of yours?"

"Actually, they're my brothers. The older man, he's my Pop." Malcolm looks down at his feet as we walk.

"Your brothers? Hmm… are you sure? Have you looked in a mirror lately?" I can't believe I just said that out loud. Doesn't my mouth have a filter? God, Clara? Don't be a bitch. You're supposed to like this guy. Malcolm lets me off the hook with a laugh. He's looking at me like he gets this question all the time.

Laughing he says, "I have three brothers' actually. Blood and genetics don't make a family, Clara. Love and loyalty do."

Well he fucking got me there.

"I'm sorry, Malcolm. Damn, you must think I'm a total bitch." I kick at a rock as we walk down the sidewalk. Keeping my head down, my hands in my back pockets, I use my left hand to reposition my braid back over my left shoulder.

"Nah, we get it all the time." His smile is big, showing his slightly crooked but white teeth.

Entering the café, Malcolm holds the door open, waiting for me to go through first. My heart beats faster as he places his hand at the small of my back to guide me through the door. I like how my face flushes, butterflies taking flight in my belly.

I'm surprised when an older man in an apron smiles and waves our way.

The café is small, with a 1950's theme. It even has half a car sticking out of the back wall that looks like they use it as a table for guests. It's setup with a small jukebox on the table, that's positioned strategically against the wall. The floors are white and black checkers. Pictures of Marilyn Monroe and Elvis cover the walls. There's a soda bar with stools in front. Wow, this place is cool.

Even the wait staff is part of the charm. They wear white aprons and black collared polo shirts with black slacks. The theme is very trendy, with an exciting hint at what it was like to live back then. This whole time I've been working right next door to this café, and I've never come in here. I've clearly been missing out. The smell in here is amazing.

The older guy wipes off the counter in front of him and says, "Hey, Malcolm! It's been a while. Why haven't you come by to see us, son? And where are your brothers? Adler promised to help me install the new security system we just bought."

"Clara, have a seat here, I'll be right back." Malcolm motions to the soda bar, his hand still nestled against my lower back as I sit. He walks toward the guy in the apron.

I can hardly hear what they are saying over the music blasting through the speakers. Trying to hide my eavesdropping, I turn toward the opposite direction, keeping my ears peeled so I don't miss anything important. I wonder how he knows this guy so well.

Walking up to lean against the bar, Malcolm's right hand meets the other man's in a shake that brings the men in for an embrace.

"Hey, Bill; I know it's been awhile. I'm sorry about that. The farm's been really busy this summer. Old Man Keating is keeping us working longer these days. How are things here? It smells great! The new menu working out like you hoped?" Malcolm says as he stands in front of Bill, his arms crossed across his chest, his stance wide, a huge smile and look of admiration on his face.

"It's been great! We have more business lately than we know what to do with. Are you two staying to eat?" The men walk back toward me as they talk. Malcolm takes the seat next to me at the bar. He sits so that his knees are straddling both sides of my body as I sit facing the bar. One of his arms rests on the bar, and the other taking its place on his knee. It's intimate in a way. Maybe it just seems that way because of how I felt when he touched me to guide me into the café.

Looking over at me, Malcolm nods and says, "Give us both the *Lost and Found* special, and two vanilla milkshakes please, Bill."

Before Bill can walk off, I say, "Wait, I want a chocolate milkshake, please!" Bill looks over at me, then at Malcolm. Smiling, I look between both of them as they stare me down. Raising my eyebrows, I look at Malcolm and decide maybe I should have stayed with the vanilla, like he ordered.

"Umm, ok. I guess vanilla it is!" I say, smiling, not wanting them to keep staring at me. There must be a story behind the vanilla milkshake. I resolve to ask about it later, my questions for Malcolm more pressing than whether to have chocolate or vanilla. I've never had someone order food for me. I mean other than my parents, and even then, they let me pick my drink.

Bill writes down the order on his pad, and then walks to the little window that shows just a small part of the kitchen. He pulls the sheet off the pad and secures it to one of the revolving clips that holds all the other orders coming into the kitchen. Waitresses move from table to table, filling water and coffee glasses and placing orders. This place is really busy.

I decide not to mention the milkshake. That is obviously something that bothers Malcolm. I have a feeling; secrets and stories are his specialty. I bet he has a ton of secrets he doesn't tell many other people; if anyone at all.

Sitting at the bar, Malcolm doesn't keep quiet. He continues to explain what happened yesterday.

But now, I'm more interested in his family. And how he knows Bill. He tells me about his tie to Baker as Bill sets our milkshakes down in front of us. I take a sip through the red straw sticking from the glass. Malcolm just nods his thanks to his friend.

"Baker and I go way back. Well actually, we all go way back. He's been a thorn in our family's side for years. So, when I saw him and his friends messing with Vinnie, I couldn't let it go."

I ask, "What's the history? Why does he set you off like that? I mean, I'm all for defending people who can't defend themselves, but what's the story with Baker?"

Shaking his head, he pauses as Bill sets two glasses of water down in front of us. Bill eyes Malcolm as if he's trying to tell him something in confidence.

"We went to school together. He's been in a fight with my brother Tate once. That's really all it is." He shrugs, "Ever since the fight, Baker has left us alone. But his father, he's had it in for our family ever since. We've just been waiting for the other shoe to drop. And now my fight with Baker yesterday might have caused that shoe to fall."

"Why is his father out to get you and your brothers? What does he think you did?"

"If beating his son wasn't enough, Pop says he needs someone to make an example out of for the election. Pop is doing his best to ensure his example doesn't involve his sons. That's all," Malcolm says, trying to play it off as if there's nothing to worry about. I have a feeling there's much more to this story.

Exhaling, I continue my questions. "What election? What is his father running for?"

"Baker's father was a lawyer back when Tate and Baker got into it. Now he's a judge and running for Congress."

"But why does he want to make an example out of you? Or your brothers?" My questions continue but are interrupted by Bill.

"Here you go kids. The *Lost and Found* special, at your service." Bill smiles as he sets the plates down. I see the biggest, most beautiful cheeseburger before me. Fries covered in seasoning and fried into perfect wedges. Cheese and bacon loaded onto the meat make my mouth water. Malcolm shifts in his seat, turning from me to face his own burger.

"Wow; that looks good!" I say.

"Yeah, Bill makes the best burgers in town." Malcolm picks up his burger, taking a huge bite. He closes his eyes, a small moan coming from his lips. The enjoyment on his face is almost contagious. It's like this is the first cheeseburger he's ever had or maybe the last one he'll ever have. I can't help but stare as he eats. His eyes closed, his dark skin slightly moist from the heat today, his lips moving with the chewing motion as he eats his burger. He opens his eyes and looks over at me; his green eyes to my blue. I'm so fascinated by the way he enjoys his food; I haven't taken a single bite yet. He motions with his head for me to eat. His hands and mouth full of the delicacy I know I'm about to enjoy. I look down, take the burger in my hands, open my mouth wide and take the biggest bite my mouth can take.

It's like a dream in my mouth. The flavors blend together, allowing me to taste each part, but only subtly. I close my eyes. I can hear my own moan as I chew. I hear Malcolm shifting in his seat beside me.

Opening my eyes, I feel the weight of Malcolm's stare. He looks at me, a very serious look on his face. His eyes bright and clear. The most beautiful green I've ever seen.

"Damn woman, do you always eat a hamburger like that?" Shaking his head, he says, "I'll be right back; going to the bathroom."

Walking away, he uses his napkin to wipe away the burger still on his hands. I watch him leave; appreciating the wranglers he's wearing today. While he's gone, I use the time to devour the rest of my burger.

Bill walks up just as I'm taking my last bite of French fries.

"Hey, Sweetie; would you like another shake?"

I didn't even notice I had already finished my vanilla shake. My burger is gone; there is only a few fries left on my plate. I can't believe I ate the whole plate.

"No, thank you Bill. I'm so full. I can't even finish these last few fries!" Rubbing my full belly, I say, "You can take the plate, I'm done."

Bill replies, "No, I think I'll leave it. Malcolm will eat those last few fries; I promise!" Smiling he walks away, swaying to the music playing out of the jukebox.

Malcolm comes back from the bathroom. His demeanor has changed a bit. He forces a smile and looks down at my plate.

"What's wrong Malcolm? Are you ok?"

Sitting back down next to me, he says, "I'm fine. Are you going eat those?" he asks about the few fries still on my plate.

Not surprised at all by his question, I motion my head from side to side saying no. He picks up the last few fries, eats them, and then finishes the rest of his own in a few fast minutes. The burger, fries, and tiny pieces all down the hatch and into Malcolm's stomach.

"Wow, I've never seen someone eat so much!" I say, laughing. I don't admit this to him, but watching him eat was exotic and sexy.

"You ate just as much as me, minus those few fries." Malcolm raises his eyebrows and smiles. Just trying to play around, I say, "Are you calling me fat, cowboy?"

His face drops, and he turns toward me. His legs are back to straddling my body, apology written all over his face. "God, Clara; I'm so sorry!"

Laughing, I say, "it's ok; I was just messing with you! It was so good! That's the best burger I've ever had." Looking down at my watch, I notice I'm ten minutes late back from lunch.

"Shit! I'm late getting back! I've gotta go Malcolm." Leaping from the stool, I grab my Tractor Supply apron and head toward the door. Malcolm gets up, throws a ten down on the bar and follows behind me.

As we hit the door, Malcolm says, "Bill, I'll send Adler your way to help with the security equipment! Thanks for lunch! See you later!" Bill waves as the door closes behind us.

Malcolm jogs to catch up to me on the sidewalk.

"Sorry I made you late getting back."

"No biggie, I just don't want Louie to call the police cause I'm late. He's not your biggest fan right now, Rocky!" I look at him sideways, my smile bright despite my full belly. I'm miserable on the inside, eating way more than usual at the cafe. I won't have to eat for a month!

"I heard what Louie said. Don't feel like you have to defend me; I can defend myself."

"I already know that, Malcolm. I have no doubt you can defend yourself and anyone else you deem needs defending. It's what I like about you." Now we're standing at the front entrance of the Tractor Supply. Malcolm looks nervous all of a sudden.

"Thanks for lunch, I've gotta go. I'll see you around?" Turning I head toward the door, hoping Malcolm will stop me. Closing my eyes briefly in hope, I walk to the door and reach for the handle.

"Clara, wait," he says. My heart pounds as I turn around, those butterflies once again taking flight in my belly. The hope that he'll ask me out again rising now that he's stopped me.

"Yeah?" I say.

"Can I see you again?" he asks. Hope is written in the form of a smile on his face.

Walking over to Malcolm, I pull a pen out of my apron and write my phone number down on the inside of his forearm. The black pen displays the numbers on his dark skin.

"Call me." Smiling, I turn and open the door but Malcolm stops me again.

"Clara, thanks. Oh, and I wanted to tell you, I don't ever want to hear you talk about yourself negatively again, ok? You're not a bitch and I can't imagine you ever could be. Your lack of a filter is a turn on. Remember that please. Never question what comes to your mind or out of your mouth. It's never wrong. Ok." Malcolm walks backwards for a few steps then turns and walks away from me.

At first, I had to think about what he said. Did I call myself a bitch?

Oh, yeah; I did. Earlier when I commented on my big mouth not having a filter. I smile as I walk in, feeling pretty great after spending that time with Malcolm. Excited at the idea we will see each other again, soon. At least I hope we will.

I can see myself diving into a relationship with Malcolm; this stranger who clearly has secrets. Secrets, I am determined to find out about. Somehow.

Chapter 25

Malcolm

Today couldn't have gone any better than it did. Spending time with Clara was just what I was hoping for. Now I can't wait to see her again. I want to spend more time discovering her, instead of her trying to discover me. If she knew my whole story, surely it would run her off. That's the last thing I want.

God, I've only been around her for a short time and I can't shake this feeling of needing to see her again. To hear her laugh. To hear that moan again. Fuck, she was turning me on just with the noises she was making. She didn't even realize what she was doing to me. She had no idea she was causing me to swell painfully. So painfully I had to get up and go to the bathroom to readjust myself. And all she was doing was eating a hamburger. I can only imagine what effect she would have if we were actually doing something that involved touching her.

Sliding into the driver side of the truck, I see Sal coming out of the barbershop, his hair really short. Sal's hair has always been long, dark and curly. He looks so different.

Sal climbs up into the seat. Looking at me, I give him a sideways stare.

"Who are you and where is Sal? Did you do something to my brother?" I say with a smile.

"Ha. I know it's short but I figure they'll make me cut it the first day of boot camp anyway. This way I have a year to get used to the idea." He runs his right hand over his newly buzzed head. Wow; he looks so different. Now his eyes seem darker than before, his face more defined. The Italian is coming out in him in full color. Getting used to this new Sal will be hard. I've only ever seen him with long dark hair always in his eyes. The motion of moving it from his brow is a signature move we've all come to know.

As I put the truck in reverse, Sal notices the writing on my arm. "Dude, what's written on your arm? Are you trying to remember when your last period was?" He laughs, "Oh wait, that was this morning, right? I almost forgot. I guess you should write that somewhere everyone can see, that way we all know when you're going to act like a pussy."

My middle finger shows him my thoughts on his comment. Nothing can ruin the high I'm on right now.

I exhale, "It's none of your business asshole." Knowing that won't be the end of it, I try changing the subject.

"Anywhere else you need to go before we head back?" I ask him.

"Nah, I've got some chores to do back at the farm. I promised Pop and Old Man Keating I'd help with the corrals this afternoon." He rolls down the window, cranking the handle over and over until the window is fully down and the summer air fills the cab of the truck. We ride back to the farm in silence, the quiet something Sal and I have always been most comfortable in.

Back at the farm, Pop steps out of the barn and motions for us to follow him into the partially finished corrals.

"These here will be bonnie when they're done. The cattle and horses should be fine with this, I think." Nodding he says to Sal, "Hey, son; can I have a blether with Malcolm a second? The Old Man could use yer help out there with that section." He points out to where Old Man Keating is sitting on an old folding chair he keeps in the back of his truck. It's just perfect for times like these when he's working out in the field and needs a break. The Old Man's not getting any younger these days.

"Sure; I'll see you later." Sal moves through the first gates of the corral, his now baldhead shiny in the sunlight.

"What's up, Pop?" I say while leaning against the same gate Sal just went through.

"Ye remember when I said yesterday that Baker's father would be doing his best to make things hard for ye after what happened? I was right. He was here earlier." He leans up against the gate, mirroring me.

"He was here? Why?" My eyes are fixed on Pop's now. Eager to hear why Judge Landry would be at the farm today and what his agenda appears to be.

"He's just tryin' to stir up trouble; says Baker was sent to the emergency room for what ye did to him." I can't hide my smile as I look over at Sal now following the direction the Old Man is giving him.

I reach up, touching my sore lip, remembering exactly what I did to Baker.

"Ye gotta stay away from him, Malcolm. One more strike with Baker and his father says he'll sue for harassment, along with pressing charges for assault." Pop lifts his old dirty green baseball hat and scratches his head, "Three strikes are all we get, son, and after Tate's run in five years ago with Baker and now this, he's determined to ruin the both of ye. He won't stop until he's got ye by the balls."

Even with Judge Landry's threats, there is nothing that can ruin this day.

"It's all right Pop, he's all talk. His bark is bigger than his bite. I'll stay away, only because you asked me too. But if I do have any issues with Baker, I'll be smart, ok? He won't have any reason to push any further."

"Ye better hope not. Yer future depends on ye staying out of trouble. It's one year, son. One year and ye'll be traveling the world, seeing things people like Baker will only dream of. Keep ye nose clean, I beg ye." Patting him on the shoulder I say, "I will Pop. Promise. Now I got a call to make. I'll be back out to help with the corrals in a second." I smile at him as I walk toward the main house. He raises his eyebrows, his green hat haphazardly sitting on his head. "Aye, don't make any plans away from this farm until next week, kid; these corrals aren't going to finish themselves. That girl can wait."

Still walking toward the house but turning to walk sideways as I yell back, "What girl?" Playing dumb, I raise my hands and shrug at his attempt for more info.

"Ye can't fool me boy. That number on your arm was written by a lass. I wasn't born yesterday."

Smiling, I return my gaze to forward, ignoring the continued comments behind me, raising my hand and waving as I walk up onto the porch, I walk inside and head straight toward the phone in the hallway.

I've got a girl to ask out.

Chapter 26

Clara

Heading home after my shift is always one of my favorite times of the day. My father's struggle with his grief is having me worry more and more each day. The moments we have together feel so much more important these days. Every time I come home I have a feeling of dread. I guess it's just leftover worry from when Mama was sick.

Pulling my car into my assigned spot at the apartment, I get out into the fresh air, inhaling deeply. I stand outside the car with the door still open, lifting my head up I feel the sun heat my face. Taking deep breaths, then exhaling, I shut the door, grab my purse and head up the stairs. We live on the second level of the building. I would've preferred the bottom level, but we took what was available in the short time we had to move.

I hear the phone ringing as soon as I reach the door. As I try to insert the key, my keys drop to the ground in my rush to get the door open.

"Fuck." My second attempt at putting the key in the lock is successful and I hear the answering machine pick up just as I get the door open.

"You've reached Stan, Gayle and Clara. We're not home but if you leave a message, we'll call you back." My mother's voice causes that familiar ache in my chest to return. Daddy and I both agreed it's too painful to change the message. I know we should. This is part of why my father is struggling to move on. But it doesn't matter, I still don't have the heart to change it.

The familiar beep chimes and then I hear Malcolm's deep baritone voice. "Clara, it's Malcolm. I hate that I missed you; call me back. I'm headed out to help with the corrals so I won't be near the phone until to…" Dropping my purse and keys on the floor, I answer the phone, a little out of breath, "Hello… hey, Malcolm. Are you there?"

"Hey, yourself. What are you doing? You sound a little winded."

"I was trying to get to the phone before you hung up. You were saying on the message that you wouldn't be near a phone for a call back. Where are you going?"

"Oh, Pop has us all on lockdown for all of next week. We're building new corrals for the livestock. The old farts need us young ones to help out." Malcolm says as he laughs before continuing, "I'd like to see you again though. I had a great time at the café."

I smile so wide with excitement, and knowing that he can't see me, I dance a little in place. "I had fun, too. I wish we would've had more time to talk." I have so many more questions I would like answered. Clearing his throat, he says, "Yeah; me, too. How about next weekend, we could hang out? Maybe go fishing? My family has a pond on the back forty, stocked with catfish and bass."

Rolling my eyes and covering the phone receiver so he can't hear me, I groan. What is it with men and fishing? God, if I weren't so interested in getting to know Malcolm better, this relationship would be over before it starts.

"Eh…Ok. Fishing, sounds fun." I smile to make my voice not sound so disappointed.

Malcolm then digs deeper into my nightmare. "I'll pick you up, say 7 am? Saturday morning?"

"Wait, What?" This time I don't try to hide my apprehension. "7 am? Are you crazy? On a Saturday that I'm off work?"

"Best time, that's when the fish bite."

"Malcolm, you're lucky you're so damn good looking or I wouldn't be going anywhere with you that early on a Saturday." Grumbling, I hear him chuckle on the other end of the line.

"Great. I gotta go, duty calls. See you next weekend, Clara." The excitement for what's to come now coming through in his voice. Maybe this won't be so bad. If this gets him excited then I can make the best of it, I guess.

"Bye, Malcolm." Hanging up the phone, I plop down in the recliner next to the small end table where the phone rests.

Fishing. Damn, maybe I should've paid closer attention to Daddy all those times we went fishing together. I should've tried to show interest in the sport Daddy loves. Just as I'm getting up, the phone begins to ring again.

I answer on the second ring, "Yeah, Hello?"

"Hey. How am I supposed to pick you up? I don't know where you live." Laughing, Malcolm's baritone is back on the other end of the line. Sitting back down on the chair, I tease him a little.

"Well, that does make things hard for you doesn't it? How are your investigation skills?"

"Stalking isn't a specialty of mine, but I could probably find out where you live. My Pop does know the owner of Tractor Supply…." Malcolm teases, trailing off as if making a threat.

Giggling, I say, "Not necessary, breaking the law by stalking me won't get us anywhere. 515 Blue Bass road. Apt 210. See you next weekend, Malcolm."

"Bye, Clara. See you later."

Hanging up, I resolve myself to try. Just try to be happy and excited about fishing. Man, if Mama could see me now. She wouldn't believe any of this, that's for sure. I lift my eyes to the sky, sending a silent prayer, *"Mama please give me the strength not to make a fool of myself."*

Chapter 27

Malcolm

"So, today's the day huh?" Sal stands outside my bedroom door, holding up the doorframe with his large body.

"Yeah. I'm leaving here in a few minutes. After I pick up Clara, we'll head straight to the pond." Looking down at my watch, I see it's 6:15 am. Plenty of time to pick up Clara and get to the water before the fish stop biting. She doesn't know it yet but what we catch today is what Pop will make for dinner tonight. And I'm hoping she'll stay long enough to eat with us.

It may seem too soon to bring a girl I just met here for a family dinner, but this family is non-conventional. Pop and Old Man Keating always say the more the merrier. They like having our friends around. They've always welcomed any additions to dinner. Tate's been dating Rebecca, a girl from school. She's been to dinner a few times now. We all like her and it's been nice to have a female presence in the house.

Clara will fit right in. Rebecca is a lot like Clara in that they both speak their mind. I'm just grateful to be in a place where we have dinner at all.

"All right, have fun and keep your dick in your pants. We don't need a little Malcolm running around. See you two at dinner tonight. If you catch anything, that is." Laughing he pushes off the doorframe with his shoulder, I manage to flip him off just as he heads down stairs to do his morning chores.

I got up extra early this morning. My chores today are less taxing than Sal's. With Pop knowing I had this planned with Clara, he had Tate and Sal split my harder chores. I do it for them when they need me to, so today they are just repaying the favor.

Grabbing a light jacket off my bed, I shut the door behind me and head down the stairs. The house is quiet, with everyone already outside, tending to the farm.

The weather is beautiful. No clouds, just clear blue morning sky without any haze to obstruct the view. The pond will have a beautiful reflection of the distant mountains. The only thing breaking this image will be the fish jumping in and out of the water.

Pulling into the apartment complex Clara lives in, I see her white Dodge parked under a covered space. It's now that I see the Susan G Komen sticker on the passenger side of the back windshield. The pink ribbon, which symbolizes women and their battle with breast cancer, taking center in my mind.

She must know someone who died or who is currently battling breast cancer. The foundation was founded only a few years back and I only know about it because the school did a fund raiser last year. Pop and Old Man Keating donated truckloads of fresh food and produce. They also send some of the proceeds from our Fall Festival to the foundation. Pop and Old Man Keating feel it's their duty to help find a cure. Unfortunately, Mrs. Keating fought and lost her battle with breast cancer when Tate was just a young boy.

Parking the truck, I see Clara coming down the stairs.

I enjoy the view as she walks toward the truck. Looking her up and down, I like what I see. She's wearing jean shorts with tiny holes on the thighs, frayed edges, with white sandals on her feet. Her tight yellow tank top makes her blonde hair glow brighter in the sunshine. Her hair is pulled back in two braids, each one lying over her shoulders. Tiny yellow bows are tied at the end of each braid. I open my door and jump out, running to the other side to open her door before she can reach for the handle. She's carrying a small lunch pail.

"Hey!" She says as she reaches me. I can't help but stare at her. She's so beautiful. Her blue eyes a stark contrast against the yellow of her shirt and the blonde of her hair.

"Hey, yourself. You ready?"

"Yep; let's go!" She takes my offered hand and I help her into the truck. I hold on a little longer than needed once she is safely up and in the seat. She smiles softly at me as I climb into the seat beside her. I look over at her as I maneuver the truck onto the highway, heading west toward the farm. "What you got there?" I ask.

Her face reddens a little, as she pats the red and blue lunch pail in her lap. "Well, you didn't mention anything about lunch, so I brought sandwiches. My Daddy always says fishing makes him hungry so I thought… sandwiches and potato chips would be good to have." She trails off as she looks at me across the console between us. "I hope you like ham and American cheese, with mayo?"

I don't tell her that I will eat anything you put in front of me, scared that one day I will again not have anything to eat. The fear makes it easy to like all food, no matter how bland or dry. I like a greasy cheeseburger like everyone else, but I'll never turn down any kind of food.

"My favorite," is all I say, hoping she doesn't see the look on my face I always get when food is involved.

"So, Malcolm, tell me more about your family and how you came to live on a farm with three brothers and a father you look nothing like?" The curiosity on her face makes it easier to answer her questions. She clearly is interested in my secrets and if she keeps looking at me like that, I just might tell her all of them.

"Well, I met Sal and Adler in foster care." That gets her attention. I didn't think she could be any more focused on me before, but now she's all ears. Her blue eyes widen with pity. This is always the reaction I get. It's why I don't talk about my years in foster care. It made me who I am now, and gave me the family I never thought I'd have. So, I wouldn't change anything and I sure don't want anyone's sympathy or pity. If I'm not sorry about my upbringing and entry into the world, no one else should be either. The only thing I wish I could change is that Lucy would be here with us now.

"Pop is Tate's father. We met at school while Sal, Adler and I were in foster care. Pop was our guidance counselor at Jefferson Middle School. At the time, we lived in, let's just say, an uncomfortable and unimaginable situation with foster parents the State of Colorado placed us with. The day I met Tate was the day our lives changed forever. That day was also our first run in with Baker. So, like I said, we go way back. We lived with Jeff and Jenny until the incident and then Pop took us in. The rest is pretty much history. What about you Clara? What's your story?" I glance over at Clara, while still driving toward the farm, just hoping I gave her enough information to change the subject. I know it won't be forever but for now will do.

"Not much really, I live with my dad, Stan. We moved here from North Carolina. End of story. Nothing else to tell." She shifts in her seat, obviously uncomfortable with my questions. She tries to hide her discomfort with a smile but I can tell she's bothered. I wish she would open up to me. I was hoping that if I gave her something, anything, she'd open up in return. Maybe her story is newer than mine. Maybe it just happened and the wound is fresh, still bleeding, making it hard to talk about.

Turning the corner, we drive past the fields where the corn is planted. I love the corn growth at this stage. It makes me feel like anything can grow and be fruitful. With enough love and care, that is. The stalks stand so proud, so ready and eager to please. Their crop gives us health and wealth; it's like they know their purpose. Since Clara clearly doesn't want to discuss her life, I try to make the conversation lighter somehow.

"These fields here belong to the farm," I point out as Clara leans on the console to look out my window. She places her right hand gently on my forearm. With butterflies in my stomach, my blood begins to boil. Her touch is like fire on my overheated skin.

I tell her all about how Nexus Farms came to be what it is now. Hoping to keep the conversation off of me for now and making her feel better about my questions. I explain how Old Man Keating begged Pop and his wife to move to America. "He needed help with the farm. The chores and the overall work far too exhausting for an aging Scottish man. Pop and the Old Man hadn't spoken in years; their relationship estranged. One day, Pop's wife Blair, also Tate's mother, reached out to her father-in-law. Secretly, Blair had kept a semblance of a relationship with the Old Man, unknown to Pop. Blair had been diagnosed with cancer that summer. And in Scotland, they didn't have the same curative mentality and mindset with breast cancer treatment they did back in the states."

Clara stares at me, her eyes telling me she wants to hear more. I continue, "Blair continued to keep the illness from Pop. They had Tate, after all, and he was still so young. Blair was scared, and had no one to turn to. So, she confided in the Old Man and asked him for help. He was able to find a doctor in Denver doing a clinical trial. Now remember, it was the early 70's at that time and the Vietnam War was going on hot and heavy. The conflict in the U.S. made it hard for immigrants to come into the country. Refugees were pouring in, and the amount of Vietnam refugees hindered the amount of people able to come over."

Swallowing, I continue on, "They actually ended up getting married. That was the only way they could get to America. Blair had been accepted to the trial and they were desperate to get here." I look over at her and see confusion written on her face. She pauses then says, "Wait, they got married? Who got married exactly?"

I responded, "Old Man Keating and Blair. Tate's mother. Pop's wife."

The shock on Clara's face is one I've seen so many times. Actually, every time that Pop tells this story. Her eyes widen, the blue orbs becoming oceans as they grow so wide. Her jaw drops and she shakes her head in disbelief, "But how Malcolm? How could they get married? She was already married to his son?"

"Marriage at that time in Scotland didn't carry over into America. So technically here in the U.S., Blair and Pop weren't considered married. This gave them a way to get here and stay here."

"Blair, Mrs. Keating, died five months later despite the treatment and work the Old Man had done to help with her illness. The cancer was too far advanced for the trial and she had waited too long for any conventional treatments to be effective. The whole situation brought father and son to forgiveness. They have been closer than ever since then. That was years ago. Then we came along, and like I said before." I smile, proving my earlier point, and then say, "All the rest is history."

Shaking her head in disbelief, she says, "Wow, Malcolm. I can't believe that story. What an amazing thing to do for your family."

"Oh, and just wait; you'll hear that story again. It's always better when Pop tells it anyways. His Scottish accent is the best and his memory never fails him. He remembers a new detail every time he tells it." Laughing, I look out the window again. The time it's taken me to tell her about Pop's history has made the rest of our drive fly by.

A few minutes later, we come to the end of the cornfields and pull up to the main property gates. *Nexus Farms* signage hangs proudly on the closed gate that opens as I pull forward. The gate's electronic and convenient but malfunctions often. These are the times that piss everyone off, having to put in extra work to manually open it when it decides to not work properly.

Clara unhooks her seat belt and leans her slender body out the window, looking in awe at the property surrounding her. Her blonde braids flow loosely down her back as she presses up against the passenger side door and window.

"Wow, this place is amazing!" Staring out the window, she watches as I drive past the barn, the new corrals, the horse stalls, and the cattle in the front pasture. I see Sal leaning up against the barn door, his hands in his front pockets as he watches us drive down the road towards the pond. Waving at him and at Pop as we drive past, I continue down the dirt covered road and park the truck close to the shore.

It's a little after 7 am on Saturday but the farm is just as busy as any other day. The constant business of farming never stops. No rest when you own a farm this large and one that feeds so many families.

Getting out of the truck, Clara carries her lunch pail and follows me to the back of the truck. I grab the small cooler I packed with some bottled water and sodas. I hand her the cooler and grab the folding chairs, one in each hand. Once I get those settled on the shore under the huge willow tree that shades the pond, I head back to the truck to get the fishing poles and tackle box.

Clara continues her look around, her eyes wide and her mouth slightly open in shock.

"Malcolm, this place is wonderful. It's so beautiful. I have to admit, when you said we were going fishing, I had my doubts. But damn, this place is heaven."

"Not one for fishing, huh? Why do I feel like I should've known that?" Grinning at her, I ask her the questions I already have the answer for. I'm positive by the sound of her voice previously on the phone that fishing isn't on her list of favorite things to do. Her strangled attempt to make light of the activities I suggested was not lost on me. I'm hoping I can change that today.

"You caught me. I hate fishing." Laughing, she looks over at me as I sit in the chair next to her.

"Well, today is a very important day for fishing. Today, we catch dinner." Raising my eyebrows and widening my smile emphasizes the importance of our task and makes her laugh even harder. Her response doesn't surprise me. Only makes me like her even more when she says, "Ok, bring it on. Give me that pole! Let's catch some fish! I have a feeling I'll be hungry later."

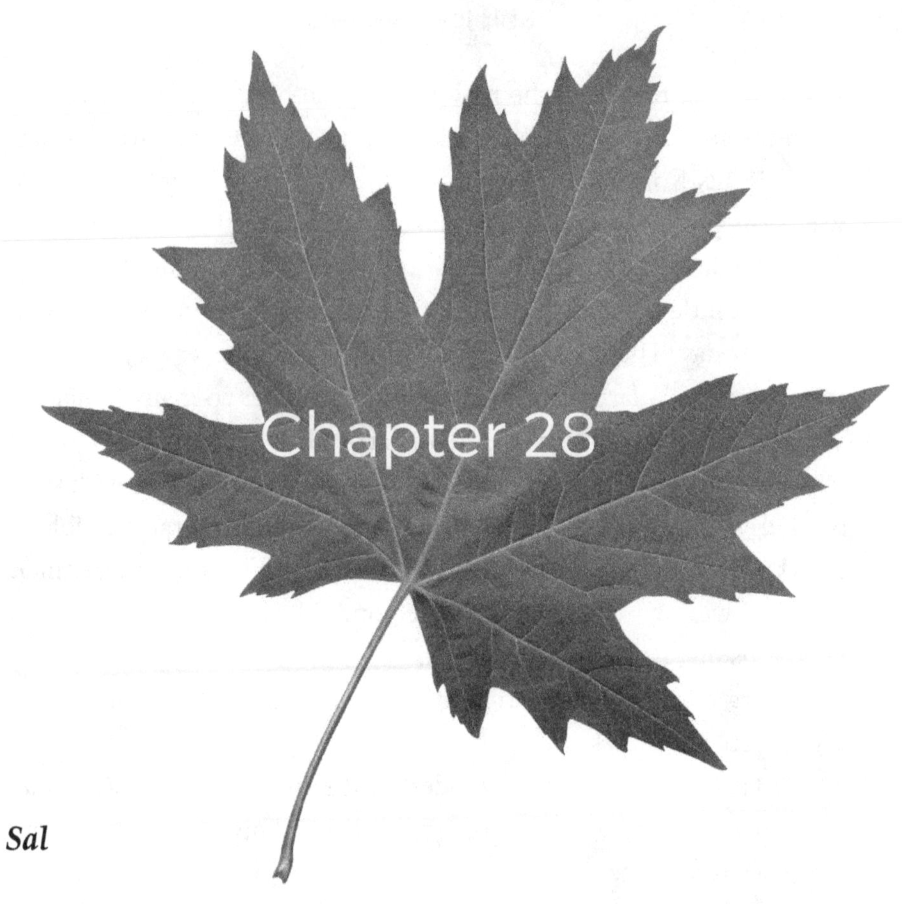

Sal

Shit. This is not good.

Fuck, I'm in trouble. Slamming my fist into the wood framing of my bathroom door, I punch it twice. Hoping the pain will help my anger subside.

Malcolm's date, the girl he brought to the farm, is the same girl I almost ran over with the truck at Tractor Supply. The very blonde haired, blue-eyed ghost I've been seeing in my dreams.

In every damn dream I've had since that day. I haven't been able to stop the flow of images going through my head. With each dream more vivid and more real than the last. All images of a woman I've never met! All of a woman my brother and best friend just had riding in the very truck I almost hit her with.

Punching the frame once more, I feel the blood start to swell under the skin. I don't even know her name. I know nothing about her. But Malcolm obviously does.

He's on a date with her. And it makes me angry. Crazy angry. Pacing the floor of my bedroom, I've never been so happy to have my living space in the barn, far away from prying ears and nosey family.

God, I have no right to feel like this. She's not even mine. I've never even met her. Groaning, I grab at my now buzzed head. My frustration grows because I can't pull on my long dark hair.

Squatting with my hands on my head, I look down at my dirt covered boots and inhale then exhale slowly. My groans slowing with each breath I take.

That's when I hear a throat clearing behind me. Those prying ears I thought I had freedom from now standing behind me. Rising, I turn to see Tate standing in the doorway.

He walks over to me, handing me the red bandana he keeps in his back pocket. I wipe away the blood from my fist, holding pressure at the middle knuckle. He doesn't wait long to speak; his Scottish accent isn't as strong as Pop's but still evident nonetheless.

"What's happening brother? What's on yer mind? And what the hell did that doorframe do to ye?" Tate's red hair hangs over his ears and brushes his collar. The color is more potent in the summer, the sun making it a deeper red.

"Have anything to do with that bonnie lass Malcolm came driving through here with?"

He sits in the chair next to the bed, leans back, his feet outstretched. He's calm and confident in his movements. Man, I have always wanted to be that smooth.

"God, Tate. I don't know what's gotten into me. I don't even know that girl. I've never met her, but I want to beat the crap out of Malcolm for having her here." I lean against the wall, my eyes lifting to the sky. Looking for guidance from whom, I don't know.

"It's like I know her from somewhere. Like I've known her forever and I feel the need to be protective of her. It's the strangest feeling."

"Hmmm, Adler says that's the same girl ye almost killed a few weeks ago. In a parking lot?" Tate asks. He sits up, his elbows resting on his knees, his hands folded into each other in front of him.

"Yeah. I almost ran her over, by accident of course. At the Tractor Supply. I only got a quick look at her. Then she ran off, crying. And man, I don't know why but it physical pained me to see her crying. Now, she's taking over my fucking dreams. Dude, I can't get her out of my head." With my hands now back up on my head, my anger rises again. "And to make it worse, she's HERE.WITH. HIM." I point angrily out toward the pond.

"Well, that girl looks a lot like a lass we used to know. The very same one ye got yer arse beaten over when we were kids." Tate stands, and says "Be careful brother, that girl is in your mind and dreams because she reminds ye of Lulu. That girl will cause trouble for ye and Malcolm both, if ye not careful. Remember, no girl is worth breaking apart the family we've built here. Promise me. Promise you'll stay away as long as she's with Malcolm. And promise that if it doesn't work out between them, ye'll talk this over with Malcolm before you make a move." Placing a hand on my shoulder, he accepts my nod as a promise.

Tate exits, leaving me to relive the same pain I had all those years ago the day Lucy died. The anguish I felt then mirrors my feeling now. This girl is with my brother and there is nothing I can do about it.

Chapter 29

Clara

Well, I made it through fishing today.

I still can't say I like fishing, but after catching three catfish I might consider doing it again. If it's with Malcolm that is.

I had a great time out at the pond with Malcolm. In between reeling in fish, I was able to find out a bit more about the real Malcolm. Although it seems he left out several major details about growing up, I know more now than I did before. I guess as time goes by, Malcolm will loosen up and tell me everything there is to know. I was surprised at my own reaction to his questions about me. I suppose we both have things we want to keep under lock and key. I want to share my life with him and what has happened in my past but the events are just too raw. My grief over Mama is a slow closing wound I'd rather not re-open for now. The last thing I want is to have a breakdown on our official first date. God; that would be embarrassing.

It's late afternoon when we return to the house. Malcolm's family is nowhere to be found. He assures me I'll meet them at dinner tonight though. Entering the house through the front door, we're bombarded by laughter. A female voice comes from the kitchen along with a smooth Scottish accent I assume must be Malcolm's father. Curiosity has me walking farther into the room, hoping to get a look at the people having such a great time. My hope of joining the fun is short lived as Malcolm stops me from going farther and ushers me back toward the front door. Laughing the whole time, I know he's just embarrassed by what he apparently knows I'm about to witness. Continuing to push me so that I'm walking backwards, my chest against his, Malcolm tries to cover my view into the living room.

Smiling, his slightly crooked teeth on display he says, "No way. Out you go! Turn around Clara. Trust me, you do not want to see this."

He continues pushing me out of the room, laughing the whole time.

Next thing I hear is singing. Loud obnoxious singing. I don't understand the words. The lyrics are in a language other than English. "Malcolm what is that singing? I can't understand the words." Giggling while I continue pushing against Malcolm's chest, I do my best to peek around his toned body. Malcolm groans and rolls his eyes up to the sky as I hear what sounds like… bagpipes?

"Oh my God Malcolm, are those bagpipes?" Covering my mouth with my hand to hide my chuckle, Malcolm groans again before saying, "Yes. It's bagpipes. And they're singing in Gaelic." The music continues, the singing and bagpipes getting louder and louder. Giving up, Malcolm grabs me by the shoulders and turns us so that my back is to his chest and I now have a clear view of the living room.

Malcolm's so close, his hands on my jean covered hips. His touch causes those butterflies to take flight again. Goosebumps cover my arms and legs as Malcolm's hand moves from my hip to my shoulder. I like the feeling of him so close.

Suddenly a man enters the living room, the kitchen door swinging on its hinges. Another older man follows behind him, holding the bagpipes we've been hearing since we came in the house. They're both wearing kilts, the plaid covering the skirt with deep blues, tans and greens. Once they notice us staring at them from the other side of the room, the first man stops suddenly causing the older man to run into him from behind. The old man's arms are full of the instrument that's blaring out the Scottish tunes. A dark-haired girl about my age laughs hysterically behind them.

The old man curses, his movements halted by the other man. "Hey you bugger, why'd you stop?" Following the other man's eyes, the old man sees us staring at them, laughing. "Oh. That'd be why."

Malcolm grabs my hand and pulls me forward stopping us in front of the two men.

"Hey Pop. Old Man, this is Clara." Malcolm's smile beams down on me, proud to introduce me to his family.

"Clara. My, my aren't ye a bonnie lass. It's a pleasure to meet ye." Mr. Keating reaches out a big paw, inviting me to shake his hand. I accept the offer. His grip is firm, but gentle at the same time.

"Hello. It's nice to meet you both." Mr. Keating releases my hand and the Old Man takes it next, his wrinkled tan palm showing his age.

"It's nice to meet you Clara. I think I'll just go over here and put these away." The Old Man takes the bagpipes and deposits them on the floor by the fireplace. The dark-haired girl comes up to me next, also reaching out to shake my hand. "Hey, Clara. I'm Becca. Nice to meet you." Giving me a smile, she turns her attention to Malcolm next. "Hey Malcolm."

All he says is, "Hey, yourself."

"So..." Pop says his arms spread out in front of him. "Where's dinner?"

A few hours later, Mr. Keating, Becca and I have the fish cleaned, filleted, fried up and ready to eat. That was the most disgusting thing I have ever done.

I could have lived my whole life and been ok with not having done that.

But I can't wait to tell Daddy how I helped clean the catfish. If anything will cheer him up, maybe that will. Malcolm sat at the kitchen table, laughing at the many faces I was making, my disgust at the task apparent.

Two of Malcolm's brothers came to join us at some point. In my distraction I didn't see them enter the kitchen. Tate and Adler joined the laughter of my first fish cleaning experience. Wiping her hands on a dish towel, Becca walks over and sits on Tate's lap. He plants a quick kiss to Becca's nose, the motion making me keep my eyes on them longer. I get the feeling they are already pretty serious. I'm excited to get to know her better, to finally have a girlfriend I can talk to. Also, Malcolm says she attends Jefferson High School as well. The same school we all will be going to this fall.

When Malcolm asked about their other brother Sal, all Tate said was he wouldn't be in until dinner was on the table. Tate mentioned Sal was out helping with a delivery of hay. When Malcolm offered to go help, Pop just shook his head, saying Sal could handle that by himself.

To compliment dinner, we've made hushpuppies, fresh green salad, with steamed zucchini and squash, all fresh from the garden. The aroma has my stomach growling and my body shivering slightly in hunger, the sandwiches Malcolm and I ate earlier now gone.

We all talk and Tate tells jokes that make us all laugh while we set the table. Looking around I notice each man has their assigned place at the table. I look over at Becca. Knowingly she nods at the seat next to Malcolm. He's already set his plate down, motioning that it's ok for me to sit next to him.

"If ye sit there lass, ye'll be sittin' next to Sal too. Watch em' lass, those boys will likely eat yer plate too. Don't say I didn't warn ye." Laughing, he rests his hand on his big belly as it shakes with laughter. Smiling, I take my seat next to Malcolm.

Sitting down I wait until everyone else starts putting food on their plates to get my own. A courtesy Mama used to always say was so very important when dining at someone else's table. Mama used to say waiting showed respect to the host.

Suddenly and out of nowhere, the hair on the back of my neck stands up and chills go down my spine. I shake away the feeling and look over at Malcolm who is now staring at me.

"You ok? Are you cold? Sal just came in, letting some cool air through the front door."

Using my hands to rub my arms from the chill, I motion my head saying no. Attempting to ease Malcolm's worry. "I'm fine, really." Satisfied with that answer, Malcolm returns his attention back to his food.

The feeling that someone is staring at me is heavy. I look around the table but don't see anyone paying any attention to me at all. I guess it's all in my head. I reach across Malcolm to add hushpuppies to my plate. The smell of him overwhelms my nose and I close my eyes, inhaling. Enjoying the warmth and comfort only Malcolm can provide. But when I open my eyes, I look right into the face of Malcolm's brother Sal.

Sal has just walked into the dining room from the kitchen, and oh my god; I can't breathe. Our eyes meet as he walks toward me, coming around the table. He doesn't look away as I stare back at him. The rest of the table continues their conversation, enjoying Tate's jokes, the laughter in the room increasing with each new joke he tells. Sal sits down next to me and I have to take a deep breath to settle my nerves. I continue to watch him; Sal's dark eyes invading my mind. Mesmerized by the dark orbs, I can't make myself look away. I know I should, but I can't seem to do what my brain is telling me too.

"Hey, I'm Sal." He says, reaching over to take my hand. The

gesture is so simple but for some reason feels like it has something forbidden behind it this time.

"Hi. I'm Clara, it's nice to meet you." My hand shakes slightly as my palm meets his.

I don't know why my heart pounds so fast as I shake his hand in return. And I'm even more confused that when he pulls away, sadness fills my mind. I don't want to let go of his hand; my palm somehow feels at home against his. But I do let go. I have to.

The way I'm feeling at the smallest touch from Sal is scaring the hell out of me.

Chapter 30

Sal

I thought I was angry before. That was nothing.

Now, sitting next to her while she laughs and looks longingly at my brother, I'm furious.

If I were a volcano, I would erupt and cause significant damage. But this is my family, I can't be mad at Malcolm. I'm mostly mad at myself, for feeling this way. For knowing what I have to do. I have to tell Clara exactly how I'm feeling about her.

This girl is it for me. I knew it the second I came out of the kitchen and our eyes locked. I knew it when I almost ran her over with the truck. Her blue eyes were unfocused and full of tears. But I knew it even then.

My entire body reacted to her stare.

My blood raged through my veins, my heart pounding, and sweat covering my body. God I've never been so angry. I just want to touch her, kiss her, and show her how much she makes my blood burn in my veins.

Just sitting here, I have to control what effect she is having on me. I haven't even touched her and all I can think about is having Clara all to myself.

But she's here with him.

I finally look away from her. My eyes are burning to return as soon as I look away. I turn my focus to Tate who stares at me, so much written on his face.

Tate slightly shakes his head, telling me silently to behave. I look down at my plate, suddenly not hungry.

How can I sit here, with her next to me and not react? It takes all the restraint I have not to reach out and touch her hand. I've never felt like this before. Never had anyone I felt so protective over. Except for Lucy.

I vaguely make out what is being said at the table. Having a new person to impress, Pop tells the story of how he and the misses came to America. Looking over at Clara, I notice she's not eating either. She just looks down at her plate, glancing over at Malcolm or over at me every few minutes. Clara engages in the conversation every once and a while. She smiles and laughs at something Pop or the Old Man says. Even though I don't know her, I can tell she's really uncomfortable.

What am I thinking? God Sal; No, you DON'T know her. And that's part of the problem.

But I can sense her though. I can feel her discomfort. I can sense her thoughts. God, I sound crazy even to myself. I can feel her eyes every time she turns toward me. Somehow, I have to find some time alone with her.

I have to see if she's rocking in the same boat as me, or if she wants to stay in Malcolm's. One thing is certain, wherever she decides to be, it'll be a rocky fucking ride.

No matter how torturous this is, I'm not leaving this table while she's still sitting next to me. If this is as close as I can get to her right now, I'm not moving from this spot until she does.

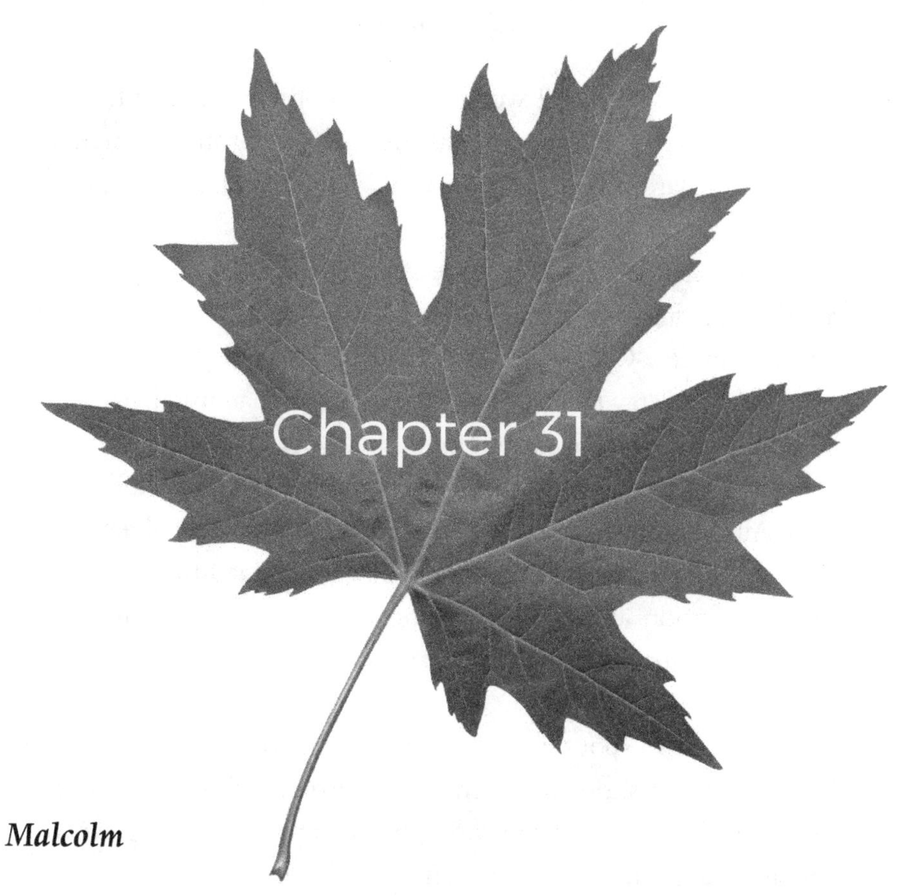

Chapter 31

Malcolm

Everyone is laughing, joking around and having a good time, but I swear tension grew when Sal came into the room. He's pissed. Flaming pissed. If he were a color, right now he'd be a dark shade of red. Blood red.

Living with him for so long, I can always tell when his fuse is lit. He doesn't get angry often. Rarely actually, but today, his anger is so palpable I think even Clara senses it. My fear is that it'll scare her, and she won't want to come back around.

After my outburst and anger toward Baker, and now Sal's anger over only God knows what, this thing between Clara and I could end before it really gets going. Especially, now that she knows about our past. Today's been one of the best days I've had in so long. I just don't want anything to ruin it.

Sal's never acted like this before. At least he introduced himself, and was polite to Clara. I wonder what's bothering him. I'll find out later, one-way or the other. We just need to get through dinner. Then after I take Clara home, I can find out what has him in tangles. And hopefully we can fix it.

Trying to make the tension less, I lean toward her slightly. Under the table, I reach over to hold Clara's hand. She jumps a bit but looks over and smiles. Clara turns her hand to interlock her fingers with mine. Our eyes stay locked for a second longer than usual, like she has something she wants to say but thinks better of it.

It only takes us twenty minutes to eat the fish Clara and I caught today. All the hushpuppies and vegetables gone as well; albeit surprisingly. Having two women at the table surely helped that cause. Even with the tension and anger radiating off Sal, he's stayed for dinner. Then even helped clear the table and is now joining us in the living room.

Adler finds a spot on the floor next to the fireplace. I sit in the recliner with Clara sitting between my knees on the floor in front of me. Sal stands at the back of the room, brooding and watching everyone. Tate and Becca take up the couch. Pop decided after dinner that his concert earlier wore him out and he went off to bed like the Old Man. Really, he was just giving us some time to get to know each other.

Clara and Becca whisper every so often, the sound of laughter louder after each secret told. Clara has to stretch herself across my left knee for Becca to reach her ear. Every time she leans across me, she wraps her arms around my thigh and leans in. With each lean, I run my fingers down her braid. Her hair is so soft in between my fingers.

It's the best feeling in the world. I'm on cloud nine, I'm so happy she feels comfortable enough with me to sit so close, and make intimate movements like she is.

I worry though because I swear, Sal grunts every time Clara touches my leg.

He hasn't moved in the last hour except to pace back and forth behind us, always keeping his eyes on Clara and me.

I try to ignore his nervousness by listening to Tate talk about the new school year.

"Ye know, we go back for senior year starting in just a month now." He says.

"Yeah, one more year at Jefferson High, and we're gone," I say, as I reach across to high five Tate. Our excitement about joining the military shared.

"And a fast year it'll be, before we know it, it'll be festival time. Hey Adler, I can't wait to see what ye've done with the music this year. The stage ye built is bonnie. Pop says ye have all new equipment out there." Tate shifts on the couch, looking over at Adler on the floor, a piece of straw hanging from his mouth.

Pushing up his glasses, he pulls the straw from his mouth before answering, "Yeah, it's going to be epic this year. It's bitter sweet actually. It will be our last year at this festival. It's going to be hard to be away for that length of time, while in boot camp and all." Looking down, he puts the straw back into his mouth.

Tate and I share a quick glance. I look back at Sal, who has stopped his pacing to look over at Adler. We share a quick knowing look, trying not to be obvious that we're all thinking the same thing. That's when Sal finally talks for the first time since we sat down to dinner.

"Yeah, it'll be a quick year for sure, then on to live and create our own futures." Sal leans up against the doorframe for the kitchen entrance and crosses his arms across his chest.

A few moments go by, all of us silent. Then Clara shifts on the floor in front of me.

"Malcolm, I really need to get home. Will you take me now?" She asks? Her blue eyes are penetrating my soul. I swear she can see all my flaws, secrets and dreams with just one look.

"Sure, let's go." Standing up, I reach my hand down, gently lifting her off the floor. Clara pulls her shorts down her thighs as she stands, the creamy skin of her thighs calling my name. Man, she makes me crazy.

We all walk outside to the two trucks parked haphazardly in front of the main house. Becca and Clara share a hug. Taking the pen from Becca's hand Clara writes her phone number on Becca's palm. Her handwriting perfect, the way it was when she wrote her number on my arm the other day. Clara looks over at Sal who leans against the porch post, still quieter than usual. She says, "Bye Sal. See ya."

Tate and Becca get into the red Ford pickup Tate always drives; the country music blaring as they drive off toward town. Adler stands on the porch next to Sal, watching us as we get ready to leave. I reach over, opening the truck door for Clara to climb in but Adler interrupts us.

"Hey Clara," he jogs down the porch steps coming toward us. He holds out his hand, and she places hers in his larger one. "Hey, Adler." She says.

He lifts her hand, kissing her knuckles softly. "It was nice to meet you. I think maybe you'll be good for my brother; I hope you stick around for a while." Smiling he stands in front of her, not letting go of her hand.

"Ok, ok; Bro. That's enough. If I didn't know better, I'd think you were trying to steal my girl."

"It's hard to know you have such hard competition isn't it, Malcolm?" Adler jokes, his playfulness contagious. He then jogs back up to the porch, pushing Sal's shoulder on his way up, as he goes inside the house. Sal just stands watching us. I nod to him as I laugh. As I'm helping Clara up into the truck she says, "Wow; Adler sure is a Casanova huh? Who would've thought? He's so quiet most of the time." She settles herself into the seat, and I imagine her doing that a lot more after today. Running around the front of the truck, I jump up into the driver's seat.

"Yeah, he's a good guy. We all worry about him though." The truck engine roars with massive power as I turn the ignition, the truck coming to life.

"Why would you be worried?" She asks, her eyebrows rising with her curiosity. The glow of the trucks dash on her face make her eyes look lighter and brighter, translucent even.

"We worry about what his life will be like when we leave for the Marine Corps." The confusion on her face has me continuing before she has to ask any more questions.

"Adler has always been the mentally strong one of us. He's smart. Like really smart. He should be going to college instead of the military. He's just not built for a future like that. You know, one so physical."

"Haven't you heard that saying, Malcolm; *don't judge a book by its cover*? Maybe you're worried over nothing, maybe he will do great in the Marine Corps." I love her positivity, her need to encourage me to see with my heart and not just my eyes.

"I wish I could be that sure. I can't risk it; I have to protect him. He's my family. I would never forgive myself if something happened to him. And neither would Sal. We can't go through that again." Closing my eyes briefly, and scolding myself for having a loose tongue, I hope she didn't hear that last part. I don't want to have to explain about what happened with Lucy. Not yet anyway. Her expression doesn't change. She just looks out the window as we drive back into town. But then, just when I think the conversation is done, she turns toward me and says, "How'd you get stuck with the responsibility to protect everyone in your family? Who says you have to be the one to make the decisions?" She sounds irritated now. I'm not sure why.

"I don't make the decisions solely on my own Clara. The only family I have is back on that farm and I'd do just about anything to protect each and every one of them. Sal and I have always been on the same page where Adler's concerned. Pop and Tate agree, but leave it up to us for the final decision. It's never a burden and it's never just my decision. Love and loyalty, remember."

"I get it, I do. It just seems like a lot for one person to take on, or in your case, for two of you to take on. And you're teenagers, not adults. I have my dad, so I guess I don't fully understand what you guys live with on a daily basis." The words are softer now, more understanding.

"You grow up fast when you depend only on a select few people." I say.

She responds, sadness in her eyes, "Yeah, I know."

The rest of the drive back to her apartment is quiet; neither of us saying much, just enjoying each other's company.

After parking the truck, we get out and I walk her to the door. My hand slips into hers and she welcomes the contact. Standing outside the door, I keep a hold of her hand, not ready to let go just yet.

She looks up at me, that same look on her face, as if she wants to say something but she doesn't. I know what she wants. And knowing I would give her anything she asks for; I lean down and place my lips to hers. She closes her eyes, her head tilting slightly to the right. Her lips soft under mine. I don't try to further the kiss; I just pull her closer to me, her chest against mine and I stay pressed up against hers. Small pecks to her lips as I show her the respect a first kiss should have. She feels so good against me, so soft and responsive.

I pull away, she follows me, asking for more but letting me go all the same.

"Goodnight, Clara." I say as I push a piece of hair that's escaped from her braid behind her ear.

"Goodnight." The look on her face makes me pause. When she opens her eyes, she almost looks confused. Not wanting to ruin the moment, I turn and walk away. Clara watches me leave, the same look on her face. Making me wonder, why did she look so disappointed the moment she opened her eyes?

Chapter 32

Clara

When I closed my eyes, I had every intention of kissing Malcolm. But when they actually shut and his lips met mine, all I could picture was Sal.

I'm a horrible person. I couldn't hide the disappointment I felt when I opened my eyes, only to see Malcolm's beautiful face instead of Sal's. And he could see it, written all over my face. The disappointment. I'm such an ass.

I can't believe this is happening. Malcolm is the best guy I've ever met. His love for his family, and the loyalty toward his brothers takes my breath away. How can I not want to be with him? How can I be thinking of Sal when I'm with Malcolm?

No matter how much I adore Malcolm, he isn't Sal. And that makes my heart hurt.

The realization that Malcolm will never be in my life as anything other than a friend, is almost more than I can take.

I can't believe how fast this is all happening. I've only known Malcolm for a couple of weeks now, and Sal even less. But I've never been more sure about anything in my life.

I have to tell Malcolm about how I feel about Sal, and soon. I just don't know how.

If I don't do it soon, I risk being that person who causes bad blood between brothers. If that happens, I'll never be able to forgive myself.

But I don't think I could give up Sal either, if it comes down to that. Not that I even know if he feels the same about me. If he even feels anything for me at all.

I guess that's what I'll have to find out first.

Damn it. This is a no-win situation.

Standing in the break room, my break almost over, Louie comes in with a concerned look on his face. I turn away from the window I was just looking out of and face him.

"Hey Louie! How are you?" I ask.

"Clara, what's with you and cowboys?" He's dead serious. I laugh as I respond, "Um, I'm not sure what you're talking about Louie. Care to elaborate?"

"Well, you have another cowboy out there asking for you. Second one, if I recall correctly. This one's not the trouble maker though, it's a different cowboy."

A different cowboy? Heat spreads across my skin, my heart reminding me it's still in my chest. Taking a few deep breaths, I will my heart to slow its gallop.

It must be Sal. Excitement fills my body and butterflies take flight in my belly.

Is Sal here? I go over to my locker to look in the mirror before possibly meeting with Sal. Pinching my cheeks to add a little red to them, a trick Mama taught me. I close the locker and head toward the break room door.

I wore my hair down today. The curls long and reaching down

my back, resting on my waistline. My blue jean overalls cover the red t-shirt I wore underneath. White Keds finish off the outfit I hurriedly threw on after getting little to no sleep last night. Man, I wish I would've worn my favorite jeans; they make my butt look good. Then I'd at least appear like I tried to look good this morning. Uh!

Looking around the main store, I don't see Sal anywhere. Disappointment ices down my heated flesh as I walk down the front of the store, looking down each isle.

Where did he go?

Just as I'm about to turn around and look down each isle again I hear my name.

"Clara. Hey pretty lady! I almost didn't recognize you with your hair down." It's Adler. Not Sal. My heart sinks into my feet. But I try my best to be happy to see Adler.

"Hey Adler! What's going on? How are you? Can I help you find something?"

"Nah, I'm just waiting for Pop to pull the truck around. We're loading up from the back dock. Just thought I'd say hi."

"I'm glad you did!" Punching his arm slightly I say, "Where's Malcolm, didn't he come with you?" I search for him, as if maybe he'll jump out from somewhere.

"Nah, he stayed home with the Old Man. Sal and Pop are here though." Blushing he looks down. Realizing he already said that he was here with Pop.

After pushing his glasses up his nose, he stands with his hands planted into his back pockets.

"I'll walk out with you." Grabbing his arm and pulling him to walk with me, he joins my stride. No longer embarrassed and back to himself, Adler loops my arm in his as we walk toward the back-dock. His confidence boosts as he looks down at my arm, wrapped in his.

"So, you wanna make my brother jealous and go out to dinner with me? Maybe go dancing? I'm a way better dancer than Malcolm." Shuffling his feet forward then backward, I giggle at his attempts to dance himself into my heart. We're enjoying the banter between us as we exit through the broad swinging doors leading to the outside of the store.

The wind catches my hair, blocking my vision. I untangle from Adler and use both hands to sweep up and tame my unruly locks. That's when I see Sal.

He's wearing dark jeans, black boots and a white t-shirt, a black cowboy hat covering his dark hair. He's leaning against the back of the truck, his muscled forearms resting on the truck bed. It's the same truck he almost ran me over with. I laugh to myself, thinking about how that day has led me to where I am right now.

It was the worst day of my life. Saying goodbye to Mama, but it was also the first day of the rest of my life. I miss Mama every day, and now I thank her for bringing these men into my life just when I needed them the most.

Sal looks over as Adler and I are coming down off the dock. Adler jumps off, forgoing the stairs. I take each one, keeping my pace slow. I'm so nervous being this close to Sal, I'm afraid I'll fall flat on my face if I go down them any faster. He stands to his full height, one arm still resting on the truck bed, the other now on his hip.

His eyes flash to mine. My stare matches the intensity of his. He lifts his chin, a half smile on his lips, saying a silent hello. Goose bumps cover my arms.

Adler breaks my concentration on Sal when he says, "Hey! Look who I found." Pop turns my way, looking over at me with a big smile on his face.

"Clara! Nice seeing ye lass. How are ye?" He walks over, giving me a side arm hug.

"Hi, Mr. Keating. Good to see you again."

Sal looks at me, his face unreadable. He doesn't look upset but he doesn't have the half smile from before on his face either.

"We've just about finished loading up. Ye talked to Malcolm today?" Mr. Keating asks.

"No, I came into work early this morning and I don't get off until five."

Pop looks over at Sal then Adler, as if silently asking them a question. Neither of them say a thing, then Pop asks, "Ye should come out to the farm tonight. Break bread with us! We'll be havin' a Scottish feast!"

"Oh yeah? A Scottish feast? That'd be a first for me. But I'll have to pass, I've got to get home to my Dad."

"Bring him along. The more the merrier."

"Ok. I'll talk with him. What time is dinner if we decide to join you?" My hesitation is only because I know Daddy will say no to going.

"Seven sharp. Hope to see ye." Pop opens the driver side door, jumping up into the seat.

Adler stands next to me. His arm reaches behind me and rests on my shoulders. I release the hold I have on my hair and wrap my arm across his lower back. The weight of his arm holds my hair down, keeping it from blowing in the wind and back into my eyes.

"See you tonight, Clara," Sal says as he joins Pop in the front cab of the Ford truck. I stay quiet. I squeeze Adler's waist and look up at him. He winks at me. His glasses falling slightly down his nose. He pushes them back up and says, "Gotta run; they may leave me here if I don't get in soon." That gets another chuckle out of me, "You better go then, see you tonight Adler."

"See you tonight. Make sure you wear your dancing shoes! I'm planning to steal you away with my moves tonight!" Getting in the truck, he winks again at me and waves his goodbye.

I stand there on the dock, watching the truck drive away and all I can think about is how the hell am I going to get Daddy to agree to going to this dinner.

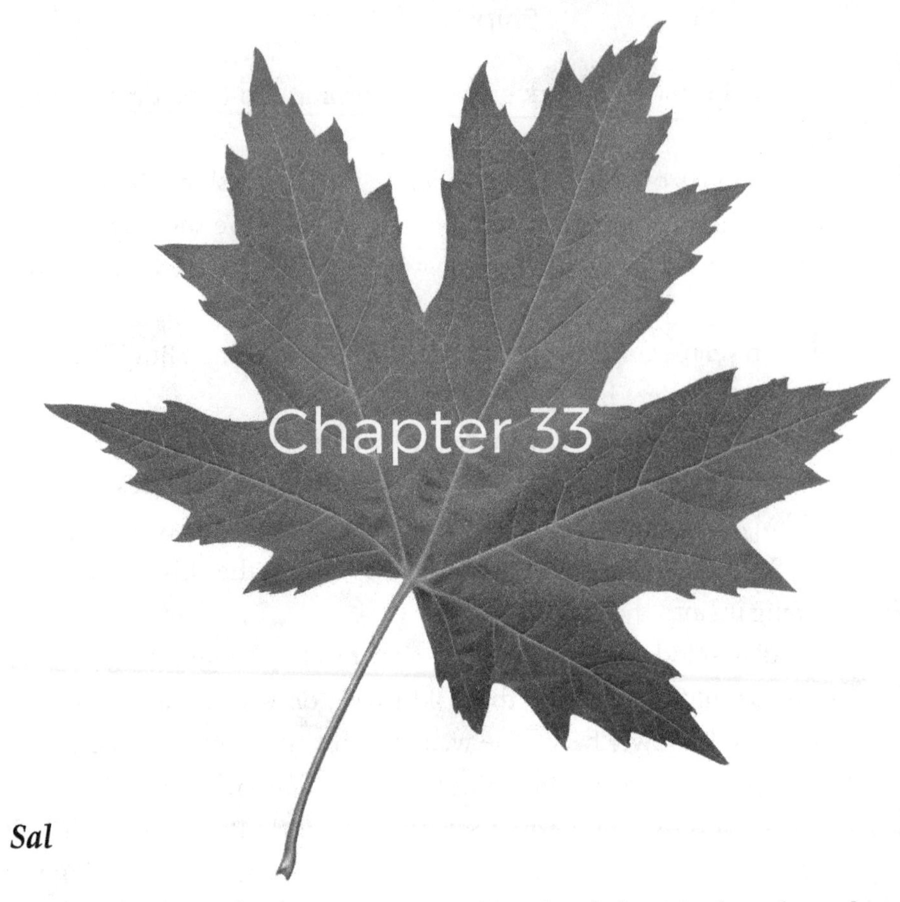

Chapter 33

Sal

Coming back to the house, my mind is clouded with thoughts of Clara.

Seeing her today was a surprise, but a welcome one. I know she works at Tractor Supply, but I was doing everything I could to avoid going in there to see her. I have to restrain myself. I've got to find a way to get her away from Malcolm before I pursue her. I've got to find a way I can have Clara and not ruin my relationship with Malcolm.

I can't lose either of them.

After Clara left with Malcolm the other night, my dreams where once again full of only her.

Now that I know it's Clara in my dreams, I welcome them. I can't get enough. In my dreams I'm the one kissing her, holding her. Not Malcolm.

I woke up uncomfortable and needing relief only she could give me. A cold shower and farm chores aren't nearly enough distraction to keep me from thinking about Clara.

Then seeing her today, her long blond hair flowing in the wind. The pain and anger were back, only ten times as intense. The real Clara is overshadowing the ghost of her from my dreams.

The need I feel for her is overwhelming. So no; I wasn't going to go find her today. It's just self-torture until I can be with her for good. But damn Adler. He had to bring her out to the dock. Clara, in all her beautiful glory.

Now I can't concentrate, the anticipation of seeing her tonight keeps me distracted. Somehow tonight, I must get her alone. I know she feels the same for me, I can see it in her eyes. While alone, I'll let her know exactly how I feel about her.

Then, we can figure out how the hell to tell Malcolm.

Chapter 34

Malcolm

After leaving Clara at her door a few days ago, I haven't had the desire to see her. I haven't called her; I haven't gone by Tractor Supply. I don't know what to say to her. I don't know what to do about the other night.

She clearly doesn't feel the same way about me. The hardest part, I don't want to be with someone who looks at me with disappointment after I kiss them. So, I've been avoiding her. Avoiding the inevitable truth. This relationship may be over before it's even gotten started.

But I'm at least relieved to know we won't be taking this any farther, risking hurting us both beyond repair. At this point, we can move on. Nothing has happened between us, not yet.

I'm cleaning out a horse trough when Pop pulls the truck around. Sal and Adler jump out and I walk over to help unload. I didn't go with them, my attempts to avoid Clara successful only if I actually avoid the one place she is most.

"Hey Bro! Guess who we ran into at Tractor Supply?" Sal asks while lifting himself into the back of the truck. He lifts bags of feed over the bed and hands them to Adler and me. I don't answer Sal; of course I know who.

"Yeah, Pop invited her and her Dad over for dinner tonight." Adler's excitement about this news takes away some of my disappointment in the fact that I won't be avoiding her for much longer.

"Oh yeah? That's great." I smile, trying to mask my reaction. I was hoping to get more time to come up with how to let her go. Despite knowing she doesn't feel for me what I feel for her, I still want to be with her.

We continue to unload the truck, Adler talking nonstop about stealing Clara away from me. Little does he know; he doesn't have to steal her away. If she were interested, he could have her because she isn't mine. She never was.

Sal laughs at Adler's attempt to ruffle my feathers, looking shocked when I don't take the bait. I tease him for good measure though, not able to completely lie down at his feet.

"Oh please, Adler. You couldn't steal anything of mine, no matter how hard you try." Laughing, I push his shoulder as Sal throws down another bag.

"Whatever; I'm twice the man either of you assholes will ever be! Once I get to show the ladies how good I am in bed, they'll line up for a piece of this!" He motions to his crotch, making Sal and I both laugh hysterically.

Meeting Clara has definitely brought out a new side to Adler. She boosts his confidence in ways no one ever has. It's good to see. Too bad he doesn't have a chance in hell with her.

Tate comes up, his red hair glowing bright in the sun.

"Hey, where's Becca? You two are never away from each other these days." I ask.

"She had a family police fundraiser. Her brother banned her from here today. The douchebag says she spends too much time here. He can kiss my arse."

"Tate, you better start separating yourself from her a little. In a year, you're off to the military. And she's going to the police academy. Maybe her brother has a point." I hate being the reasonable one. It's not a role I like, Tate usually takes that responsibility, but I guess we have to keep each other in check sometimes.

He grimaces. I don't have to tell him; he already knows. Doesn't make being away from her any easier for him.

He's already said he's going to marry her as soon as he's done with boot camp and she's done with the academy. I'm not real sure how they plan to live separate lives. Both career paths will take them in different directions at least for a while.

The afternoon goes by fast. Work on the farm never stops. The corn is getting taller, the ears starting to appear on some of the stalks. They stand so tall that the stalks reach up to the center pivot irrigation sprinklers, almost touching the water source and drowning out the tops of the corn plants. This late in the season, and being the end of July, the corn is close to ready for harvest. The first batches are anyways.

The newer fields won't be ready until October. These fields are the ones the Old Man does the corn maze out of for the festival. Signs of a heavy winter are on us; the red maples already turning a beautiful shade of yellow. Their leaves are readying themselves to turn the darkest of red. This is my favorite time of year.

School will be starting in a few weeks now. That realization is making me even more excited because that means my teenage years are almost behind me.

Finishing up my evening chores, I go into the main house and up the stairs to shower. My anticipation of what tonight will bring is causing a bit of anxiety. My fear that I've read Clara all wrong and will hurt her when I break things off makes me take pause. What if I did read her wrong? What if she does feel the same for me? The only thing is, I know I didn't read her wrong. I saw it clearly in her eyes after I kissed her.

Shaking off my thoughts, I dry off the water droplets dripping down my chest and clear the steam off the mirror. Standing in front of it, I run my hand over my shaved head.

Dread isn't a good look on you; stop being a pussy. She's going to thank you for putting her out of her misery.

I pull up my jeans as I hear the doorbell ring. I resolve myself to the fact that it's time. Time to see what Clara thinks about all of this, find out if what I felt the other night is the end of our short relationship.

Chapter 35

Clara

While I'm not surprised my father didn't want to come tonight, I'm still disappointed. I really wanted him to meet my friends. To meet the guys who have given me back my life, and the pieces of myself I lost when Mama died. Mentally I can check off another item on my list. And it feels good. I do dread coming over here tonight though. I'm terrified that I have to tell Malcolm that I only want to be friends. Also, afraid that when I tell Sal how I feel about him, he won't feel the same for me. My greatest fear is that admitting all of this will somehow take away the happiness I just recently found.

Standing at the front door, my nerves have me messing with my braid. Wondering if I should have worn a different dress or maybe a pair of different shoes. Maybe I should've just left on my overalls. Then I wouldn't feel like I'm trying too hard.

My fears are forgotten though, as soon as Sal opens the front door. I swear he can see right through me. The heat in his gaze just might set my body on fire.

"Clara." That's all Sal says as he stares into my eyes. I feel my face heat up; my palms start to sweat as goose bumps cover my arms.

"Hi." I wipe my hands on my dress as I stare back at him.

"I'm glad you made it. Come on in." He moves to the side to allow me to enter. He stays so close that our chests touch as I move past him. He grabs my hand as I move toward the kitchen. My purse catches on the doorknob stopping me from moving away from his touch. My first reaction is to pull away, the feel of his palm against mine, sending a shock up my arm. But I don't pull away. Instead I find myself moving closer to him. He reads my body's reaction and pulls me closer still. His hand is still entwined with mine, as he reaches to put our joined hands behind my back. Resting them on my rear, the feeling of his thumb rubbing small circles on my skin makes my blood pound in my veins. I can hear the blood rushing fast through my ears.

I swallow and look up at him. The way he looks down at me, I feel everything he wants to say but can't.

"Clara, I'd like a few minutes to talk to you before you leave tonight?" He lowers his head so that he whispers the words in my ear. Involuntarily I nod my answer, now certain I would give this man anything he asked for. He gently kisses my cheek.

My eyes close and my head moves toward his kiss. I don't even realize what's happening. Sal kisses me one more time then pulls his hand away from me.

I feel the loss of his touch immediately and I'm shocked at how that makes me feel.

I knew I was drawn to him; knew he was the one for me. But I never could have imagined it would feel like this, when he touched me. My heart aches to be back in his arms.

He smiles and we walk into the kitchen, the festivities already going on. But I laugh when I see that we aren't having a Scottish Feast, we're having pizza. There are at least five big pizza boxes on the counter.

"A Scottish Feast huh? That looks a lot like pizza." Adler and Pop turn at the sound of my voice.

"Ye caught me lass. But it's still considered a Scottish Feast. As ye get three Scotts to feast on pizza with!"

Malcolm comes down the stairs. He's wearing jeans and his feet are bare. His button-down shirt is open showing the white t-shirt underneath.

He comes straight over to me. "Hey," I say.

"Hey yourself. Glad you made it. Where's your dad?" he asks and looks around.

"Oh, he decided not to come."

"Maybe next time." Malcolm says, as he looks over at the pizza on the counter, licks his lips then says, "You want to eat? I need to talk to you, but we can eat first if you're hungry?" The green of his eyes seems lighter tonight. He searches my face, trying to read my thoughts. I guess we should just get this over with.

"No, I wanted to talk to you too. We can eat after." Malcolm nods and tells the others to start without us. Taking my hand, he walks us out of the kitchen and into the living room.

Sal stands in the doorway of the kitchen, his arms crossed across his chest. Much like he did the first night I met him. He's brooding and watching Malcolm really closely.

Malcolm stops at the couch, puts socks on his feet then slips them into his boots.

"Let's go out to the pond. It'll be quieter there."

"Ok." I swallow around the lump that has settled into my throat. Breaking up is never easy, but this breakup feels awful. I feel like I need to hurry and get out my apologies before he says anything. But the words won't come, not while we're still in the house.

We go outside and jump into the Ford truck I've become so accustomed too.

Malcolm doesn't say anything while he drives us through the pasture toward the pond. He parks by the willow tree and jumps out.

We stand under the tree, the leaves flowing in the breeze. He just looks out over the water, the weight of what we are about to say heavy around us.

Before he can say anything, I blurt out my apology.

"Malcolm, I'm so sorry about the other night. I feel really bad about my reaction to your kiss." Putting my head down, I twist my fingers around themselves, the tips going white with the force of my anxiety.

He looks over at me, disappointment clear on his beautiful face. He looks back out over the water. "I have to say, that's the first time I've gotten that look after I kissed someone." He laughs under his breath. The smile he gives me helps relieve some of the tension and guilt I feel.

"I'm so sorry. I can't believe this is happening. I wanted you to kiss me, so bad. I didn't expect to feel that way after it though."

"At least we're finding this out now. At least this hasn't gone any farther. It would make it so much harder to end if it had." He stands with his hands in his front pockets. A stance I'm finding out is a frequent one for him. He turns to me and looks me straight in the eye.

"Is there someone else, Clara? I swear you were into the kiss until you opened your eyes. It was like you were imagining someone else kissing you instead of me." Somehow there's no judgment in his eyes, just a true curiousness about my thoughts and feelings.

I debate with myself on whether I should be honest and tell him I was picturing Sal. I decide against being that honest, but I do tell him thc truth.

"Yes. There is someone else." Grabbing onto to his arm, I try to explain without going into detail.

"I'm so sorry Malcolm. I didn't expect for this to happen. This other guy, he just kind of... happened. Well, nothing has happened yet, but I'll be totally honest with you. I want it to. And that makes me an awful person, I know. But it's how I feel. You mean so much to me though. Since my mother died, I haven't felt like myself. I've felt like a shadow of who I was when I found out she was sick. There's a part of me that's glad I've changed from the brat I was, but I finally feel a little more like myself. And that's because of you." I lay my head down on his arm, hoping he can feel the affection I have for him and his friendship.

He lays his head down on mine in return and wraps his arms around me.

We stand there under the willow tree. The same spot where he taught me that fishing really can be fun. We hold onto each other as if this is the last time, we'll ever be able to.

"Clara, you're very special to me. Nothing you say or do could take that away. You have my loyalty. As your friend, and as your almost boyfriend." He smiles down at me and my heart cracks open just slightly. Malcolm slips into the space where friendship is most sacred. The space where the only thing better, is love.

"I'm sorry about your mother. I wish you would have told me sooner. It makes sense now, why you're so closed off sometimes."

I decide then and there from today on, I'm not going to fear telling my story. It may still be an open wound but if I can move on from it, maybe my mother's experience can be helpful to other women with breast cancer.

For the next hour we sit on the grass surrounding the pond and I tell him all about my life in North Carolina, and how I reacted to moving haunts me on a daily basis. I tell him how I didn't want to come to Colorado and that I actually threw a tantrum with full on kicking and screaming, and he laughs. I explain how the mountains made me feel the first time I saw them and how they made me feel when Mama was sick and dying.

It feels good to let go of all I've kept inside. To say the things, I fear the most.

Fear that my father will never recover from the loss of my mother.

The fear he didn't come tonight because he'd rather take a handful of pills and slip away into a fitful sleep he may not wake up from.

"Thank you, Malcolm." I wipe away the tears that have suddenly pooled and escaped, traveling down my cheeks. Wiping a few stray tears, he says, "For what?"

"For listening. You're a good listener."

"Anytime Clara." He lifts my hand, placing a kiss to my knuckles. Getting up he says, "We should head back, I'm ready for some pizza." He helps me up and we get back into the truck. I watch him as he drives us back to the house, realizing I'm at peace. I know that one day, he's going to make some girl really, really happy. I'm just sorry that it won't be me.

Chapter 36

Clara

The pizza is delicious. My stomach has been asking for food since I first got here. The smell of cheese and pepperoni covered pie fills the entire house. My mouth waters as we come into the kitchen. Malcolm takes out four slices, heating them in the microwave.

"That was so good!" Still chewing my last bite, as I talk with my mouth full.

"You want another slice? I can heat up some more; there was plenty left." Malcolm gets up and places his plate in the sink. I get up and do the same, rubbing my belly for effect.

"No, I might pop if I eat anymore."

"You want to watch a movie? I think Tate and Adler are in the living room watching something. It's probably something gory like Nightmare on Elm Street or Fright Night but I bet we could convince them to watch something else."

"Nah, I really should get home. Check on my Dad."

"All right, I'll walk you out." I grab my purse and head toward the front door, saying goodbye to Tate and Adler.

"This was a really good night for me, Malcolm. Thank you again for listening and not hating me after everything that's happened."

"Don't mention it, just remember that if this other guy doesn't appreciate you and know how special you are, then he's not right for you, ok? And if he hurts you, he'll have me to deal with." The seriousness on his face makes me laugh.

"Goodnight Clara. Drive safe." Malcolm shuts the door to my car. Walking back up the porch steps, he turns and offers a slight wave before going back into the house.

Just as I'm putting the key in the ignition, I remember I promised Sal I wouldn't leave without talking to him first, but I have no idea where he is. Malcolm mentioned once that Sal lived in a small room in the barn. I didn't see him in the living room with the others so he must be in his room. Knowing I shouldn't be going into a man's bedroom alone has my heart racing. Sweat gathers on my forehead, despite the cool breeze coming through the car windows.

I'm so nervous but I push forward and enter the main sliding doors to the big red barn.

Looking around I see random tables and chairs, hay bales, a tractor, and what looks like electrical equipment spread out over a stage. Over to the back of the barn is a small room. That must be Sal's room. There's one small window next to a door that's slightly ajar. Walking up to the window I peek inside. There's a bed, armchair, and a dresser. There's no sign of Sal anywhere.

I lightly knock on the door and it opens more from the force of my fist on the wood.

I go inside feeling guilty for entering when no one is here to give me permission. The feeling that I'm breaking the law somehow over comes me and I reconsider going in.

My curiosity wins so I wonder around his room, looking at the pictures he has taped to the mirror. Pictures of him with Malcolm, Tate and Adler as young boys. A few more recent ones of them doing all different things around the farm.

I would have loved to meet them when I was younger. It would have been great to grow up with them in my life. I pull one picture down off the mirror. It's a picture of Sal, Malcolm and Adler when they were very young. A little blond headed girl is perched onto Sal's shoulders.

I smile.

I can see and feel the affection on his face as he smiles at the person taking the photo. I can also see the same love and affection on Malcolm and Adler's faces as they look up at her. Malcolm is reaching up to hand her what looks like a milkshake.

In the background I can barely see what they are standing in front of, but don't get the chance to look closer because I hear a door shut behind me. Standing up straight and looking into the mirror, I see Sal standing behind me, wet from a shower. His chest is bare with the exception of a thin silver chain, a cross attached and dangling from his neck. The only thing he has on are gray track pants, hanging low on his waist, showing the perfect shape of his toned hips and slender build. The definition of muscle from his chest to his stomach as it makes its way down his body has my mouth watering.

God, he's perfect.

He has a towel in his hand, the motion of drying his short hair halted at the sight of me in his bedroom. His dark eyes burn into mine. I can feel his stare all the way to my toes. Those familiar goose bumps are back and covering every inch of my skin.

Without breaking eye contact, I explain my intrusion into his personal space, "I…I um, the door was open." He looks over at the door then back at me. Heat rises up my neck and I feel it coloring my cheeks. I turn to face him, my face red with embarrassment. The tension is heavy that I came in without being asked and found him half naked.

"You said you wanted to talk to me? Before I left."

He doesn't say a word, just walks towards me and puts the towel onto the chair next to his bed. As he passes me, he lays a hand on my waist. Sal pulls me closer to him as he turns. His arms wrap around my waist and I'm surprised at the intimate way he hugs me.

Sal holds me tight, like he's missed me. It's strange but feels so good.

His hand moves up my back and rests on the back of my head. I sink deeper into his arms. My hands come up to rest on his chest, my cheek pressing against him just below his neck. He holds me as if I'm cherished, as if I belong here in his embrace. Inhaling deep, I'm lost in the sweet scent of sandalwood, sawdust and fresh cut grass.

He pulls away from me a little, just enough so that our bodies still touch. His forehead comes down to rest against mine. My eyes are closed, and I can feel his breath against my lips. I don't move, I don't breathe.

Sal removes the band holding my braid at the base of my spine, releasing my unruly hair.

I exhale the breath I'm holding as his hands separate my braid section by section. He slightly pulls on my hair as he climbs his fingers up toward my scalp. The curls surround me, the smell of lavender from my conditioner overtaking his scent.

He rubs my scalp, keeping his forehead against mine. It's the best feeling. The tenderness of my head from the heavy braid easing a little from his attention.

His hands move around to my neck, his thumbs caressing my jaw. His voice is like gravel when he finally speaks.

"You. Are. So. Beautiful." Each word he says as a statement, with so much passion behind each word.

"When I'm around you and I can't hold you like this, I can't breathe." He lays a kiss on my forehead, then each of my cheeks.

"I want to take you somewhere. Will you go somewhere with me, tomorrow?" His hand now rests on my cheek. The look in his eyes makes me feel needed. Wanted. I can't believe that so quickly I would feel this safe and secure with Sal. Just knowing that no matter what he asks of me, I won't deny him.

"I would go anywhere with you."

A grin spreads across his face and he hugs me tight again. This time putting his nose into my hair and inhales deeply. He pulls away and rests his hands on my cheeks again. I can feel his heart beating faster as he comes closer to me. As I wrap both my arms around his waist, I close my eyes in anticipation of his kiss.

But I'm left wanting when his kiss lands on my cheek once again, then a second one on the corner of my mouth. They never land where I desperately need them too. His lips are soft and moist on my skin, making my neck and chest break out in a sweat.

The heat between us is like fire; the flames burning us from the ground up.

"We can talk about what all this means tomorrow, ok? You should get home. We'll leave early. I'll pick you up at 9."

"All right."

With one last kiss to my cheek and forehead, he releases me. We walk to the barn doors and out into the mountain air. The air hits my overheated skin and gives me chills.

Sal runs his hands down my bare arms, his palms re-heating my skin as they move. My hand stops his movement, the need to hold him overtaking me. I turn and wrap my arms around him once more.

Squeezing me tight, he embraces me with a laugh. "We're in trouble, Clara. It's getting harder and harder to say goodbye. Now go. I don't think I can push you away if you touch me again."

I turn on my heel and head to my car, holding onto his hand as long as I can before opening the door and getting in. My feelings of how well this night went are then overshadowed by the person who was watching us from the porch.

Chapter 37

Sal

I didn't notice Pop standing on the porch watching us until Clara was safely in her car and driving down the gravel driveway. Lifting my chin, I acknowledge that I see him standing there and run back into my room to slip on some shoes and grab a t-shirt.

Walking across the yard, Pop sips on a cup of what I assume is tea with a little Irish whiskey.

"Ye sure are cozy with your brother's lass, son." There's no judgment in his tone. Somehow, he never passes judgment on us even in situations that he should. If it was my girl and I found my brother embracing her, I'd be pissed. Well, that already happened and all I could see was red. So, if Pop were to scold me or judge me, I'd have to say it's warranted. I still feel the need to explain why he saw me with Clara.

Sitting behind Pop on the porch swing, I wait for him to continue. I'm surprised when he doesn't say anything else.

"Pop, I know what you must be thinking and what you just saw isn't that."

"Aye. Why do ye think ye know what I'm thinking? Huh?" Shaking his head, he continues, "Am I that easy for ye to read these days? Aye!" Laughing, he comes to sit next to me on the swing.

"What I think son is that ye're on dangerous ground. Aye, anyone with eyes could see the way that lass looks at ye. From the day we met her, even when Malcolm took her fishing. I know ye better than anyone lad and yer anger that night had everything to do with that bonnie lass." He raises an eyebrow, side-eyeing me.

"I can say ye two look great together. Ye brother might see it differently unless ye find the balls to admit ye love the lass. Don't ruin ye loyalty with him for her. It's not worth it, son. Love and loyalty made ye family. That's a bond too strong for a lass to break, ye hear." Patting me on the knee, he slowly gets up; Pop's knees not so strong in his increasing years.

"Yeah, ok Pop. I'll talk to Malcolm, promise."

Settling into my seat and crossing my legs at the ankle, I decide it's better to tell Pop where I'll be tomorrow.

"Oh, hey; Pop." Catching his attention, he faces me again, "I'm taking Clara to the church tomorrow. Leaving around 9."

Taking another sip of his tea he says, "Aye. Be careful lad." Blowing on the hot liquid in his cup, he waits a second then takes one more sip. Then he warns me again about Clara.

"Don't forget what I said, talk to Malcolm, son; the sooner the better." Now standing next to me, he pats my head, just like he used to when I was younger.

"Will do, Pop. Goodnight."

"Goodnight, son."

I sit there on the swing a little longer just thinking about tomorrow and Clara. Knowing it will be a great day but having a feeling we have a long hard road to go down before we'll reach happiness together. I'm up for the challenge and will do anything I have to, to show her I'm the one for her.

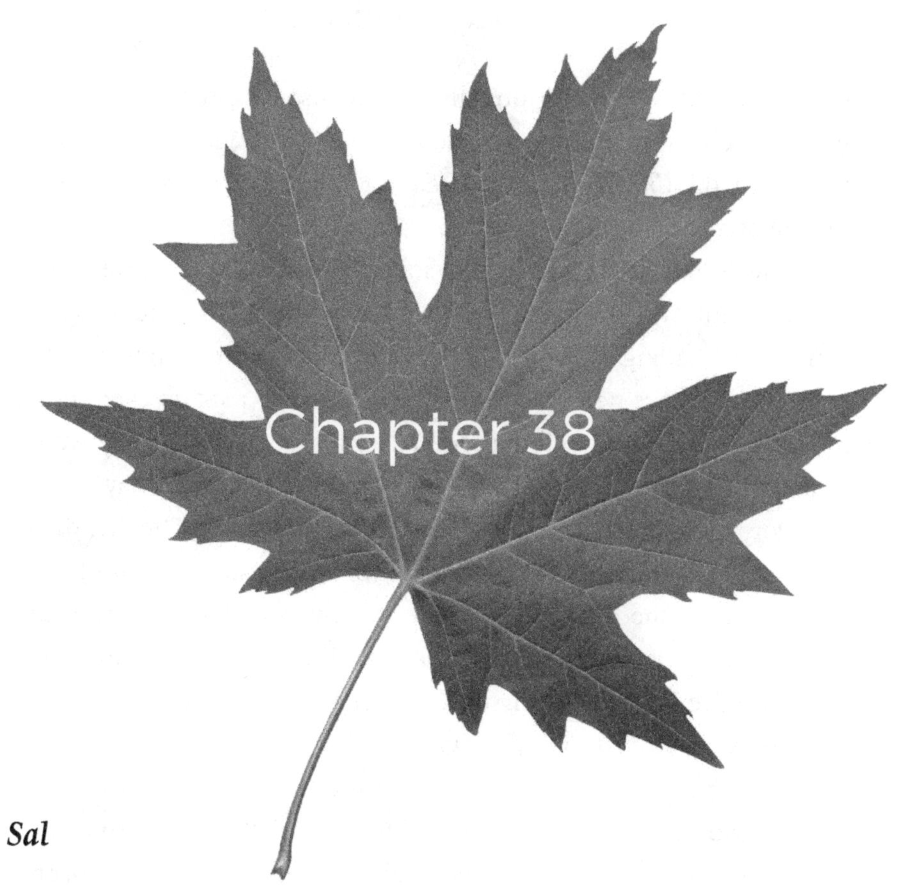

Chapter 38

Sal

The next morning I'm well rested for the first time in a few weeks. Finally getting to be with Clara has me feeling better than I have in a long time. My dreams last night were still filled with her, but they were different. Somehow, they seem brighter. More in color. Vivid color. Spending the day with her has my heart pounding so hard; I can hear the pulsating in my ears.

The need I have to touch her, hold her and kiss her is bordering on obsessive. I need it like a drug that's running through my veins. This drug being the only thing making me feel whole again. Taking her to the church today will be hard, but I'm finally ready. I haven't been there since I was little. Since before Mom died. I was only six years old back then. I don't remember the church that well, but I remember how much my mother loved it.

We went there as often as we could, at least once a week for mass, sometimes more. It was a long drive to Allenspark but Mom loved that little church so much. It wasn't until a few years ago I found out the history of the *Chapel on the Rock. Saint Catherine of Siena Chapel* is the official name of the congregation.

It feels like taking Clara there solidifies our bond and gives me the chance to introduce her to Mom. It's like getting her spiritual approval somehow. Loading the truck, it's quiet on the farm this morning. One of those rare days where work has just started to pick up even though it's early on a Saturday. I don't see Malcolm around yet. I really wanted to talk to him before I left. To tell him I am seeing Clara today.

Pop is right; I need to tell him sooner than later. The last thing I want is for him to think I've lied to him or worse, stolen what's his.

Reality is, she was never his. She was always mine; we just needed some time to figure that out. Looks like I'll have to find him later, I don't want to be late picking up Clara. It's a two-and-a-half-hour road trip I am very much looking forward to.

Pulling into the parking lot I take the first open spot I can find. Knocking on her door, I'm suddenly nervous. What if she thinks I've come on too strong? What if her father hates me? Being an orphan enters my mind, making me doubt she could love me. Whispering to myself *"Stop it Sal,"* I give myself a pep talk, which helps me lift my hand to knock again.

Clara doesn't open the door; it's her father.

He has a sad smile on his face but a smile none-the-less. His sandy brown hair is combed, and he's nicely dressed in a white long-sleeved dress shirt and brown slacks. You wouldn't know anything was off by his appearance, except for the dark circles he wears under each of his eyes. I now know where Clara gets her blue eyes from.

"Good morning; you must be Sal? I'm Stan Abernathy, Clara's father." The hand he offers shakes slightly revealing his nerves and helping me calm mine.

His handshake is firm and formal. With strength behind it, the quick motion betraying what I see is exhaustion.

"Nice to meet you, Mr. Abernathy. Thank you for allowing me to spend the day with your daughter."

"Oh, please. Call me Stan." He smiles and fiddles with the doorknob. Motioning me in, his nervousness increases as he looks toward the hallway. "Clara will be out in a few minutes. Have a seat." He motions with his arm at the brown and tan plaid couch against the far wall.

We sit in silence for a few minutes, me looking over at him every few seconds, then back toward a door that appears to lead out to a patio. Stan sits in the recliner next to me, picking at his shirt. First the buttons and then a wrinkle up near his collar.

Suddenly he gets up urgently.

Panic in his eyes as he excuses himself and walks down the hallway. I hear him knock and then say, "Hey princess, are you almost ready? Sal is here and waiting for you."

I get the feeling he's trying to get rid of us. I hear the door open and Clara responds saying, "Yes, Daddy; I'm ready. Are you sure you'll be ok by yourself today? I don't have to go if you don't want me too." The concern resonates in her voice, making red flags go off in my head. Something doesn't feel right. What in the world has happened to make her worry about him like this?

I'll find out soon enough.

"No, honey; go have fun. I love you so much. I'm so proud of you and the woman you're becoming. I couldn't have asked to be blessed with a better daughter. I can't keep you locked up in this apartment day and night. Thank you for the offering to stay and thank you for taking care of me all this time." I can't see them, but his words are loud in my ear.

I hope one day I can be the kind of father who praises and loves his daughter like Stan loves Clara. Feeling guilty for eavesdropping on what they're saying, I stand from my seat on the couch and walk over to the door I was just staring at and peer out the window.

Clara's voice again sounds in my ears, and I realize this apartment is too small for me to get out of earshot.

"I love you, too. Thanks Daddy, I'll be home this evening ok?"

Footsteps have me turning to watch her walk into the room. Stan follows behind. Her blond hair is down, the curls wild but composed at the same time. Her blue eyes are so bright in the morning sun coming through the windows; I lose my breath just looking at her.

My heart skips, and my skin heats up as I admire her from her head to her toes.

She's wearing a white sundress with pink lilies covering the fabric. The neck of her v-shaped dress shows her flawless white skin and her neck is covered with silver chains all stacked with tiny crosses dangling toward her breasts.

With the amount of light coming in through the apartment windows, she's glowing. Her blonde hair is radiantly bright and beautiful. Not being able to breathe from looking at her has my heart beating even faster every second I stand here.

When she sees me standing by the back door, she comes straight over to me. And without any hesitation at all she wraps her arms around my neck. Then places the simplest most intimate kiss on my lips. Grabbing her by the hips, I pull her against me, wanting no space between our bodies.

It's as if she doesn't remember her father is standing right behind her watching us. I love that she doesn't care that he is.

"Hey. I'm so happy to see you." She says as she gets closer still and embraces me in a tight hug. I respond likewise, with no hesitation.

"Not as happy as I am to see you." Taking her hand, I turn her so we're facing her father again. Even though I thought he'd be unhappy about Clara's public display of affection, he seems relieved somehow. The smile he's wearing seems forced because of the tear that drops from his eye and runs down his face.

Clara notices and rushes to his side, "Daddy, I'm so sorry. I didn't mean to upset you."

In a show of affection, he touches her cheek, another tear falling as he says, "No princess, I'm not upset, I'm happy. It's so great to see you shine so bright. I needed to see that you're trying to live again by allowing someone to love you."

Clara looks over her shoulder at me, happiness at his answer clear on her pretty face. "Well; you two better get going. You said this church is a few hours away right, honey?" Stan asks, wiping the tears from his eyes as he walks us to the door. Clara looks at me to confirm what she's already told him. "Yes sir; a couple of hours in the car and then at some point we'll stop at a café in Allenspark to eat lunch. I'm guessing I'll have her home by five or six o'clock tonight."

"Sounds good, take care of my girl, Sal." Stan offers his hand again and I gladly take it. This time his handshake a bit weaker, showing Stan's exhaustion tenfold.

After Stan hugs Clara one more time, I take her hand in mine and we walk to the truck. The drive goes quick. Knowing so little about each other keeps the conversation going. We discuss school starting in a few weeks, Clara's work schedule at Tractor Supply and she fills me in on how much she misses North Carolina. She doesn't ask me any questions, just answers all of mine without hesitation.

I'm engrossed in her. Nothing else matters in this moment but what she tells me and how she feels. I envision my life will revolve around making her happy and keeping that bright blue sparkle in her eye. Half way through our drive, she lifts the center console between us and scoots over to sit closer to me. I hold her hand, my thumb tracing circles on her soft skin.

A few times on our journey she asks me to pull over to the side of the road. She hops out of the truck and excitement fills her as she looks out at the wildlife and aspen trees. I love coming to the mountains. There's a certain peace that comes over me when I'm in the fresh clean mountain air. Watching her in this element makes me ready to see her in all our experiences. My hope to provide her the chance to be this excited every single day of her life.

Pulling into the church parking lot, I don't have any trouble finding a spot as it's late enough on Saturday that all the other early visitors have already headed home. We walk up the steps that lead to the church, hand in hand. The feeling of her skin against mine feels like home.

We enter through the main door and into the chapel. It's small. Quaint. I love it. The chapel is empty when we enter. Standing at the end of the aisle between two sets of pews, we look around. Clara's face says her thoughts. She's as in awe as I am. I've been here before, but I don't remember it ever being this beautiful. The image my mind conjures as we stand here is of Clara in a white dress. Yellow flowers in her hair, promising to love me forever in front of our friends and family. I can't believe the thoughts going through my head. I've only known her for a short time, but I already can't imagine my life without her. As I stand in the chapel with Clara by my side, I can only imagine marrying her in a church just like this one.

I head down the aisle, pulling Clara behind me. She's mesmerized by her surroundings. The meaning of this place is heavy in every heart that walks through the door. By looking at her pretty face, I know she's been taken in by the power of God just as I have been.

I don't know the proper procedures of prayer in any church, let alone a church like this, so we sit on the first aisle and stare up at the man on the cross. I move so that I'm slightly turned toward her, my arm around the back of the bench resting on the back of the pew. Our legs touch at the knee and she rests her hand on my leg. I like that she wants to always be touching me. It feels good to know she needs that connection as much as I do.

Instead of waiting for her to ask why exactly I brought her here, I begin with explaining about my mother and her love for this church.

"I bet you're wondering why I've chosen to bring you here. This place is special to me. My mother loved coming here. Before she died, we came up here once a week, typically on Saturdays for Mass. I was young so all I really remember was the outside of the building and the statue on the hill. I remember her praying on her knees, a rosary in her hand, but I was so young I don't remember anything else."

My eyes stay glued to the crucifix hanging above our heads, the candle sticks on the pulpit. They stand tall, waiting for someone to light them.

Crossing her legs and turning in closer to me, she asks, "How old were you when she died?" Looking down at her hand still resting on my knee, sadness settles in, making me regret the decision to talk about my mother. "I was six." Swallowing the lump in my throat, I feel the urge to change the subject to something more positive and hopeful.

"I'm going to marry you in a church like this someday." Her head snaps up in my direction, surprise at my honesty evident.

"You think so, huh? Well; we should probably be together longer than one day before we talk about marriage." I look down at our hands and entwine my fingers with hers, tightening my grip and squeezing tightly. She laughs at her own comment, then looks back up at the pulpit.

"I don't need longer than a day. I know today that I'm going to marry you one day. I can already see you walking down the aisle wearing a white dress with yellow flowers in your hair." I figure I've already probably scared her with my honesty so why stop now.

"White dress huh? What If I told you I don't want to get married? What if I said that I don't believe in marriage?" Running her hand through her hair, she blushes a little. The smile on her face showing me she doesn't mean that, she's testing me.

Being as serious as I possibly can, I say, "Then I'd tell you I have at least a year to change your mind on that."

"Well you're in luck; I do believe in marriage. I just think you have to know the person you're marrying before taking thc plunge. I mean, what if you end up not liking the old ball and chain? If you don't know who you're marrying, then the marriage is over before it ever begins."

I see her point, but I have no reservation that if I were able to marry her today, right now, we'd be together for as long as we both live. Nodding, I say, "not a chance. I guess we better start working on knowing each other then. Let's get started on that now." Leaning down, I lower my head and place a kiss to her lips. It's quick and simple. "Let's go upstairs and ring the bell. The sign when we came in said if each new person to the church goes up stairs, sends up a prayer and a wish then rings the bell, the wish will come true."

On the balcony, Clara sits on a stool that is clearly provided for the choir and closes her eyes. Her hands press together in prayer in front of her. Her lips move as she says her wish and prayer, but no words come out. I stand by the stairs leaning on the rail of the balcony and just watch her. She must feel the weight of my stare because she opens one eye, looking sideways at me with a smile that's changing her mood from serious to playful. The chain for the bell touches her shoulder, waiting for us to pull on it.

"Come over here, make your wish, say a prayer and let's ring this bell!" Clara says to me.

"I already made my wish and prayer; they've already come true." Another bit of honesty from me. She keeps me unfiltered; I'm not able to hold back anything from her.

Her eyes narrow as if she doesn't believe me. So I move to sit next to her. Not blinking or missing a beat I say, "I have a family, three brothers I never thought I'd have. And I'm here with you, aren't I? All my prayers and wishes were granted the day I met Malcolm and Adler. Then I had prayers answered I wasn't even praying for. That day Pop took us to live at the farm, was the first day of the rest of my life. Which all lead me to you. You literally dropped onto the hood of my truck, and one look into your beautiful blue eyes was it for me." Trying to lighten the mood now that I got so serious, I say, "It's a good a thing that old truck has good breaks, or we wouldn't be sitting here."

Sadness now covers her face, but she recovers quickly.

Not sure what I said to have her mood shift so fast, I reach up and grab the chain. She smiles and wraps her hand around mine so we're holding it together. "Ready?" I ask. She nods a smile back in place.

We pull the chain and the bell rings out load. Chiming each time, we pull the chain down toward us. Her smile widens as we pull a third time and then release the chain. Our hands stay locked as I pull her toward me, our bodies pressing against each other.

"My prayers have been answered, and God sent me you, Clara. I will spend every day for the rest of my life working to deserve to keep you." With my heart pounding, and blood rushing through my body, I wrap my arms around her waist and lower my head to kiss her. This time, our kiss is different from the other kisses we've shared. My mouth opens, my tongue running along her lips gently, urging her to open up to me. She does and our lips slide against each other, our tongues in a steady dance. The passion of our kiss has her body melting into my arms. The love I feel for her comes out strong and true in our passion to get even closer than we already are. Pulling away, her face is red and flushed with need and passion. I can feel her kiss touch my soul, the look in her eye says she feels the same and that she needs me just as much as I need her. Hugging Clara to me tightly I say a silent thank you for the trust she has already put in me in such a short time.

"Sal? If I told you I don't know what love really is, and that I'm scared of what you make me feel, what would you say? Would you want to still be with me? If I told you I don't know what this feeling is, would you still love me as you do now?" Worry and regret shadow her face. Fear evident that my answer will be anything but what she's hoping for.

I don't hesitate in my answer. Taking her face in my hands I say, "I will love you no matter how long it takes for you to figure that out. And then I'll be here waiting when you finally do." Her reply comes out as a whisper, "If this is what love feels like, I don't ever want to be without it, or without you."

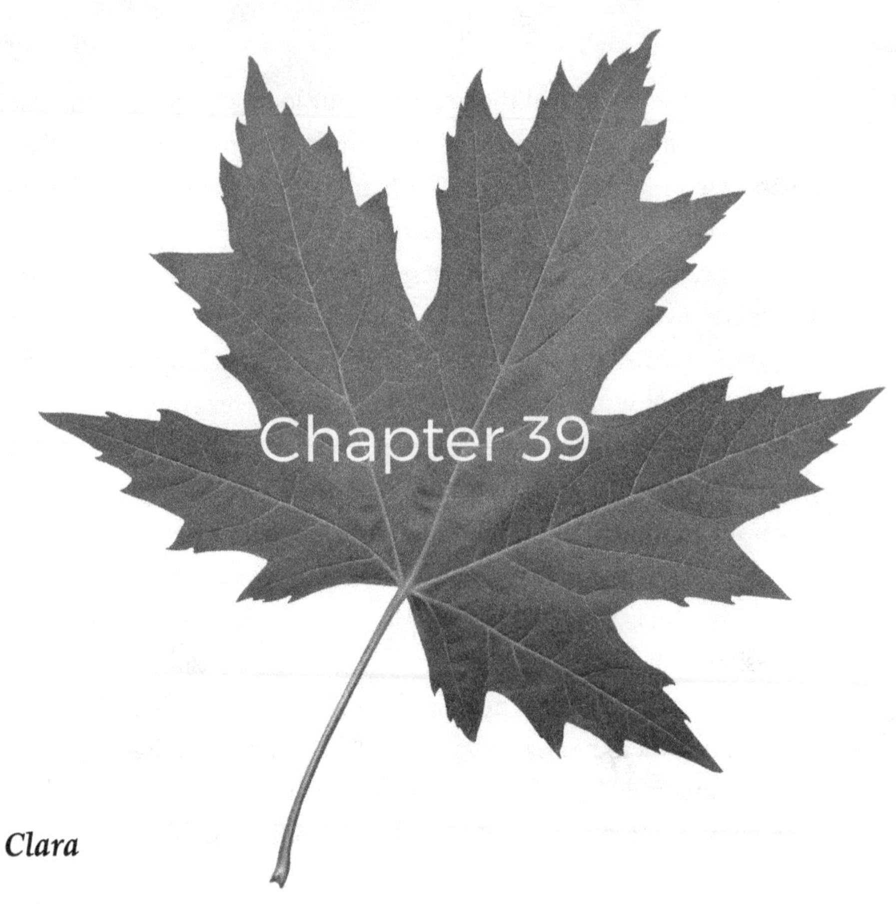

Chapter 39

Clara

I've never been kissed with so much need and emotion. The times before when he'd kiss me, it was always on the cheek or forehead and felt so amazing and intimate even though it was only PG rated.

As a little girl, I always wondered what it would feel like to be truly kissed, with passion and hunger. When I kissed Malcolm on my doorstep that night, I felt good and wanted inside but I didn't feel the desire I needed. Even with my mind playing tricks on me, the disappointment when I opened my eyes overshadowed what I was feeling when I looked up at Malcolm. Then when Sal touched me, kissed me gently for the first time, I never would have thought this is how I'd feel. Malcolm's kiss was gentle and friendly. Sal's kiss was passionate. Needy. And Possessive. It left me wanting more, more of him and more of his kiss.

Coming out of the church, we sit on the steps outside. I sit close to him and tangle my arm in his. I can't seem to stop touching him. The need to have him touching me in return feels more like desperation. God; get a grip, Clara.

Sitting on the steps I think back to when I was in his room last night. The pictures he had on his mirror have been on my mind ever since. I decide now is a good time to ask about the one that I keep seeing over and over again in my mind.

"Hey Sal, can I ask you something?" Kissing the top of my hand, he nods.

"You can ask me anything you want."

"Who was the little girl in the picture with you, Malcolm and Adler? The one you have hanging on your mirror from when you were kids?" His body tenses and his eyes widen at the question, making me regret asking him about the picture as soon as the question comes out.

"I'm sorry, Sal; it's none of my business. You don't have to answer." Getting up, I straighten my dress with my palms and take the next two steps down before Sal stops me.

"Not so fast, Clara. It's ok, I'll talk about Lucy, it's just a sore subject, that's all. Come back up here, sit next to me." He pats the concrete step next to him and I sit back down. I keep my hands on my knees this time, thinking he needs space for this conversation, but he takes my hand in his instead.

"I didn't realize you saw that picture, so it just surprised me that you asked about her."

"Really, you don't have to tell me. It's ok if you don't want to talk about her."

Shifting so he's facing me, his knee now up on the step bent toward my hip. I move to match his position our bodies facing each other, hands locked between us.

Swallowing as if a lump has formed in his throat, I feel guilty for bringing this up. The topic is obviously hard for him to talk about. I have to admit that while I feel guilty and regret the question, he has my mind wondering about what happened to her and where she is now.

"The little girl. That's Lucy. Lulu, we called her. She lived at the foster home I moved into that Malcolm and Adler was already living in. It was a horrible place. It was bad enough for three young boys but even worse for a little girl. Living there killed her."

I didn't expect his last words. They make my head snap up to look at him. His eyes are wild with anger. I don't say anything just continue to listen to him tell me about her.

"She was only six years old when I moved into Jeff and Jenny's. Jeff was an alcoholic and a creep. Jenny was a crack head, a heroin addict. How they actually got to become foster parents is beyond me. Pop to this day is still trying to prevent people like Jeff and Jenny from being in the system. Anyway, we lived with them for months. Lucy was a tiny little thing and it wasn't uncommon for us to find Jeff trying to molest her. I became her protector. We all did. We protected her and never left her alone with him. But one day, Lulu was sick when we dropped her off at school. I tried to get her to skip class with me. I told her I'd stay with her the whole day. We could even go to Bill's for a milkshake. Chocolate milkshakes were her favorite. But she refused; she wanted to try and go to class."

Knowing this story is taking a devastating turn, I look down at our joined hands, hoping to channel strength to Sal so he can finish. He looks out across the parking lot, the pain making it hard to continue.

"We all went to class that day. Malcolm has always had a sense about things. He knows when something is off and on that day he had a bad feeling. He knew something wasn't right. I tried to go about my day and not worry, but it turned out Malcolm was right." Swallowing again, Sal looks over at me. His eyes start to fill with tears.

"We met outside after school like always. Malcolm was pale and scared, his fear making us all nervous all over again. Tate was also with us; we had decided earlier in the day to go get Lulu from the elementary school and then go to Bill's for that milkshake. We went almost every day after school, trying to avoid going home. But when we got to Lulu's school, her teacher was outside ushering kids to the busses, but we couldn't find Lucy. She wasn't anywhere to be found. My worry grew as I ran over to her teacher. She smiled and said hello like always, but she could see the worry on my face. I asked her where Lucy was. Then my worry turned into panic. She said Lucy had become ill. She was vomiting while in the nurse's office, so they called the fosters to come pick her up."

My heart is pounding so fast, I close my eyes with fear of what he's about to tell me. I cover my face with my hands, tears welling up in my eyes. I look up at him as gravity pulls a tear from my eye and down my cheek. He doesn't wipe it away, just continues telling me what happened to Lucy.

"I couldn't breathe. God, Clara; I've never been so scared in my entire life. I looked over at Adler. He was already crying. Malcolm and I took off running toward the house, panic and adrenaline running through our veins. When we got to the house, Jenny was dead. She was lying on the floor in the living room, a needle in her arm. She had overdosed. When I ran into the bedroom where we slept, Jeff was on top of Lucy. I knew she was already dead but if there were any chance, she wasn't, I was going to try and save her. I was only twelve years old at the time, but I jumped on Jeff's back and we began to struggle. He punched me several times, kicked me and knocked me to the ground unconscious. Malcolm had run in behind me, covered Lucy's tiny exposed body with a sheet. He then used his own body to shield Lucy as Jeff spiraled out of control and crashed through the window above my usual spot on the floor."

My tears come so fast and hard now, I can't breathe. I can't believe what they've been through. Everything life has thrown at them. My mother dying was traumatic and heartbreaking and I will never be the same after that experience, but hearing about this is unbelievable. My thought goes immediately to the beating Sal got and what happened to Malcolm.

"Where you hurt badly? What about Malcolm?"

"I was bruised up pretty good. Had some broken ribs, but I survived. Malcolm had some cuts on his arms, but he was ok, too."

I'm scared to ask but I do anyway. "What about Lucy?"

"She didn't make it." He runs his hands across his shaved head, then down his face. When he looks back at me, his face is as it was before. He's calm now, with no hint of the tears I saw in his eyes from before. The years that have passed by have clearly helped him keep his feelings regarding Lucy in a box for safekeeping.

"I spent one night in the hospital and was released the next day. Malcolm and Adler stayed in the room with me. Pop worked tirelessly to get custody of us, all three of us. To say we were shocked is an understatement. We moved to the farm the day I got out of the hospital, then a few days later we buried Lucy. And now here we are."

"Wow. Sal, I had no idea what you guys had been through. I'm sure each of you have your own past too. Like before you knew each other. That one experience, what happened to Lucy, is something that no one should have to face, let alone three twelve-year-old boys."

He looks thoughtful now, like he has so much on his mind. I'm sure his story and our talking bring up so much more than just Lucy.

"I take it Malcolm never mentioned any of this to you?" His arm shifts, coming around my neck to pull me closer to him. Still sitting on the stairs, the pressure from sitting here for so long is taking its toll on my butt.

"No, he didn't mention anything. Malcolm has never been an open book. He's kept things locked away. He did mention Mr. Keating and how him and his wife came to America. And that he's worried about Adler wanting to join the military. But other than that, he's been a closed book. It's like he has secrets he doesn't want anyone to know about."

"Yeah, Malcolm thinks that the past is the past. He doesn't dwell in it. He just moves forward, always moving forward. After Lucy died, we vowed to always take care of each other and each other's families as well. When we have them that is. It's our pact between us brothers.

Malcolm believes everything that happened in our early years should stay in the past. The only thing that hasn't changed from the past is Bill."

I can't place that name but it sounds so familiar to me.

"Who's Bill? The name is familiar but I can't place it." I ask.

"Bill owns Rocky Mountain Soda; the little café next to Tractor Supply. That's where we used to take Lucy for milkshakes and Bill would sometimes put us to work after school. He'd pay us under the table so we'd have a little money in our pockets." Sal scratches his head, seeming uncomfortable sitting on the steps of the church. Now I remember who Bill is. Malcolm and I ate at Rocky Mountain Soda a few weeks ago. That hamburger was the best I've ever had.

"I ate there. With Malcolm. I've met Bill. That's why he sounded so familiar! Oh, that burger, Sal. My mouth waters just thinking about that burger." I rub my stomach in a dramatic attempt to show my affection for the greasy meal.

Sal laughs. "Yeah, Bill makes the best burgers all right. Did you guys have the *Lost and Found* special?"

Thinking back, I lift my chin to the sky trying to remember. Bill and Malcolm had a moment after he ordered for us and now looking back, I wonder if Bill was trying to hint to Malcolm that he was about to have to answer some tough questions. "Yeah, you know what. I think it was called that. Is there another story behind that burger, Sal?"

"Oh, Clara; there's a story behind everything," he says still laughing. "The *Lost and Found* special was what we always ordered when we went in. It wasn't called that then, of course. But the first time we ever went into the café, Bill asked if we were lost. Then after we had been going there for a while, Bill would give us free burgers and milkshakes along with a little money for working. He said one day that he had found the best workers in us. We were his lost and found kids. Hence, the name of what he'd been feeding us. When he upgraded and remodeled the café, he dedicated that burger special as The *Lost and Found* special."

No wonder I liked Bill just from meeting him once. Now the love and affection I saw Malcolm had for him makes sense. Man, Malcolm is a closet full of secrets. Walking back to the truck, it feels good to stand and stretch.

We get in the truck and Sal takes us towards Allenspark. Driving through town, we find a small restaurant tucked away in a shopping center and go in for some lunch.

Now. Knowing that Malcolm keeps his past as close to him as his family, I understand why he believes moving forward and not living in the past is so important. I vow to be the same. To do my best to live in the moment and for the future, not dwelling on what's happened to me in the past. Moving on and enjoying life is what Mama would have always wanted.

I know the conversation is going to turn to me and my sad story as soon as we walk in. We're seated at a booth against the far wall of the restaurant, secluded from other diners. It's almost romantic in a way. But I have a feeling everything Sal and I will do will feel romantic in some way.

We get situated in our booth and Sal asks the question I've dreaded answering. The one Malcolm never asked, and I was thankful he never did. But Sal is different. After hearing his story, I want to tell him mine. Doesn't make it easy, but it encourages me a little to open up to him.

Reaching across the table, he takes my hand in his. "So, Clara. Tell me what made your family move all the way to Colorado from North Carolina?" He places a kiss on my hand, a gesture that's becoming a routine I'm beginning to crave.

"Well. My parents moved us here when I was twelve. My mother was diagnosed with breast cancer and needed special treatment. The only place that had the specialist she needed and that my father could transfer his job to was in Denver. So here we are."

The resolve on his face is clear without him having to ask where my mother is today. Instead of waiting for him to ask, I say, "My mother battled cancer for five years. Then she died peacefully at home with Daddy and me by her side."

"So, that means your mother died recently? Clara, God; I didn't know. I'm so sorry."

I'm surprised that tears aren't threatening me. That I can talk with Sal about this without falling apart. Just as I'm about to tell him he almost ran me over the day my mother died, our waitress comes up to take our order.

Sal orders a burger with bacon and fries, a coke to drink. I order a patty melt with sautéed mushrooms added, steamed broccoli as a side with a sweetened iced tea.

"So, you like mushrooms, huh?" The playfulness on his face is infectious. His smile is broad and beautiful, his dark eyes shining brightly and drawing me in. The need to kiss him is strong and overwhelming. Leaning across the table, I tilt my head and close my eyes, inviting him to meet me in the middle. He does and our lips join in the softest kiss. His tongue gently touches my lips and I open up to his kiss. Pulling away, I lick my lips; he tastes good, like mint- flavored toothpaste. "Yeah, I love mushrooms. On everything!"

"Duly noted, princess." He winks at me and sits back against the booth. His pet name for me gives me goose bumps. I didn't think I'd like a man calling me pet names, but from Sal's mouth, it's heavenly. My Daddy calls me that too, which could get a little weird. I guess I'll have to tell Sal to pick another name. Not realizing it, I wrinkle my nose at the thought. Princess is what my Daddy has always called me. He stills at my reaction, "What? What did I say?"

"Well, my father calls me princess, so if you do too, it could get a little weird." Lightening the mood, I laugh hoping he'll see the humor in all this.

"Yeah, I guess it could. Duly noted again, BABE." Sarcasm fills his voice, making me laugh. "Much better!" I say.

"So, tell me more about your dad. Now that I know why he seemed so sad but trying like hell to pretend he's not. What does he do?"

"He's a political analyst." Sal has a look that tells me he has no clue what that is. I didn't either for the longest time.

Laughing, I explain, "I didn't know what that was either until a few years ago. He was a lawyer that became a journalist. So now he does political analysis for news studios. So, long explanation short, he gets paid to give his opinion on the government and on government officials." Leaning back into the booth, Sal nods his head in understanding. "Ok, that sounds cool, I guess. So, he's like really smart huh?"

"Yes, you could say that."

"And what does Clara plan to do when she's out of school?" Looking at me, one eyebrow raised in curiosity, he looks so handsome. I love his playful side. It's hard not to reach across and kiss him again.

"The same as my Daddy, really. But I want to be a lawyer first, work as a public defender then go into politics. I want to run for office one day." Holding my head high, I pray my future plans don't disappoint him. They're huge goals but I know I can make a difference if I try. I already know Sal plans to go to the military with his brothers. The thought puts sadness at the forefront of my mind. We just met and began a relationship and in less than a year, he'll be leaving for boot camp. I hope my big life plans don't scare him away.

"Those are beautiful dreams Clara. I know you can do anything you set your mind to." There's no judgment or doubt on his face, and that gives me hope that no matter where our lives take us, we can figure out how to make this work. I already know Sal will be joining the military. But I haven't asked any details so I decide to pry into his future just like he did into mine.

"I know you're going into the military, but I don't know what you want to do when you get there."

"Me? I plan to do Special Forces. Join the Marines, move up the ranks. Then I'll marry you and help you with your campaign while I take care of our kids." Wow. I didn't expect that answer. Well; I guess he already has our life all figured out. Smiling like a loon at Sal, I can't hide my pleasure at his answer. I don't elaborate because the waitress is bringing our lunch out. The conversation is lighter as we eat. Nothing serious is being talked about and I'm grateful for the emotional reprieve. The feeling that I've had enough sad stories and enough heartache in one day is very heavy on my heart. We finish eating and make our way back to the truck.

Climbing in, exhaustion hits me. I slide into the seat and back across where the console would be. Sal gets in and turns the ignition. As he drives us back, I watch out the window, enjoying the scenery moving past quickly, the mountains putting me in a pattern of being awake and asleep in intervals. The light sound of Willie Nelson's *Seven Spanish Angels* comes through the speakers. I look over at Sal driving and find it hard to stay fully awake. He pats his leg, inviting me to lay down across the seat. As I lay down and rest my head on his thigh, I drift off into the most sound, peaceful sleep.

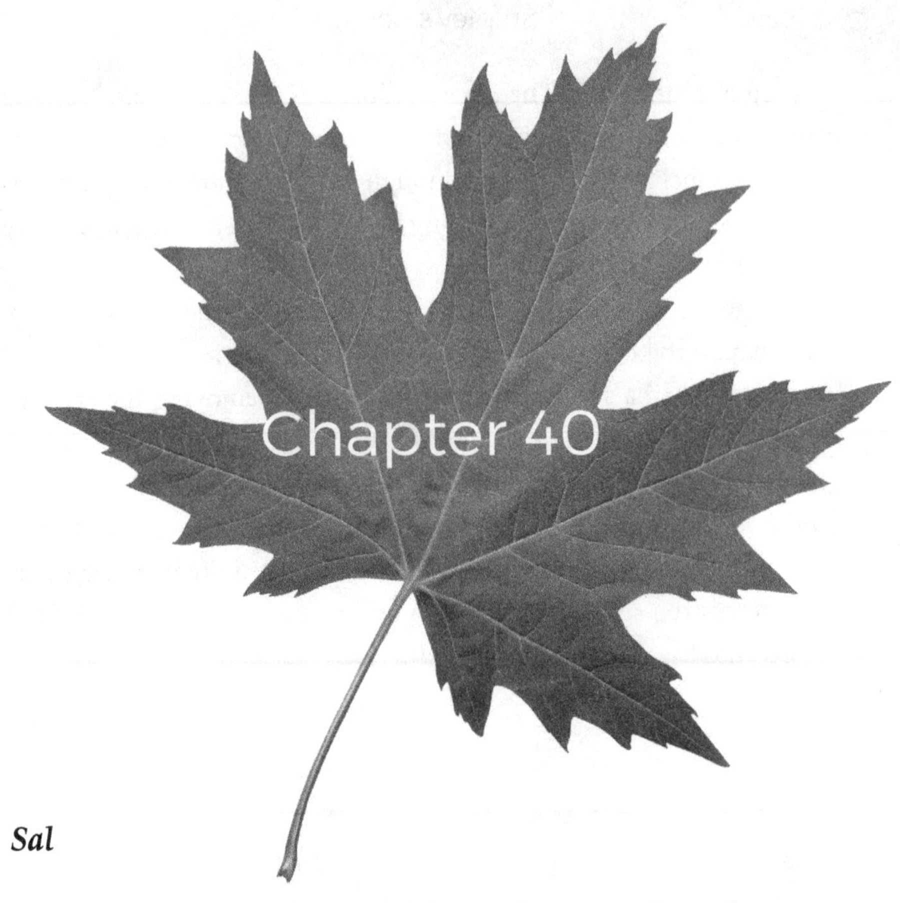

Chapter 40

Sal

Clara's sound asleep when I pull the truck up into the parking space at her apartment. She's lying on her left side. Her head on my thigh with one arm out straight, the other bent at the elbow and tucked under her cheek. She's so deep in sleep I don't want to wake her but I promised Stan I'd have her home no later than six. It's six-twenty now. I've already broken my first promise to her father.

I run my fingers through her long hair. Her curls soft and smooth, allowing my finger to pass through each time without meeting tangles. All I can do is sit here and watch her sleep. Her chest is moving up and down with each breath. Her dress is perfectly in place despite the position she's lying in, the tops of her thighs just barely visible. The white skin is making my mouth water at the thought of running my lips across places on her body that would make her moan out my name. At some point, she kicked off her sandals, her yellow nail polish shining brightly on her bare feet. I wish we could sit like this forever.

The ache I now have for her strains in my jeans, making me need a quick adjustment. Trying not to wake her, I move just barely enough that it causes her to shift on the seat. Now lying on her back, she blinks a few times and turns to look up at me. Her big blues eyes look at me with so much affection, my heart pounds. She gives me the most beautiful sleepy smile.

"Hey. Are we home?" Placing her hand on the seat, she lifts herself up to look out the front window.

"Yeah." Involuntarily I reach out and grab her hand, pulling her closer to me. She slides over, thigh to thigh. I touch her face, warning her that I'm about to kiss her. My body reacting to her so strongly has me ready to lay her back down on the seat so I can work out my desire and sexual need on her. But I respect Clara too much for that. Doing my best to keep myself in check, I take a deep breath then lean my head down and press my lips to hers. Her response is different from the last few times I've kissed her. She kisses me back with fervor, matching my hunger stride for stride.

Before I can move to get closer to her, she turns around in the seat. Bringing her knees up on the seat next to me, she holds my face in her hands as she tortures my mouth. Needing to be as close as possible, I grab her by the waist and pull her across to straddle my lap. The steering wheel keeps her from being able to fully climb on, so I slide over to the middle seat and pull her on top of me.

The feeling of her that close drives me insane and I kiss her harder, without any control. The need comes out so intense I can't hold in my urgency, running my hands up her thighs and under her dress where I feel the soft lace of her panties at her hips. She moves against me, making me moan into her mouth. I run my hands up and down her thighs and around to grip her ass. The skin there is the softest skin on her entire body.

She wraps her arms around my neck then runs her fingers through my hair. Now that her chest is against mine fully, I can feel the hardness of her nipples pressing against the fabric, the urge to touch each perfectly shaped mound is too much for me to handle. She continues to gyrate on my lap, making me harder with each rotation of her hips. I moan into her mouth again.

Her panting breaths are heavy and hot in my ear and on my neck. God, I want her so bad. But I know I have to stop this; our first time can't be in this truck. Kissing her again, I almost change my mind and lay her down across the seat. My mind and my heart are warring with each other. One telling the other to shut up and get the relief I've needed ever since I first laid my eyes on her. Mustering up all my self-control, I use my palms and apply pressure to stop the rotation of her hips against me. She doesn't get my hint right away, increasing the motion and applying more pressure down on my lap with her hips. The motion is making her breath come harder and I can tell she's close. What kind of man would I be if I denied her this?

Releasing the pressure, I was putting on her to stop moving, instead I help increase her movements and she moves faster. As her hips jerk, her lips kiss me with so much passion. I know she's close by the little bites she's taking on my bottom lip. She starts moaning, small little moans that make me almost lose the little bit of composure I still have.

To help get her where she's trying so hard to go, I move my hands up from her thighs to her breasts. Squeezing gently, and rubbing her nipples between my fingers, she gets to the highest peak of the mountain. She throws her head back and rides the wave high into the sky before coming back down slowly. She stills in my lap and my heart soars. She's an angel and even more beautiful while in ecstasy, if that's even possible.

She lays her head on my shoulder, catching her breath as I push the hair from her face. Sweat that accumulated across her brow sticks to her hair. I run my fingers across the top of her head to push back her blonde locks.

Looking at me, her face reddens in embarrassment. The reality of what just happened crashing down on her. She tries to turn away but I stop her from moving from my lap. We've got to get one thing straight right now. I never want to see her embarrassed by what we do to make each other feel good. To feel loved by each other.

"Hey, don't hide from me. Don't ever hide from me. Why are you embarrassed? That was the hottest, sexiest experience of my entire life," I say.

Shifting on my lap, I still her motion with my hands. Glaring a warning at her that her movements are now painful.

"Don't move like that, babe." The words come out as a growl.

"Sorry." With her face turning even redder, she shifts to move off my lap completely. I stop her one more time. Pulling her down, I kiss her gently. Trying to put all my love in this one kiss. She looks at me and smiles.

"Thank you, Sal. For ah-you know." Kissing me again, she removes herself from my grasp and this time I let her go.

The sandals she was wearing are dangling in her hand as we walk toward the apartment. Holding her hand, we walk slowly toward the door, both not wanting the night to end just yet.

"I don't want you to go yet. Can you stay awhile? Please? We can watch a movie."

"Sure, I don't want to leave yet either." Taking our time on the stairs, we move slowly. Enjoying it being just the two of us for a moment longer, knowing Stan will be in the apartment with us once we go in.

At the door, Clara is surprised that the door is locked. It sets something off in my mind.

"What is it?" I ask.

"I'm just surprised Daddy locked the door; he knew we'd be here around six."

"Well it is six-forty. Were forty minutes late, babe. Your dad's never going to let me take you out again." I laugh, trying to ease the sudden fear that trickles down my spine. What the hell is wrong with me?

"True Story. Yes, we're late. And for the record, Daddy wouldn't try to keep me away from you." Taking her in my arms again, I say "Oh yeah? How can you be so sure?" I play along, her mood is infectious, but something still nags me as we stand here.

"Because he knows I'd find a way to defy him and be with you anyway!"

"You're such a rebel, babe. You better watch out; defiance turns me on." Clara turns the key in the lock and turns the nob as I kiss her again. Stealing one more kiss before going inside.

Clara drops her keys as she turns and enters the apartment, so I pause outside the door to pick them up. Her piercing scream from inside startles me and I'm not prepared for what I see when I push the door open.

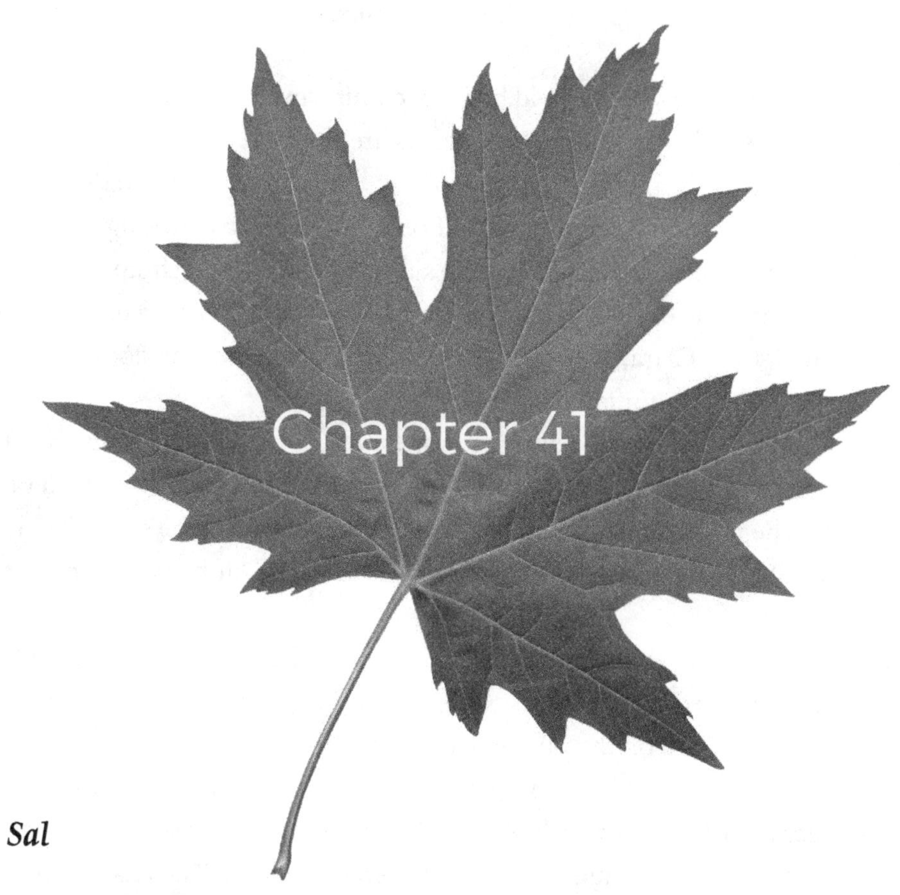

Chapter 41

Sal

Shock and surprise keep me rooted in place. Keeping me from moving at the sight of Stan Abernathy hanging from the main center beam in the living room. A rope is tied around his neck; the weight of his body, held only by the thick wood of the beam. The decorative holes throughout the beam being what he used to pass the rope through to take his own life.

Clara's screams break the thin glass of my shock, causing adrenaline to course through my veins. Body and mind click into place and I run full speed toward him. Grabbing a kitchen chair, I pull it close to Stan's dangling feet and legs, then use it to stand on. I try to relieve the pressure of the rope on Stan's throat by lifting him up by his legs.

His skin is still warm so I use all my strength to lift him up to release the tension around his neck. Clara continues to scream; the sound making it hard for me to continue what is probably a useless futile task. The need to hold her is becoming over bearing. Clara drops to her knees by the chair. Her screams are nonstop.

Just as I'm about to give up, my arms tired from holding the weight of his body, Stan coughs. Loud whole-body wracking coughs. He's barely conscious but manages involuntarily to reach up and pull slightly on the obstruction to his airway. I muster all my strength to lift him higher. "Clara, get up and call for help." I yell, but she doesn't hear me over her continuous screams.

After coughing a few more times, his arms go limp again and I fear this time his body will give out for good. Looking down at Clara, I see she notices Stan trying and failing to reverse what he's so selfishly done. She runs up to the chair, trying to help me lift her father higher in the air.

"No Clara; go call 911. Hurry! Hurry, babe! Tell them to hurry!" The continued weight of his body makes my muscles shake and shiver. I can hear Clara on the phone begging someone to help us.

Through her tears she pleads, "Please, come. It's my father; he needs help. He tried to kill himself. Please help us! Send someone fast."

My arms continue their goal of holding up Stan. The chair is rocking back and forth a little from the heaviness of the body I'm holding in my arms. I balance on the chair and chant in my head, "Please don't fall, please don't fall." He hasn't regained consciousness and I fear we didn't get here in time. Clara stays on the phone, talking to the 911 operator and it only takes a few minutes until I hear the sound of sirens. The relief I feel that they're close is nothing compared to the feeling of them relieving the pressure of Stan's weight off me. As soon as they have a hold on him, I jump down off the chair and drop to the floor next to Clara. I hold her tight as the paramedics place her father on a stretcher, remove the rope from his neck and begin CPR.

It feels like decades that they work on him, but in reality, it's only a couple of minutes. Clara's cries fill the entire apartment and I hold her tight trying and failing to ease her worry. The paramedics stop every minute to assess if Stan is breathing and if he has a pulse. Then after two rounds of CPR, we hear Stan cough. Clara's head shoots up, tears streaking down her face. We sit there on the floor, hoping that's a good sign but scared it's not going to be enough to support life.

The paramedic standing closest to us says, "We got him back. I can't say what the damage will be but there will be some lifelong consequences to his actions here today. I'm sorry we couldn't do more."

"But he's alive, right?" With hope beaming in her eyes, my girl's big blue eyes still hold so much sadness but now have the slightest amount of faith that Stan will pull through.

"Yes, Ma'am; for now. But let's get him to the hospital. His chances of survival depend on him getting to a doctor within an hour of injury." Patting her on the shoulder, showing sympathy to the situation, he continues, "I think we just made it here in time." Smiling sadly at us the paramedic continues out the door.

Clara and I follow the stretcher out and wait for Stan to be loaded into the rig before jumping back in the truck and heading toward the hospital.

Man, I would give anything in this moment to take away the pain Clara is in right now. And as we drive, I can already feel the guilt building up that I kept her later today then I should have. Just knowing that the forty minutes we were late could have been the precious minutes Stan needed us around to keep him from doing what he did.

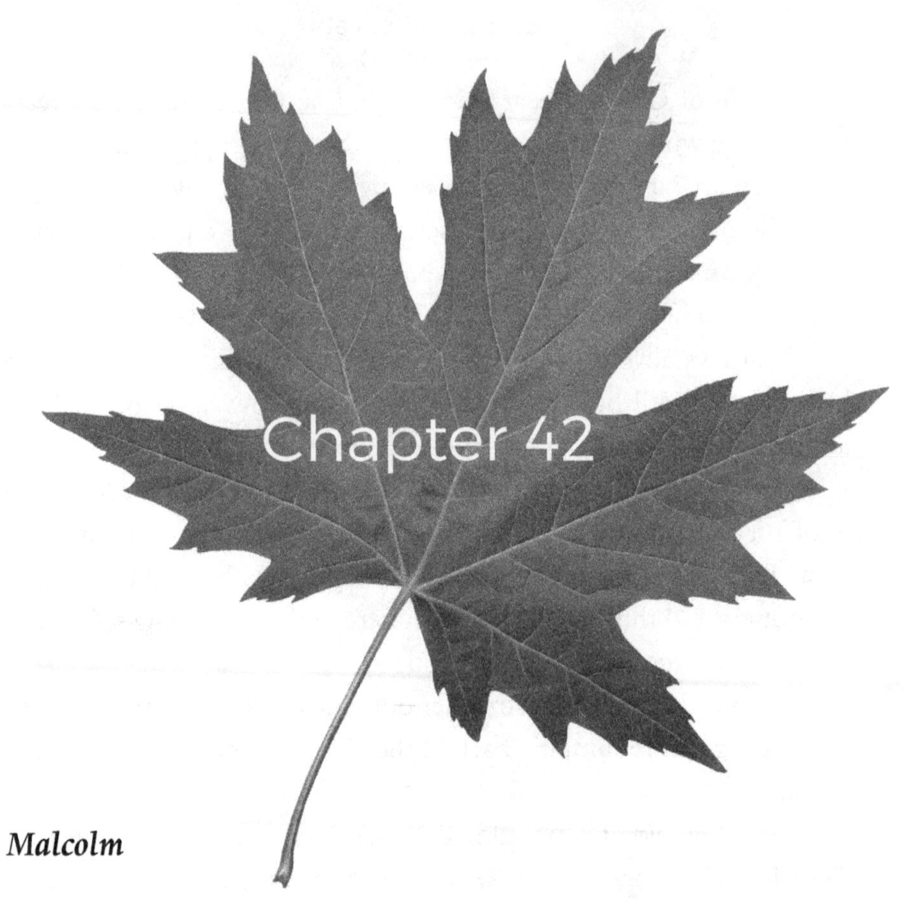

Chapter 42

Malcolm

Waking up this morning something feels off and has me feeling like I have a hangover. The only problem is, I didn't have a single thing to drink last night.

Rolling over, I glance over at the alarm clock. The numbers are blurry; the red color isn't bright enough for my eyes to comprehend due to the sleep in my eyes. Rubbing with my knuckles, trying to clear the nights rest, I finally blink enough to clear my vision.

I think my eyes are playing tricks on me and I have to rub my eyes again, blinking quickly because I swear that clock said 10:15 am. Looking back over at the clock, yep; it says 10:15am. I rarely sleep this late, unless I'm sick. Or I have that random and rare day off. This is not a day off and I'm not sick, so my brain must be foggy from too much sleep. Hence the hangover feeling.

Somehow my body must have needed the additional rest. Not

dwelling on the fact that I'm still in bed, and that I should be out there helping with chores, I get up and go into the bathroom down the hall. Running the shower to cold, I brush my teeth and wash my face, the washcloth I use letting off the smell of cotton that's been used a few too many times. I toss the rag into the basket full of clothes I need to wash today and get into the shower.

The water is cold and soothing on my skin. I wash off yesterday's dirt from my body using the white bar of scented soap that sits on the tub's ledge. I make a mental run through of everything I have to do today, along with everything I missed while I slept in this morning. To say I'm surprised no one came in to wake me is an understatement. Pop normally would have sent one of the guys up here to get me up.

Rinsing the soap and shampoo off my body, I let the water spray against my face, the cold water waking me fully. Bringing my head out of the water, it's now I feel it, something's off. My senses heighten all of a sudden. The feeling that something's not aligned right somehow makes my heart skip a beat and heat covers my skin. Shaking my head and letting the water run over me one more time, I turn the nob and reach out to grab a towel.

Getting dressed, the feeling that something isn't right somehow grows and lingers, making me wonder what's got me so uptight this morning. Maybe I am sick? I hope it's that and not my intuition speaking loudly. Trying to tell me something terrible is about to happen.

Going outside, my eyes move around the farm, searching for Pop or one of the guys. I don't see anyone but I can hear the tractor going back behind the barn. The roaring engine is flat from sitting in the barn unused for this season so far. It's close to harvest time so I suspect they're back there doing tractor maintenance and care. Coming around the corner, my already dirty boots kick up more dirt. I never would have thought I could get more dirt covering the steal toe of my boots, but sure enough that's what happens. Pop leans over the nose of the tractor, dictating to Tate what screw to tighten and which wrench to use. Tate lies flat on his back under the tractor, the only part of his body showing being the bottom half of him.

"Hey Pop. Tate." Shielding my eyes from the sun, I walk over and lean up against the tractor, trying my best to get under some shade.

"Malcolm, ye decided to wake up from yer coma eh? Thought maybe ye'd sleep all day, son. Are ye sick or something?" Pop asks, his tone outlined with worry, not irritation that I hadn't been out here helping them earlier this morning. "Nah, just needed the extra rest I guess." Standing tall, Pop looks at me. Narrowing his eyes, he says "Ye sure? Ye look a little pale, son." Not wanting to worry either of them with my lingering fear that something is off, I change the subject.

"Where's Sal? And Adler? How'd those assholes get out of working on the tractor this morning?" Grinning, Pop side-eyes me. "Aye, Sal went to Allenspark today. Won't be back till late. And Adler went over to Bill's. Was asked to help with some security equipment or something. Tate dropped him there a few hours ago. Can ye go over and pick him up? I need Tate to finish this up." Tate turns his body so only his head pops out, frustration clear on his face.

"Ye sons of bitches did this to me on purpose. Now he's got me in tractor hell. I'll be lucky if this old thing works at all once we've finished." Returning to his work under the tractor, Tate doesn't say anything else, just grumbles his dissatisfaction of the task at hand. Pop laughs and kicks Tate's black Justin boot, a warning to just shut up and do what he's been told.

"Sal went up to the church, huh? He hasn't gone up there in a long time. Is everything ok, Pop?" The uneasy feeling, I woke up with just intensified at the knowledge that Sal's made a day trip to the one place he still feels close to his mother. He only ever goes up there when he's got something on his mind. The need to be closer to his mother is very strong as he seeks approval or forgiveness for something he's done or something new that's come into his life.

"Aye. Did ye see him before turning in last night? Or this morning, lad?" Pop knows I slept in this morning so now I'm skeptical about his prying. There's something he knows that he's not telling me.

"Noooo," I draw out the word for effect. "I was in a coma, remember?"

"Aye! Aye, ye sure were." Trying and failing to not look like the cat that ate the canary, Tate saves him from this conversation. "Bro, would ye please stop distracting the old man, I need his help with this." Pop rolls his eyes, "Ye could do this with yer eyes closed. Don't be a bugger, lad; it's not becoming of ye." Pop gives Tate's boot another kick, resulting in another groan coming from under the tractor. Resolved in the fact that Pop doesn't seem to have any concern over Sal's trip to the church, I decide to head on in to town. See how Adler's fairing with all that security equipment.

Driving around to the back of the shopping center, I pass by the Tractor Supply and wonder if Clara is working today. My mind says I'm allowed to wonder; our break up doesn't mean were not still friends, but my heart says to distance myself from her. My need and attraction to her is still strong. We may not be together but I do still care about her. More than I should admit.

Parking in my usual spot behind the Café, I jump out of the truck. It's usually busier back here on a Saturday, but today the lot is deserted. I can see where Adler has installed the cameras and there's electrical equipment boxes all over the ground, but Adler's nowhere to be found. He must have gone inside to test out the newly placed camera or grab some different tools he needs to complete the job.

Just as I'm getting to the door, the unsettled feeling comes back. Hard and fast, the hairs on the back of my neck rise to attention. I stop my pace toward the door and reach up to place my hand on my neck. Taking a deep cleansing breath and hoping the motion calms my nerves, I'm suddenly knocked to the side. Something grabs ahold of both my arms, pulling them painfully behind me. It happens so fast I don't have the chance to look behind me before something is pulled over my head. Black fills my vision and my already erratically beating heart tries to open my chest and make a run for it. "What the hell?" I manage to get out before I feel a painful kick to my stomach. The pain causes me to hunch over and fall to my knees. My arms still being pulled behind me has my right shoulder popping out of socket. Pain shoots down my back to settle in my stomach. Nausea causes my once dry mouth to water profusely.

Swallowing down the bile in my throat, dizziness wraps me in a cocoon of false safety. My mind is playing tricks on me that my attacker is done beating me.

Realizing that's not the truth, kicks come fast hitting my rib cage over and over again. Curling into a ball, my shoulder and ribs screaming, I do my best to pull my knees up, protection needed in any form. My arms are still being held behind me.

The kicks keep coming. Kicks to my face, my stomach, my back, and my already tattered arms. My assailants keep muttering words I can't understand through my already cloudy brain, but they're vile. Vile words as they beat me and torture my already bruised body. As unconsciousness tries to take me under, my mind goes to the farm and my family. Unable to move, I resolve that I may never see any of them again. Knowing I need to move, to try and get away somehow, I make a feeble attempt to fight back. It only irritates my attackers, causing the kicks to come even harder and faster. With one last attempt, and using all the strength I have left to kick out a foot at my attackers, one final blow to the side of my head has the darkness taking me to the point of no return. The already dark environment becomes darker still as I finally lose consciousness and pass into a deep hole of sleep.

Chapter 43

Sal

Pacing back and forth across the ER waiting room, the wayward thoughts my mind is producing bounce around like a pinball machine. Clara watches from the hard waiting room chairs. I pray we got there in time. The medic was hopeful we did but we still haven't heard anything about Stan. For over an hour we've been here, waiting.

Pacing.

And waiting.

My heart bleeds for Clara, her fear of losing her only living parent almost too much to bear. Losing my mother was hard, but at six years old, I didn't understand it. I can't imagine what it would feel like to lose her now; now that my brain is able to understand the implications of not having parents. I tell myself that if Stan dies, at least Clara is old enough to care for herself. At least she has me to help her get through this. As comforting as those thoughts are to me, she doesn't need to hear that right now. She just needs a fucking update. Where is the damn doctor? With hands in my buzzed hair, pacing is doing nothing to ease the tension in the room. Resolved to the fact that my pacing is not speeding up the doctors, I take the seat next to Clara. She immediately curls up into my side, my arm wraps protectively around her.

"What's taking them so long, Sal? We should've heard something by now. At least that he's alive. Or dead." Her tears fall faster, more intense at the reminder that her father is likely dead and not alive.

"I don't know, babe. I'll go see if I can find out anything; ok? Will you be all right here by yourself for a minute?" Nodding her head yes, she wipes again at her wet face. I kiss her gently and stand. Walking out of the stuffy waiting room, I look down the hallway in both directions. There's not a soul in sight in either direction. Taking a left, I walk toward the little bit of noise I hear. God, they must have put us in the basement when we got here. I thought ER's were supposed to busy. Turning the corner at the end of the hallway, I pause. The distinct frame and red hair of Pop has me blinking and thinking I'm hallucinating. I rub my eyes and when I open them, he's gone. Man, I must be going crazy.

Deciding to find a pay phone to call Pop and let him know what's going on, I look around hoping to find a phone. This is a hospital after all; there should be phones all over the place. Just as I spot one down the next hall, a nurse comes towards me. Her steps are fast and in a hurry. The white of her uniform is bright against the cream-colored walls. Without hesitation she comes up to stand in front of me and I know she has news about Stan.

"Mr. De Luca? I'm nurse Janice, I have an update for you on Mr. Abernathy." My reply comes out solemn, the fear of what she'll tell us making it hard to be strong. "Ok, yeah. But can we go back to the waiting room? His daughter is waiting in there. I just came out to see if I could find someone."

"Of course." She begins walking toward where Clara waits. Her fast pace and straight face give me hope that maybe the news isn't so grave. Entering the room, Clara sees us and stands, her hands balled up in her dress. The tears she's cried in fear make her eyes red and swollen.

"Ms. Abernathy? I'm nurse Janice. The doctor will be down in a few minutes to give you details and next steps on your father's care. But we wanted to at least update you that your father is alive." Relief flashes across Clara's face. The nurse notices her reaction and continues, "He's alive but this will be a long road to recovery. Your father had a stroke on top of his other injuries. His blood pressure was just too high after the stress the attempted suicide put on his body."

"But he's alive? And you think he'll make it out of here?" My heart breaks at the hope on Clara's beautiful face. She obviously isn't hearing anything the nurse says besides that Stan is alive. "Yes Ms. He is alive and he will be released. Those details you'll have to work out with the doctor. He'll be down as soon as your father is stable."

"Can I see him? Please; I need to see him."

"You can, but not until he's stable and in his assigned room. Just wait here; the doctor will be by soon with another update." Leaving the room, the nurse hurries back to Stan. Clara returns to the chairs, sitting heavily and leaning forward to rest her head in her hands. I squat in front of her, and put my hands on her knees. Tenderly rubbing her leg, I hope I can give her the strength she's about to need to get through the next update. I have a feeling this is just the beginning to Stan's long battle. The aftermath of his attempt to take his own life is nothing compared to the feeling and thought of losing him all together. But scary all the same.

A short few minutes later, the nurse was true to her word. The doctor comes in, his brown tie and dress shirt covered by a white coat. His name is embroidered onto the left breast above a pocket holding pens. "Hello. I'm looking for the family of Stan Abernathy?"

"That's me. I'm Clara Abernathy." Standing again to address the doctor, he shakes her hand. Then reaches across to shake mine too. "I'm Dr. Traister. I've been caring for your Dad here in the ER. Please sit, Clara. I know this must be hard. I have an update, and I wish I could say your father is going to be fine. But in reality, he's got a real battle ahead of him. As do you, dear." Clara and I sit, Dr. Traister taking the chair next to Clara. He turns slightly so he's looking her straight in the eye.

"The damage done to your father's body in his attempt to take his own life is extensive. While the medics got to the apartment in time to save him, they had no idea the damage the hanging had done. Your father's throat was damaged from the pressure of the rope. If that wasn't enough, the stress of the situation caused your father to have a stroke. That's where a vessel in the brain bursts from an increase in blood pressure. Has your father ever been diagnosed with high blood pressure, Clara?"

"No, never. He's always been healthy. At least I thought he was." Looking down at her hands, embarrassment on her face that she didn't know more about her father's medical history.

"It's likely he didn't have a history, but it helps me treat him if I know if he was on any medications for high blood pressure."

"No, nothing like that. He takes a daily vitamin, but that's all."

"Thank you, Clara. Is there anything else you can tell me about your father's medical or mental history? Sometimes the smallest details can show us a larger picture. Any depression history? Has your father ever tried to commit suicide before?"

"No. I knew he was sad but I never would have thought he would do this. You see, my mother died recently from breast cancer. She died after a five-year battle. Ever since, my father has been sad, but I didn't think it was depression. The doctors treating Mama wanted my father to go to a support group but he wouldn't. He always said having me around was support enough. I should've made him go." Returning her head into her hands, the tears start again, the feelings of guilt hitting her hard now.

Trying to ease her burden, the doctor continues, "There's nothing you could've done, Clara. Depression is a battle that must be fought by the person having the symptoms. They're usually really great at hiding it and not wanting to burden anyone else with their feelings or problems. It's not until a suicide attempt or success that the family knows the depth of their sadness."

"So, what's next? If he had a stroke, what does that mean? Will he be ok? Will he go back to being normal?"

"Well, that's a hard question to answer. Your father is showing signs of left sided paralysis and cognitive deficit. We will manage his symptoms and blood pressure to prevent another stroke but your father has a long hard recovery ahead of him. He's going to need rehabilitation to see what function can be re-taught and restored. Luckily your father has long term insurance that covers a nursing home. That will ensure the burden of care doesn't rely completely on you."

"A nursing home? No, he would never agree to going to one of those. Nursing homes are for old people anyway. He's so young!" Clara's panic at the idea of putting her dad in a home has the tone of her voice coming up. I rub her back, hoping I can channel some calm energy her way.

"It'll only be for rehab initially, Clara. He needs extensive therapy. He will have to re-learn how to talk again, use a toothbrush and eat with a fork. This is not an easy diagnosis to recover from. I recommend sending your father to the nursing home temporarily and then once he's getting function back, you can make other arrangements for him, ok?" Dr. Traister smiles, trying to encourage Clara this is just temporary.

"I'm transferring your father to the 5th floor of the hospital. He'll get great care and start therapy immediately. You can see him once he's settled up there. Just know, Clara. He's not the father you knew even just this morning. Prepare yourself. Be strong. He needs you to be strong for the both of you." Standing Dr. Traister reaches down to shake my hand again. As he leaves the room, Clara takes a few deep breaths, overwhelmed with the news just delivered to her.

"What am I going to do, Sal? My father in a nursing home. I can't believe this. I mean at least he's alive and going to be ok, but I'm scared.

It's been hard enough without Mama here, and now I have to figure this out. Alone." Tears pool in her blue eyes again, and I feel horrible that she feels alone when I'm sitting right next to her. I'm failing her in this relationship already.

Cupping her face in my palms, I urge her to look at me as I say, "Clara, you are NOT alone. You will NEVER be alone. You have me. You have Malcolm. You have my entire family behind you. We will always be here for you." By some miracle, she smiles. It's weak and unsure, but it's a start. Kissing her, and putting as much love into the kiss as I can, I tell her without words how much she means to me. How much I adore her, and how I will never leave her.

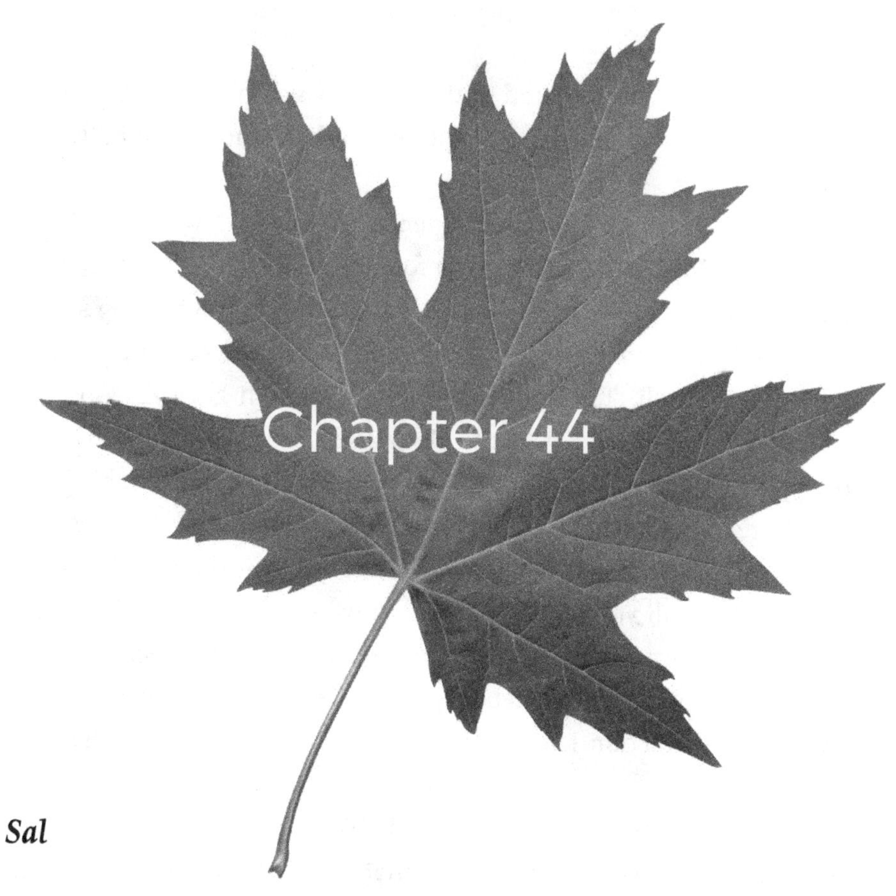

Sal

Finally, a half hour later, Clara gets approval to see Stan. We leave the waiting room and walk down the same way I did earlier with nurse Janice, toward the elevators. As we walk, there's a commotion in the hallway. We can't see what's going on but can just barely hear something. The worried and angry voice sounds familiar though I can't place it. The voice is still too far away to be clear. Continuing our stride, with my arm around her neck, I look down at Clara. The expression she gives me tells me she recognizes the voice too. I swear that voice is Scottish. It takes my mind a minute to understand what I'm hearing, but when it does my blood drains from my body. Worry and fear increases my stride. Clara does her best to keep up with my pace. My heart pounds like a thousand racehorses on a track as adrenaline pounds in my veins. I turn the corner and see Pop, Adler and Tate standing in the hallway. Pop's worry is easily seen written on his face. He stands, his face red with anger. Hands placed firmly on his hips. Pop's anger causes him to spit his words on the doctor in front of him.

"Ah want to know what happened to my boy? What the HELL happened? Why did it take so long for ye to call me? Ye better start explaining ye wee bastart!" The man taking Pop's verbal beating shrinks back as if he's been slapped. Scared to reply and cowering against the opposite wall. Tate interrupts, "Pop, Pop! Ah got this. Go! Take a walk. Ah'll find out, ok? Go!" He pushes Pop down the hallway, in the opposite direction from us. Pop paces down the hallway, his hands now tugging on his red hair.

"Pop? Tate, what's going on? What are you doing here? I was just about to call you and let you know we were here." Calling out to them, I slow my pace and settle up next to Tate. The doctor quickly replies, "I'll let you know when you can see him." He walks briskly away in the direction I just came from, passing Clara in his haste to leave.

"Sal?" Tate asks, looking shocked. "What the hell? What are WE doing here? How'd ye know to come?" Tate drops his arms to his sides, defeat making his body sag. My worry kicks up as I notice the tension surrounding my family. Tate obviously tired of trying to keep everyone together, Adler chews on his bottom lip, fear evident in his movements.

"I didn't know. I'm here with Clara and Stan. What's going on? We were just going to call Pop and tell him what's happened to Stan. Where's Malcolm?" Looking around I don't see him anywhere. Tate's face is pale as he explains, "Malcolm was attacked, Sal. Outside Bill's. In the back lot. He'd gone to pick up Adler but didn't make it inside before someone attacked him."

Adler steps up, his face white with grief and guilt. "I was putting in the camera's and security system for Bill. I knew Malcolm had gotten there because I saw him for a second when I first turned on the camera. It caught him walking up to the door but then shut off after only a second. I messed with the wires and connection device, it wouldn't turn back on so I didn't know what was happening. When he didn't come in a few minutes later, I thought he'd gone to see Bill before coming in to tell me he was here to pick me up. When I was done setting up the system, the camera flicked on and that's when I saw him lying on the ground."

As if sensing my need for her touch, Clara places her arms around me from behind. Her touch settles my nerves and calms me enough to think about what Adler said. Malcolm attacked? That doesn't make any sense.

"Is he ok? Where is he?" I say looking around again for Malcolm. Pop comes back to where we stand in the hallway, his worry no less than it was a few seconds ago when he was lashing out his anger at the doctor.

Pop says, "Wee bastarts aren't saying anything. Just that he's stable and with the doctor." Sighing heavily, he continues, "They didn't call me for hours, Sal. Hours. Saying that he'd been attacked and to come to the hospital. They kept Adler locked in a room, without a phone. Ah'm so mad!"

"I just don't understand. Malcolm attacked? By who?"

Tate responds, "We don't know yet. But we'll find out. And then that arsehole better hide, cause I'm coming for him." His tiredness and defeat melt away, replaced again by anger. Adler stands taller, trying to match Tate's determination.

As if just realizing what I'd said about Clara and Stan, Pop separates the group, getting closer to Clara and I.

"Clara. What's going on with ye father?" Pop asks. Clara looks at me, not able to verbalize the horrible events we witnessed just a few short hours ago.

"We went to the church and to eat in Allenspark today. I told Stan I'd have Clara back by six. When we got home, we found Stan. Found him after he'd attempted suicide." I decide not to include all the details now. Not wanting Clara to have to relive the awful reality again so soon. Pop doesn't hesitate, just takes Clara and pulls her into a tight hug. She accepts his affection, holding on to him just as tight. Her tears come again. More tears as she cries for not only Stan but for Malcolm as well.

"Oh, ye sweet child. Good God, give us strength to get through this terrible day."

For the next few minutes we all just stand there. Adler, Tate and I lean up against the wall. Pop sitting in the chairs across from us, Clara still wrapped tight in his embrace. Recent events distracted me from where Clara and I had been headed when we found out about Malcolm. Remembering that Clara can now see Stan, I encourage her to go up to the fifth floor. Sensing she doesn't want to be alone, and seeing the state of Adler's worry, I ask him to go with her.

"I need to stay here, babe, but you go up. See your dad." Turning toward Adler I ask him, "Hey bro? Will go with her? Please. I'll be up as soon as we get an update on Malcolm."

"You bet." Adler's jaw tightens. He accepts my request with renewed purpose. Having something to do other than just sit and wait is a huge relief.

Handing over Clara feels like a betrayal. I shouldn't leave her right now, but having Adler with her gives me some comfort in knowing that she's being taken care of. My brother adores her. We all do.

Needing to get to the bottom of what happened with Malcolm and now that Stan is stable, I can focus my attention on finding out who did this. Another doctor comes out to update Pop. Taking a deep breath, the doctor prepares himself for what I am sure he's been told would be a repeat of Pop's yelling and frustration.

The doctor clears his throat before saying, "Mr. Keating, your son has been beaten severely. He suffered multiple broken ribs, a dislocated shoulder and a concussion. It appears his attackers came up from behind him, and did not give him any chance to defend himself. He has no obvious signs of defense or struggle. It was a surprise attack; he didn't realize what was happening until it was too late. He will be fine, I assure you. His shoulder has been reset, his ribs will heal with time and his concussion will resolve on its own. I don't have any details from the police but they were here this morning after Malcolm was brought in by ambulance. I apologize for the delay in contacting you, but police procedure prevented me from doing so. Again, I do apologize."

Sighing, Pop stays quiet so I ask, "Can we see him?"

"Please go ahead and go in. Mr. Keating; I will discharge him to your care this evening. The police have all they need for now."

Pop waves a hand in acceptance, dismissing the doctor to return to his work with other patients. Then, suddenly it hits me. If Adler was able to see Malcolm for a second on the camera before the attack, maybe the camera caught something during or after the attack that could help us find out who did this.

Stopping Pop and Tate before going into Malcolm's room, I tell them my theory. "Ye're right, Sal. Maybe that camera caught more than we think. It's worth another look. Ye two, go back to Bill's see what ye can find. I'll stay here with Malcolm. If he gets discharged before ye get back, we'll see ye at the farm." Placing his large palm on my shoulder, he squeezes, showing me affection while dismissing me at the same time. His impatience to find out what happened make my determination even stronger and more urgent.

Peeking in the room, I see Malcolm lying on the bed, not moving. His arm is secured tightly against his chest, his face bruised and battered. My anger rises, boiling me from the inside out. I'll find out who did this, and they will pay the price. And the cost will be extremely high.

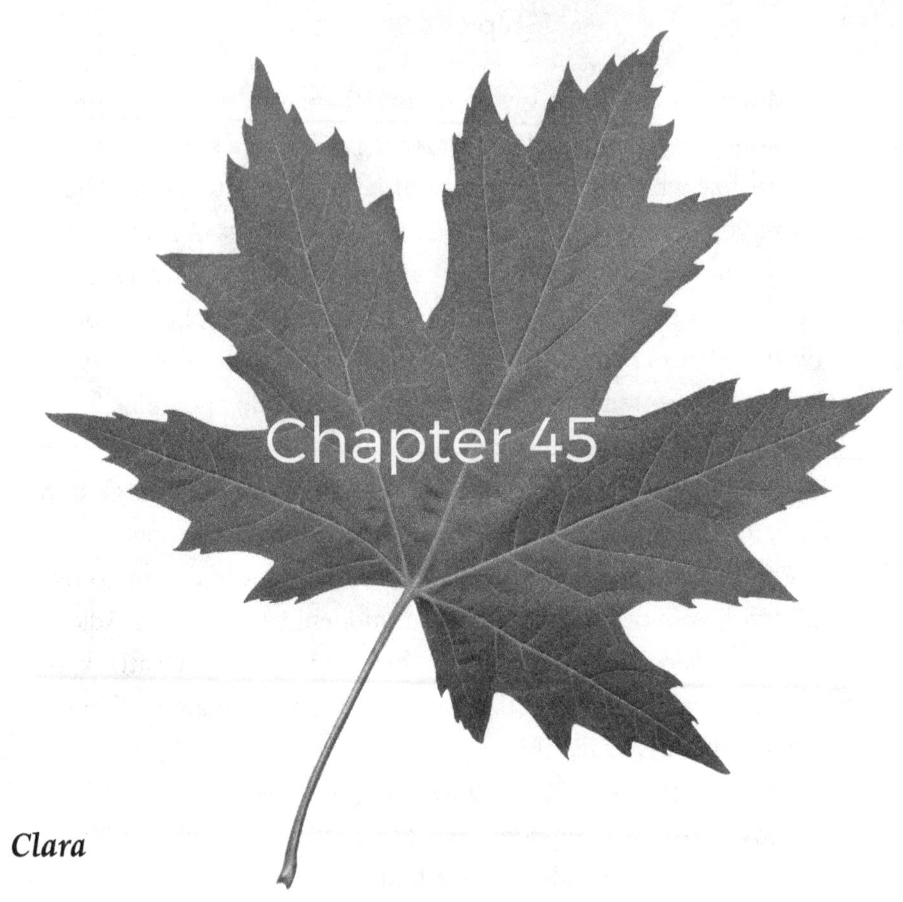

Chapter 45

Clara

Nothing could've prepared me for what I saw when I walked in my father's hospital room. Luckily Adler was with me, to catch me before I hit the ground. Before the uncontrollable sobs over took my body. Such sadness and pain all wrapped up in a tiny package. Now that package lies in a bed across the room from me. Not moving, not feeling. Just lying there. Still as can be.

My sobs ebb away into deep-seated anger, anger that Daddy would do this to himself and selfishly to me. Losing Mama was bad enough, but at least I had time with her before she died. At least I knew what the end result was. It didn't change the fact that her death was hard to accept or that I would miss her when she was gone. But my father, he knew this would be a shock. He knew this would destroy me. And he did it anyway. No clues to tell me how sad he's been. No time to try and help him past this. And now all I feel toward him is anger. Deep anger.

Adler has stayed with me for the last hour, never leaving my side. He even stood outside the bathroom and waited for me. I'm grateful for the support. I wish it was Sal here of course, but Adler is a great substitute. I still haven't heard anything on Malcolm. My earlier grief is overwhelming me with the worry of what will happen with Daddy. I thought my worst day ever was when Mama died. But I was wrong.

While I'm sad that Mama died and I miss her every day, I now feel blessed that I got to say goodbye. One last chance to really have the time to process her illness and death. Now I know, having that time made it easier to deal with her being gone, for me anyway. If Daddy had died, it would have haunted me for the rest of my life.

While I'm pissed at how this day has gone, I can't help but be thankful Daddy is alive. I may be pissed at him but I love him and I can forgive him for this. It will just take time.

Moving across the room, I sit in the chair next to his bed and hold his hand in mine. He hasn't moved at all. The only sounds are his breathing and mine, with the occasional chime from the machines measuring his vital signs. He looks normal, except for the dark red rope marks on his neck and the drooping of the left side of his face. The nurse already warned me the facial effects of his stroke would be more prominent once he awakens from this deep sleep. His brain needs rest and relief from his deep depression and the trauma from the stroke.

Adler comes up behind me. He places a warm and welcome hand on my shoulder; I cover his hand with mine. Drawing strength from him a sense of peace comes over me. Adler sits in the empty chair next to me. We keep a tight grasp of each other's hands, drawing support from each other. Sighing, Adler asks what I knew was coming. I've been dreading having to explain myself without Sal here.

"I was surprised to see you here with Sal. I think we all were. What's going on, Clara? I thought you were dating Malcolm? I hope you know what you're doing, playing my brothers against each other." I suck in a breath, radiating a glare over to Adler. How could he think that? I've reached my limit today. I know he has every right to ask me that and to be protective over his family but he doesn't really know me. I've never given him any reason to accuse me of playing them against each other. My anger reaches its peak. The day's events are too much, causing me to lash out, causing all those emotions on the floor to gather up and release in a rush of outrage.

"You know what, Adler? Fuck you!" Pushing his hand away from mine, my chair slams against the wall as I get up quickly and forcefully. Heat rises up my chest and smothers my face.

"Hey! Hey… Wait a minute. I meant no offense, Clara. I just know how much Malcolm cares for you. And then today I saw the way Sal looked at you and man…I realized that he doesn't just care for you, he loves you. I could see it all over his face. I just worry about what this will do to Malcolm. You guys obviously haven't told him yet." Adler stands in front of me, hands up in surrender.

"No, we haven't told him. We haven't had the chance to. I wasn't thinking about that today. Sal and I just wanted to have a day to see what we are. What we have together. If this relationship is worth the risk of Malcolm hating us both." Resolved in the fact that Adler wasn't accusing me of anything, my anger ebbs. And I realize my fear mirrors his.

"And?" He waits only a second for my response before he continues, "To me it's obvious but what the hell do I know?" Shrugging Adler leans against the wall, shoving his hands into his jean pockets. He keeps his focus on me. Sitting back down in the chair I so abruptly rose from, I respond with the first thought that comes to my head.

"It's all happening so fast, Adler, but I've never been so sure about someone in my entire life. Sal's it for me. I know it. I care for Malcolm; he's become my best friend. But I can't ignore what I feel for Sal. I won't." Putting my head in my hands, I do my best to relay all my heart and soul through this one declaration, hoping Adler can see that I'm telling the truth about how I feel.

"Besides, Malcolm and I broke up."

"You did? When?" He asks. "You were just at the house with

Malcolm last night. You guys didn't say anything. Neither of you acted like you had just broken up."

"That's because we both realized we just aren't fit for each other. We realized we're better as friends. And it felt good to admit that to each other. I'm sad it didn't work out. Really, I am. But now I know why and it's because of Sal. I would have always felt drawn to Sal. And that's not fair to Malcolm. He could see it too. He could tell that I had someone else on my mind."

"So, when are you going to tell him?" Adler asks.

"Not sure, after all that's happened today. And now Sal's occupied with finding out who did this to Malcom. I don't know what to do. Should I wait for Sal or go ahead and tell him? When he's awake that is." My worry over telling Malcolm about Sal and me is interrupted by movement from my father's bed.

I pull my chair closer to the bed as Daddy opens his eyes and looks up at the ceiling. His left eye opens only slightly and it's now that I see what the nurse was warning me about. The facial droop is more severe now that he's waking up. Daddy turns his head toward me. The devastation on his face lessens my anger at him. A single tear falls from his good eye and my heart breaks into a thousand pieces. Why didn't I see his pain? Why didn't I see his struggle to survive a life without Mama? My anger is replaced with deep-seated guilt. I was too busy trying to move on and live my life. I've neglected him and his needs. It's all my fault we're in this mess.

Touching his face, I lean over and kiss his cheek. Tears pool in my eyes, threatening to spill over, and I do my best to keep them from falling. To prevent more hurt and heartache over something we can't go back and change.

"Oh, Daddy." Laying my head down on his shoulder, my desperation to heal him has me praying to God to forgive us both for our actions today. Judge and jury have condemned us both to live with the guilt of our mutual neglect of each other.

"Sooorrry. So sooorry." Slurred words come out of his mouth

slowly. The left side of his mouth is still, not moving with his words. Shaking my head for him to stop, he ignores the tears now falling without regard and tries to explain why he's done the unthinkable.

It takes him a long time to formulate his words and get them out. "It's been so hard…to be without her. I'm… I'm so sorry." He pauses after every couple of words to catch his breath. "I… I didn't plan… this, Princess. When… when I saw… how much that boy loves you, and I…I knew you'd be all right." Taking a deep breath, he continues, "I decided I would go be with your mother. It's where I…I belong." Swallowing, his words get trapped and he struggles to get anymore across. He closes his eyes, giving into the rest his brain so desperately needs. It's then that it dawns on me. His behaviors and actions from this morning. The way he hugged me, and told me he loved me as we left. That must have been when he decided on this fate.

Adler is there again. Giving me strength in the feel of his hands lying on my stiff stressed shoulders. He leans down and whispers in my ear. "I'm going to check on Malcolm and then see if I can help Sal and Tate. If you need anything, Pop's still here. All you have to do is go to him, ok? Anything you need, Clara. Pop will be there for you." Leaning down, he kisses me on the forehead then turns and exits through the heavy wooden hospital door.

Looking back at Daddy, I'm overcome with the severity of his condition. Knowing Adler is right, I resolve myself in the fact that I may have to cash in on the knowledge that Mr. Keating is so generous and helpful in stressful times. Because I'm realizing there's no way in hell, I can handle all this by myself.

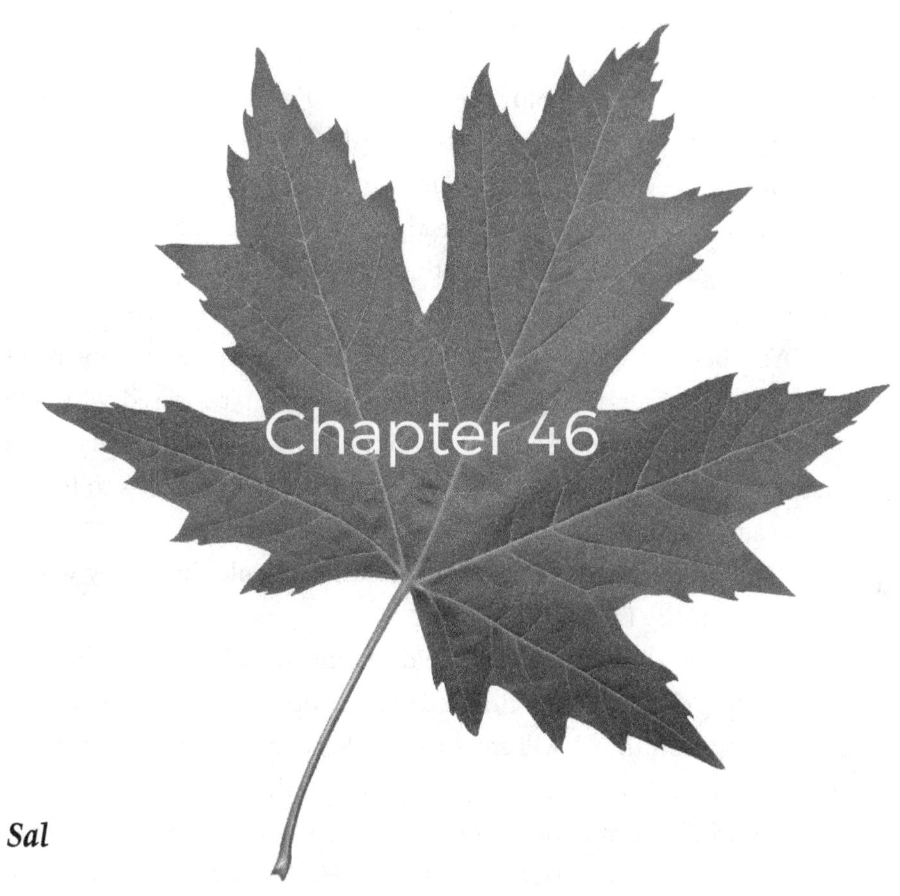

Chapter 46

Sal

Tate pulls the truck into the parking lot behind Bill's restaurant. As we get out, we look around. What we're looking for, I don't really know. I guess anything that could tell us who did this to Malcolm. Except for the yellow police tape strung around the orange cones that surround where Malcolm was found lying, there are no signs anything even happened here.

Bill opens the back door as we're walking up. Tate goes in first as I take one last look around the parking lot, hoping to see something, hoping for any clues to jump out and help us identify the attackers. But my eyes don't fall on anything of use.

Tate's already explaining what we're hoping to find as I enter into the back-stock room. Bill stands next to the rack full of large cans of tomato sauce, ketchup bottles and Styrofoam take out containers. Full of worry, Bill explains what Adler had already told us. The camera wasn't running at the time Malcolm was attacked. "I'm sorry guys, Adler had just started the install. We got a quick flash of Malcolm on the camera but that's it. We couldn't see anyone else out there but Malcolm."

"I know. Adler said the same thing, but maybe after the install, before you guys found him, something can be seen. It's worth a look, right?" I ask.

"You bet it is. Let's go in where all the security equipment is set up, see if the camera picked up anything. I haven't messed with any of the equipment since Adler left with the police. He didn't even get a chance to show me how to use any of it." Bill motions for us to follow him to another back room, this one just off the kitchen.

"Did the police ask about the cameras? Ye would think they would have asked, too." Tate asks.

"No; they didn't. But like I said before, we didn't even think to bring it up. Adler had just finished setting up the cameras when the attack happened. But I will say I'm a little surprised the police didn't ask; they know I've been having problems with break-ins. They were the ones who recommended the cameras to begin with." Bill reaches into his pocket, pulling out a set of keys. He puts one in the lock and turns it. The door opens to reveal a huge security setup. Two large TV screens and a computer keyboard are set up on a desk. A VHS recorder sits on top of a shelf next to one of the TV screens. Bill goes over to the chair in front of the desk and plops down into the seat. He pushes various buttons on the keyboard, but nothing happens.

"Hey, Bill. Let me try." Tate sits down in the seat Bill stands up from. Doing the same as Bill just a minute ago, Tate pushes buttons in no particular order on the keyboard. Again nothing happens. Frustration builds as I contemplate what to try next. "This is useless. We need Adler. He's the only one who can get this stuff working." Tate's accent comes out stronger with his mutual frustration. Pushing buttons faster and harder, Tate pounds his anger into the keys, prompting Bill to intervene.

"Hey. Careful. It may not be easy to work, but don't break it before we see if there's anything on that tape." Scolding Tate, Bill gives the back of his head a swat. We all jump at the sound of knocking on the door. Without pause, the door opens. The person on the other side not waiting for our permission to enter. My frustration grows, that is until I see it's Adler coming through the door.

"Thank God, dude. We're having hell getting this stuff to work." Tate stands, letting Adler come into the room and sit in the chair in front of the desk. Releasing the breath, I didn't realize I was holding, relief that Adler is here is short lived when I think about Clara alone at the hospital. But really, this is where Adler needs to be. Helping us find who's guilty of hurting Malcolm. I realize that now. I also know he wouldn't have left Clara there with Stan alone if she couldn't handle it.

"Of course, I'm here. Can't have you assholes breaking this fine equipment, now can I?" Side-eyeing Tate, Adler reaches up and hits a button on the wall. Obviously, he heard the pounding Tate was giving the keyboard just seconds before he entered the room. Suddenly the TV screens light up. Gray lines and static cover each screen. Silence settles over the room, anticipation of what might come up on the screen our priority over any further discussion. Bill and I lean in toward Adler, flanking him on each side. As if getting closer will help us see something faster. Tate stands behind us, being the tallest one in the room makes it easy for him to look over our heads as we all stare at the screens.

"Ok. Here goes. Remember guys, I had just set all this up when I saw Malcolm lying on the ground. After that, I took off out back to help him. I'm not sure if I even pushed record on the camera before running outside." Adler shifts in his seat. Like his nerves are making him antsy and jittery.

"Let's hope you did. This could be our only chance to find out who did this," I say. Anxiety settles in as we stand there and wait for the picture to come up on the screen.

Adler stands up, turns the power on for the VHS recorder. Sitting back down, he takes a deep breath and stares up at the screen. Following his eye movement, I look up at the two screens. The gray static starts to clear on one screen, allowing us to see the back-parking lot. Focusing on the one screen, I'm fascinated at the clarity of the picture. The yellow tape around the orange cones is in black and white but as clear as a Rocky Mountain river.

Adler pushes a few keys in front of him and the screen covers with static again. It takes my eyes a minute to realize he's rewinding the tape. The movement is so fast I can't make out anything on the screen. As he continues to rewind, Adler keeps his finger on the button until the screen turns black. Suddenly, static shows again, and then a blurry picture before a clear view of the back-parking lot appears. It looks just like it did on the live footage except for the police tape and orange cones are now gone. It's footage from before Malcolm was attacked. The image is clear with just a few cars going across and an occasional person walking by.

"The camera picked up more than I thought it did after I initially mounted it. These cameras are hard wired into the breaker out back. They come on as soon as the power is connected but I didn't think it had recorded anything. Not after I first saw Malcolm walking up." Adler continues to stare up at the screens. A second later, the second TV screen pops up with the same static and gray lines as the other one did. Then suddenly a picture of the front of the restaurant pops into view.

Adler does the same with the second screen. Pausing the first one, he presses down on the keyboard and the second screen copies what the first one did. As it rewinds, I stare at both screens. It's unbelievable what this security system can do. I see now why Adler has a passion for security and electronics.

Once the front camera is finished rewinding, Adler presses pause again, stalling the images on the screens. Each screen now showing a different view. "Watch closely guys. It could be the smallest detail that could lead us in the right direction." Pushing play on the keyboard and squinting his eyes, Adler focuses all his attention to the screens above. Doing the same, I stare without blinking so long my eyes begin to water. The strain is too much without allowing my eyes to recover from the stress I'm putting them under. Blinking rapidly, it's then that I see Malcolm walking up to the back door. He stops just in front of it, reaches up and places his hand on the back of his neck. Just as Adler said, the camera captures him walking up and then goes black again. The front camera never falters, it just continues to show us the front of the restaurant.

"The screen went black Adler. Is that all it got?" Tate asks.

"I don't know. Hold on, let's see if it comes back up." Refocusing his attention to the screen, Adler gasps when the image does come back up. Seeing that it did in fact record more than Adler first thought, I cringe, knowing what I'm about to witness.

Malcolm is on the screen, his arms pulled behind his back, a black cloth covering his head. All three attackers have black hoodies on, keeping their identities hidden. One stands behind Malcolm, holding him still. The other two stand in front of Malcolm, positioned for a fight. After a few seconds, one of the assholes swings around his body, gaining power then lifts his leg in a forceful round kick to Malcolm's stomach. Malcolm falls to the ground and his trapped arms bend unnaturally behind him, his right shoulder popping and twisting in the wrong direction. He falls to his knees, then to the ground. There's no sound so we can't hear his anguish, but I can feel his pain. They continue to kick him over and over again.

Time slows, making it feel like it's been hours that I've been watching these cowards beat my brother to within inches of his life. It only lasts a few minutes but that's long enough. Enough to dislocate Malcolm's shoulder and break several of his ribs. To disable him so badly he can't defend himself. Just as the doctor said, they snuck up on him. He had no chance of avoiding the attack. Anger rises up my body. Starting in my toes and lighting me up so hot the room starts to go dark around the edges of my vision. Taking deep breaths, I step away. Bending over at the waist, I catch my breath then look back up at the screens.

"These dickheads have hoodies on; I can't see their faces," Adler exclaims, his own anger coming through.

"The twats. Covering their faces like asshats. Damn it! Who the hell are they? This is pointless if we canna see their faces!" Tate turns the other direction from us in anger.

"This was clearly planned, you guys. Right from the very beginning. These assholes planned this attack and they planned it to be brutal. It's someone we know. Someone Malcolm knows. It has to be. Somehow, they knew he'd be by here eventually," I say.

Bill, Adler and I continue to look at the screens. Once the beating ceases, Malcolm lies on the ground, not moving, his body a mangled mess of limbs. His arms lie painfully behind him even after his attacker has released him. The black cloth stays loosely over his head. The attackers run off in separate directions, trying to hide their next move.

"This is where the footage came up when I was installing the gear. I took off outside as soon as it came up. The camera must have been recording the whole time, even though the inside equipment was still being set up. Thank god for that." Pain flashes across Adler's face. The guilt he feels for not getting to Malcolm faster present in his posture.

Standing back up straight and taking another deep breath, I look up at the screen showing the footage of the front of the store. I can't believe my eyes as I stand there and watch the three sons of bitches that did this walk casually across the screen. The three of them walk right past the camera facing the front lot. Their black hoodies are hanging down toward their backs, showing their faces clearly.

Now it's clear who did this to Malcolm. I know who hurt my brother, and he will pay for this. I swear to God, he will pay for this. Tapping Adler on the shoulder and pointing up at the screen, Tate and Bill follow our gazes to see what we're looking at. Adler presses pause on the keyboard again, stilling the attackers faces on the screen and my vision goes red.

Tate gasps. Bill swears under his breath and I just stand there and look into the face of the enemy. It's a familiar face, one which shouldn't surprise me, but does based only on the brutality of this assault. I wouldn't have thought he'd have it in him. Wouldn't have thought he could be so evil. But I was wrong. He is pure evil. And he showed us all how evil he is today.

Staring at the screen, my hand forms a fist. Slamming it into the desk in front of Adler, an angry growl escapes as I turn and head toward the door. It creaks and moans as I throw it back and exit into the hallway.

Jumping up, Adler follows with Tate and Bill on his heals.

"Sal! Sal, wait! Where are you going?" Adler asks. His question stops my hurried pace, turning to face them, my words come out through gritted teeth.

"To find Baker Landry."

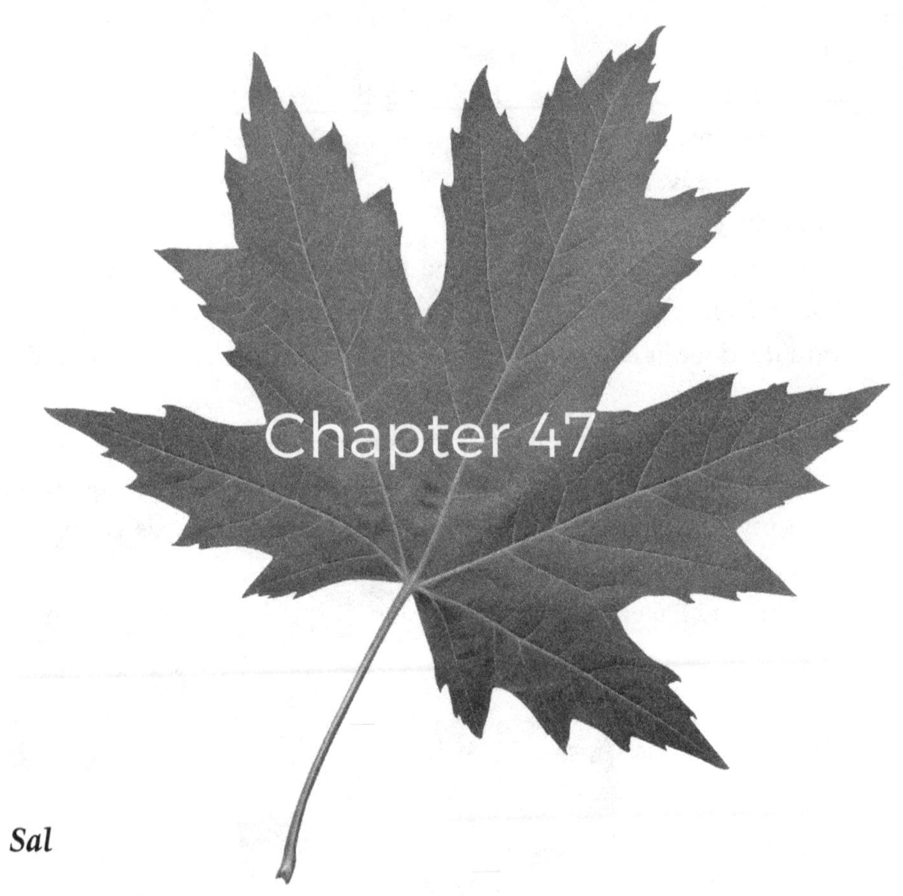

Sal

With heavy footfalls on the black and white checkered floor, my anger grows. It makes my thoughts become irrational and violent. Baker Landry. Not only did he beat Malcolm to the point of unconsciousness but he did so in the most brutal and cowardly way. Masking their faces to prevent being caught is the truest form of cowardness. The truest form of premeditation I've ever seen. He won't be able to get out of this, no matter who his daddy is.

Adler continues to call after me as I continue my determined stride toward the door. Every step gets me closer to Baker. My lip curls in disgust, my brain playing the video of Malcolm's attack over and over in my head.

"Sal! Wait up bro; just wait." Feeling the weight of a hand on my shoulder, I slow my pace to a stop. Breathing hard I turn toward Adler. My nostrils flare as the air goes in and out of my lungs. Tate and Bill come up behind us.

"Now let's think about this, brother. What will you finding Baker and killing him accomplish?" Always the one trying to keep peace and avoid trouble, Adler tries to convince me not to walk out that door. Tate doesn't say anything, just stands there listening to us argue.

Staring at him like he's lost his mind and the answer to his question is obvious. I say, "Revenge Adler. You know, an eye for an eye. I'm not going to kill him but he deserves to feel every bit of the pain Malcom is feeling while he lies in that hospital bed."

"I agree, Sal; really I do. But there's a process we have to follow and before you end up in jail, we should probably let Pop know what we've found. We'll take the security tape home to Pop and then turn it over to the police. Don't you think Malcolm should also have a say in what happens? Baker attacked him. Not you." I know he's trying to reason with me, but that just pisses me off even more.

"He did attack me, Adler. He attacked all of us. Don't you see that? If one of us gets hurt, we all get hurt! That's what loyalty is. Adler!"

"Ok! Ok! I get it. Calm down. Let's just go, take the tape to Pop, ok? Then we can all make a decision about what to do next, together. As a family."

Tate nods his head in agreement, "Ah agree, Sal. We canna react too fast and risk being foolish. Especially with the proof we have now it was Baker who did this. Don't forget who Baker's father is. We have to be careful, Sal. We need to turn this tape over to Pop."

Tate has a point and now that I've had a minute to calm down, I see what they're saying is true. Baker's father will do anything to turn this around to make it Malcolm's fault. And we have to be careful with this new information we have.

"Ok, let's go home. We'll see what Pop and Malcolm want to do. You got the tape?" Looking at Adler, I make sure he grabbed the tape before following after me.

"I got it, it's right here." Waving the black box in front of me, I grab it out of his hands. I trust him to keep it safe but still won't risk anything happening to this tape before I can get it home and into Pop's hands.

"All right; let's go. Pop should have Malcolm home by now. Let's head to the farm."

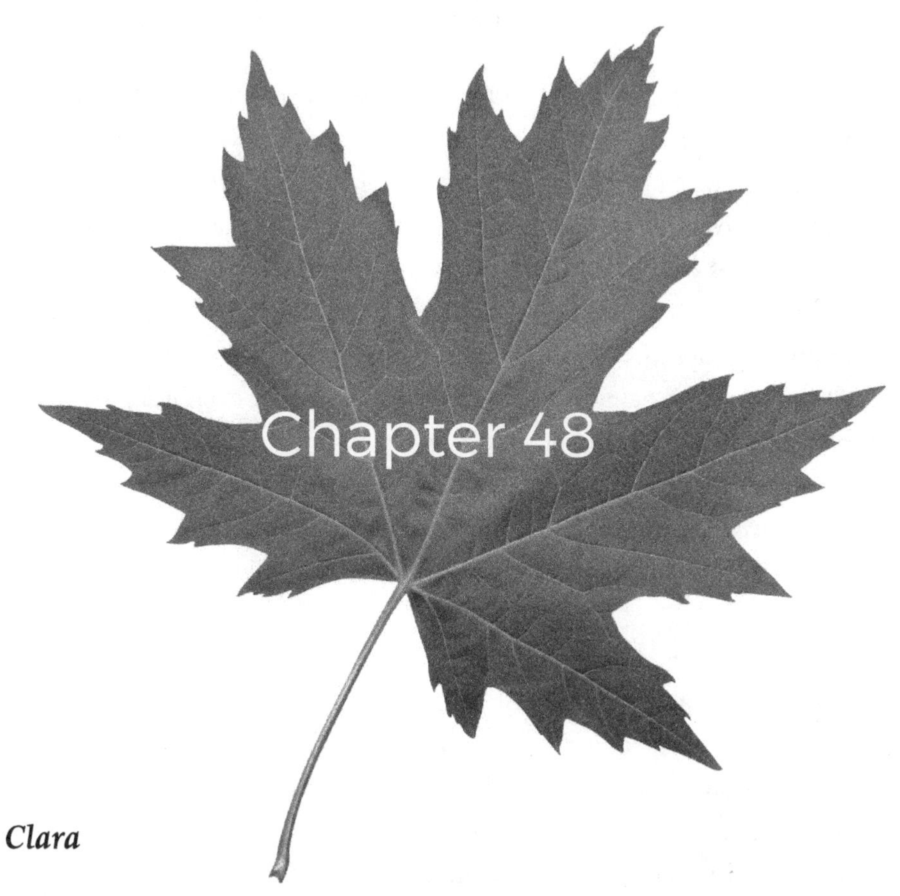

Chapter 48

Clara

Pacing the hall outside daddy's room, the doctor walks away in the opposite direction from me. Tears threaten as I think about what the doctor just said and how my life is about to change. As the tears fall and cloud my vision, I don't see Mr. Keating walking toward me until he gets close enough for me to reach out and touch.

He doesn't hesitate, just walks straight up to me and wraps me up in his strong arms. Curling into him, I feel safe and young again. Back to the little girl I was when we moved to Denver and I realized my life would be different. I feel like that same confused and scared little girl I was then. Pulling away from me, he looks down at my face and wipes the tears from my cheek.

"Come sit here, lass. Tell me what has happened. How is yer father?" Pulling me from the hallway, we sit in the hard-plastic waiting room chairs. Pop pulls me into him, holding onto me tightly. I use the opportunity to rest my tired head against his shoulder.

"The doctor just said daddy has three to six months of rehabilitation in a hospital before he can come home. Then when he does come home, he won't be able to be alone. I'll have to hire full time nurses and caregivers to stay with him twenty-four hours a day." More tears fill my eyes and fall in fast succession. "What am I going to do, Mr. Keating? I can't afford our apartment on my income from the Tractor Supply by myself. And then when I have to hire someone to take care of him, I won't be able to afford anything. I can't even imagine how I would get him up and down the stairs. We live on the second floor." Mr. Keating hands me a tissue. Where he got it from, I have no idea. I didn't even see him reach in his pocket.

"Oh lass. What will you do? Do ye have family ye can call for help with this?"

"No. It's just the two of us. My mother died not that long ago from breast cancer." The look on Mr. Keating's face looks almost painful. He recovers quickly and hugs me tighter. Remembering what Malcolm once told me about how Mr. Keating's wife Blair had died of breast cancer, his reaction is what I had expected. It's never easy to lose someone to such a terrible and incurable disease.

"Well ye canna take care of him alone, Clara. Don't ye fret. There's time to plan it out. Ye hear? Just know ye won't have to do this alone. Ye got family in us Keatings. Dry those tears, lass. Ye canna let Stan see ye upset." Drying my eyes, I don't have any idea how he'll help me figure this out. But I know he will and that gives me the relief I need to get through at least today.

Then I think about where I'll go tonight when I leave here. I don't want to go home to that apartment alone. Just the idea of being where daddy tried to take his own life has my lunch coming back to haunt me. The relief I was feeling is short lived, replaced by nausea and an unsettled feeling. Mr. Keating takes notice. He doesn't miss a thing, I've realized.

"What is it now lass?" Concern is back on his face. His blue eyes filled with worry.

"I can't go home, Mr. Keating. I can't be there, where it happened." I say, dread lacing my words.

"Do not worry. There is room for ye at the farm." Winking he smiles. "But ye canna stay with Sal. That's where ah draw a line. Plus, ye two haven't told Malcolm about ye have ye?"

I don't know why but shame fills me as I look at Sal and Malcolm's father. Shame that I didn't tell Malcolm about my feelings for Sal before today. I told him I had feelings for someone, I just purposely left out that I had those feelings for his brother. I didn't know until today where those feelings would lead us. I didn't know the magnitude of what was happening and at the time I didn't care of the consequences. But now I sure do.

"No." Looking down at my lap and shaking my head, I try to defend what Sal and I have to Mr. Keating. "It's so new. What Sal and I have. We didn't even know if "we" were a thing until today. That's why we haven't told Malcolm yet. But I know we should have told him by now."

"Ya, ye should have said something. But that's all in the past. I know ye will tell him now that ye know for sure there's something to tell." Winking again, he gives me the same reassuring smile he did a few minutes ago.

"Now. Malcolm's been released. Let's get ye both home. Ye said goodnight to ye father? Are ye ready?"

"Yeah, he's asleep for the night. The nurse gave him a sedative to help him fall asleep. So, I'm ready."

We stand and begin to walk toward Malcolm's room. Feelings of gratitude and genuine appreciation fill me and I reach up to stop Mr. Keating before we get to the end of the hallway.

"Mr. Keating? Thank you. Thank you so much. For everything."

"Ye welcome, lass. And call me Pop, child. I've already told ye, Mr. Keating is an Old Man. And that Old Man's not me!" Laughing, he pulls me in for another hug and for the first time tonight, I laugh too.

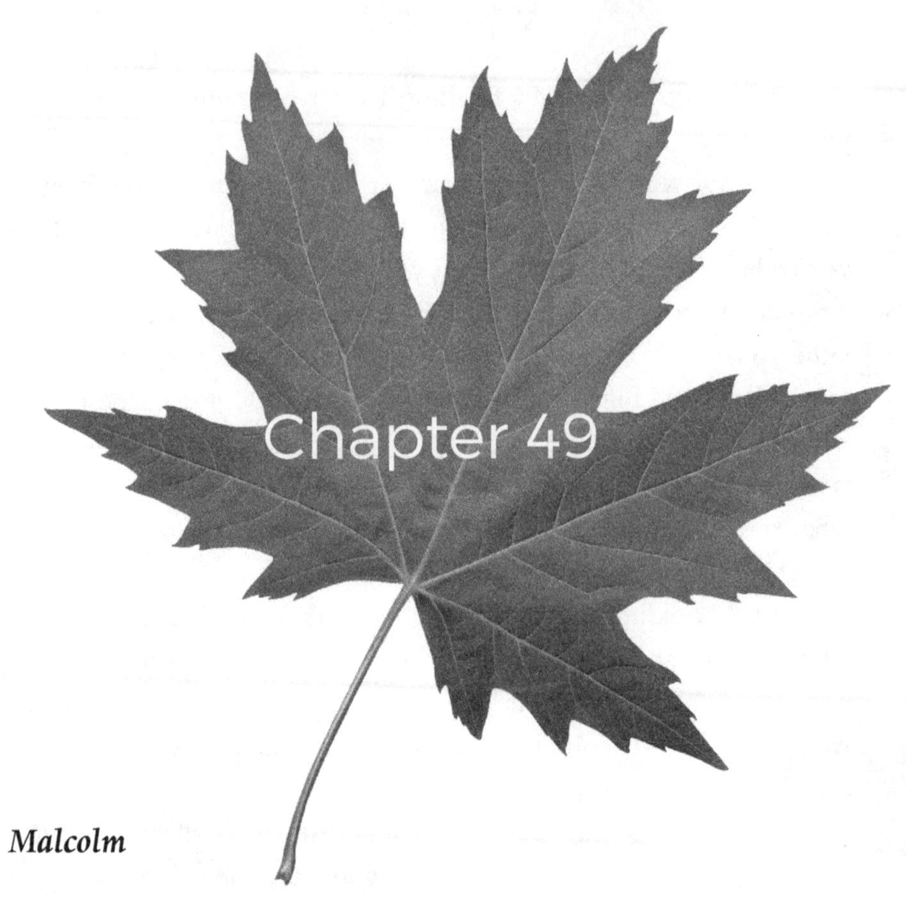

Chapter 49

Malcolm

God, my body hurts. Deep seated pain like I've never felt before. Getting back home to the comfort of my own environment helps the pain a little. Thank God for these pain killers. I have a feeling I'll be living off them for a while.

Pop settles me on the couch when we get home. The idea of being alone in my bed for the next 24 hours with no TV fills me with dread. So, I ask Pop if I can just lay here until later tonight. Pop agrees, afraid of leaving me alone after the diagnosis of a concussion. Even though the doctor said I was out of the danger timeframe, Pop isn't taking any chances. With my arm strapped to my body to prevent the movement of my shoulder, it's almost impossible to adjust myself and get comfortable laying here. My ribs fill with pain every time I try to move.

Pop comes into the living room to bring me some tea. He lights up the fireplace and covers my lower half with a blanket. The slight fever I've had all day gives me a chill. Turning on the TV he adjusts the channel, then sits in the recliner next to me. The Old Man is nowhere to be found. Pop says he's been outside torturing the new farm hands. The temporary hired hands, here to pick up the slack from all the work we've missed since I was attacked this morning.

For the next fifteen minutes we sit, watching the first part of the six o'clock news. My thoughts turn to Clara. She was with Pop when he came to take me home. To say I was shocked is an understatement. Then, when I heard about what happened to her father, I couldn't believe that this day could be any worse. Clara was a wreck. Her hair matted, mascara staining her cheeks and her dress wrinkled with her beautiful white skin pale from fear. Her only request on the way home was for a nice warm shower. Her hopes of washing away this horrible day almost nonexistent but there none the less.

Resting my head against the couch's armrest, I listen to the reporter on the screen tell the city of Denver a play-by-play of my attack. Pop watches too.

"Today in Jefferson County, a teenage boy was attacked suddenly in the parking lot of a busy shopping center. It has been reported that the teenager's name is Malcolm Shipley. Malcolm is seventeen years old and about to begin his senior year in high school. Malcolm suffered a concussion, broken ribs and a dislocated shoulder in the attack. He was released from the County hospital this afternoon. The investigation is ongoing, as there are no suspects at this time, and unfortunately Malcolm is not able to recall the events that led up to his attack. There have been no witnesses that have come forward as of yet."

Listening to her recount my attack pisses me off. The fact that I have no idea what happened makes me angry. The only thing I remember is walking up to Bill's and then everything going black. Pop interrupts my thoughts when he grunts and points up at the screen. The same reporter is on the screen again but this time has none other than Judge Landry standing next to her. His pressed suit flawless for the camera. Man, I wish I could I punch that asshole. I turn my thoughts to what I'm hearing from the TV set. Judge Landry spews what Pop and I know is such bullshit.

"The attack on Malcolm Shipley has us all very worried about what Denver is becoming. With the inflation of residents from other states, our crime rate has increased by twenty-five percent in the last two years. While we do suspect that gang violence could have something to do with Malcolm's attack, we are determined to find out who did this horrible crime against one of our very own teens. It is my mission to assist law enforcement in finding out who did this and to ensure they pay for the crimes committed against Malcolm." God, he's such a liar. He was just telling Pop a few weeks ago how he'd end us after my fight with Baker. I guess this is what someone has to do to get elected to public office though.

Lies. Typical politicians.

The reporter changes the subject suddenly. Changing the topic to Judge Landry's campaign and his efforts to clean up this district in Jefferson County. Angrily, Pop mutes the TV and slams the remote down on the small table next to the recliner. "The twat! Such a liar. God how ah wish someone would expose that arsehole." Mocking Judge Landry Pop says, ""It is my mission to assist law enforcement in finding out who did this and to ensure they pay for the crimes committed against Malcolm." My arse! More like ye'd like to finish off my boy for beating up ye precious Baker. He's just as big a twat as ye're!"

Pop's reaction makes me laugh. It also makes pain crush my ribs and shoot up my arm. Putting my head back down on the armrest, I see Pop get up in a rush of frustration and head into the kitchen, cussing in Gaelic the whole way. After he slams a few cupboards, it's silent in the kitchen again. He doesn't return to the living room right away. I'm grateful for the quiet. My head is pounding.

Just as my eyes close and sleep begins to take me to a restful place, the front door opens. Sal, Adler, Tate and Bill enter the living room. Sal comes around the couch and squats at my side. Worry and fear covers his face.

"God, Malcolm you look like shit, brother. How's it feel to be home?" He asks.

"Great. I couldn't wait to get out of that hospital bed. Man, those beds are brutal." Moving up slightly so I'm sitting up instead of lying flat with my head on the armrest, pain shoots up my back. My temples pound with the force of blood rushing into my head. Grimacing I put my one good hand on my forehead before asking Sal to get me another pain pill. Rising he goes into the kitchen, joining Pop. Adler and Bill sit across from me on the floor in front of the fireplace. In Adler's favorite spot. He always sits there any time we hang out in the living room.

"Malcolm, do you remember anything? Anything at all?" Adler asks. Bill watches me in concern as I continue to grimace in pain. I need that pain pill.

Now.

Sensing my need, Bill gets up. "Malcolm, I'm going to see what's taking Sal so long to bring you that pill. Be right back." He smiles as he leaves the room. I turn my focus to Adler. Suspecting he knows something I don't, I shake my head no and through gritted teeth, try to relay to my brother what I do remember.

"Nah; all I remember is walking up to the back door at Bill's place. I'd come to pick you up. Pop said you were there installing some security equipment or something. After getting out of the truck, I was close to the door when someone covered my head and everything went dark. That's the last thing I remember."

The kitchen door sways back and forth as Pop, Sal and Bill come back into the living room. If I thought Pop was pissed before, I was wrong. He looks murderous now. He comes over and squats down in front of me, his anger palpable. He hands me a pain pill, then a glass of water.

"Son. Take this then we've got quite a story for ye. And there's video to go with it."

"Um, ok. What's going on?" The suspicions I had that Adler knew something were just confirmed. I fear I'm not going to like what I'm about to hear.

Before they tell me what the hell is going on, Clara comes down the stairs. Her hair is wet, and she's wearing one of my t-shirts and a pair of my favorite boxer shorts. Entering the living room, she pauses behind the recliner and stares out at all of us.

"Eh, Hey!" She says and waves her hand to all of us in the room.

Trying to ease the obvious surprise in the room that Clara is here, I clear my throat and speak. "So. Guys. You have something to tell me? To show me?"

Clara comes further into the room and sits in the other recliner. The Old Man's recliner. She sits with her legs folded under her running a brush through her long blonde hair. Her presence is no longer a distraction. Except to Sal. He keeps looking at her. Like he can't take his eyes off of her for too long. It's weird; they've only met one other time and he was pissed off the whole time. But I swear he looks at her with so much familiarity. Putting those thoughts away for another time, I focus my attention on Adler. He begins telling me what he remembers from my attack earlier today.

"I saw you outside Bill's place, Malcolm. But only for a second. I had just placed the back camera and come back inside to work on the system. The camera came to life briefly then shut off. I saw you for only a second on the screen as you were walking up. I didn't think anything of it until a few minutes later when it came back up. That's when I saw you lying on the ground, your arms behind you. With a black cloth over your head."

Not knowing what happened next even though I was there, I urge him to go on. I'm starting to get tired and drowsy from the pain meds. The faster we get through this story the better. I'm rethinking not going straight to bed after all. Rolling my head across my shoulders and closing my eyes, I'm relieved the pain has dulled slightly now.

"Ok, go on," I exclaim. Curiosity peaking now that the pain is dulled a bit.

"I ran outside. Bill ran out after me then immediately went back in and called 911. I uncovered your head and stayed with you until the police and paramedics came." Adler looks over at Bill.

"I ran to call for help. You were bleeding and unconscious but Adler was there with you, so I left you guys there. Police got there so fast, thank God." Bill's relief is clear on his face. He's always been a part of this family, since before the Keatings, so I can imagine how worried he was to see me lying on the ground bleeding and broken.

"They kept Adler in police custody all day. Twats didn't call me until hours later. Tate and Ah came to County as soon as they called." Pop looks over at Tate. Tate nods back, confirming what happened. "I need to go call Becca. We may need her brother's help later. I'll be right back." Tate leaves the room, heading upstairs to use the phone. It's quieter and more private up there than when everyone's in the living room.

"What does he mean, we may need her brother's help later?" I ask.

Sal squats again in front of me on the couch. My brother. My best friend. Why does he look like he's about to give me bad news?

Looking back at Clara for a second, he returns his gaze back to me. The fact that he looked at her with concern tells me, this is going to be hard to hear.

"Malcolm. You were attacked in brutal fashion today, brother. And we have it all on tape."

The shock of hearing this makes me tremble. My battered brain isn't hearing clearly what Sal said. At least I don't comprehend what he said. They have my attack on tape? What kind of tape? Damn, now I wish I had waited to take the pain meds. These meds make my brain cloudy.

"Yes. We have the whole attack on tape. And Malcolm; it was premeditated. Pop hasn't seen it yet. He stayed with you while Tate and I left the hospital to try and find evidence of the attack. Adler had said he was setting up the cameras and that he initially saw you walking up, then the screen went black. We had hoped that somehow the attack recorded. And we were right."

"Ok, so where is it?" I ask. All I can think about now is that they have a tape. And I want to see it.

Sal looks at Clara again. She nods. What's with that?

Then he looks at Pop. Pop nods his approval and Sal walks back over to the recliner. He picks up a VHS recorder tape. It's black and bulky.

He walks over to the VHS player and slides the tape in. The machine accepts it and immediately displays static on the TV. Sal hits rewind until the tape stops. He then hits play and sits down next to the couch facing the TV. His arms are wrapped around his knees, crossed in front of him. He looks over at me and I can feel his anger. I look back at the TV and watch.

There's static. Then the picture comes to life. All I see on the screen is…me. I move toward Bill's back door then the screen goes black. Nothing happens for several minutes. The screen just stays dark.

"What's going on? Why is the screen still black? You said you saw who did this to me." Confusion makes me irritated and the meds are taking a toll on my mood.

"Just wait, Malcolm. It's coming." Adler says.

Looking back at the screen, I see the static clear and a picture comes up.

Gasps around the room are heard as I'm beaten bloody on the parking lot floor behind Bill's and the Tractor Supply.

I can hear Clara cry out in horror. Bill rushes to her side, Sal turns to look back at her. I keep my focus on my attack. Their faces are covered. I don't recognize their movements or their mannerisms; I can't see their faces.

The video is quick and leaves me exhausted. It's like I was beaten all over again. My vision narrows. I fear I'm going to black out. I've just relived the trauma and pain from earlier today and I don't know if I can handle it a second time. I need some fresh air. I move to stand, but Sal stops me.

"Hey, wait. There's more."

"I don't think I can relive that a third time Sal. Please just let me up." I beg.

"Just wait. This part's the best part. If there is any part that's good, that is." He sits down beside me and focuses his attention on the screen. I decide to do the same. Looking at the screen, Adler explains why the picture is different.

"So, I installed front and back cameras at Bill's. When we realized the back camera had captured the attack, we figured the front might have caught something too. And sure enough, it did. I recorded the two on one tape somehow. I still haven't figured out how, but I did." Adler looks at me; his sympathy and love apparent in his expression.

I look back and see the image on the screen change. Now, it's the front of Bill's restaurant.

I see three guys I don't immediately recognize in black hoodies come across the screen and then they're gone. Not understanding what I've seen, I ask Sal to rewind it. My family stays silently watching as I try to wrap my scrambled brain around what I'm seeing.

It's then I realize. The video of my attack revealed three guys in hoodies. The cloth blinded me so I never saw them. The guys on this last part of the video didn't have their faces completely covered, but they were still wearing the black hoodies down around their backs. Their faces are no longer covered and reveal their identity.

Oh God.

Those are the guys. The guys who attacked me.

"Did you see him, Malcolm?" Sal asks. His anger keeps growing, and I can feel it. It's strong and forceful. But I don't know who he's talking about. I ask him to rewind it one more time.

Sal stares at me as I see what they've already realized. The person who attacked me; he's clear in the video. It's Baker. Baker fucking Landry.

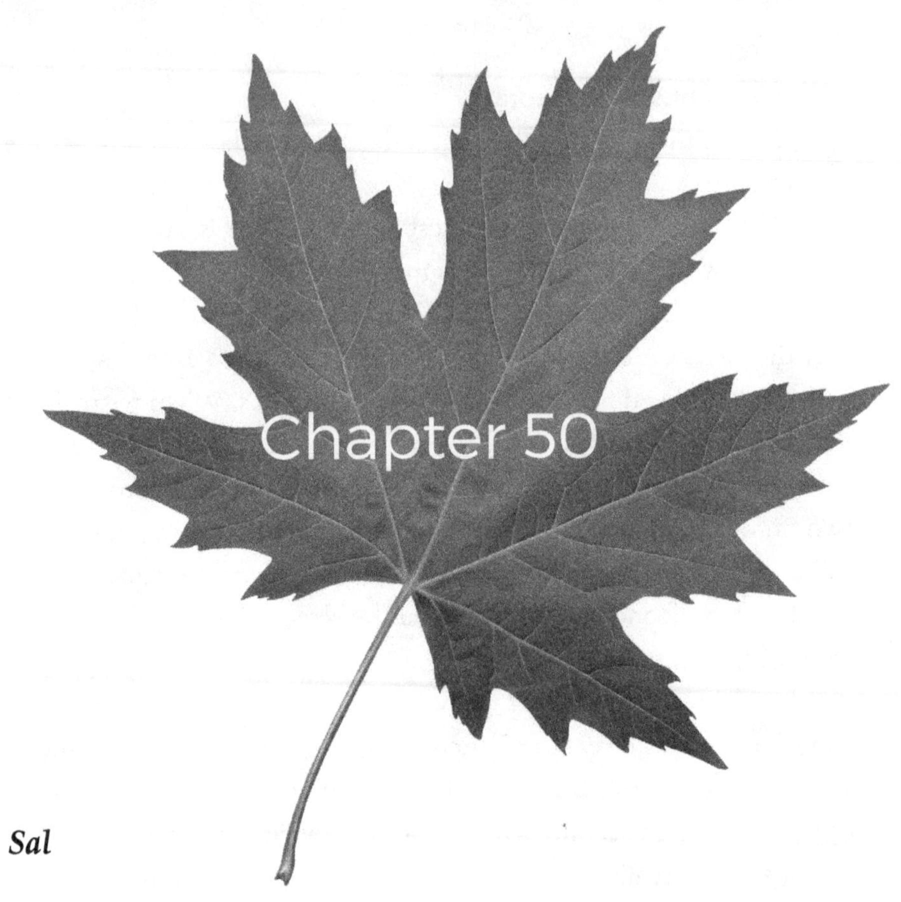

Chapter 50

Sal

Seeing Malcolm's reaction to finding out Baker did this to him wasn't exactly what I had expected it to be. Rubbing the back of his neck with his good hand, Malcolm's deep breaths tell me he's either trying to stay calm or his pain is still severe. The medication isn't completely through his system yet. Standing up from my spot on the floor, I walk over to where Pop is standing. The television screen is black once again, its job now done. Looking around the room, I'm surprised at how quiet it is. It feels like we've just entered a room full of explosives that could detonate at any moment.

Pop had moved over to stand behind Malcom as the video played. Looking over at me he too takes a deep breath. Malcolm clearly gathers himself and moves his body to sit on the side of the couch. Throwing his legs over to meet the floor, he grimaces and then says what we're all thinking.

"So? What now?" he asks, tiredness shining in his eyes.

"Aye. What now?" Pop places his hands on his hips, thinking of what to do next. I have a feeling we aren't going to like what he suggests. If his solution doesn't include Baker bleeding and then thrown into jail, then I don't want to hear it.

"Ah, best be making a call to Judge Landry. Good place to start," he says. Yep; I don't like it.

"Pop, we should be calling the police and handing over the tape. Calling Judge Landry isn't going to get us anywhere." Frustration and outrage consume me.

"Aye, but we've got to tread slowly and carefully, son. There are sharks in this water ye don't even know about. Ah, canna risk this coming back on Malcolm or one of ye somehow."

Tate comes down the stairs and leans up against the railing. We all turn at the sound of his voice.

"Aye. I have to agree with Pop. Becca says Judge Landry has contacts at the station. She said her brother's been trying to catch him in something shady for a while. She also said if we turn over that tape, it'll likely disappear."

I hadn't thought of that. But still. We can't just sit on this and do nothing. What's to stop Baker from doing this again?

"Ok, it's settled. "Sweat accumulates on Malcolm's brow. "Pop will go talk with the Judge. Let him tell you how I brought this on myself. Go ahead. I already know it's what he'll say. Then we can decide where to go from there."

"Malcolm's right. He did beat the crap out of his son after-all." All eyes shoot to Adler. His comment is surprising.

"Adler!" Pop chastises him for speaking his mind. Rolling his eyes, Adler continues to be the voice of reason. "What? It's the truth. I'm stating the truth here! Malcolm did beat the crap out of Baker. Not that long ago if I remember right. So, I'm just putting it out there. It's obvious Judge Landry will say they're even now." Leaning back on his hands, Adler changes positions.

"And I'd have done it again if Baker and his friends hadn't been pussies and covered my head so I couldn't see them," Malcolm says before moving to stand up from the couch. Pop and I move at the same time to help him up. As if dizzy from standing too quickly, Malcolm grabs onto my forearm. He smiles at me, accepting the support.

"I'm headed upstairs, guys. I've had about all I can take for one day." Pallor sets in across his face. Man; he's always been so strong. Seeing him so weak and broken is heartbreaking to witness. Clara stands up, as Malcolm and I get closer to where she's seated.

"I got him, Sal. I'll help him upstairs. Get him settled in while you guys finish your talk." Her eyes move to Malcolm. There's so much there. So much I can't explain. She obviously has feelings for him. But I know in every fiber of my body, those feelings are nothing like the feelings she has for me.

Malcolm looks back at us one last time as he takes his good arm and wraps it around her neck. As soon as Clara has helped him up the stairs, I focus my attention back on the topic at hand.

"Pop. I'm coming with you. When you meet with Judge Landry."

"Nah, I don't think so, son. Ye should stay here with Malcolm. I'll meet with him, get a resolution and be home." He can see I'm not happy with that answer and immediately starts shaking his head in refusal.

"Come on, Pop. Let me come with you. You're going to need someone to witness everything he says. Let me do this with you, for Malcolm." I sigh heavily. Hoping and praying Pop will change his mind and let me come with him. I know I've got him when he drops his head in defeat.

"Aye. All right. But ye'll keep yer damn mouth shut ye hear. No lip out of ye. Ah do the talking. Understand."

Raising my hands in surrender, I say "You bet, Pop! I won't say a word. Cross my heart."

Feeling like I won this time, I go upstairs to check on Malcolm and Clara. Bill says his goodbyes while Adler, Tate, and Pop wonder off to their respective rooms. Everyone is feeling the effects of today on their bodies, the need for sleep taking control for the remainder of the night. Peeking in Malcolm's room, I see Clara helping him remove his shirt. She then pulls back the covers on his made-up bed. He walks over to climb in and I realize Clara will be sleeping on the couch so I better get it ready for her. Grabbing some sheets and a pillow, I look in at them one more time before heading downstairs to make up the couch.

Seeing her in my brother's clothes should piss me off, but strangely it doesn't. For something so intimate, I know it doesn't mean anything. Not in any way other than friendship. In quick time, I have her spot ready for her to climb in. Wishing instead she'd be in my bed with me, I set the stage so that if she decides to come sleep with me tonight, there will be no signs she didn't sleep here come morning. Pop tried to warn me, defer us from sleeping in the same bed. That doesn't mean I won't ask Clara to sneak out to the barn in a few hours, because that's exactly my plan.

Damn just the thought of her in my bed has me going crazy.

We've got to talk about how to tell Malcolm about us. We haven't had the chance to talk at all since the hospital. I want to know about Stan; about what his prognosis is. I want to hold her, kiss her and help her slip into a peaceful restful sleep. Give her some relief from this terrible day. I know being here, helping Malcolm get settled, is just what she needs to help distract her from worrying about Stan.

Just as my thoughts are turning back to the tape, and meeting with Judge Landry tomorrow, Clara comes down the stairs. She shuts out the light on the stairs as she comes to the last step. Walking over, she stops in front of me. Her blue eyes tired and seeking relief. I don't hesitate to take her in my arms and into a strong loving embrace. Pulling back, I run my hands up her arms to her neck. She shivers at my touch. Pushing her hair behind her ears, I kiss her gently. I kiss her slowly. Our movements are just as slow as molasses and just as sweet. I almost forget where we are until she pulls away and looks down at our feet.

"Sal, we have to stop. What if Malcolm comes down the stairs and sees us?" Fear of being caught causes her to look back over at the stairs. I don't care who walks in. I will proudly show anyone who interrupts that Clara is my girl. Do I want us to tell Malcolm that we're together and not have him find out any other way? Yes, of course I want that. But if he were to come down the stairs and catch me kissing her, I wouldn't apologize for it.

"Ok. Ok. I'll stop. But just know, I don't WANT to stop," I confess.

"I know, but Pop already told me you were off limits if I stayed here. We have to behave or he'll never let me come back." She's serious. And it makes me laugh.

"He would let you come back. He would have to."

"And why is that? If we break the rules, he could forbid us from seeing each other. And that would be awful. I don't think I could handle that, after everything that happened today with daddy and Malcolm. I can't risk not being able to be with you, Sal." Tears pool in her eyes and my laughter dies in my throat. She lowers her eyes to our feet again and it crushes me.

Lifting her chin with my fingers, I place another kiss on her lips. Knowing my future is already planned and set, I give her the insight she needs to feel confident that no matter what happens, she will always be welcome here.

"Clara, listen to me. I'm going to marry you someday. I know it. And after tomorrow, they'll all know it too. That means no matter what, you will always be welcome here and nobody can tell you that you can't come back around. Ever." I kiss her again, quickly just to seal my point and end that line of thinking.

"Now, crawl in those sheets. Get a bit of rest, because in a few hours I expect you to sneak into the barn and into my bed."

Her blue eyes widen. Disbelief in my expectation of her tonight is written across her beautiful features. Turning, I walk out of the main house and toward my room in the barn. Damn, this will be a long few hours while I wait for Clara to join me. Entering my room, I remove by boots and drop them next to the chair beside the bed. I take off my shirt and faded Levi's then go into the bathroom to wash up. When I'm done, I go over to the window and peer out. I left the barn door open slightly giving me the perfect view of the living room. Clara stands at the window, her body glowing in the light from the lamp still on in the house. Her blonde hair shines bright and lights up my thoughts as I lay down on my bed and wait for her to join me.

Chapter 51

Clara

Watching Sal through the window, I see him turn the light out and go to bed. My thoughts are consumed with the idea of sneaking over there and climbing into bed with him. Guilt swallows me as I lie on the couch and cover my body with blankets. How can I be thinking of this? On a day like today. On a day when daddy tries to kill himself and Malcolm gets attacked. I'm being selfish. Just like today when Sal and I got back to the apartment. I should've gone right in. I should've gotten out of the truck and gone inside. I might've been able to catch daddy sooner. I could've prevented his stroke.

God. Grabbing and pulling on my hair with both my hands in frustration as I lie here, I know my thoughts are bullshit. I know I couldn't have done anything more than I did. And I know that taking a few more minutes to enjoy Sal, to be free and feel amazing didn't have any effect on the events from today.

Daddy was saying constantly that he wanted me to move on, to find happiness and to try and live my life. Hell, living life was on my list! So that's what I was trying to do. Live my life. And it was starting to seem like life was going to be good. But where I messed up, the part that haunts me most right now, is that my list was supposed to be living life-for both of us. I neglected him and his quality of life. I won't make that mistake again. No matter what. Now I have to figure out what I'm going to do. I can't afford our apartment, the bills, or the caregiving daddy will need once discharged. Groaning, I roll over and do my best to put the stress aside. I'm exhausted despite it being so early. It's only eight o'clock but my body is so tired that sleep consumes me, taking me away for a much needed few hours of sleep.

The sound of beeping wakes me from a deep, deep sleep. Startled at the noise, I roll over and look around. The room is dark. There was a lamp on right before I fell asleep but now it's off. Someone must have come down and shut it off while I was asleep. Sitting up, I move my legs over to rest on the floor. I stretch, my muscles needing the pull and release of the motion. The beeping I heard must have been in my dreams. It did sound vaguely like the monitors daddy was hooked up to tonight. Damn, my mind is playing tricks on me. Standing up I go over to the window and look towards the barn. The clock says it's one a.m. Man; I sure was tired.

Having an internal debate with myself on whether I should do as Sal wanted me to and sneak out to the barn, I wrestle with the idea of just staying put. That's what I promised Pop. I know going out there is wrong. It will only lead to one thing. Am I really ready for that? Am I ready for that level of commitment and devotion? Once I give myself to a man, that's it. I can't imagine ever giving myself to more than one man. Mama was only ever with Daddy and I have always vowed to live under the same expectation. Staring out the window, I make my decision.

I told myself to live. To live life. That's what Mama and Daddy both wanted for me. To take the hardest of days and live through them and not let them crush me. Just like it has Daddy. I won't live with regret or guilt that I can be happy. Confident in my decision, I take one last quick look around the living room then head to the front door.

Opening it slowly, it creaks slightly on its hinges making me cringe. Slowing my efforts to open the heavy wooden door, I open it slowly. The door is quiet now as it opens and I push the screen door thinking I'm home free in my deception. I was wrong. The screen loudly creaks, sounding like nails across a chalkboard and I fear I've woken the entire house. Stepping out onto the porch, I decide the best thing to do is to run across the yard as fast as I can. Hoping that if I'm quick enough, and if anyone wakes up from the noise, they won't catch me wondering across the yard. Jogging across the yard, my bare feet become cold and wet from the cool moist grass. Once I get to the barn doors, I turn and make sure I haven't been caught. With my heart pounding in anticipation, I peak inside Sal's room. He lies on his back, one hand behind his head the other resting on his bare chest. My mouth waters to kiss him. Entering the room, I tiptoe to the bed trying my best not to wake him. He's lying in the middle of the mattress, not giving me much room to slide in. My worry is put to rest when he opens his eyes and looks at me standing over him. The room is dark but I can still see his face in the shadow of the open barn door through his window. He moves onto his side, allowing me to slide in next to him. We lie there and stare into each other's eyes. Sal settles my nerves when he says, "Did you manage to wake the entire house when you opened the door? The screen?" His smile is infectious. He laughs and I smack his stomach to show my disapproval that he hadn't relayed that tiny bit of info before he left the house earlier.

"You could've mentioned that. I had to plan my own military mission to get over here after all that racket." Laughing, we look at each other. The moment quickly changes from something funny to something full of passion and love. It feels so good to be here with him.

Deciding that living is much better than not, I kiss Sal. With passion, love and deep-seated appreciation for each other, we make love. Heat covers my body and my heart pounds as Sal shows me what true love is and what it feels like. My earlier release in the truck is nothing compared to how he makes me feel right now.

The questions I had earlier at the church about whether Sal could wait for me to catch up to the same feelings; by knowing that what I am feeling right now is love. All melt away and disappear as I fall deeply into the abyss that is Salvatore De Luca.

Malcolm

As I stand in the kitchen at the stove, the teakettle sings a peaceful song, letting me know that the water is ready and hot. I grab the kettle and pour the hot liquid over the tea bag in my mug. Only having one good arm and broken ribs makes even simple movements hard and painful. Putting the pain medication bottle in my mouth, I use my teeth to hold the bottle as I turn the cap to open. Knocking a pill from the bottle to the counter, I leave the open bottle there and put the pill in my mouth. The pain awakened me about an hour ago. I lie there trying to refrain from taking any more meds. But the pain is just too intense.

Looking up at the clock above the stove, it reads one a.m. and I'm grateful I got as much sleep as I did after going to bed so early. Clara was an angel, helping me upstairs and into bed. My battered body is unable to care for itself. After tonight I can't help but notice all those feelings coming back. I know after our kiss I said I wouldn't push her to feel something more for me. I wouldn't pursue her. And yes; she did tell me there was someone else, but damn if I don't care about that after tonight. The feel of her gentle hands and her loving care for me in my time of need, has me changing my mind. I want her.

I can help her with Stan. I can help them both through this hard time. Seeing her in my clothes doesn't help me stay away either. God, she looked good wearing my shirt. Taking my tea, I push open the kitchen door that opens to the living room and quietly enter the room. Just to sit there across from her and watch her sleep would be a dream come true so I enter the room to do just that. I'm surprised to see she's not lying there. When I walked through the living room a few minutes ago, she was sound asleep. Maybe I woke her when I turned off the lamp.

Thinking she's gone to the bathroom; I sit down in Pop's recliner to wait for her to return. Sipping my tea, I allow my mind to wander a bit and I picture what it could be like if I actually fought for her. Fight to be the man to make her happy. My thoughts are interrupted at the creaking of the front door then the screen. Getting up, albeit slowly, I walk over to the window and look out to see Clara running across the yard. What the hell is she doing?

She stops at the barn door and turns back toward the house. Her blonde curls wild and free as she turns. Taking a fast look around, she enters the barn. I decide I better go see what's going on. Leaving my mug on the table next to the chair, I follow where Clara just ran across the yard. Turning back, I look at the house before entering. Clara's nowhere to be found. It may be dark but there's really no reason she'd come out here at this hour.

That's when it dawns on me. Every look and every moment of tension from Sal. Every second of hesitation from her since I've met her. Why he was so angry that day we went fishing. Why she had disappointment written on her face when I kissed her. It all comes crashing down on me. It all makes sense now. Knowing that I'll only be torturing myself by looking, I walk to the window anyway. Needing proof even though I know what I'll see. Peering inside, my hope of being with Clara is shot down. Shot with a thousand arrows through my chest. My heart their target. My chance to fight for her over before it even began. Just like our relationship.

As I watch my brother, my very best friend, make love to the girl that was mine first, I decide to keep my feelings a secret. The best thing I can do now, is become her closest friend. To be the one she needs when he can no longer be there for her. If the only way I can be close to her is to give my approval for their relationship, then that's what I'll do. Because I truly love them both.

Chapter 53

Sal

As I lie here, looking over at Clara who is sleeping soundly next to me, I dread the day I have to leave her. I know the next year will be the best of my life. Spending this time together will mean everything to both of us. Next year will also be life changing for all of us. The military will come calling and life will change from a life of choice to a life of duty. But first, we have to finish this thing with Baker. Getting justice for what he's done to Malcolm is my first and only priority for today.

I don't know what Pop has in mind for this meeting with Judge Landry today. My gut tells me things will be settled somehow. Not sure how that can happen. I expect nothing less than notifying the police of what happened yesterday and handing over the recorded tape. A nagging unease is telling me though, to be ready, because it likely won't be that easy.

Running my fingers through Clara's curly hair, I think about how

I don't want to leave this room or this bed. I could lie here with her all day. Leaning down over her sleeping form, I kiss her gently, hoping to wake her from her slumber. She doesn't know it yet, but it's past eight a.m. and if she doesn't get herself back to the house, everyone will know she's in here with me. She stirs slightly, but doesn't awaken, so I kiss her again but add a little pressure this time. Turning over and away from me, she groans. Laughing at her I prop my head on my hand and use the other to run my fingers down her back. She stiffens and turns back to face me, her face bright red with embarrassment. This seems to be a pattern with her after the bliss of our actions wears off. Laughing, I reach out and pull her into me. She comes willingly and molds against my body. God, she fits perfectly against me.

"I've told you before, Clara, you should never be ashamed of anything we do. We should be happy we've found each other. We're the lucky ones. Not everyone can say they have a soulmate."

Kissing her on the nose and pulling away from her, I sit on the edge of the bed, my back to her. She comes up behind me, wraps her arms around me and says, "I'm not ashamed Sal. I've just never woken up in the bed of a boyfriend before. It's a little strange." Smiling up at me, her face lights up the entire room. She's so beautiful it's almost hard to look at her. Knowing every second gets us closer to caught, I rise from the bed and slide my faded Levi's up my legs. Sitting back on the mattress, Clara wraps her arms around my middle again. Pulling my socks then boots on quickly, I rub her arm reassuringly and finally tell her what time it is.

"Clara. You do realize the sun is up, right? It's a little past eight and I would bet money Pop is already up and knows you're not still sleeping on the couch." Panic grows on her face as she realizes that my words are true. Releasing my waist, she jumps out of bed, her curly blonde hair tangled and wild from our rolling around in my bed. Laughing, I get up and move to the other side of the bed where she is frantically looking for the shorts she was wearing when she came in here last night. Seeing them hiding under the comforter hanging half on and half off my bed, I pick them up and dangle them in front of her.

"Looking for these?" Smirking, she takes them and pulls them up her body. The size is larger than her tiny waist and she rolls them down to fit better. It doesn't really help. That's when I remember those are Malcolm's boxer shorts and that we still need to tell Malcolm about us. I ready myself to come clean to my brother. I'm dreading this. It won't make any difference if he's upset or not; I won't give Clara up. But I really want his support. Damn; I'm such an asshole for even thinking that. How can I ask for his support when I stole his girl right out from under him?

"Meet me out behind the new corrals in twenty minutes. There's a spot on the large sprinklers at the back of the pasture where I'll meet you and we won't have to worry about anyone seeing us together. We'll figure out a plan to tell Malcolm about us then I'll go with Pop to settle things up with Judge Landry."

"All right. I'll see you in a few minutes," she says.

After I kiss her again, she leaves my room. I watch her out the window as she crosses the yard, opens the front screen and enters the house. Giving myself a mental pep talk, I prepare to hear what Judge Landry will say regarding his precious Baker and the fact that he almost killed Malcolm.

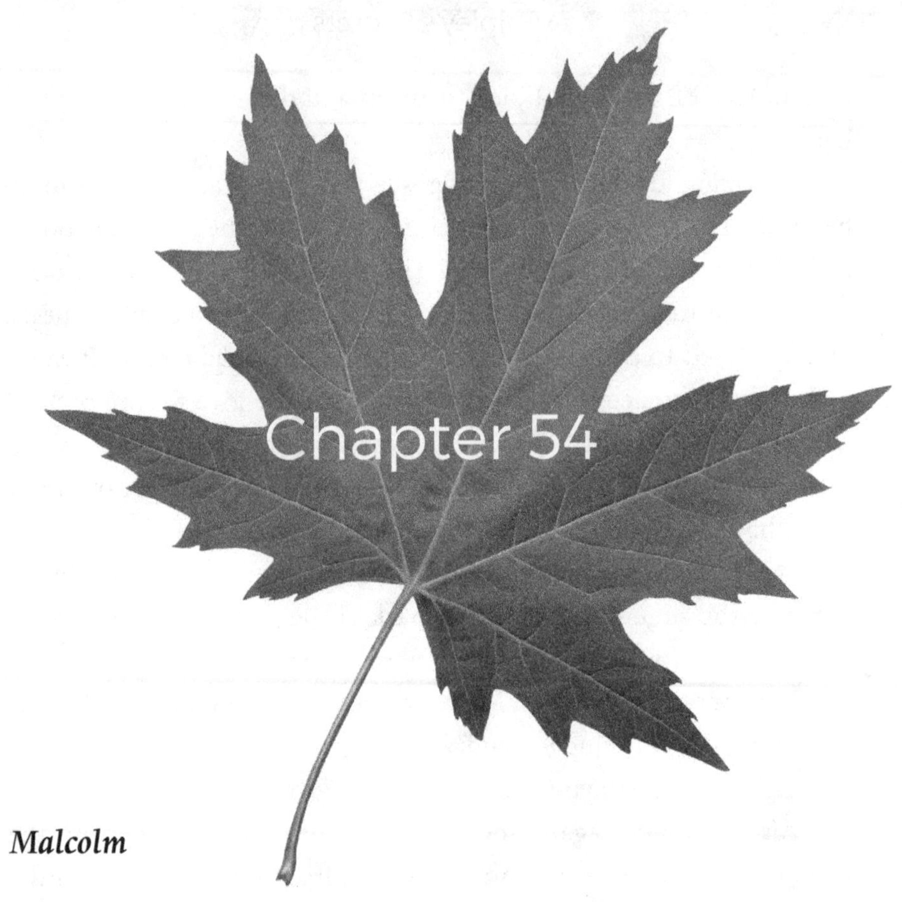

Chapter 54

Malcolm

Yesterday was a horrible day. Not only did Baker get evil and beat the crap out of me, but I also witnessed Sal and Clara together for the first time. Seeing them having sex was not exactly how I would've wanted to find out about them. I stood there and stared in at them for only a second but as the images of last night play over and over in my head, it feels like I'm still standing there watching them even now. My feet planted and cemented into the barn floor, not able to move away from the window, even though I'm dying to walk away. I can't get them out of my head. The sight of them plays on repeat, just like the tape of Baker and his buddies attacking me in the parking lot.

No matter how hard the day was for me, it took a toll on us all. I'm sure of that because I woke this morning to find Adler sleeping again on the floor at my feet. He hasn't done that in a while so I know yesterday's events hit him harder than he will ever admit. This morning Adler got up and bounced out of here like he hadn't just been sleeping on the floor of my bedroom. It was like nothing had happened; he was back to his normal joking self.

My body has been trying to reject my activities all morning. I can't do anything as fast as usual, and I need help with the simplest things since my arm is in this sling. And it's pissing me off. Frustration as I try to remove the cap on my toothpaste has my face red with anger and pain jetting up my arm. Not to mention my bruised ribs. God, they hurt.

Deciding not to even try to get the lid back on the tube, I leave the toothpaste open next to my wet toothbrush and slowly walk back out to my bedroom. Attempting to put on a shirt is impossible to do by myself, but I try nonetheless. Epic failure occurs and my frustration grows even greater.

"Damn it!" As I throw the t-shirt across the room, Pop comes in and interrupts my temper tantrum. He picks up the shirt as he comes further into the room.

"Ye need some help, son? Ye should take it easy on this shirt; it canna fight back." Smiling, he walks over to the closet and hangs the shirt back up. He grabs a short-sleeved flannel that buttons off the hanger and comes over to help me put it on.

"Here, hold ye arm up as I take the sling off to help ye get this shirt on."

Doing as I'm told, I use my left hand to hold my right arm against my chest as the sling falls from my body. Immediate relief comes as the cool air in the house touches the heated skin of my arm. I so badly want to extend it and stretch the muscles up to work the soreness out but I know it wouldn't help. It'd only do more damage probably. Pop gently grabs my battered right hand. I release it from my grip and he slips the open shirt up my arm. Giving my arm back to my other hand, he pulls the shirt around my back and rests it on the opposite shoulder. As Pop replaces the sling to my right side, allowing my arm to rest comfortably back in its stable position, he surprises me with the topic of conversation he chooses.

"Ah, see ye were up in the wee hours having tea. Did ye see Clara leave the house while ye were in the kitchen?" Sensing in his eyes that he's measuring up how I feel about Sal and Clara, I keep the promise I made to myself to pretend that it doesn't bother me and that I'm supporting their decision to be together.

"You know about them, huh?" I ask.

"As do ye," Pop says in return. I'm thinking he's known about them for a while, by the look in his eyes.

"Yeah, I know. And it's ok, Pop, I just want them to be happy. I think we've all had enough heartache and trauma in our lives. It'll be good to see something good come out of all this." Trying to show him I'm telling the truth; I give him a small smile. With my face bruised I'm hoping he doesn't see right through my bullshit.

"All right son. Ye canna lie to me lad, cause that girl and her father need some help and we can help them. And we will, but ah canna do it if you won't be ok with it." Not entirely understanding what he's talking about, I nod so he knows to continue.

"Clara can't afford the rent on their apartment on her own, and Stan will need extensive therapy after he is able to leave the hospital. She needs support and a place she can finish high school. A place she doesn't have to worry about money and healthcare costs. Ah talked with the Old Man. We can build another room off the barn, opposite of Sal's place. Section it off for two rooms with a handicap bathroom, and Clara and Stan can move in there." Staring at me, he's looking for conformation I'm not going to freak out over this.

Shocking even myself, it doesn't piss me off. It gives me relief to know Clara and Stan will have support and a place that's safe for them both. Even if it means she'll be even closer to Sal. And that it'll mean I'll have to see them together all day, every day. I guess I'll get good at hiding the torture I'm feeling when I do see them together.

"I think it's great, Pop."

"Ye sure son? Ah won't offer if ye need to think about it. Make sure ye can live with seeing them together every day." Goddamn it's like he can read my mind. Doing my best to reassure him it's ok I say, "Really, Pop; I think it'll be great to have them here. And I'll get used to seeing Sal with Clara. It'll just take some time, that's all."

"All right, ye better go talk to Sal. He's been trying to find a way to tell ye. Whatever happens son, just as ah told him, no matter what, ye boys canna let her come between ye. Clara is great, but ye are brothers; best friends. That means more than either of ye even realize."

I know what he's saying, and my promise to myself will keep the three of us together, despite my feelings for Clara. Because at all costs, loyalty to my family is all that matters to me. So, I will love her from afar, all because of how much I love my brother and because of how much our relationship means to me. I can suffer to make sure they're safe and happy.

"Ye need to move around. The doctor said to walk around as much as ye can, get those muscles working to heal ye. Sal and Clara are out behind the corrals. Ye go, get Sal. It's time to go meet with Judge Landry." Walking back to my bedroom door, he turns around just as he gets to the hallway. "Adler sleep in here last night?" He asks.

"Yep. I think he's taking all this harder than he's letting on."

"Aye. All right, go get Sal, ok?" Pop heads down the stairs, his footfalls heavy as he takes each step slowly.

I take one last look in the mirror at my battered body, then I head down the stairs myself.

Walking through the living room, I look over at the couch where Clara was sleeping when I went into the kitchen this morning. The blankets and sheets are all folded nicely and lie on the very spot I was sitting last night when we watched the tape. Taking deep breaths, I prepare my broken heart to relay all the love and support to them I possibly can. All while I lie and tell them I'm ok with all of this.

I can't see them as I walk up to the large irrigation system. They look and act like a regular garden sprinkler but are much bigger and release a ton more water. The system covers the entire back part of the property, stretching hundreds of yards. The water pressure and watering schedule are set on a timer that can be manually turned on if needed. It's set to water this part of the pasture in a few hours. But knowing that Sal and Clara are back here somewhere, I decide to turn it on early. Fish them out from wherever they're hiding. Opening the panel on the irrigation systems main section, I cancel the scheduled watering and hit the on switch. The system comes to life. The water coming through the pipes is loud and forceful as it makes its way up the pipes to the sprinkler heads that stand above me. I watch for a minute as the water coming out of the sprinklers causes the light from the sun and the green of the crop to form a rainbow. The colors dance across the silver of the irrigation system. It's beautiful and happens every time the water comes on. Looking down the system as the water makes its way down the pipes and turns on the sprinklers one by one, I see some commotion a few yards away. Continuing to look down in that direction, I notice the commotion is actually Clara. She screams and runs in my direction, her clothes soaking wet from the water. I can't help myself; laughter bubbles up and comes out as she runs frantically away from the spray.

Sal laughs too as he walks slowly this way. Laughing so hard, my ribs throb and remind me they're broken, so I take deep breaths and grimace through the pain. Clara looks furious with me as she makes her way in my direction. It makes me laugh again.

"Those aren't supposed to come on for another couple of hours. Dude; what the hell?" Sal asks, without any anger in his voice.

"I just thought you two needed to cool off." Sarcasm drips from my lips.

Clara stands before me now, her hair wet and stuck to the skin on her face and her shoulders. Looking down I see the water has made her cold, making her nipples visible through her white dress. The same dress she was wearing yesterday. She sees my eyes go to her chest, causing her eyes to follow. Realizing her nipples are now visible, she quickly covers her chest with her arms. "Oh, my god. This is so embarrassing." Red covers her face and brightens her white skin, the contrast getting darker against the white of her dress. Sal goes over and puts his arm around her, then looks at me.

"Well, I guess this is as good a time as any, Malcolm. Clara and I uh, are uh, dating." I didn't expect it to be so easy for him to admit that to me. I think if they weren't standing in front of me soaking wet, I'd be mad about that. But this situation is too damn funny. And after yesterday, I think we all could use some laughter.

"Yes, Sal; I can see that." Sal and I laugh as Clara huffs her irritation.

"You two stop laughing. This is not that fucking funny. I'm soaked through. And my dress is WHITE!" Slapping Sal on the stomach, she stomps off toward the house. Sal and I follow behind her. Our pace is much slower due to the pain in my ribs and shoulder. I decide to do my best to keep the mood light, so I continue my sarcasm regarding the situation we now find ourselves in.

"So, you're dating my girl now, huh?" Side-eyeing Sal, I smile so he knows I'm kidding.

"Look Malcolm, we didn't plan this. It just kind of happened. I wanted to talk to you first, but then everything happened yesterday and I didn't get the chance. I'm sorry we hid it from you for this long."

Speaking a little of the truth I'm hiding, I respond without hesitating, but still with humor in my tone, "Well, I'm glad you didn't because if you had told me in any other way, I might have been pissed." For good measure I throw in, "Besides, if Baker hadn't kicked my ass and I found out about you two, it may have been you in the hospital after I kicked your ass."

"Like you could ever kick my ass, little brother." Sal jokes.

"It was never proven that you're older than me, so leave the little out that statement please. That is unless were talking about your dick." Widening my eyes for effect, Sal laughs and says, "Oh, hell no; my dicks twice as big as yours. Just stop right there."

We walk for a second in silence when a sharp pain shoots up my arm and down my side. Grimacing, I grab Sal so he'll pause his steps and let me take some deep breaths. "Are you ok?" he asks.

"Yeah, I'm all right. The laughing just hurts, man. Hurts so damn much." Clearly there's double meaning in that statement, but I don't tell him that. "Hey, Pop said to come find you. It's time to go meet with the Judge. You better go change, then find Pop."

"You're going with us, right?" he asks me.

"Nah, I'll stay here or I might end up in jail instead of Baker." No sarcasm this time, only the truth. My anger will get me in trouble where that guy is involved.

"Clara wants to go to the hospital. Will you go with her? I don't want her to see Stan alone. It tears her apart." Just the fact that he trusts me around her even though technically she was my girlfriend first makes me even more confident in my decision to keep my feelings hidden. "Malcolm, she's so scared of what's going to happen when Stan goes home. I'm trying to reassure her but it's hard. There's not much I can do. I've thought of asking Pop and the Old Man to help. What do you think?"

"They've already talked about it. Pop told me this morning the Old Man wants to build onto the barn, opposite your room, for Stan and Clara to move in there. Then we're all here to help while Stan recovers and Clara can finish high school without worry." Even though we've been a part of this family for five years now, Sal still has trouble accepting what the Keatings will do for their family. And now, Stan and Clara are considered just that too. Family.

"Wow; I knew they'd help but I never expected to that degree. It always seems to amaze me at the lengths Pop and the Old Man will go to help others. It makes me feel even more grateful to call them family." Placing my hand on his shoulder, I nod as I take in another deep breath and begin walking again back toward the house.

Sal turns toward the barn to go change for the meeting as I continue back to the house. Suddenly I remember I didn't give him an answer on going with Clara to the hospital.

"Hey Sal, I'll go see Stan with Clara. After we leave the hospital, I'll take her by the apartment to pack a bag. Don't worry; I'll take care of her. I promise."

"I know you will; thanks, brother." He disappears into the barn, leaving me standing in the yard where Clara ran across last night.

As I enter the house, Clara and Pop are sitting on the couch. Pop has his arms wrapped around her as she cries softly into his shirt. Fear rises in my chest and I wonder what's happened now? We can't take any more bad news. But just as quickly as that fear tried to overtake me, relief washes over me as I see Pop is smiling. Clara just keeps crying and says, "Thank you Pop. Thank you so much! I don't know how I'll repay you, but I will."

"Oh lass. Ye can repay us by graduating with these knuckleheads next year. Don't fret over it, lass. This is what family does for each other, and ye are family now. Ah figure if these two love ye, then ye must be good stock. Dry those eyes, lass."

Sal now stands beside me in clean dry clothes. Seeing how he looks at Clara and how much he adores her, I'm satisfied that no matter what, we will get through everything that's happened over these last couple of days. We will all survive and, in that survival, we will keep each other safe from any further harm. Sal goes over to Clara, taking her from Pop's arms.

Standing Pop says, "Ok, lad; let's go." Sal kisses her gently, making me need to look away at their public show of affection. Putting my focus back on them, Pop stares at me, a knowing look on his face. He walks past me, puts a strong hand on my shoulder and squeezes his reassurance as he winks at me and goes outside to wait for Sal.

Clara and I stand on the gravel road outside the house and watch as the truck drives down the driveway. My only thoughts now on are that tape and what will happen with Baker after his father sees what he did to me. Hoping that jail is in Baker's future, I suddenly have a terrible feeling. The feeling that says things are about to get a whole lot messier.

Chapter 55

Sal

Driving to downtown Denver is usually a short drive, but today it feels so miserably long. As Pop maneuvers the truck through the parking garage, I feel my anger rising. It's going to be hard to listen to Baker's father make excuses. Because I'm sure that's what we are about to hear; excuses.

The Capital building is busy today with the hustle and bustle of downtown at lunchtime at its peak. Business people in their suits walking to grab a sandwich and get back into their busy day. We go through metal detectors and pass a large reception desk before getting to the elevator. Entering, we ride up to Judge Landry's floor in silence. There's nothing left to say between Pop and I. We both know this is probably a wasted trip. At least Pop is giving him the chance to do the right thing. Not that he'll do it.

Coming out of the elevator, we enter an office with wall-to-wall windows. The words "The Honorable Judge Landry" proudly painted on the door. Rolling my eyes, I look at Pop as he pauses outside the door. He smirks as he reaches for the handle and pulls the glass door open.

An attractive young woman sits at a large dark wooden reception desk. Large white signs with red and blue stars and stripes that read "Landry for Congress" are stacked up behind her at the desk. She looks up as we walk up, her voice small and quiet.

"How can I help you?" Her smile is kind; she's very pretty and young. Younger than I first thought. I'm surprised someone so young works in a place like this.

"Aye. We're here to see Judge Landry. He's expecting us." Pop says, his Scottish accent causing a small smile to cross the young woman's face. It's the same reaction he always gets.

"You have a great accent. Where are you from?" She asks.

Pop loves this. Besides telling people that he was married to his stepmother and spreading his coming to America story, this is his next favorite topic.

"Scotland. The Highlands." Laying on his accent even thicker, I roll my eyes for the second time in minutes. Seeing my annoyance, the woman side-eyes me, smiles and gives Pop one last look then says, "Judge Landry will be right with you. Please have a seat."

Sitting in the waiting area, my eyes find multiple chairs around the room, a water dispenser and a dozen or so magazines on top of a small table. Pop sits down next to me and picks up a magazine. He flips through the pages one by one, not really reading anything just looking at the pictures. I do the same, just to keep my hands busy. My palms are sweaty, causing me to run my hands across my jeans to dry them.

It takes forever for Judge Landry to call us into his office. He's purposely making us wait I'm sure.

"Mr. Keating? Come on in; sorry to have kept you waiting. Busy day here at the Capital." Flattening and smoothing his silk tie and buttoning his fancy suit jacket, Judge Landry guides us into his office. The inside is much like the reception area. All large dark wooden furniture, glass doors and mirrors along one wall. He ushers us in, offering the seats in front of his desk, then rounds to the other side and sits in an equally large brown high-backed chair.

Pop, not being one to beat around the bush or talk pleasantries with someone he doesn't much care for, gets to the point fast.

"Thank ye for meeting with us, Judge Landry. This is a pressing matter that needs our immediate attention. I'm sure ye're wondering why my son and I are here today?" Keeping his composure and speaking slowly as to keep his accent from overtaking his speech, he continues to explain our presence here. Pop sits with his elbows on his knees, his hands clasped between them.

"Ye are aware that my boy was attacked outside Rocky Mountain Soda yesterday and spent the day in the hospital. Ah saw ye on the news last night." Sitting back in his chair, all smooth and collected, Judge Landry looks at Pop with a skeptical eye. He taps his pen on the desk in front of him, already wondering why were really here.

Unbuttoning his suit jacket, he rests his arms on the chair's armrests. As if trying to prove what he said on the news cast last night, his response is predictable. "Oh yes. I am fully aware, and have the Denver police keeping me with updates on the case. I am very sorry about what happened to Malcolm. Even after his past discretions where my son was involved, I would never believe anyone deserves what happened to Malcolm yesterday. How is he doing?"

"His ribs are broken, right shoulder dislocated, but he's alive. That's all that matters." Pausing, Pop continues after a deep breath. "Ah do recall ye saying about how ye going to make it a priority to find out who did this to Malcolm and to bring that person to justice. That is what ye said to the reporter, wasn't it Judge Landry?"

Narrowing his eyes, Judge Landry answers but keeps uncertainty behind his voice as if he knows what's coming next. "Justice for Malcolm is my priority Mr. Keating, just as I said. The safety of our youth, as I have been promoting in my campaign, is the staple of our future here in Denver. I'm basing my entire platform on our youth and their roll in this city." Changing his position, Judge Landry now sits with his elbows on the table, his fingers steepled in front of him.

Pop also moves, now sitting with his back against the chair. His posture more relaxed. "Well, there's a new development in Malcolm's case. We happened to realize that the cameras that had just been installed at Rocky Mountain Soda had captured the whole incident on tape. Those cameras were installed at the police departments request." Watching Judge Landry closely, he tries to hide his bristle and the fact that his back stiffens. But I see it. And so, does Pop.

Pulling the tape out from under his arm, Pop lays it on the desk across from Judge Landry. Knowing he has him nervous, Pop goes right for the jugular.

"Would ye like to watch the video? I've got it right here."

"Why is it Mr. Keating that you have that tape and the police do not?" Returning to sit back in his office chair, Judge Landry smirks. "I guess it really doesn't matter why the police don't have that tape, because now, we can hand it over to them. I'll call the detective right now. Have him come on over here and pick it up. Add it to the evidence."

Clicking his tongue in disgust, Pop's lip curls as he responds. "Aye. That would make ye very happy, huh, Judge Landry? Hide what ye boy did to my son." Pop's resolve is gone now. His face is red with anger as he stands and slams his big meaty hand on the desk.

Still ever so cool and calm, Judge Landry stares at Pop from across his desk. I watch in amazement at the situation unfolding before me. If I didn't already think Judge Landry was evil, I do now. I do after his next words. "Well. All I can say is Malcolm got what he deserves after he jumped Baker outside the Tractor Supply. Eye for an eye, Mr. Keating. It's the oldest justice in the book. My boy only did this to Malcolm because of what Malcolm did to him. They're even now. We can move on."

Not believing what I'm hearing my anger overflows and spills out on the floor in front of me. "The hell they're even. Fuck that! Malcolm didn't cover Baker's head before beating him. Malcolm didn't dislocate Baker's shoulder while his buddies kicked him in the stomach and broke his ribs." Putting out his arm to stop me, to calm me down, Pop keeps me from getting in Judge Landry's face. And from doing something I'd likely regret. This guy has it out for us, he always has.

"That's just the cop-out Ah expect from ye, Judge Landry." Shaking his head, Pop reaches over to grab the tape off the desk but Judge Landry beats him to it. Snatching it up, Judge Landry stands, opening his suit jacket and sliding the tape into the side pocket. The size of the tape causing a bulge that can be seen as he stands in front of us. My shock at what's happening is dulled by the look on Pop's face. Relief comes over me when I realize that Pop is so calm because he has a plan. And Judge Landry is falling perfectly into his plan.

"All right, ye can have that tape. Ah canna make ye hand it over. But what are ye going to do for us in return? Ye can't expect to just take my only proof of what the lad did to Malcolm and expect me to walk out of here empty handed," Pop says. I've never seen him so conniving. It's awesome to watch.

"I'll tell you what, Mr. Keating. If you forget all about this tape and what Baker did to Malcolm, I won't ruin your boys' chance in the Marine Corps. You can go home, get these kids through their last year of high school and ship them off to California like they want. But if any word gets out about this tape or our meeting today, I'll ruin them. All of them. And you too, just for the fun of it."

Looking from Pop to Judge Landry then back again. Pop stares him down, and I know he won't take the bait. Baker's father is just threatening to interfere with our enlisting in the Marine Corps to keep Baker out of jail. He couldn't really do anything to interfere.

"Aye. All right. Ye got a deal. But I will warn ye, if ye boy so much as looks at any of my sons wrong. I'll go to anyone who will listen and tell them every crooked thing I know about ye and ye family. It might be hard to win an election if the community ye plan to serve doesn't trust ye."

Judge Landry's eyes widen slightly, the fear of being slandered in the community a real threat to his campaign. He reaches out his hand to Pop. Waiting for Pop to offer up a handshake to seal their mutual deal. Pop laughs under his breath and turns away. Walking out of the room in record time. I follow behind him in shock and anger that he'd give up so easily.

"Pop. Wait. What the hell was that? Why'd you give in?" Brushing me off he looks at me and mouths, "Not now, Sal. Just let it go."

Riding down the elevator in silence, my anger grows as Pop ignores my silent pleas to go back and change how that whole situation ended. By the time we get to the parking garage my anger is boiling over. Justice for Malcolm feels lost and left back there on the floor of the Capital building. I can't keep quiet like Pop wants any longer.

"Pop? Pop; please stop. We have to go back. We need that tape. We can have Becca's brother help us find someone, anyone who will listen and help us get Baker thrown in jail." When he doesn't stop and doesn't even acknowledge that he can hear me, I yell out at him. I let all my anger spill over and I yell out, my voice echoing in the large space.

"Pop! STOP, NOW!" Getting his attention, he turns. Grabbing my arm, he pulls me toward him but doesn't stop walking. "Shush. Shut up lad! Get in the damn truck and shut ye trap." He pushes me toward the passenger side door and goes around to his side. I open my door and jump in.

"What the hell, Pop? Why ignore me? We have to go back up there. We can't let Baker get away with this." Pleading with him, I'm even angrier when he still ignores my request to go back to the Capital building. Deciding I'll just go by myself; I open the truck door as Pop puts the truck in reverse.

"Sal. Get ye arse back in the truck. Damn ye boy, gotta learn patience, son." Putting the truck back in park, Pop looks around before showing me why he's in such a hurry to leave here. Opening his jacket up he pulls out a smaller tape, black like the other one but smaller and newer looking. "What's that Pop?" I ask.

"It's insurance, boy. Insurance ye dumb ass is going to cost us if ye don't shut the hell up and let me get us out of here."

Noticing now that I was right and the reason Pop was so calm was because this is what he had planned all along. He knew how that meeting would go and Judge Landry played right into his hands. He was prepared and set things up perfectly.

Sal

Driving back to the farm, my admiration for Pop grows to epic heights. As he explains that he had Adler make a copy of the tape this morning, and that Adler had slipped a voice recorder into the breast pocket of his shirt so he could record the whole thing, I look at him in awe and admire his bravery at going up against someone as powerful as Judge Landry.

When we get home, Clara and Malcolm are back from the hospital already. Walking up to them, I don't hesitate to kiss Clara hello now that everyone knows the truth. I do notice that Malcolm flinches slightly. He recovers quickly though, like it never happened.

Clara has changed from the dress she was wearing when we were soaked by the sprinklers earlier into jeans and a white tank top. Her blonde curly hair is pulled back into her signature braid. God, she looks good, her jeans tight in all the right places, making my mouth water.

Pop motions us all into the house, so he can relay the events that just happened and what they mean. Tate and Becca come out of the kitchen, laughing at something and eating out of a huge bowl of popcorn. They join us as we enter the living room.

"Ok, ye sit. The lot of ye. Tate, go grab the Old Man." Pop sits down into his recliner. Removing the tape and the voice recorder, he lays them down on the small table next to his chair.

Clara and I sit on the couch across from him. The same couch she's supposed to be sleeping on but never will again. Malcolm sits next to Clara. A grimace covers his face as he sits, his ribs aching at the movement.

Adler enters the room next, his boots loud as he comes down the stairs. Jumping down to skip the last two steps, he lands hard with a thud into the living room. Coming over to Pop he raises a hand, giving Pop a high five and says, "so, it worked? Pop, did you get the tape?" His excitement is infectious and I smile. Pop nods and says, "Sure did. We got him Adler. Yer plan worked perfectly." Man; Adler has proven he's smart, talented and able to use his skills with electronics in ways none of us would have ever imagined.

Maybe our worries of him joining the military with us are over-exaggerated. Hell, he's smarter than all of us put together. I'll have to mention that later to Malcolm and Tate. Maybe encourage the idea of Adler joining us instead of continuing to push him away.

Old Man Keating comes in the house from out in the field, Tate on his heels. He sits himself down in the other recliner. "Now we're all here. Let me explain what happened today. Adler had a great idea and it worked perfectly." Pop goes on to explain the events that took place. Then he lays down the Keating law as he tells us it could take up to a year to build a case against Baker and his father.

"A year, Pop? Really? We'll be getting ready to go California at that time. Why do we have to wait that long?" Tate asks. Malcolm answers, his focus on that long timeframe as well.

"Because, after a year, Pop can release the tapes to Becca's brother without the threat of Judge Landry interfering. We will already be well into boot camp by then. And Baker will be going to jail instead of starting his post high school life. Adler and Pop bought us some time."

"Yeah but that means we have to put up with Baker for the next year." Dread that we have to see that prick every day at school next year sets in.

"Aye, I'd say Baker will keep his distance. There's only one thing Judge Landry loves more than Baker. And it's his campaign. He won't let Baker risk that for him. He'll keep him in check." Pops words ring true.

Malcolm wipes sweat from his brow, and rises from the couch. "Sorry guys, but I need a pill and my bed."

"I told you that you were over doing it Malcolm. You shouldn't have carried my suitcase in from the truck. I told you not to." Clara says, concern written on her beautiful face. "I'll help you get settled. I'll be right back, guys." Clara wraps her arm around Malcolm, helping to steady him and guides him up the stairs.

I love that she wants to help Malcolm. That she has a heart so big that even after the horrible scene we witnessed with Stan, she's able to be here and not be a complete mess. Clara is the strongest person I know. It's likely that taking care of Malcolm is keeping her mind off Stan and the long road they have ahead of them. Getting up, I go over to where Adler and Pop are whispering about something. Inserting myself into their conversation I listen as Pop tries to decide where to hide our insurance policy.

Adler voices his thoughts on the tape first. "Where will you stash them, Pop? If it's found out where they are, someone will try their best to steal them, to keep Judge Landry on the offensive instead of the defensive."

"Aye, we could keep it here somewhere but that's just not safe enough. I'm thinking the Old Man and I will take a ride into town. Maybe clear out that old safety deposit box Blair opened when we first moved to the U.S. These should be safe there. The only people with access to that box are the Old Man, me and ye boys." Pop winks as he holds up the black-recorded tape. "And in the meantime, ye boys should try to go back to ye lives. Act normal. Do as ye were before all this happened. We've got an addition to build on to the barn. That starts tomorrow."

"Good plan Pop. I'll go check on Malcolm. Then I'll go start the plans for the add on. After that, Clara and I will start some dinner."

Pop nods, dismissing me. He and Adler stay there, still talking over the recorded tapes, Pop praises him for his smart idea and fast thinking. Taking the stairs two at a time, I enter the hallway headed to Malcolm's room when I hear Clara and Malcolm laughing.

The sound is music to my ears. When Clara and I decided to be together no matter the cost, my fear was that Malcolm would never forgive me. But hearing them laugh together and seeing the smile on my brother's face when I enter his room, justifies my willingness to risk everything to be with Clara. My need to protect him is just as strong as my need to protect her. And in this moment, I know that from this day on, not only will Malcolm protect me but he will also always protect her. And that realization is enough to give me a lifetime of relief.

Chapter 57

Malcolm

Getting up this morning is much easier than it was yesterday or the day before. My body is on its way to finally healing. It's been a month since Baker and his buddies attacked me behind Bill's. While my shoulder remains in a sling, my ribs and bruises are healed. My physical features back to normal, for the most part.

Sal, Pop and Tate have been busy building the add on to the barn. It'll be a few more months until Stan is discharged from the rehabilitation hospital he was just sent to a few days ago. His recovery is only starting and it's a long road he has to travel. I'm just happy we get to be the ones who help him and Clara find the right path.

Clara has been so attentive to me since she moved in here. It took some convincing from Pop but Stan finally approved of moving to the farm and letting go of their apartment lease. Since then, she seems to have a huge weight lifted off of her. She walks around here lighter and with renewed purpose. Her only goal to make this the most comfortable home she can for Stan when he's released. Sal has been happier than I've ever seen him. I wouldn't change anything that's happened, if it means I didn't get to witness the happiness they have right now.

I've decided to go into town this morning and get a haircut while everyone finishes the morning chores. I still can't do much because of my immobile shoulder and being here watching everyone else work makes me feel guilty. It is now easier to get dressed and do every day normal activities like brushing my teeth. I recently started doing therapy on my shoulder but it's still not ready for normal movement and activity just yet. Heading down the stairs I run into Adler who's been busy setting up a new entertainment center in the living room. The old TV is now gone and replaced with a nicer and much bigger one. Adler says we will love the sound that comes out of the new speakers he's installing. This new technology makes watching horror films feel like you're actually there instead of just watching. I'll believe that when I see it. He's excited about it, that's all that matters.

School starts next week so I figure this is a good time to get a haircut and grab a couple of items I still need for classes next week. Waving at Clara as I jump up into the truck, I can't help but stare at her a minute longer as I look out the windshield. God, she's beautiful. Clearing the fog out of my mind, I start the engine and head into town still trying to figure out how the hell I'm going to stop thinking about Clara and how much I want to be with her.

Fresh from a haircut, I feel so much better now that my hair is short again. Leaving the neighborhood store, I walk with my one good arm full of bags, the items I need for classes divided between the bags equally. Walking towards the pickup, I'm shoved to the side by a kid on a bike screeching his tires as he hurries away. The sound of voices behind me causes the hairs on the back of my neck to rise to attention. I know that voice.

Walking a bit faster hoping to get to the pickup and avoid the confrontation that's about to occur, I feel someone push me from behind. Not hard, but enough to cause me to stumble forward just a bit. Catching my balance, I turn around and face Baker who is flanked by his two friends, the same friends that beat me up. Like cowards, their faces hidden to ensure they wouldn't get caught.

"Well hello there, Malcolm. How's the arm?" Squinting his eyes, he looks at me with disgust and hatred. His friends laugh, knowing the cause of my pain and injury.

"Much better, thank you. I'm healing despite your attempts to disable me." I return his look with a smile, trying to show him that even though I'm still recovering from their last attack, I'm not afraid of them. Breathing slowly in and out of my nose, I watch him and his friends, keeping them in my sights. Ready just in case they attack me again.

"Oh, come on, Malcolm. You know you had it coming. You can't jump someone and not expect a payback. Eye for an eye and all that." Baker smiles, his demeanor is calm as he looks between his two friends. They both nod in agreeance.

It's now that I remember what Pop said and that I should avoid this at all costs. One year Malcolm. One year and he'll get what's coming to him. I decide to walk away, no matter how hard it is. Giving them a sarcastic smile, I say "Ok, Baker; whatever you say, bro. You got me!" Turning I walk to the driver side door. I bend over to drop the bags to the asphalt, so I can open the door. Just as I'm about to pull the handle, Baker comes up behind me. Standing, I lean up against the pickup door. Still trying, but failing at avoiding the inevitable. Baker is so close I can smell the mint on his breathe as he makes a threat that he will regret for the rest of his life.

"Just thought I'd give you a little warning Malcolm. My father says to stay away from you so I will, but keep this in mind, you have three brothers I'm dying to put in the hospital just like I did you. Oh, and let's not forget that beautiful blonde with the nice tits' you guys hang out with. Clara? Yeah, that's her name. There are so many things I'd love to do to her, too." Licking his lips, he continues, "And I will if you so much as look at me wrong. Do you understand?"

I don't move or say a word. My wrath is building up and threatening to spill over. It's bad enough he threatens me but Clara and my family? Hell no! Taking deep breaths, I stare into his eyes. Hoping he sees my unspoken promise that if he hurts anyone in my family, I'll kill him.

With a laugh, he pats me on the shoulder and steps back. The space now between us isn't helping my anger lessen any. Just when I think he's going to walk away, he turns rapidly and lands a hard punch into my right rib cage, re-breaking the same ribs that just healed. Falling to my knees, he squats in front of me and says, "Don't forget what I said, Malcolm. Cause I would gladly take Clara on the ride of her life." He laughs with his buddies and finally walks away.

Standing, the pain in my ribs resonates all the way up my body. But not all the pain is from my now re-broken ribs. It's also from the fear that Baker will indeed cash in on his promise and hurt Clara. I can't let that happen. I have to protect her, just like I would protect anyone else in my family. Opening the truck door and putting the bags into the back seat, I climb up into the driver's side and start the engine. Wincing from the pain, I drive out onto the main street.

But instead of driving home, I turn the truck in the direction of Channel 10 News Station.

Chapter 58

Malcolm

It's been a week since my last run in with Baker. School starts tomorrow so we're all getting ready to set the table and eat dinner. Pop always says a good meal and a good night's sleep before the start of a new school year is key to its success. Pop, with the help of Clara, has a made an Italian feast of spaghetti and meatballs, French bread with garlic butter, and crisp salad with cucumbers and tomatoes from the garden. Apple pie for desert tops off our feast.

Since leaving the store the day Baker threatened my family, I haven't heard anything related to my attack. I guess they didn't believe me when I said I knew who had attacked me. The journalist I sat in front of that day didn't seem too impressed with my allegations of assault and battery by Jefferson County's finest Judge's son. Not to mention I didn't have any proof. I've been watching out for Clara extra close. She doesn't know it, and neither does Sal, but I follow her to work when she's scheduled and then follow her home when her shift is done. If I told Sal the threats Baker made on her, we'd have bigger problems than the assault and battery on me. Baker would be dead; at the hands of Sal.

Setting the table, Tate tells his usual jokes, keeping us all laughing. These are my favorite times, sitting down for dinner with my family. We've grown by two; Clara now a permanent member and Stan close behind her. We still don't have a date of discharge from the rehab but their added-on room is close to finished and ready for Stan whenever that discharge happens. Clara attends counseling sessions twice a week with her father. They've been trying to work through Stan's attempted suicide all while he works to strengthen his body from the stroke. Clara is positive after each visit saying she believes the therapy is helping him a little more every day. She says it's even helping her cope with it all.

Just as Pop comes in to sit down at the table, spaghetti loaded on every one's plates, the phone rings. The Old Man answers it then yells over at Pop to come take the phone.

"Hey Keating, phones for ya!" Setting the receiver down on the table the phone rests on in the hallway, the Old Man comes and takes his seat at the head of the table. We continue laughing at another joke from Tate, this one funnier than the last. The atmosphere is light and relaxed. Everyone ready and eager to get the new school year started so we can follow through with our future plans. That relaxed atmosphere is shattered though when Pop comes back into the dining room, a stern and worried look on his face. He stares at me. The hair on the back of my neck stands telling me that call was not a good one.

"What is it Pop? What's happened?" Knowing the call likely involves my trip to Channel 10 News last week, I ask him what's happened anyway. Not wanting to give myself away.

"Malcolm, let's go son. It was a detective with the Denver Metro Police. They need to speak with us. Baker has been arrested and charged with assault and battery. They need yer statement." Pop's face is pale. I've never seen him look so worried. The fear of what Judge Landry will do now is heavy in the room. I don't care about the consequences though. If this keeps Baker from hurting my brothers or Clara, then it's all worth what happens next.

Walking into the police station with Pop next to me keeps me grounded and less worried of what's to come. Just being here to give a statement about Baker and his attack on me should make me happy, but it doesn't. Pop didn't say a word on the drive here. I tried talking with him, to get out of him what the detective said on the phone, but he'd just shake his head and say, "Not now, son."

We are taken to a small investigation room, a large rectangular window on one wall. I sit in one seat while Pop sits next to me. Two cups of coffee are on the table in front of us. I don't drink it, and neither does Pop. A few minutes later, the door to the investigation room opens. A slender dark-haired woman and tall skinny man enter the room.

"Mr. Keating, thank you for coming tonight." Reaching out, she shakes Pop's hand before looking at me and repeating the gesture. Pointing at the other detective she introduces them both. "I'm detective Watts; this here is detective Taylor."

"Malcolm, it's nice to meet you. I know tomorrow is the first day of your senior year and it's late so we will make this quick and get you home, ok, son?" Nodding, I entwine my fingers and lay my hands in my lap. Pop sits back in his chair, now calm and cool. The worry I saw in his eyes before is now gone.

"What's this about? We were sitting down for dinner with the family when ye called, detective Watts." Pop asks, not wanting to beat around the bush.

"Well we got an anonymous tip from someone saying they knew who had beaten your boy so badly a few weeks ago." The detective pulls out a chair and sits across from us. Detective Taylor does the same, but he stays silent for now.

"Ye don't say? And what did this tipster say about Malcolm's attack?" I can tell Pop is trying to play dumb, not lead on that he already knows who did this.

"Well, the information we have is that the attack was premeditated and that the whole thing was caught on tape. But you already know that don't you Mr. Keating?" Bile rises up from my stomach. She seems to be accusing Pop of something.

"It appears that the attacker is none other than Baker Landry. The Honorable Judge Landry's son." Detective Watts looks over at detective Taylor. She nods for him to continue.

"Mr. Keating, the tip stated that there is a tape hidden in a safety deposit box at the very bank you keep your farm's funds in." So that's where he hid the tapes. But if they know that, then it wasn't my tip to the journalist that's brought us here tonight. I sit back in my seat, a little less nervous now that I know someone else has also leaked the information.

"We've arrested Baker Landry; he is in a holding cell waiting to be processed into County. His father is pissed and wanting heads to roll. Your head to be exact." Detective Taylor laughs a little then looks at me. I get the feeling detective Taylor is not at all impressed with Judge Landry.

"Judge Landry claims you came to him after Malcolm's attack and threatened him and his son with the tape. He says you threatened his life, Mr. Keating. Says you threatened that if Baker came anywhere near any of your family again, you'd kill him." Detective Watts speaks next. "I think you've got this covered from here, Taylor. I've got to go deal with Judge Landry." She gets up and leaves the small room. Pop's demeanor doesn't change with the information they've provided. He's completely unfazed by Judge Landry's accusation.

Once detective Watts is gone, detective Taylor becomes more forth coming with information and less accusatory toward Pop. He sits back in his chair, and looks across the table. The same smile from before is planted on his face.

"So, here's the deal, Mr. Keating. My sister is Rebecca Taylor. She is dating your son Tate and things seem to be pretty serious. My sister assures me there is no way in hell you'd threaten anyone, let alone a public official. So I'm prepared to give you the benefit of the doubt. Not to mention, when all this with Baker started a few weeks ago, Tate called and asked my opinion so I already knew a tape existed." Detective Taylor sits back up, his elbows on the table and looks straight at Pop. I forgot Becca's brother was a detective.

"Can I be completely transparent, Mr. Keating?" Taylor asks Pop.

"Please do, detective." Pop's answer is curt.

"Judge Landry is crooked. He's using his campaign to do some, let's just say, not so legal activities related to this election. We suspect some election tampering may be going on. Or maybe he's bribing people with The Landry Foundation funds to increase voter turnout. We're not completely sure. Now I know this isn't exactly legal, but I'm about to ask you to help us out." Taylor keeps his focus on Pop.

"Go on; I'm listening." Pop leans forward and rests his hands on the table, prepared to hear whatever detective Taylor is about to say.

"We need something on Landry to warrant an arrest. We need him to admit to something, something illegal. It can be small; it can be huge, but it just has to be illegal. I was hoping you'd help by wearing a wire and meeting with him. To, you know, try and push some info out of him."

Pop and I look over at each other, knowing that illegal admission already exists. It's in the safe deposit box with the tape. A smile breaks out on both our faces as we realize detective Taylor is giving us a way to get both Baker and his father at the same time.

Nodding, I give Pop my permission to let the detective in on our secret. Not that he needed my permission, but that's how this family works. We make decisions together. Especially the ones that affect us all on some level. Pop looks back over at Taylor.

"Well, ye in luck, lad. We already have that admission." Pop smirks.

"Oh yeah? You do?" Detective Taylor is more intrigued now than before; his curiosity is evident in the form of hope on his face.

"Ye know about one tape from Tate, but did ye know there's a second one?" Pop teases him with the idea that there is already a confession of some kind out there.

"No, Mr. Keating. I was not aware of that, obviously. Since you're here now, me asking for your help." Taylor laughs.

"Well, I will turn over both tapes to ye. Given that Judge Landry gets what's been coming to him and his awful son. But only with a promise from ye." Detective Taylor's eyebrows raise a bit but he doesn't look away from Pop, just matches his intensity. The need to end Judge Landry as important to him as it is to us.

"And what promise would you like me to make, Mr. Keating?"

"Promise my boys that their futures will be protected if I turn the good Judge over to ye." Hope to finally be done with the Landrys flashes in Pop's eyes. I can't help but feel the same hope growing for me as well.

"I can't make promises, Mr. Keating, but I will say I'll do everything possible to help protect your boys. Especially since their futures involve my sister's future, as well." He nods firmly at Pop, then rises from the table. "Well, if we've got a deal, Mr. Keating, I'll wait for you to bring me the tapes." Pop and I stand, too. Reaching over, detective Taylor shakes both our hands and turns toward the investigation room's door. Knocking, someone from the outside opens the door. Pop leaves first, and as I attempt to exit the room, detective Taylor stops me.

"Hey son. I just want to say I'm proud of you. Your anonymous tip to the journalist at Channel 10 News last week is what heated up this whole investigation. If you hadn't been brave enough to meet with her, none of this would be happening." He smiles genuinely at me. His appreciation is welcome.

"Well, I don't take threats lightly against my family. I love them too much to allow someone to threaten them. They're all I've got. Loyalty is the bind that keeps us together and will forever, detective Taylor. I plan to keep it that way."

Turning to walk out behind Pop, he stops me again and says, "I know, Malcolm; that's why I don't worry a bit about Rebecca being a part of this family. I know you and your family will protect her, at all costs."

Nodding again, I leave the room following Pop. We get into the truck and head back to the farm and the family we both love so much. The family we have protected, possibly at the cost of our future.

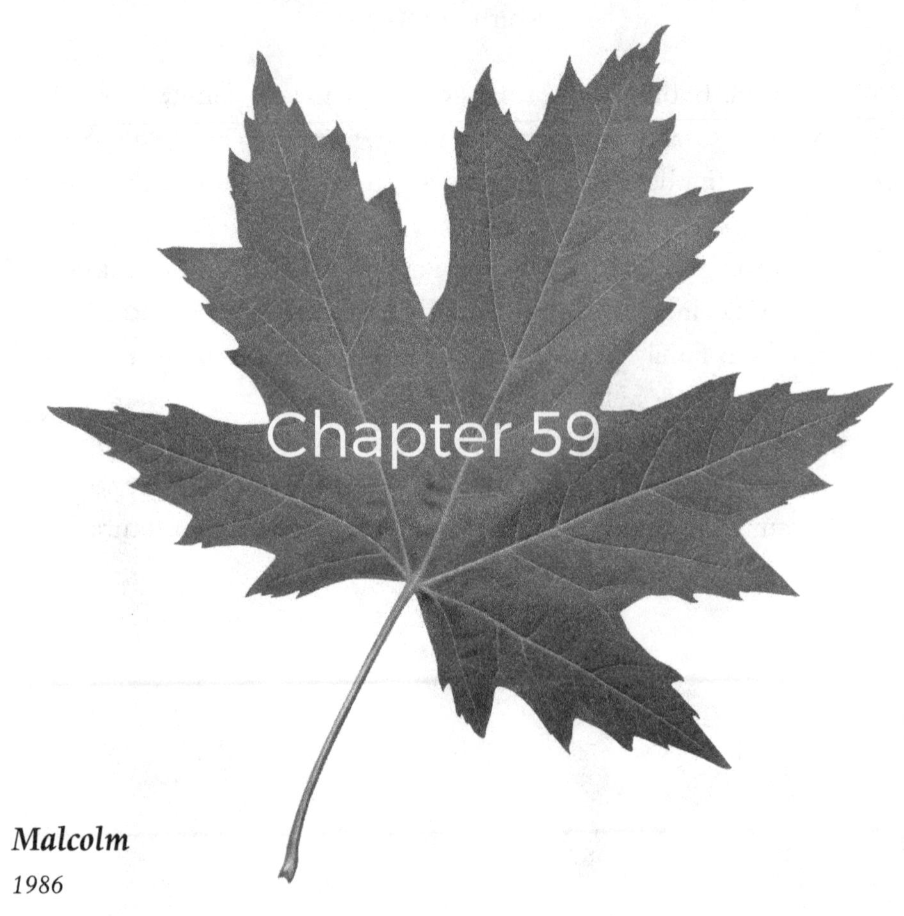

Chapter 59

Malcolm

1986

At this time last year, we didn't think we'd see another fall festival at Nexus Farms for at least a few years. That makes this one even more special. Originally for boot camp, we were scheduled to ship out in July. However; due to court appearances and testifying in the Landry trials, our ship date changed to October. Other than that, I've been surprised Judge Landry hasn't been able to influence any part of our future. Not yet anyway.

The trial for both Baker and Judge, no wait; *Charles* Landry, has lasted the entire last year. Of course, Charles Landry tried to turn the tables on us. His lawyer tried everything to have the focus shift from him and Baker to Pop. No matter the tactic, he couldn't win. And now, they are both off to jail. Baker received five to ten years in a plea deal. He was originally charged with second-degree attempted murder as the attack was deemed premeditated. But after the little influence Judge Landry still had, Baker took a plea deal and pled guilty for first degree assault and menacing. Charles Landry also got five years for election tampering, along with a two thousand dollar fine. The sentences handed down to them in punishment was enough in my book. At least we have five to ten years before we have to worry about that family messing with us again.

Leaning against the open barn door, I look out at the community that stood behind us during the trial and feel such appreciation for the support we got. Charles Landry was such a powerful influence in our community that not one person wanted to stand up for us in the beginning. But once one came forward with evidence of election tampering, others followed. Next thing we knew, The Landry Foundation was dismantled and broken up. Charles Landry's younger brother was given the impossible task of taking over the only living pieces of The Landry Foundation that still exist. There's not much left.

Tomorrow my brothers and I get on a plane to California, the Marine Corps calling our names to join them. I'm so excited to start this journey in my life. After we turned over the tapes last year, Tate, Sal and I made it our mission to help Adler prepare for boot camp and a life in the military. He's gained fifty pounds, and muscled up better than any of us would have expected. Still smaller than any of us, he's much more physically prepared for the demands the military will put on him. And we feel better about having him join us in California tomorrow.

Watching the dance floor, I keep my eyes on Sal and Clara. They're dancing slowly to Willie Nelson's *Last Thing I Needed First Thing This Morning,* holding each other tight. Sal is excited about leaving but scared to leave Clara here alone. Stan is doing much better, he's been walking a bit more and not having to spend so much time in the wheelchair. Clara has been so focused on his recovery and therapy I think she almost forgot we were leaving, until this week when it all started to sink in. Now she cries often, the weight of being without Sal almost too much to bear. Sal holds her tightly as they sway back and forth and he kisses her softly every few minutes. Tate and Becca are just as they usually are, all jokes and fun. He swings her around like the song is faster and more upbeat instead of slow. She laughs as he dips her dramatically. When he pulls her back up quickly, Tate plants a hard kiss to her lips, making her sag against him.

Seeing my brothers so happy is the highlight of every day. My fears that they wouldn't forgive me for tipping off the police were forgotten as soon as Pop and I got home that night. No forgiveness was needed once I told them the threats Baker had made, and that those threats were what caused me to go against Pop's directive.

My feelings for Clara haven't changed. She means more to me now than she ever has. Has that changed my pursuit of her? No. She's Sal's girl. And I'm ok with that. Not like I really have any other choice than to be ok with it. Clara is my best friend, besides Sal. I confide in her about things I'd never tell anyone. Even Sal.

She knows my deepest secrets. And she assures me she'll always keep them safe. The only secret she doesn't know and she never will, is that I love her. And that if my brother wasn't in the picture, she'd be mine. I'd make sure of it.

Walking over to Sal and Clara, I raise my chin at Sal in a silent question. Can I dance with your girl? Sal smiles, then pushes Clara away from his chest. She looks at him, disappointed until she sees me standing waiting my turn to dance with her. Taking her hand, I pull her toward me and Sal lets her go. Clara and I wrap our arms around each other and hold on tight as Heart sings *These Dreams* in our ears. God I'll miss her.

"Malcolm I'll miss you. I don't know what I'll do without our morning walks around the pond. I've come to depend on them for my sanity." She laughs as she looks up at me, her beautiful blue eyes showing so much grief.

"Oh, Clara; you'll be fine. Boot camp is only thirteen weeks, and then you'll see us before we get stationed. It'll go fast. Your classes at

CU Boulder will keep you so busy and you won't even think about us." I know that's far from the truth, but I say it anyway, hoping to lessen her sadness.

"I sure hope you're right, Malcolm. And what about Adler; are you sure he's ready? Are you sure you guys will be able to keep an eye on him?" Clara's eyes flash darker blue as her tone of voice becomes deeper. The need to relay her concern is strong. I've already told her Adler is our priority. We all have, but she still asks.

"I promise, Clara; we will take care of Adler."

Satisfied with my answer she lays her head on my shoulder just as Sal comes back to reclaim his girl.

"Ok, cowboy. That's enough. I only get one more night with her for like weeks, Bro. Give her back." Laughing he reaches out and Clara willingly goes back to Sal.

I walk over, lean against the barn door, and watch as my family says goodbye to all of the people, we love the most.

Watching Clara say goodbye to Sal was the hardest part of this whole day. Hell, she had Pop, Adler and even Tate crying. God, that woman pulls at all of our hearts. She cried against Pop as we loaded the plane. He released her into the trusting arms of Rebecca as the plane took flight and took us away from the only place, we've ever called home.

Now, here we sit. The four of us. Scared but oh so excited about the journey we're about to embark on. As the plane lands in San Diego, I can't help but look around in amazement. The palm trees stand tall, humid air causes sweat to cover my arms and torso. Coming off the plane, we're bussed to MCRD San Diego. Sal, Tate and Adler sit in the seats next to me. When we arrive to our destination, we exit the bus and are instructed to stand at attention on the yellow footprints painted onto the concrete. The Drill Instructor stands in front of us as we all line up.

It's eerily quiet.

I stay staring at the palm tree across the way from me trying not to draw attention to myself. The Sergeant standing in the front begins to speak, and my anxiety kicks up as he says, "Hello, girls; welcome to hell!" Tate laughs softly. So softly that I can't imagine anyone could hear him, but I was wrong and in two seconds flat, the Sergeant is in his face. Spit shoots from his mouth, covering Tate's face as he asks, "Do you have something to say Recruit? Go ahead, speak now. This is your only chance."

Tate responds with a strong voice, "No, sir; nothing to say, sir." The Sergeant then asks, "What's your name Recruit?" Tate answers, his voice strong again. "Keating. Sir."

The Sergeant's facial expression changes to shock briefly. He hides it well and I wonder why he had that reaction to Tate. Looking at Adler then Sal next to him, he then focus' his eyes on me. With his head turned in my direction, his body stays facing Tate. His hat is tilted down severely showing the back of his shaved head. My heart starts pounding as he stares at me.

As the Sergeant comes to stand directly in front of me, my heart beats so fast I can hear the blood flowing in my ears. He yells out at me for the first time.

"And, who do we have here? Speak your name son. Don't keep me waiting or I'll make you pay for it later!"

Without hesitating I answer, still looking straight ahead at the palm tree.

"Shipley, Sir."

Laughing, he bends at the waist and I look down at him without moving my body. My nerves are hyper aware, the same terrible feeling I've had only a few times in my life hitting me hard and fast as the Sergeant stands in front of me. He continues laughing before getting in my face and screaming, "Well this should be real fucking fun Recruit!" I look up and that's when I see who he is.

Sergeant Landry.

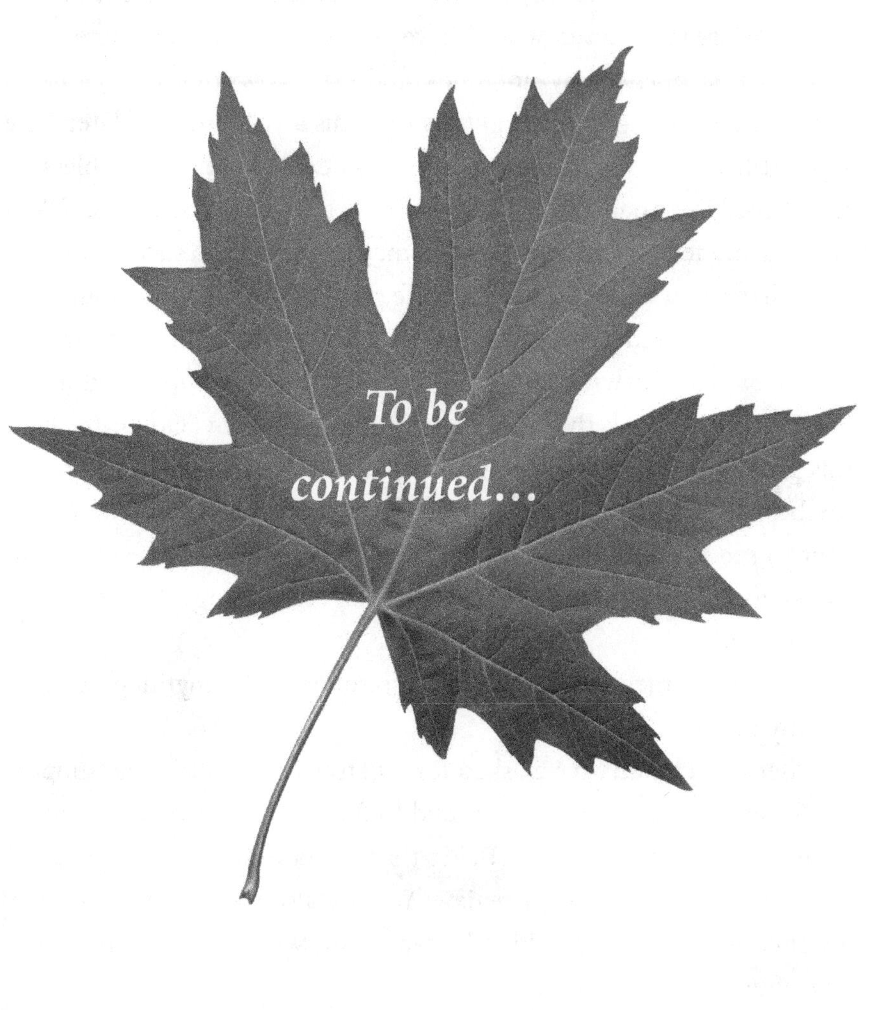
To be
continued...

Acknowledgements

Thank you to everyone who has taken the time to read *Shipley's Secrets.* This is a dream I never would have thought could ever come true. When I first opened my notebook and started writing ideas for this book, I never thought it would turn into this a year and half later. The support from the writing community has been an even bigger blessing than I could've imagined. Thank you to the bookstagrammers, fellow authors and fellow readers that have made this book so successful.

Thank you to the love of my life, Jason Simmons. Without your support, love, and inspiration this wouldn't have gone this far. My dream of being a writer became real, because you supported a few notes in a notebook that turned into our book baby. Going through this process with you, working alongside of you to make this project the best we can, has been the most satisfying time of my life. I can't wait to see what other books we work on together. I hope we get to spend every day writing and perfecting the crazy things that come out of my head.

To the women in my life who inspire me to do anything I've ever put my mind to. Thank you!

Becky, I couldn't have asked for a better role model. The support you've given me to be who I am and to do the things I've set my mind to, means everything to me. Being that you are such a huge reader, I am anxiously awaiting your review! You are also the best mama-in-law a girl could ask for. I wouldn't be who I am without you in my life. I love you!

Mom. Thank you for giving great support to a crazy daughter with big dreams and an even bigger attitude. Your genes are the creative ones, despite what Dad says. I love you.

Alyssa, my beautiful baby girl. I want you to know that you can do anything you set your mind to. Nothing is off limits. Let the last 18 years you've watched me be your motivation to know you can succeed in anything. Let the last 18 years of watching Jason and I be your example of what marriage and love should look like. Right now, your dream is nursing school and in 10 years it could change to anything you want! Never settle and never depend on anyone else to make your dreams come true. Study hard, work harder and support your dreams and aspirations. Women are powerful and can move mountains. All we need is a little support from those who love us and you have that in abundance. I can't wait to see where life takes you. I love you so very much.

To my beta readers—Danielle, Tessa, Sharon, Kimberly, Ron, Jason and Anthony. Thank you for taking the time to read and give me the feedback that has made this book so much stronger! Your support has given me the confidence to publish *Shipley's Secrets* and be confident that other's will want to be a part of this story.

Thank you to Champagne Book designs for the beautiful formatting and interior design. This has been the most amazing experience and I appreciate you being a part of it all.

Thank you to Books and the Bear for your help with promotion and editorial services. The support to make this story its best means the world to me.

Thank you to Ari with CoverIt designs. This is the most beautiful cover! And your willingness to design this, when I had no clue what I was doing, saved me!

Thanks to all you for supporting me and my crazy ideas! I appreciate you coming along for the ride! Cheers to the next one!!

About the Author

Jen was born in San Diego California and was raised in Lubbock Texas. Jen's life took her into a career of nursing. In 2008 she earned her Registered Nursing degree and began caring for patients in a fast-paced Intensive Care unit. Her dreams led her to obtain an undergraduate degree in Nursing followed by a Master's degree in Nursing Leadership and Organizational Management. Jen has always loved to read and enjoys mostly contemporary romance books. The idea suddenly came to her one day to sit down and start writing *Shipley's Secrets*. The process at first, was just a release from the busy day to day life of a Registered Nurse in healthcare management.

Jen's inspiration to finish and self-publish came in the form of encouragement and love from her husband Jason. Jen gets her inspiration from authors like Pepper Winters, Jamie McGuire, and Colleen Hoover. Jen hopes that the inspiration from writing *Shipley's Secrets* will inspire her to keep writing in the young adult and contemporary romance realm.

Jen likes to read, write and watch movies in her free time. Any chance to drink champagne and eat pasta, she jumps on. Jen lives in Northern Colorado with her husband Jason, daughter Alyssa and their dog Lady Simmons.

CPSIA information can be obtained
at www.ICGtesting.com
Printed in the USA
LVHW110711290522
720020LV00017B/105

9 780578 608327